Talk Show

Also by A. O'Connor

Talk Show

A. O'Connor

POOLBEG

Published 2012
by Poolbeg Press Ltd
123 Grange Hill, Baldoyle
Dublin 13, Ireland
E-mail: poolbeg@poolbeg.com
www.poolbeg.com

1

A catalogue record for this book is available from the British Library.

ISBN 978-1-84223-499-0

Typeset by Patricia Hope in Sabon 11/15
Printed by CPI Group (UK) Ltd, Croydon, CR0 4YY

www.poolbeg.com

About the author

A. O'Connor is the author of five previous novels – *This Model Life*, *Exclusive*, *Property*, *Ambition* and *Full Circle* – and is a graduate of NUI Maynooth and Trinity College Dublin.

Acknowledgements

A big thank-you to all at Poolbeg – especially Paula Campbell, Kieran Devlin, David Prendergast and Sarah Ormston, for all the work bringing *Talk Show* from start to finish. Thanks to Paula and Nicola for the valued advice on the story direction. Thank you, Gaye Shortland, for your excellence as an editor. And my continued gratitude to the booksellers, reviewers, and of course readers.

For Gina

1

Kim Davenport surveyed the television studio audience. They weren't a hushed audience, or a respectful one. They didn't sit in quiet concentration, carefully listening to the show's guests before deliberation. They were the opposite. A baying mob, fired up with excitement, that would do justice to the crowds who used to sit in the ancient Roman Colosseum. And that was the way Kim liked it. The more fired up, the better. The more bloodthirsty, the better the ratings. *The Joshua Green Show* depended on audiences like these; confessional talk shows always did. There was no point in having people on the stage divulging their deepest darkest sins, if there wasn't a rampant public there to offer their loud chorus of disapproval and outrage. Kim knew the formula well, it was one she had helped pioneer, and it had now brought *The Joshua Green Show*, and her as its producer, to fifth place in the national ratings.

Kim leaned towards the cameraman. "Give me a close-up on Joshua when he goes on the attack."

The cameraman nodded with a grin.

Kim liked to think she had discovered Joshua. He had already been working in broadcasting when she'd met him, but buried in radio on some night-time shift. When she had been searching high and low for a presenter to front her new show, she had nearly given up on finding someone in Ireland. Everyone she had interviewed had been too polished, too pleasing, too charming. She didn't need that for her show. She needed someone who could be rough, arrogant, commanding and in control – and yet combine this with an almost pious, holier-than-thou attitude. That was a hard combination to find. She should know, as she had looked far and wide. And then she had come across Joshua with his backroom radio talk show. And voila! A star was born.

Joshua Green walked up and down in front of the first row of audience seats, a microphone in one hand. A man of forty-two, he was fair-haired and brown-eyed and very well turned-out in a designer suit.

He looked directly at the camera as he spoke.

"My next guest, Glen, started dating his best friend Aidan's sister, Donna. He broke up the relationship after a month. But recently Glen claims that Donna won't let him go, refusing to give up the relationship. He says he's caught in a trap, with his friend blaming him for the situation. Ladies and gentlemen, please give a warm welcome to Glen!"

The audience began to clap and cheer enthusiastically as Glen walked onto the stage and sat on one of three chairs positioned facing Joshua's empty one. Joshua generally preferred to stay on his feet, the better to prowl around his victims.

Glen was a good-looking young man of about twenty-one with a confident air about him.

Joshua sat on the side of the stage and looked up at Glen.

"Right, first things first, Glen, how did you meet Donna?"

"I suppose I've known her for years. She was my friend Aidan's little sister. I never paid much attention to her really, she was just always there. Then one night me and Aidan and the gang were out in our local bar, and she kind of tagged along. I guess I always knew she had a thing for me. One thing led to another and we spent the night together."

"Probably not the wisest of things to do, Glen, with her being your mate's sister – but, by the sound of it, you weren't too fussed about that at the time."

"I know that now, Josh, and if I could turn back time I would. I suppose I must have liked her in the beginning. We arranged to meet again and things went from there. But it was always just a fling to me, and I thought it was just a bit of fun for her as well."

"When did you realise it meant more to her?"

"I noticed pretty quickly that she was needy and clingy. So after a couple of weeks I tried to distance myself from her, but she was having none of it. It was really awkward, because of Aidan being my friend. So I couldn't be as direct as I wanted to be with her."

"Don't you think you should have been honest with her? It would have been the decent thing to do."

"Yeah, I do now," Glen nodded.

"Sometimes you have to be cruel to be kind, Glen. Continue."

"Then she started talking about us moving in together, and I was like – steady! Then Aidan warned me how much she was into me. So I told her that I wasn't in love with her and I didn't see us having a future. But I said I wanted us to be friends."

"And what happened?"

"She threatened to kill herself."

The audience began to gasp. "*User*!" one male voice shouted.

"And how did you deal with that?"

"I continued to see her for a while because I was worried about her. But she became so clingy again, I had to get away from her. So I sat down one evening and told her I didn't want to see her again, not even as a friend. I stuck to my guns this time."

"And that was the end of it?" asked Joshua.

Glen shook his head and looked down at the floor. "No, she refuses to let go. She turns up at my workplace and sends me texts saying we're meant to be together."

Joshua stood up quickly. "Okay, we're now going to meet Donna and her brother Aidan, who is Glen's best friend."

The audience clapped loudly, and some cheered while others jeered as Donna and Aidan walked onstage. Donna was a blonde girl of eighteen with an air of fragility. Aidan was Glen's age, and looked agitated and reluctant to be there. They sat down on the spare chairs near Glen while Joshua nimbly ran up the steps leading to the stage.

"You're a total liar, Glen! You're only telling one side of the story!" Donna accused loudly.

"No, *you're* the one who's deluding yourself, love!" snapped Glen. The audience began to jeer loudly.

"Give her a chance to speak, please," insisted Joshua, making cool-it gestures to the crowd. "What's your side of the story then, Donna?"

"He's making out there was nothing between us. That he was doing me a favour going out with me. He was the one who pursued me the first night in the bar when we started seeing each other."

Glen sat up and glared at her. "I don't deny I chatted you up, but I didn't realise I was chatting up a nut-job!"

"Watch your mouth!" warned Aidan loudly, causing the audience to jeer again.

"Everyone shut up and give Donna a chance to say her piece!" said Joshua loudly. "Go on, Donna!"

"The first night we were together, he couldn't stop saying beautiful things to me!"

"Yeah, and then I sobered up!" snapped Glen.

"*Using bastard*!" shouted a loud voice from the audience as the place erupted into laughter and heckling.

"I don't believe you mean those things!" Donna wailed. "There was – there is – this special magic between us. If we just spent some time together you'd see we could be great together!"

"Not in a million years!" insisted Glen.

"Did you say flattering things to Donna in the beginning, Glen?" Joshua pressed him. "Did you lead her on?"

"I always say flattering things to the girl I'm going out with. At the time anyway."

"You just totally used me then?" Donna shouted at Glen.

"Look, you're not even my type! Now get over it and get a life!" Glen shouted back.

"User! User! User!" the audience began to chant.

"You strike me as somebody who plays the field, Glen," said Joshua. "Don't you think it was really stupid of you to add your friend's sister to the list?"

Glen looked at Aidan, embarrassed. "It was a lousy move. But we live and learn."

"A move that may cost you your friendship." Joshua turned to

4

Aidan. "And, Aidan, you're in the unfortunate position of being caught in the middle of all this?"

"I'm just angry with both of them. I can't believe Donna won't accept it's over. She's making a fool of herself and me." Aidan turned to Donna and spoke loudly. "Get over it, Donna. He's not all that, you know. He'll never settle down!"

"But I could change that," insisted Donna.

"*Sad cow!*" a woman's voice shouted from the audience, causing everyone to laugh.

"You've had a lucky escape, Donna," warned Aidan.

"I wish *I* could get an escape from *her*!" said Glen, rolling his eyes.

"Stalker!" a man hissed from the spectators, causing more people to clap loudly.

"Everyone calm down!" demanded Joshua. "Aidan, has what happened affected your friendship with Glen?"

"Of course it has. His ego always has to get in the way. He's one of those guys who needs female attention and as soon as he gets it, he moves on . . ."

"That's not true!" Glen defended himself loudly.

"You can be a complete asshole, Glen! And you were treating Donna as just another conquest, with no regard for me. And you've bitten off more than you can chew with her!"

"Donna, Glen claims you've been relentlessly phoning him, is that true?" asked Joshua.

"I rang him a few times, but he's exaggerating," said Donna.

"We put a trace on Glen's phone. . ." Joshua turned and looked at the audience, tantalising them before revealing the result of the trace. Then his voice adopted a loud accusatory tone: "You phoned him sixty times in one week, Donna!"

"Donna!" snapped Aidan angrily.

The audience gasped at this revelation and started heckling Donna loudly.

"Lock her up! She a nutter!" came a call from the crowd.

"You don't understand!" Donna shouted, trying to be heard over the crowd's roaring. "I've approached him a few times to try and talk to him. But I'm not a stalker!"

Joshua put his hands in the air and shouted at the audience to be silent before turning his attention back to his prey.

"Aidan, what's she been like at home?"

Aidan looked at her wearily. "She's not sleeping well, or eating. She took the break-up very badly. We've all tried rallying around her. Plenty more fish in the sea, kind of thing, but she fell for him very hard and he shouldn't have given her any encouragement."

"It all got on top of you, didn't it, Donna?" said Joshua.

Donna nodded while staring at the floor.

"It was her idea to come on this show, because it was the only way she could get to talk to Glen," said Aidan. "I don't know what she thought would happen here today. That they would fall into each other's arms and declare undying love?"

Joshua had the audience under control and, as he approached Donna, his voice adopted a soft tone.

"Look, Donna, sweetheart. I'm getting the impression here that you haven't had much experience with relationships, and Glen was probably your first love. It sounds to me you were just another notch on Glen's bedpost. We all have to cope with rejection, Donna, it's part of life and it's part of growing up."

Aidan put an arm around Donna as she wiped her eyes.

"Glen, you need to lay your cards on the table now and say to Donna here, in front of the audience, in front of her brother, without being either kind or cowardly, how you feel about Donna."

Glen leaned forward and looked at Donna directly. "I don't love you, I never did. I want you to stop contacting me. *Now*!"

"Do you now accept your relationship with Glen is over, Donna?" pushed Joshua.

Donna said nothing but continued to wipe her eyes.

"Donna, now you have to admit it to yourself and everyone else so you all can get on with your lives – do you accept there is no future for yourself and Glen together?"

"Y-y-yes," whispered Donna.

"Good girl. And Glen, it's time you grew up and realised that actions have consequences. People aren't just there to be played with to flatter your ego. You've had a lucky escape here with Donna, next time you might not be so lucky."

He turned to the audience and raised his arms.

"Ladies and gentlemen, a round of applause for Donna, Aidan and Glen!"

The audience started to clap and whistle energetically as the closing music began to play and the show ended.

2

Joshua walked quickly through the wide corridors of the television studio, RTV. The programme's researcher Brooke Radcliffe walked beside him, carrying a clipboard. She was aged thirty, a slim attractive girl with long chestnut hair.

"Well, how did it go?" asked Joshua.

"You were excellent, well done," congratulated Brooke.

Joshua untied his tie and wiped his forehead as he was sweating profusely.

Kim Davenport came marching towards them, smiling broadly.

"I've just taken a quick look through today's take. Brilliant! Lovesick girl bordering on stalker behaviour."

Kim put her hand in the air and Joshua slapped his hand against hers in a high-five fashion.

"I'm running really late today, so I've had to put back our meeting for next week's programme until five this evening. Sorry!" Kim pulled a sympathetic face.

"That's impossible, Kim!" Joshua looked unhappy. "I'm meeting Soraya and the kids this afternoon – I can't put them off."

"Listen – I've just had a word with the ratings department and they said we just missed the Number 4 slot last week."

"Number 4!" Joshua was delighted.

"Yes! So I think if we could just up our game a little, the slot is

8

ours for the taking. And that's what I want to discuss in the meeting. Now," she coaxed, "you're not going to let a few little things like a wife and kids get in the way of your march to the top, are you?"

"Okay, see you at five," said Joshua.

"Good man! That's my professional!" Smiling broadly, Kim strode off.

In his dressing room, Joshua took off his suit jacket and took out his mobile.

"Select me a new suit, will you?" he told Brooke.

She went to his wardrobe and started looking through his suits as he phoned his wife.

"Soraya, it's me. Listen, cancel this afternoon, will you? Something has cropped up at the studio, and I can't make it . . . Yes, I know I promised . . . There's nothing I can do, Kim's called a late meeting . . ."

Brooke held up a navy suit for his approval. Joshua nodded and gave her a thumbs-up.

"I'm sorry, love, but there's nothing I can do. I'll try to be home as soon as possible. Listen, I'd better run, I'm doing an interview with the *RTÉ Guide* in ten minutes. Love you!" He turned off his mobile. "Take some advice, Brooke – don't ever get married!" He began to take off his shirt as he walked into the en-suite bathroom.

"I don't plan to! Your show has put me off marriage for life!"

She heard Joshua put the shower on. "I'll just leave your suit hanging on the door!" she called. She didn't get any answer and turned to leave.

"Oh, and get me a McDonald's!" Joshua shouted from the shower.

Kim walked through the double doors leading into the reception of the television centre. She looked much younger than her forty-five years, with her long well-groomed black hair and trim slender figure kept in shape by frequent visits to the gym.

Donna was being comforted by Aidan on one couch, with Glen sitting across reception on another.

Kim halted and addressed all three.

"Thank you so much for coming on today and sharing your story with us. We've been inundated with people ringing in and sympathising with you all."

Aidan looked up, annoyed. "I told her not to come on this show. I told her it would lead to public embarrassment for her."

"There's no embarrassment in expressing our emotions, Aidan," Kim said, nodding earnestly. "We all need to get in touch with our inner selves, like Donna has been doing today. Now – has reception called you a taxi?"

"Kim," began Aidan, looking deeply unhappy, "yourself and Josh said there would be a counsellor here to talk to us after the show, to help us cope with all this. We'd really like to see the counsellor."

Kim looked surprised but still smiled. "Oh! Okay! Em – yes, I can see how you might want to discuss your problem a little more. I'll get somebody to talk to you now."

At that moment Brooke came through the glass doors from outside, holding a McDonald's takeaway bag.

"Ah! And here she is!" said Kim. "This is Brooke who is our counsellor for the show and she's going to take you to a room and talk out your issues. Glen, would you like to join them?"

Glen looked horrified at the thought. "No, thanks!"

"Kim, could I talk to you for a moment?" asked Brooke, looking surprised and unhappy.

"What is it?" asked Kim as she and Brooke headed to a corner of reception.

"Kim! I'm not a trained counsellor! I can't talk to these people about their problems!"

"Of course you can! You dealt with them before they came on the show, didn't you? You're probably the best person equipped to talk to them."

"But I'm not trained to counsel anyone!"

"Well, I'm afraid you've no choice! We haven't replaced Richard since he quit and we don't have anyone trained at hand. To be honest, I think all this psychotherapy is a load of old bullshit anyway. All they need is somebody to pour their hearts out to. Just order them a taxi when they're through and send them on their way."

"But I have to bring Joshua's lunch to him." Brooke held up the McDonald's bag, looking distressed.

"I'll make sure he gets it." Kim took the bag from her.

They walked back to the show's guests.

"Now, Aidan and Donna, if you'd like to follow Brooke? She's going to give you all the help you need."

Aidan and Donna stood up and followed a smiling but uncomfortable Brooke back into the studios.

Kim turned to Glen. "Glen! You must be delighted with today's programme?"

"I'm over the moon if it puts a stop to her haunting me."

A taxi pulled up outside the front doors and beeped loudly.

"That must be my taxi. I'd better be on my way," said Glen.

Kim put her arm around Glen as she walked him to the door. "Keep me informed how it goes. In my experience of these situations, this is really where the problems start. People who get obsessions rarely give up at the first hurdle."

"You're not serious!"

"What I'm proposing is a follow-up programme, if she starts her stalker-like behaviour again. Think about it, and let me know."

"I will, and thanks for everything, Kim."

"That's what I'm here for!"

Kim waved him off, before looking down at the McDonald's bag Brooke had handed her. She flung it into the bin and went back into the studios.

Kim stood at the top of the table in the boardroom, looking at the production team of *The Joshua Green Show*. Joshua was seated to her right and Brooke to her left.

"Ladies and gentlemen, I'm sure you've all heard we're at Number 5 in the ratings. A big congratulations to us all!"

Everyone grinned broadly.

"But this is no time for complacency," Kim continued. "I think

11

we could even achieve the Number 1 slot. It's in our grasp! All we have to do is reach out and grab it!"

Kim sat down and looked at the stack of papers in front of Brooke.

"So what have you got for me?" she asked.

Brooke stood up and handed out paperwork to all around the table, starting with Kim.

"These are the calls we've received in the past week from viewers looking for us to air their problems," said Brooke, as she arrived back at her seat and sat down. "I've ticked the ones that seem to be of most interest."

Kim scanned down the first page and flicked over to the next one.

Joshua read aloud: "*My sister is pregnant and the father could be any one of three.*" He looked up. "Sounds a bit *Mama Mia*, doesn't it?"

Kim turned to Brooke. "Are the three potential fathers prepared to appear on the show?"

"Only two, I'm afraid."

"Get me the third, and I'll consider it." Kim moved on to the next item. "*My son is a drug addict,*" she read. "We can't revisit that old territory again . . . Sister a prostitute, we did that last January, and March come to think of it. It's too soon to parade another brasser looking for her family to redeem her."

"What about this one?" asked Joshua. "*I have five children by five different fathers.*"

"That's not a talk show – that's a fucking circus!" snapped Kim. "What does she want us to do about her situation at this stage – introduce her to the sixth daddy?" Kim looked at Brooke accusingly. "These are all a bit lame, Brooke. Is this the best you could do?"

Brooke looked slightly hurt and defensive. "All I'm doing is giving you an outline of the viewers who rang during the week. I can't make up something that's not there, Kim."

"Then maybe you need to be a little more proactive about finding good guests, rather than just sitting back on your pert little ass waiting for them to call!" Brooke sat forward, her face flushed, to say something, but thought better of it and sat back again.

"The trouble is this is our fifth year on the show and we've covered so much already," said Joshua. "It's hard not to repeat old territory."

Kim looked angry. "I don't accept that for one minute. Good television is about good innovation. Now I've got that Number 1 slot within my greedy little grasp, and I want it. So what are you going to do about it, Brooke?"

"I can't invent something that's not there, Kim. I can only give you the guests who ring in."

Kim threw her hands in the air. "Then your best is not good enough, Brooke. The proof of the pudding is in the eating, and your pudding is tasting decidedly off to me." She stood up and began to walk around the table. "As you are all aware a new Director of Programmes is starting at RTV soon. A man called Guy Burton. A man who will decide what goes on RTV and what doesn't. He could cancel our show on a whim if he wants to. This is a change of management, people, and I think we should all be very scared."

"Come on, Kim, you're being a bit overdramatic," said Joshua, folding his arms. "We're the Number 5 show – he's not going to even think about cancelling us."

Kim picked up Brooke's paperwork. "Well, if this is the standard we'll be producing in the future, I wouldn't bet on that, Joshua."

3

It was nine o'clock that night and Joshua was waiting outside the main entrance of the television centre. Kim came marching out. She had changed out of her business suit and was now wearing skin-tight black-leather trousers, high-heeled shoes, and a tight jacket, her handbag thrown over her shoulder.

"Do you not have your car with you?" asked Kim.

"Not today, no," said Joshua.

"Well, Jasmine will be here in a second to collect me – can we drop you off?"

"Nah, thanks. Brooke is giving me a lift, she's just getting her car from the car park."

"I see."

"You heading out on the town?"

"Of course! There's a bottle of Bollinger with my name and Jasmine's on it somewhere."

Jasmine was Kim's twenty-two-year-old daughter. It amused Joshua that mother and daughter were best of friends and were always hitting Dublin's night spots together.

Brooke pulled up beside them.

"Well, enjoy your night," said Joshua as he opened the passenger door.

"Will do, see you tomorrow. Give my love to Soraya!" called Kim as he slammed the door.

She stared at the car as it sped off.

Brooke lit up a cigarette and Joshua looked disapprovingly at her and opened the window beside him.

"She wants me out, Joshua. Kim wants me out," she stated.

He glanced at her disbelievingly. "That's bullshit! She's just being the usual demanding bitch she always is, that's all."

"No, this is something else. I can feel it. She's always trying to demean me. The other day she put me on reception for an hour. Reception! I'm a researcher, not a receptionist!"

"She just demands a lot from the team. It will be somebody else's turn to be picked on next week. She just wants to maintain the show's standard."

"But what does she expect? I can only present real guests with real stories."

"Well, prove her wrong. Get her something original. Find her stuff she can't criticise."

"That's easier said than done, Joshua . . . I think she wants to give my job to that bloody daughter of hers."

Joshua looked sceptically at her. "Jasmine? Nah!"

"Yes, Jasmine, or Mini-Kim as I call her. If I hear Kim saying once more that Jasmine has just graduated from media college, I'll scream. Graduated and looking for a job. My job! You've seen Jasmine – she's so up her mother's arse, it's sickening. My job would be a nice start for her in the industry."

Joshua guffawed. "Who the fuck would want their kid working with them? I couldn't think of anything worse than my son at the studio."

Brooke smiled sympathetically at him. "Things still bad with Lee?"

"Give me one of those cigarettes, will you?" He reached forward, took a cigarette from her pack and lit it, closing up his window at the same time. "Lee drives me mad. He's in the middle of doing his final school exams and he doesn't give a shit about

15

them. He's not going to get into university, he did no study at all. And no plans for the summer. All he does is lie around all day, watching TV, or hanging around those deadbeat mates of his."

"Well, he's just turned eighteen, what do you expect?"

"I was out working when I was eighteen. I didn't have the luxury of school, or going to college like he has. He lives in a beautiful home, has a loving family. I mean Soraya loves him as if he is her own. And things aren't that easy for her with the two toddlers. But she always put him first, not that he ever appreciated it."

"She's a star alright," Brooke dragged on her cigarette. "Try and go easy on him, Josh – he hasn't always had it that easy."

"Neither have I!"

"Yeah, but you were the adult, Josh. Whatever happened with Lee's mother, you were an adult dealing with it, he was a kid."

"What's this, are you taking that counselling you did earlier to heart and found a new talent in life?"

She glanced at him and pulled a face before smiling. "Hardly. . . Speaking of which, that girl Donna was in a bad way after the show."

"She seemed to have fallen hard for her ex-boyfriend, alright."

"No, it was something more than just unrequited love. She was still insisting that she and Glen could have a future together. I don't think she's stable."

"I don't think anybody who appears on our show is particularly stable, do you?"

Kim strode through the bar at the Shelbourne with her daughter Jasmine following on behind. People were calling over to her and she greeted them back.

A man caught her arm as she walked by. "Kim! When are we going to have that lunch?"

"I'm busy all this week, Peter, but I want to catch up soon. Call me tomorrow and we'll fix a date."

She swept by and headed for the bar.

"Hey, Ryan! How we doing?" she said to the barman.

"Doing great, Kim. What can I get you?"

16

"Two Cosmopolitans to start off with . . . each!" She slid up on a stool and Jasmine sat next to her.

"So, where we going tonight? What club are we heading to?" asked Kim.

"Wherever you want, Mum! The city is your oyster!"

"Where's your father tonight?"

"I left him at home. Watching some programme about quantitative easing."

Kim raised her eyes to heaven. "I guess it makes a change from gardening programmes."

The Cosmopolitans were put down in front of them and Kim took a long drink.

"Oooh, I needed that!"

"How's work?"

"Great. We're shooting a classic next. 'My brother-in-law got me pregnant' – shock horror!"

"Can't wait to see it!" said Jasmine gleefully.

"I'm having a lot of trouble with that researcher though."

"Brooke?"

"She's just not up to the job. She doesn't have that sense for the outlandish you need."

Jasmine tutted. "How did she get the job in the first place?"

"I don't know. But I know how she's keeping it – she's fucking Joshua Green."

"So you've been saying," said Jasmine.

"I mean, if she was just an incompetent researcher, I could put up with her. But she's an incompetent researcher who's fucking our star, and that makes her very dangerous. If it ever got out, imagine the scandal! Joshua Green having an affair on his perfect wife and family! After all that pontificating! The show would be axed, his career would be over . . . and so would mine for that matter."

"She's a liability," stated Jasmine.

"Joshua doesn't realise the great things I have planned for him, and me by association. The position for the Friday night *Tonight Show* is becoming vacant soon and I think Joshua would be perfect for it."

17

"Do you?" Jasmine was surprised. "But that's the station's flagship show, interviewing all the big stars and dealing with serious issues. That's a big jump from what Joshua is doing now."

"It's a big jump but one he can manage, especially with me pushing him. Because if Joshua gets the show then so do I – I'll be the new producer of *The Tonight Show*. I'll have reached the top."

"Ohhh! How exciting!" cooed Jasmine.

"I'm going to start canvassing the new Director of Programmes as soon as he starts. And I'm not going to let a grubby little affair with a little slapper like Brooke ruin all that . . . You know, I look at her sashaying around the studio, and I think 'Is this what we fought for? Is this what feminism has brought us to? A girl who still thinks using her body will get her ahead? A girl who thinks she will climb the ladder by sleeping with the star of the show?' It makes me want to puke."

"So how are you going to get rid of her?" asked Jasmine.

"I'm not sure yet, but I will. And when I do, there will be a nice new position for you there to take over as the new researcher."

Jasmine smiled broadly and giggled.

Kim jumped off her stool and sank back the rest of her Cosmopolitan. "Come on! Let's go party! Let's rock!"

Joshua lived in a very large Victorian three-storey semi-detached on a leafy street in Sandymount. Brooke pulled her car over outside the high railings at the front.

"Thanks for the lift," said Joshua, opening the car door and jumping out.

"No problem, see you tomorrow," said Brooke.

"I'm off tomorrow, so I'll see you the next day," he said as he closed the door.

Brooke drove off. It was only when she had turned out of the street that she realised she had an important document for Joshua to sign and, if he was off the following day, she needed his signature now. She sighed, turned the car around and pulled up once more outside his house.

She walked through the gateway into the short gravel drive.

Joshua's BMW was parked there alongside Soraya's Range Rover. She hoped Joshua would answer the door, quickly sign the document and she could get on her way. It wasn't that Soraya wasn't always nice – she was nice to a fault. She had often been around to their house, getting something signed, or delivering or collecting something. She just wasn't in the mood to press her nose up against the window-pane of their perfect life that night. As she climbed the steps to their front door, through the large Georgian windows she could see the tasteful luxury of their home: the warm glow from the chandelier lighting up the gold-and-cream themed interiors, the fire in the large fireplace at full blast even though there didn't seem to be anyone in the room.

She pressed the doorbell and waited.

The large door swung open and there stood Soraya.

"Hello there!" Soraya's face creased into a big smile.

"Hi, Soraya. I forgot to get Joshua to sign something. Could I disturb him for a second? If he could come out and sign it?"

"Well, come in!"

"No, it's alright, I –"

"Well, he just got into the shower, so if you don't mind waiting?"

"Oh – okay." Brooke groaned to herself as she stepped into the wide hall, her shoes sinking into the thick-piled gold carpet.

"Come on into the kitchen and have a coffee while you wait. Joshua takes for ever in the shower."

Brooke followed Soraya down the hall towards the kitchen. Double doors opened to the mahogany-panelled dining room on the left, the lounge to the right. In the kitchen the au pair was playing with the two children, Danielle aged three and Daniel aged two, on the cream porcelain-tiled floor. The kitchen was expansive and was a Clive Christian design.

"Ulrika, it's way past their bedtime," said Soraya. "Would you mind taking them up?"

"Sure thing," said Ulrika, getting up. Gathering up the children, she took them over to their mother to kiss.

"I'll check on them in a little while," said Soraya.

Brooke smiled at the children and waved at them as Ulrika carried them out of the room.

"Ulrika is a treasure," said Soraya. "I found her on this wonderful website called *scandinavian-au-pairs-in-a-hurry.com*. Take a seat, Brooke."

Brooke sat up on one of the stools at the island. Soraya set about making the coffee as Brooke studied her. She was a tall willowy woman in her mid-thirties, with long cascading natural-blonde hair. She had a refined beauty and her skin was almost luminous. Brooke was sure that it wasn't a face that had ever, or would ever, be touched by Botox. She imagined her radiant skin was the result of being protected ever since childhood, never exposed to the sun. She guessed Soraya had never had a cigarette, had always eaten well, and always had a restful night's sleep. Dressed in light jeans and an oversized white shirt, she looked the ultimate yummy mummy.

Brooke looked at the array of photos on the wall, a lot of them happy family portraits. There was a large one of Soraya aged around fourteen, a willowy beauty even back then. In the photo she was leading her pony in the countryside. Brooke reckoned the photo had been taken in Soraya's family's holiday home in the South of France – the one Joshua always went on about for weeks before they headed off there every summer.

As Brooke looked at Soraya and her pony, she thought the nearest she herself had come at that age to a pony was watching repeats of *Black Beauty* on TV. And that was only after she had managed to successfully fight off her brothers and sisters for the remote control. In another large photo, Soraya, aged around eighteen, was dressed in a stunning ball gown. She was surrounded by other well-dressed people and at the base of the photo was an inscription: *The Irish Embassy in Paris*. Brooke guessed the photo was taken when Soraya's father had been ambassador to France. Yes, Brooke knew all about Soraya's life.

As she studied the intricate design on Soraya's gown in the photo, she remembered that the only time she had worn a ball gown at that time of her life was going to her school graduation dance. And that night had turned into a full-scale Gothic horror.

The lad she had finally persuaded to bring her to her debs had proceeded to get mindlessly drunk on a self-made concoction of extra-strength lager and sherry. Yes – sherry! She had spent the night nursing him in the toilets as he chucked up. By the time they finally emerged, the dance was over, the lights were off and everyone had gone home. They had also missed the last coach and had to spend an hour and a half walking home, her propping him up. By the time she arrived home her crinoline dress resembled Scarlet O'Hara's after arriving back to Tara from the Civil War.

She quickly dismissed any further thought of that awful night and smiled at Soraya as she came over to the island and sat a mug of aromatic coffee in front of her.

"So I hear big changes are coming?" said Soraya, sitting up on another stool at the island.

"Sorry?"

"The new Director of Programmes at RTV, Guy Burton."

"Oh! Yes!" Brooke smiled.

"Nobody knows anything about him seemingly. Let's hope the show is safe."

"Joshua's show? I can't imagine any threat to it – the ratings are going up all the time."

"Hopefully. You never know what new bosses want or think though, do you? They always want to make sweeping changes and make their mark." Soraya smiled again.

Brooke thought she didn't look a bit worried. "As I said, I think Joshua is safe," she said.

"Well, we'll all get to meet the new man soon at the reception at The Four Seasons next week to greet him."

"I doubt I'll be invited to that," said Brooke.

"Oh, I'm sure you will," said Soraya, and she made a mental note to get Joshua to put her on the guest list.

"No, I don't think researchers will be at that. It's only for senior staff."

Soraya smiled sympathetically at Brooke. "It's a thankless lot being a researcher, isn't it? You get the blame when things go wrong and none of the credit when things go right. I should know!"

Brooke nodded and smiled. Soraya had been a researcher on Joshua's show in its first season. That's how they met. She'd heard that Soraya got the job through a family friend. It irritated Brooke, when she thought of how long and how hard she had fought for her position, that the opportunity had just been gifted to Soraya. But that was life, thought Brooke.

"Do you miss it? Working on the show?" she asked.

"Not in the least. I wasn't a very good researcher as it happens, as I'm sure you've been told," Soraya giggled.

On the contrary, everyone had always said what a brilliant researcher she had been.

There was suddenly an outburst of shouting upstairs, breaking up the peaceful ambience of the house. Brooke could hear Joshua's raised voice and his son Lee's.

"Oh dear, here we go!" Soraya pulled an apologetic face and got up and walked out into the hall.

Brooke listened as Soraya shouted up the stairs.

"Excuse me please! We have a guest – could you keep your voices to a respectable level, thank you!"

Soraya came back into the kitchen.

"I'm so sorry, Brooke, goodness knows what you think of us, with all that shouting. I imagine you never have that kind of embarrassing commotion wreck your peace at home."

No, not since I live on my own, thought Brooke, but she smiled indulgently.

She heard Joshua come pounding down the stairs and into the kitchen, dressed in a bathrobe and towelling his hair dry. "Do you know what Lee is doing upstairs? Emailing his friends! He's in the middle of his exams and he's emailing his friends instead of studying!" Then he spotted Brooke at the island. "Oh, hello, Brooke!"

"Sorry for disturbing you, Joshua. I forgot to get you to sign this, and Kim will kill me if I don't have it first thing in the morning," explained Brooke, pushing the paperwork and a pen towards him.

"Oh! We can't be upsetting Kim!" he said sarcastically with a smile. He approached the island, took the pen and started scribbling his signature.

At that moment, Joshua's son Lee came into the kitchen.

"Where do you think you're going?" demanded Joshua as Lee headed for the back door.

"Over to Aunt Helen!" snapped Lee, putting on his jacket.

"Oh, no, you don't! You've got exams this week and you're not going anywhere. Aunt Helen indeed! She's a handy excuse. You're off to hang around with those no-good deadbeats you call friends!" Joshua headed over to the back door and blocked Lee's progress.

"Oh, piss off!" snapped Lee.

"Don't you speak to me like that!" shouted Joshua.

"Then don't treat me like the people on your freak show!" Lee shouted back.

Brooke looked on, mesmerised and a little concerned, as the two launched into a full-scale argument.

Soraya had begun stirring a big pot on the range. "Brooke, will you stay for dinner with us?" she asked.

"Oh, no! No, thank you!" said Brooke quickly, jumping off the stool and grabbing the signed paperwork. She didn't know what would be harder to put up with: Joshua and Lee's rowing or Soraya's perfect cooking.

"Are you sure? We'd love to have you, and they'll calm down in a minute or two," said Soraya, nodding over to the rowing pair.

"No, thanks, I've got plans for tonight."

"Okay. Joshua! Brooke is leaving!"

Joshua broke off from his argument. "Right. Thanks, Brooke, I'll talk to you later."

Brooke nodded and quickly made her way out as the rowing started up again.

Brooke opened the front door of her apartment and slammed it behind her. She walked into the small sitting room and set her briefcase on the coffee table, then flicked on the television with the remote. She went into the kitchenette and, opening her fridge, she selected a lasagne ready-meal and stuck it in the microwave. She then opened a bottle of red wine, took it and a glass out to the coffee table and sat down on the couch. She poured herself a large glass of wine, took some paperwork from her briefcase and settled back for the night.

Just then her mobile rang and she saw that Donna Doyle's number had come up.

"Hello, Donna? Is everything alright?"

"I just needed to have a talk about the show today with you. Can you talk for a while?"

Brooke looked at her paperwork and sighed, then forced herself to sound cheerful down the phone. "Sure, Donna? How do you feel now?"

Soraya sat at the dressing table in their bedroom, brushing her hair.

Joshua was on the bed, writing his blog on his laptop.

"You know the photo shoot coming up for *Privilege*?" asked Soraya.

"Yes?" He didn't look up from his computer screen.

"How long will it take?" asked Soraya.

"How long do they usually take? Three – four hours? I've told Lee I want none of his attitude on the day either. He sits down and poses with the rest of us and does what the photographer tells us to do."

"I don't blame him for having attitude with something like the photo shoot. All his friends will take the piss out of him."

"Look, he takes all the benefits of my fame – the money, the house, anything he wants when he wants it. He can put a bit back for once and at least pretend we're one big happy family."

Soraya put down her brush and stood up. She came and sat beside him on the bed. "But we *are* just one big happy family." She smiled at him and snuggled into him.

He put his arm around her and kissed her hair.

"What gems of wisdom are you writing on your blog today?" she asked, looking at his computer screen.

"About dealing with difficult teenagers!"

She laughed. "Joshua?"

"Hmmm?" He was typing away.

"She's a nice girl, Brooke, isn't she?"

"Yeah, she is."

"I thought it would be nice if you got her an invite to the reception party for the new Director of Programmes next week?"

"Why would I do that?"

"I just think it would really excite her to be at it."

"But researchers never go to something like that."

"But I think she's talented. It would do her good to mix with people at the party."

"I can't see it myself . . . But if it makes you happy, I'll get her put on the guest list."

She smiled up at him. "Thanks, Joshua."

He smiled back and kissed her before his eyes returned to his website.

"For fuck's sake!" he snapped.

"What's wrong?"

"Listen to what somebody has written on the message board of my website! *'Joshua's show sank to a new level today. What a line-up! When is RTV going to realise the shit it is inflicting on the country and send Green and his tacky show back to the sewer where he belongs. I don't know how he can sleep at night exploiting these poor unfortunates.'*" Joshua looked at Soraya with raised eyebrows. "The writer calls himself – or herself – *Joshua's Number One Fan.*"

"Sarcastic to boot! Well, you can't expect gushing praise all the time on that blog, Joshua. Your show is controversial, so you're always going to get some criticism."

"True," said Joshua.

Soraya wished he looked more convinced.

4

Brooke opened an email from the public relations department at RTV. She read and then reread it. It was an invitation to the reception being held in the Shelbourne Hotel on Friday night to welcome RTV's new Director of Programmes, Mr Guy Burton.

Soraya put on her earrings, then stepped back and looked at herself in the full-length mirror in their bedroom.

"Will I do?" she asked, turning around as Joshua came out of their dressing room tying his tie.

He took one long appreciative look at her in her shimmering satin Karen Millen gown, her hair tied back in a bun.

"You'll more than do!" he said, and took her in his arms.

There was a beep from outside the house.

"There's the car," said Soraya, pushing him away and quickly fixing her lipstick in the mirror.

"Come on then!" he said, putting on his jacket.

Soraya picked up her wrap and they left the room.

Downstairs, Lee was stretched out on the couch texting on his mobile, while Daniel and Danielle were on the floor playing.

"We're off," said Joshua.

"Right – bye," Lee said, not looking up.

"Ulrika will be back in an hour or so. You'll be alright till then?" asked Soraya, bending down and kissing the children.

Lee nodded and kept texting.

"Soraya asked you a question!" Joshua said in a raised voice.

"Of course I'll be alright!" Lee shouted. "What do you think is going to happen? That the house will burn down or something?"

"With you in charge, there's a very good possibility!" Joshua said.

"Well, stay at home and mind your own kids then, instead of swanning off to some posh party!" Lee snapped.

The car outside beeped again.

"Thank you, everybody! We need to get a move on, Joshua, or that driver will leave without us. We won't be late." Soraya bent down and kissed Lee.

In the hall Joshua shook his head in despair. "The attitude!"

"He's fine."

"Maybe we should get his Aunt Helen to drop in to check on them?" suggested Joshua.

"No, that would be undermining Lee. Besides, she probably will be out on a date."

Outside a Mercedes was waiting for them on the gravel driveway.

"Good evening, Mr Green, Mrs Green," said the driver as he opened the car's back door for them.

They sat in.

"I thought RTV were supposed to be cutting back on these perks like chauffeur-driven cars to events," whispered Soraya to Joshua.

"They have!" He gave her a cheeky but confident smile.

"So they're still looking after you!" said Soraya. "Their Number One Star!"

Joshua's smile dropped.

"What's wrong?" she asked.

"It's just when you said 'Number One Star' . . . you remember what somebody called Joshua's Number One Fan wrote on my message board recently? Well, whoever it is has been constantly posting messages on my website. And it's really nasty stuff. Pretty vicious."

27

"Well, as I've said to you before, Joshua, when you do the kind of show you do, you're going to get insults from time to time."

"I know that. But the trouble is, this person is so relentless. They seem to write something every day. Sometimes twice or three times a day. It pisses me off. And they can hide behind their user name and remain anonymous whereas I'm totally exposed."

"Well that's the trouble with television, Joshua – you never know who's watching."

Brooke had taken the previous day off and gone shopping for a new dress for the Shelbourne party. She was so excited about going, and felt it was a great opportunity to get to know important people at RTV. She had finally found a cream satin gown and spent three hours deliberating over it in Karen Millen. The pluses were it was stunning, eye-catching and a statement. The minuses were it was too stunning, too eye-catching and too much of a statement. Not to mention the price. She felt if she turned up in it she might put people's noses out of joint. A 'Who does she think she is?' kind of scenario. She didn't think she had the confidence to wear such an outfit to this work do. Finally, with the strong encouragement of an over-zealous salesgirl, who had missed her way and would have made a fantastic life coach, she bought it.

Surveying herself in the mirror for a last time before she set out for the reception, she had to admit she looked marvellous.

Then, as she reached for her wrap, the phone rang.

It was Donna Doyle, the girl who had appeared on the show – and she was desperate to talk to someone. She began to pour out her troubles.

Half an hour later Brooke put the phone down and reached again for her wrap. Late now, she called a taxi and hurried outside to wait.

As she stood on the side of the road, it was threatening to rain again after a recent downpour. The taxi arrived promptly and swerved in to pull up beside her, but in doing so drove into a puddle, and splattered dirty water all over her cream gown.

Brooke sighed as the taxi pulled up in front of the Shelbourne and she looked down at her black cocktail dress. Her satin gown had been ruined by the earlier taxi's assault and she'd had to go back up to her apartment and change. The cocktail dress looked nice, but it wasn't a patch on the gorgeous dress she had bought. She paid the taxi driver and got out.

Jasmine was driving an extra lap around Stephen's Green en route to the Shelbourne, her mother in the passenger seat.

"I don't want to arrive before Guy Burton," said Kim. "I want to make a big entrance so he realises how important I am."

"I wonder what he's going to be like?" asked Jasmine excitedly.

"He'll be like all other Director of Programmes the world over. Enter with great fanfare, promise to change the world. Then reality hits him: he is just another cog in the wheel. So he gets on with going along with the status quo and not rocking the boat." Kim spoke in a world-weary, seen-it-all-before voice.

"You're usually right."

"I'm always right. But we'll play along with him, flatter his ego, and let him down gently."

Jasmine pulled up in front of the Shelbourne, handed the car keys to a porter and the two of them headed in.

Brooke had circulated the function room in the Shelbourne, gripping her glass of champagne tightly, realising she had never spoken to most of the people present before. She felt out of place. Finally she managed to latch onto a PR girl who she was slightly friendly with and stayed by her for dear life, offering to assist her with the night's events if she needed any help. When the PR girl moved off to deal with some disaster concerning canapés, Brooke found herself putting up with the attention of an executive in his fifties who had tried chatting her up in the canteen a few times before. As she listened to him droning on about his golf, Joshua and Soraya arrived. Brooke thought they entered the room in the way the Sun King and his queen might have entered Versailles, confident of everyone's attention and everyone's focus. Soraya seemed to have a glow about her and Brooke realised with a jolt she was wearing the same Karen Millen cream dress she had bought and just ruined. And as she watched Soraya and Joshua working the room, she didn't know whether to laugh or cry. Laugh with relief that she hadn't shown up in the same outfit as Soraya, particularly as the outfit looked so much better on her. Or cry, because it was typical that fate should intervene to save Soraya's gilded life from the embarrassment of having a lowly researcher show up in the same dress at the same function.

Soraya and Joshua were chatting with Fiona Fallon, the very glamorous and Botoxed star of the channel's successful soap, and her screenwriter husband Mike. Mike had risen to the crest of Irish film success in the nineties and even got an Oscar nomination. His career since had somewhat stalled, and he was reduced to grabbing a television series whenever he got the chance.

"I hear the new director is going to invest a lot into good drama," said Joshua.

"That's me fucked then!" said Fiona. "Pity he doesn't like bad drama, then I'd be safe!"

"Well, I'm going to try and set up a meeting with him early on. I've quite a few ideas for some good drama series," confided Mike.

"Any roles for an aging beauty with a slight booze problem?" questioned Fiona.

"Isn't that the role you play in the soap you're in now, honey?" asked Mike.

"That's the role I've always played in everything I've been in," she answered. "I played it when I was thirty and I'll play it when I'm seventy. It's a role that comes naturally to me."

"What about you, Josh? Have you any plans to present to him?" asked Mike.

"No. I'm really happy with everything just the way it is," said Joshua.

"I wonder who he's going to put presenting *The Tonight Show*?" asked Mike.

"I heard they were looking at Darren O'Keefe," said Soraya.

"No, Darren's too highbrow for *The Tonight Show*. He's too current affairs. You need someone who can get down and dirty with the stars for that role."

As the men kept talking, Fiona drew Soraya slightly aside and said, "You're looking fabulous, Soraya. Just fabulous!"

"Thanks, Fiona, you're looking great yourself," smiled Soraya.

Fiona leaned closer and whispered conspiringly, "Who does your Botox?"

Soraya continued smiling but looked perplexed. "I haven't had any!"

Fiona scrutinised her face and grinned. "Sure thing! And I'm Dolly Parton's sister! Don't be coy, Soraya." Fiona glanced over at Joshua. "Joshua is looking rather good these days. Any nip and tuck going on there?"

"No, Fiona. I've put him on a diet of fresh fruit, vegetables and plenty of water."

"I see! So *that's* the answer, is it?" Fiona smirked disbelievingly. "You can trust me, Soraya. Let's face it, I'm not one to judge. Do anything to roll back the years so you keep getting the roles, that's my motto. I heard you got the front cover of *Privilege*?"

"Yes."

"Who got it for you?"

"I don't know, Fiona. It came through the RTV public relations department."

"I heard Kim Davenport wangled it for you. Blackmailed the editor over some sex scandal he was involved in several years ago. She knows where everyone's dirty linen is hidden in this town! Mine included! And she isn't afraid to use it to get what she wants."

"Kim's a sweetheart."

"Sure she is! Let's just hope you guys never fall out with her, or you'll find all your dirty linen hung out to dry as well!" Fiona knocked back her champagne and grabbed another glass from a passing waiter.

Soraya glanced around to see if anyone could rescue her from Fiona. She spotted Brooke talking to a man in the corner. She waved over and Brooke waved back and smiled. Soraya beckoned to her. Brooke looked a bit surprised, but took her leave of the man and made her way over.

"Hello, Soraya."

Soraya bent forward and kissed Brooke on the cheek, surprising her further. "How nice to see you here, Brooke. And you look great. I was going to wear black."

"Funnily enough, I was going to wear cream!" said Brooke, looking at the replica of her dress on Soraya.

"Fiona, this is Brooke."

"And who are you, my lovely?" asked Fiona, looking her up and down.

"I work on Joshua's show."

"At least you're not an actress. I hate actresses, particularly young ones. Show me a young actress and I'll show you the beginning of a boulevard to broken dreams! You know they don't let people go up to the Hollywood sign in Los Angeles any more? Too many actresses were killing themselves by throwing themselves off it, their dreams in tatters. Life is very hard for an actress."

There was a sudden commotion at the entrance to the room and heads turned to see Kim standing there beside Jasmine.

"Time to party, everybody!" Kim called out, as she came through the room and everyone rushed to greet her.

"Oh fuck, I feel my headache coming on," said Fiona, placing an arm through her husband's. "Come on, lover, let's mingle. I feel a hurricane heading in this direction, and I need to find shelter. Joshua, Soraya!" she blew them a kiss. "It's been emotional!"

Fiona and her husband walked off.

Kim made a beeline for Joshua and Soraya, exchanging pleasantries with everyone she passed.

"Well, here we are!" said Kim.

"Hi, Kim – hi, Jasmine," said Soraya.

Kim suddenly spotted Brooke. "What are *you* doing here?"

"Eh, I was invited," said Brooke, going bright red.

"But why?" Kim was annoyed by her presence.

"Because," Soraya said, quickly putting an arm around Brooke,

"Brooke is an integral part of Joshua's team, and it's good experience for her to be here."

"I see!" said Kim, glaring at Brooke. "Anyway, where is he?"

"Guy Burton? He hasn't arrived yet."

"Shit! I wanted to get here after him, so he would see my entrance!"

A dark-haired man aged around forty suddenly joined their circle. "Oh, I saw it alright. Quite a carnival!"

Everyone stared, all at a loss for words.

"Guy Burton," he introduced himself, and smiled at everyone. He accent was mid-Atlantic.

Kim was taken aback. She expected him to be announced into the room, followed by a public introduction by the Public Relations Manager or the station head himself, Henry King. Not a man discreetly moving through the crowd, listening in. It was nearly sneaky, she thought.

She decided to quickly take back control of the situation. "Guy, it's a pleasure to meet you." She stretched out her hand for him to shake. "I'm Kim Davenport, I'm –"

"I know who you are, Kim," he cut in, shaking her hand.

"Of course you do. And of course you need no introduction to Joshua Green – and this is his lovely wife Soraya."

"Joshua, I've heard great things about you," said Guy.

"Welcome aboard," said Joshua, shaking his hand.

Soraya then shook his hand and smiled. "A pleasure to meet you."

"And this is my beautiful daughter Jasmine," said Kim.

Guy took her hand while Jasmine attempted her best to look coquettish.

"You have no drink, Guy, what do you want?" asked Kim.

"I'm just going to have a Coke."

"Right, Brooke, a Coke for Guy, a vodka and tonic for myself, and a wine spritzer for Jasmine."

Brooke stood for a second, realising she was not going to be introduced to Guy.

"Brooke?" snapped Kim.

Brooke nodded and turned to go and get the drinks.

As she heard Kim rattle on about the show's success, she wished she hadn't come.

Glancing at his watch, Guy wanted to move on. He had already spent twenty minutes talking to Kim and Joshua. There were a lot more shows on the channel and he wanted to meet and greet everyone else. Not get lumbered with Kim's plans for the future.

"Do you know, I'd love to hear the rest of your ideas, Kim, but I'm not really taking it all in here with the noise. But I'm setting up half-hour meetings with all the station's producers over the next week and so you can tell me everything then."

"Right!" said Kim, disconcerted. "I look forward to having a proper talk with you then."

"Joshua, I'm looking forward to working with you. Soraya, it's been a pleasure." He nodded at Jasmine and Brooke and walked off into the crowd.

"He's a cold fish," stated Kim, looking after him.

"I think he's kinda cute," said Jasmine.

"You need to get your contact lenses seen to, Jasmine."

"I thought he was a pretty cool guy," said Joshua. "Quite personable."

"Yes, give the poor man a chance, Kim," urged Soraya. "It must be daunting for him. Coming here and not knowing anybody."

"Oh, don't worry, I will give him a chance. I aim to be his new best friend." Kim was watching him as he made his way through the crowd. "He needs somebody like me to help guide him in his new role. I can be very beneficial for him as he settles in."

"Nobody knows this station like you, Kim," conceded Joshua.

"Look at that! Fiona Fallon has commandeered him. She'll have him booked in for liposuction if we leave him to her. Let's rescue him! Come on, Joshua!" Kim linked his arm.

"But he just left us, Kim! Quite pointedly, if politely."

"Bullshit! Let's go! We need to circulate anyway."

She hauled an unwilling Joshua off as Jasmine headed off to the bathroom, leaving Soraya and Brooke alone.

"Don't fetch any more drinks for her, Brooke," chastised Soraya.

"She's my boss, I can hardly say no," said Brooke.

"You're not here to work, you're here to enjoy yourself. Well, as much as anyone can at one of these things!"

"I thought you'd love all this – the glamour and everything."

"When you've been to as many as we have, they just become tedious. Joshua loves them, so I don't mind if it pleases him. I'd prefer to be at home with the kids, if the truth be known."

"Is your au pair minding them?"

"No, Ulrika is out on a hot date so we left Lee in charge – which brings its own problems."

"Doesn't he like minding the children?"

"It's not that, he's very good at it, but Joshua doesn't think he's responsible enough. Thinks the house will burn down while he's on his iPad. And that in turn causes big rows," Soraya rolled her eyes.

"They seem to have a volatile relationship," observed Brooke, remembering the shouting match she had witnessed in their kitchen recently.

"The problem is they are too alike. That's why they fight like cat and dog. It's the exact same with me and my mother!"

Yes, if Soraya's mother was anything like her, Brooke imagined those squabbles over whose soufflé was superior might get quite tetchy.

"But you get on with Lee?"

"Oh yes, I adore him. We're great friends. I'm not cast in the Wicked Stepmother role at all," Soraya giggled.

Brooke wondered, as she had a thousand times before, what the story was with Lee's mother, Joshua's first wife. Nobody knew anything about her and it was closed territory as far as Joshua was concerned. For somebody who made his living out of exploring other people's lives, his own past was closed shop.

"Well, I'm sure you're a wonderful stepmother," said Brooke sincerely. "Lee's lucky to have you."

"Well, Lee's had his troubles but he's a good kid underneath. I keep reminding Joshua of that. I'm lucky to have him as a stepson, although I never, ever imagined myself in that role. I never thought

I'd be married to somebody with a previous marriage and a son behind him. And neither did my parents."

"They're not fond of Joshua?" pressed Brooke. She realised she was being very nosy, but couldn't help herself.

"Me and Joshua are from very different backgrounds. I think they expected somebody different for me."

Yes, judging from the debutante photos from her time living in France, Brooke imagined Soraya's parents expected her to marry a titled billionaire who lived on the Avenue Foch.

"But we're very happy, and that's the main thing. I'm an only child and we lived in a lot of embassies growing up, so it could be lonely. I love having Joshua and the kids, and the au pair. I don't even mind Joshua and Lee's rows! They fill the house, and I love a full house. Have you any brothers and sisters, Brooke?"

"Any number of them," answered Brooke, raising her eyes to heaven at the thought of the brood she had sprung from. An embassy full of empty beautiful rooms sounded a wonderful place to grow up in, she thought.

"Then you're lucky," said Soraya.

And so are you Mrs Green, thought Brooke.

5

It was Sunday morning. Kim pulled into Joshua's driveway. It was a habit of hers to call over to the Greens' house every Sunday morning where Joshua would cook her breakfast and they could have a good catch-up after the week. She enjoyed doing it, as they could speak freely without the risk of people listening in at the studio. And it demonstrated how close they were. She rang the doorbell, and Joshua answered it, still in his dressing-gown.

"Did I wake you?" she asked, stepping inside.

"No, I've been up an hour," said Joshua as she followed him down the hallway and into the kitchen where there was a smell of a fry-up in the making.

Joshua returned to his cooking and Kim sat up at the island. The patio doors were open and outside Soraya and the au pair were playing with Danielle and Daniel. Kim imagined Lee was still in bed – the kid never seemed to get out of bed before midday, much to Joshua's consternation. Joshua took out a can of Coke from the fridge and handed it to her. She opened it, lighting up a cigarette at the same time.

"Was it a late one the other night at the Shelbourne?" asked Joshua, as he went back to tending the fry.

"I think me and Jasmine were the last to leave, nothing new there." She dragged on her cigarette and took a gulp of Coke. "I tell you one thing, I think Guy Burton was very impressed with you, Joshua."

"Nah . . . the only thing he seemed impressed with was Fiona Fallon's cleavage!"

"That's only because he had no choice, the way she was shoving it in his face all night long."

"Poor Fiona!"

"Poor Guy Burton! But, seriously, I could see from his reaction he thought you were a man going places."

"Well, that's good then. It's best to have the Director of Programmes on our side."

"Definitely . . . especially when we make our pitch for *The Tonight Show*."

"*What?*" Joshua turned around, his mouth open in disbelief.

"I think you'd be perfect for it."

"I think you're insane."

"Seriously, Joshua. They've bandied that many names around to take over that show and not one is right for it."

"And in all the names they've bandied about, my name hasn't been mentioned once!"

"That's because we haven't expressed an interest in it."

"No, it's because what we do on our show is a million miles from what they do on *The Tonight Show*."

"No, it's not! On your show we deal with the grubby details of the common people, on *The Tonight Show* we'll be dealing with the grubby details of the rich, powerful and famous. A natural progression, as far as I'm concerned."

"You've really thought this through. You're serious."

"All we have to do is make everyone else realise how good you'd be."

Joshua started to serve out the food onto plates he had lined up along the counter. "The trouble, is I don't think I would be any good at it. It's not my scene." He crossed over to the patio windows and shouted, "Breakfast is ready!"

He then took two plates and came over to the island. He sat up on a stool opposite Kim.

Kim threw the half-finished cigarette into the half-full can of Coke.

"Joshua, when have I ever let you down or given you bad advice?"

"Never." He started to eat his breakfast.

"When I found you in radio and told you that you would be perfect for television, you didn't believe me. Remember?"

"I remember."

"It took me a while to convince you. But look at you now. And you will be perfect for *The Tonight Show* – we just have to prove to Guy Burton that you are."

"And how do you propose to do that?"

"Leave it to me, Joshua. I'll fix it, I always do. . . You know that *Privilege* magazine shoot coming up for you?"

"Uh huh."

"I think I might get the PR department to suggest to Guy Burton to come for a look during it. I'll tell them to say it's important for him to see how the PR department works. But, if he comes by, he'll see just how impressive you are. Just ready to step into the shoes of *The Tonight Show* presenter. We'll announce your candidacy for the show with *Privilege* magazine and back it up with more interviews in the papers. And on your website, start being more political. Less blogs about Manchester United and more on global warming. That website will be important to project you as an intelligent and deep-thinking candidate for the new post." She noticed Joshua's face had soured slightly. "What's the matter?"

"Have you read my blog recently?"

"Sorry, Joshua, but I haven't had time to read your deepest darkest thoughts on life and the universe." She smirked over at him, then saw he looked concerned. "Why?"

"Nothing really. It's just that on the message board there's some idiot writing pretty insulting stuff about me."

"Not like you to be sensitive."

"I know. But it's a bit of a cheek, using my website to diss me. And get this – his or her user name is 'Number One Fan'."

"It goes with the territory, Joshua, unfortunately. If you land *The Tonight Show*, your profile will be much higher and you'll get much more attention. With the bad comes the good. That's one of the drawbacks of fame – you'll always get people who hate you." She had worked with enough stars over the years to know that behind their egos and bravado, they could be fragile when criticised.

Kim winked at Joshua as Soraya and the children came in from the garden.

6

Guy Burton had arranged to meet all the producers. He was allotting each producer a thirty-minute meeting, as an initial get-to-know-you chat. Kim had decided she needed a lot longer than thirty minutes to have a proper *really* get-to-know-you chat with Guy and had devised a plan to enable them to spend some quality time together. She stood with Jasmine in an empty corridor at the television studio beside a glass-encased fire-emergency button.

"Now my meeting with Guy is due to start at four o'clock," she instructed. "Give it to no later than five past four and then break this glass and press the emergency button – then scarper out of the building and make sure nobody sees you."

"Consider it done!" nodded Jasmine and Kim headed off to meet Guy.

Kim popped in to the toilets and checked out her appearance in the mirror, fluffed out her hair and added some lipstick. She was looking forward to spending the afternoon and evening with Guy. It would allow him to see her qualities, see what she was made off, and see how he could help her get to where she wanted to go.

"Guy!" smiled Kim as his secretary showed her into his office.

He stood up, reached across the table and shook her hand. They both sat down.

"They've given you the best office," said Kim, smiling. "With

41

the best views." She pointed at the extensive manicured lawns outside that stretched out around television centre.

"Yes, it's nice to have some green to look out on. In my last job, my office just looked out on New York skyscrapers," said Guy with a smile. Now . . ." he opened an alarmingly big folder full of paperwork, "I've been going through some figures . . ."

She glanced at her watch as he began to discuss viewing figures for Joshua's show. Although she was still smiling, her eyes glazed over as he moved the conversation on to advertising revenue. And he completely lost her and her smile when he moved his talk on to production costs.

As he droned on, he was in danger of putting her to sleep and so she thanked heaven that she had organised her plot with Jasmine.

Suddenly the blaring fire alarm began to siren.

Guy looked up from his paperwork, startled. "What's that?"

"It's the fire alarm!" said Kim, standing up. "We have to evacuate the building immediately!"

"Oh!" said Guy, standing up and beginning to gather some paperwork up.

"No time for that," said Kim, going around the other side of the desk and taking his arm, leading him to the door. "There's a very strict policy that we have to get out of the building immediately once that alarm goes off."

As she propelled him out the door, he resisted. "My jacket – my wallet –"

"No time for that. Let's get a move on!"

He dived back for his jacket despite her urging, then she grabbed him by the arm and hauled him down the corridor.

As the alarm continued to wail all the television staff began to pour out of the building and into the front car park which was the assembly point.

"I wonder if there's a real fire?" said Guy, looking up at the building for signs of smoke. "Could be a hoax or false alarm."

"Impossible to tell, but it will take them ages to check everything and everywhere," said Kim.

"Shit! I could do without this!" Guy was irritated.

"Best to write off the rest of the afternoon. This has happened a few times before, and we won't be allowed back in the building until they have checked every last light fitting!"

"What a waste of time!" said Guy.

"Well, there's no point in standing around in the car park with the rabble. My car is just over here – let's go for a coffee and continue our meeting." Kim walked over to her car, while Guy stood staring at the building.

Kim paused at her car door. "Guy?"

Guy turned and looked at her, then joined her.

"Where are we actually going?" asked Guy some minutes later as he realised they had been driving quite a while and passed many places that would have supplied them with a coffee adequately.

"I thought we might as well pop over to my place for that coffee," said Kim.

"Your place?" He was surprised and confused.

"Yes, it's not that far. We might as well have our meeting in a bit of comfort."

"Right!" He searched for his mobile in his jacket pockets only to discover he had left it behind in the office. "Blast! I've forgotten my mobile! Can I borrow yours? We should check on the fire – see if it was a false alarm."

"Too soon to say." Kim made no move to produce her mobile. "We'll check when we get to the house."

Guy subsided and looked ahead.

A short while after, Kim turned into her gateway, drove up a long driveway and parked in front of the house.

"Here we are!" she said.

Guy got out and looked up at the house. It was an architecturally designed flat-roofed, one-storey house that seemed to be spread out forever. There was a lot of glass and a real look of the seventies about it – signs of an architect who was trying to be too clever.

Guy followed Kim to the front door and she let them in.

"Nice gaff," he complimented as he followed her through the wide, granite-floored hallway that had lots of examples of modern art on the walls.

"I like it," she said as she opened the double doors at the bottom of the hallway and showed him into the lounge.

He blinked a couple of times as he looked around. It was a very large room on split levels, done out in complete seventies chic. The sofas and armchairs were cream leather with chrome legs, with a round glass coffee table. There was a suspended light fitting that hovered halfway to the floor. There was lava lamp sitting on the television and a sheepskin rug lying in front of a stone floor-to-ceiling fireplace. Steps led up to a dining area where there was a round glass table and cream-leathered chrome-legged chairs.

"What do you think?" asked Kim.

"It's very . . . retro."

"It's retro, it's hetero, it's metro . . . it's everything I love. I love the seventies, don't you?"

"I guess."

"It brings me right back to my youth. I just managed to catch the late seventies when I was in my early teens, so remember all the wildness." She pulled a face, "Not that there was much wildness going on where I was growing up in Malahide. But there was BBC 2, and I was allowed unlimited access to it. And that educated me to the world. My parents would be off to bed, and there I'd be glued to the television till the early hours, watching programmes that were totally unsuitable for my age, thinking back on it. But it was my education. It made me realise, at an early age, the power of television. It showed me the world that was out there, and I wanted to be part of it. To educate people and show the very different lives that people have."

"Well, I guess you certainly achieve that with Joshua's show."

"I'm glad you can see that, Guy. Because to me, making good television is so much more than advertising revenue and production costs – it's educational."

"So you see Joshua's show as being educational and not just entertainment?"

"Got it in one, Guy."

A man walked into the room and halted, startled. "Oh, hello!"

Kim turned around. "Guy, this is my husband Tom. Tom, this is our new Director of Programmes, Guy Burton."

"Hello," said Guy, smiling and shaking Tom's hand.

Guy was surprised to see Tom. He hadn't been sure what Kim's husband would be like. But, since seeing the house, he had vaguely imagined somebody wearing an unbuttoned shirt complete with medallion, with dodgy taste in clothes, jumping out of a vintage sports car and competing with Kim in who could hang on to their youth the best. Instead, Tom was a man of around fifty, with a kind and open face, a paunch and glasses, dressed in a cardigan.

"Very nice to meet you," said Tom with a smile. "Can I get you a cup of tea?"

Kim guffawed. "He doesn't want a cup of tea, for goodness' sake, Tom! We need something a little stronger than that, don't we? We've just had a shock, Tom – the fire alarm went off and we had to evacuate the building. Probably a false alarm or hoax though as there wasn't any smoke to be seen."

"Oh dear," said Tom. "How upsetting! I hope Jasmine isn't in any danger?"

"No, she wasn't even there at the time."

"Em – can we check up on the fire?" said Guy. "I'd like to phone –"

"I'll do that right now," said Kim and headed over to the drinks cabinet. She took out two crystal tumblers. "Whiskey okay with you, Guy?" She didn't wait for an answer and filled two glasses with hefty whiskies and squirted some soda in them from a seventies soda-dispenser. "It's brilliant, isn't it?" she said, holding up the dispenser. "I got it in an antiques shop in Galway. It's amazing what passes for antiques these days."

She came and handed Guy his drink.

"You media types and your afternoon drinking! You're all so decadent," said Tom, smiling indulgently. "Anyway, I'm out to do some gardening. Do let me know if RTV has burned down! Nice to have met you, Guy."

"Yes, you too," Guy smiled as Tom ambled off through the patio doors and went down the gardens.

"He seems like a very nice man," said Guy.

"Yes," said Kim. "He's my rock . . . well, more like a stone. As in – around my neck!" She turned and started laughing. "You know, I can't remember meeting Tom. I was very young and was going through a real alcoholic stage at the time. I can't remember a thing from those times, I was so drunk. I can't remember marrying him, and I can't remember getting pregnant!"

"I imagine you do remember giving birth, however," said Guy with a wry smile as he sat down on the sofa.

"That I do!" She sat down on a sofa opposite him. "I'm glad we are having this time together, Guy. It's giving us a proper chance to get to know each other. I find office environments stifling sometimes, don't you?"

"They can be." He took a sniff of his drink. "Eh, Kim, I'd like to check up on what's happening back at the studios."

"Right," she said. "I'll phone security."

She went to where she had dumped her handbag on a table, retrieved her mobile and punched in a number. After a short exchange she came back. "Yes, seems to have been a hoax. Nobody has admitted to setting off the alarm and there is no evidence of fire. However, the Fire Brigade are still going through their routine check."

"That's a relief!"

Kim sat down again and picked up her whiskey glass. "Cheers!"

"Cheers," said Guy, raising his glass.

"Okay," she then said, seizing the initiative, "to continue at the point we left off before the alarm – we had gone through advertising figures and production costs, hadn't we? But we both know you can quote figures and costs until you're blue in the face, but the only figures that matter are the ratings, right?"

"Ratings are important, yes," nodded Guy.

"And *The Joshua Green Show* has relentlessly climbed the ratings since it went on air. True or false, Guy?"

"That's . . . true," agreed Guy.

"Good, then we all know where we stand. Joshua Green is a talented man, Guy. A very talented man. They say behind every great man is a great woman, and I'm the great woman behind Joshua Green. I discovered him, I made him, and continue to make him."

Guy nodded and took another sniff of the whiskey.

"I believe we've only seen the beginning of what Joshua Green can achieve. I think he can go much further than he has."

"What did you have in mind?"

"You will be very shortly looking for a new host for *The Tonight Show* and I think Joshua would be perfect for it."

"*The Tonight Show!*" Guy was incredulous.

"I'm asking you here to think out of the square box, Guy."

"Yes, but that's a huge leap for somebody like Joshua. I mean, to take him from a confessional Jeremy Kyle type show and expect him to front our biggest chat show. I –" Guy shook his head.

"Why not?" Kim jumped up excitedly and started to pace. "He is exactly what you're looking for. He has a way with people that is second to none!"

"Yes, with a certain type of person. But he has never interviewed Hollywood stars or politicians."

"He would rise to the occasion with ease. You know, Joshua has been given a lot of other offers from other television channels, and he has always shown loyalty to RTV and turned them down."

"I appreciate Joshua is a very successful talk-show host."

"Joshua sees his future with RTV, but he wants RTV to take him seriously and give him the opportunity to expand."

"I see," said Guy, understanding the thinly veiled threat that he would have no choice but to consider Joshua for *The Tonight Show* if he wanted to secure Joshua and the associated advertising into the future. "Well, I will certainly consider Joshua for *The Tonight Show* now that I'm aware he's interested in it."

"Thank you." Kim smiled at him and sat down. "Another thing, Guy – you're in a position to do me a big favour."

Another one? thought Guy. "Yes?"

"We have a problem with a member of staff on our show."

"Who?"

"A researcher called Brooke Radcliffe."

"And what is the problem with her?"

"Well, apart from the fact she's a mediocre researcher, she's also fucking Joshua Green."

Guy's eyes widened. "I see. And what part do I play in this situation?"

"I want you to get rid of her."

"On the grounds that she's fucking Joshua Green?"

"Precisely."

"I'm not sure if that's grounds enough to fire somebody."

"I don't think I'm making myself clear, Guy, forgive me. All our futures rely on Joshua's continued success. Joshua's image is one of perfect father and husband, a real family man. If it was ever discovered that he was sleeping with a whore from the production team, he'd be ruined. He'd be exposed as a hypocrite. All that pontificating over the years! The show would be cancelled, and think of all that lost advertising revenue."

Guy sat forward, confused. "You're the producer of the show. Why don't you just get rid of her yourself?"

"I can't be seen to do that. It might cause problems between me and Joshua. You see the pickle I'm in."

So you want me to do your dirty work, thought Guy. He sat back. "And how do you know they are sleeping together?"

"Well, I've no direct evidence, admittedly. Nobody has said anything. But I just know. A woman knows these things."

"Really?" He raised an eyebrow sceptically as he looked out at Tom doing the gardening and wondered, if Kim was so in touch with her emotions, what was she doing for years in a marriage where there was obviously no common ground.

"I'll see what I can do," he promised.

"Good. And when Brooke is gone and we're looking for a replacement for the researcher job, I've got just the girl. My daughter Jasmine."

Guy made a mental note never to put himself in a position where he was at the mercy of Kim Davenport again. He was hijacked for the entire afternoon and evening at Kim's house. The TV studios were now back in action but every time he made reference to getting back there or asked to use the phone, she filled up their glasses again. Tom had disappeared off to his bridge class early on, and Guy was left alone to spend nearly five hours listening to the world according to Kim while she got steadily more drunk. He felt he knew her inside out by the time he finally got a reprieve on the arrival of her daughter at nine in the evening. He insisted that Jasmine give him a lift back to his office. Kim was far too drunk to drive by then. And the taxi she said she had called for him had never materialised.

On the journey back to the studio Jasmine proved herself to be her mother's Number One Fan over and over again by singing her praises continuously. When she wasn't informing him of the brilliance of Kim, she divulged how she had tried to go blonde the previous year, and gave him an excruciatingly detailed description of how her make-up routine had changed during that period. "It's far easier being a brunette," she had tipped him off.

One thing that had become clear to Guy, through being held hostage by Kim, was just how important Joshua Green – and Kim, by virtue of her being his producer, mentor, Svengali and best friend – were to RTV. She had laid her cards out on the table. Joshua's show was a hugely popular and revenue-spinning programme, and that meant he and Kim had power. She was letting Guy know in the firmest of terms that she was going to have no normal producer/Director of Programmes relationship, because by virtue of Joshua's success, she had power. She even thought she had enough power to get Joshua and herself the flagship *Tonight Show*.

7

Kim had spiked a big curiosity in Guy about Joshua's show. True for her, it was one of the channel's cornerstones, and as such should be of importance to him. He spent the next few days observing the show from the sidelines. He would sit at the back of the studio unnoticed, watching the production team as they rehearsed and went about their business. Kim was in complete control and he could see she was a dragon to work for. Joshua seemed narcissistic, in the way most television stars Guy had dealt with seemed to be. Arrogant, full of his own importance and yet highly strung, the smallest of things could set him off into a temper tantrum.

And then Guy made a special job of looking out for Brooke Radcliffe, Joshua's accused paramour. He heard another of the production team call out to her, and was surprised when he identified her. He remembered seeing her at the reception. She didn't look like the home-wrecking femme fatale that Kim portrayed at all. He had imagined a short-skirted, low-topped alpha female, more interested in her appearance than her job. Instead Brooke was casually dressed in jeans, white T-shirt and a cream blazer. She had long chestnut hair, often tied back in a bun, and a striking intelligent face. And rather than being a mediocre researcher, as Kim claimed, she seemed to be damned good at her job. She ran herself silly all day doing things far beyond the remit of her position, including fetching Kim's dry-cleaning at one stage. When anyone shouted at her for something, she seemed to have it at her fingertips and she seemed to have a natural rapport with the show's guests. Intrigued, he watched out for any signs of intimacy between Joshua and Brooke. He couldn't see any. They had a good normal working relationship, but no more than they had with other members of the production team.

Then one day Guy passed Brooke in a corridor as she hurried into the studio.

"Brooke," he said, stopping her in her tracks.

She seemed to get a shock that he knew her name and looked at him apprehensively.

"I wonder could you get me a schedule for the show for next week," he asked.

"Eh, yes!" she said, taken aback and she fumbled through a folder she was holding, before handing him some papers.

"That's it there," she said.

"Thank you," he said, impressed she had it in a second, and with a nod and a smile he moved on.

He asked her for a couple of other things during the week and, each time, she got him what he wanted with impressive speed.

Nevertheless, he analysed the whole situation over the following days and decided that, if what Kim was saying was correct, it was just too much of a risk to keep Brooke. He couldn't play around with a show as important as Joshua's. If Brooke was sleeping with Joshua the implications could be immense and best to get rid of her quick smart. It wasn't a risk he could take, and if Brooke was innocent of the crime she was accused of, then that was unfortunate. That was the way the cookie crumbled.

He rang HR and asked them to arrange a dismissal letter for Brooke. He then rang down to *The Joshua Green Show* and asked for Brooke to see him at five thirty. It was the earliest he could fit her in, as he had a packed day of meetings.

Brooke sat very nervously outside Guy Burton's office. What on earth did Guy Burton want to see her about? What had she done wrong? She had never even been in the company of the previous Director of

Programmes, let alone talk to him, let alone be summoned to his office. Kim had been in unusually good form all day, and that made Brooke nervous. She wondered if it had something to do with her.

"You can go in now," said Guy's secretary, and Brooke stood up, knocked on Guy's door and entered his office.

Guy looked up from his paperwork and smiled.

"Ah, Brooke, thank you for meeting me. Sorry it's so late, I was held up in meetings."

"It's no problem," she smiled.

"Take a seat," he said and she sat down.

Guy had lost count of the number of people he had dismissed over the years. In his experience there was no point in beating around the bush. Just tell them there was no longer a position for them due to re-organisation.

She looked very nervous, he thought.

He reached into the open drawer beside him and lifted the envelope containing her dismissal letter from HR.

"Brooke, due to . . ." He stopped and studied her smiling face. He paused for a second, and then laid the letter back down in the drawer. He studied her for a while and then asked, "How long have you been working on the show, Brooke?"

"A couple of years."

"You enjoy it?"

"I love it."

He watched her for a while. "Can I ask you a personal question?"

She shrugged. "I guess so."

"Are you sleeping with Joshua Green?"

Her face went bright red and he wasn't sure if she looked very angry or very embarrassed.

"What made you ask such a thing?" she demanded.

"I don't know."

"Well, something must have!"

"I just heard some talk, that's all."

"You know, I'm sure I could have a case against you or something for asking such a question," she threatened.

"I'm sure you could."

They sat staring at each other.

"Actually, I am sleeping with Joshua. Not that it's yours or anybody else's business."

He looked pensive. "I see. Can I ask you another personal question?"

"It seems to be an occasion for it."

"Don't you feel guilty about his wife and children?"

She gave a little laugh. "No! They're not my wife and children, so why should I feel guilty? That's for Joshua's conscience, not mine. I'm not cheating on anybody."

He sat forward and studied her. "Why is a bright and intelligent girl making do with somebody's leftovers?"

"I come from a large family, I'm used to hand-me-downs."

"But being fitted around his and his family's schedule? It's a bad deal."

"I don't think it's a bad deal. I get to see Joshua when he's all spruced up, in great form, when we're going out to nice places. I don't have to see him first thing in the morning when he's groggy, and hung-over and bad-tempered and looking like shit. He's gone long before the morning, I can assure you. I don't have to deal with the dirty washing, or the other boring domestic details. That's her role. I think I get the sweet end of the deal."

"Don't you want a husband and a family of your own some day though?"

"Well, yes, one day, when the time is right."

"You know, time passes by very quickly, Brooke. People not that much older than you thought they could delay finding the right person while they attended to career, fun, whatever. They thought there was all the time in the world to secure the great catch, and now they are in danger of getting none at all."

"Speaking from experience?" she snapped.

He shot her a warning look.

"Well, what do you suggest I do then? Give up Joshua and concentrate on finding Mr Right? Position myself at a bar every night and fight off lecherous drunks? Or maybe I'll post my photo and details on the internet? That will give my old school friends a good laugh when they come across it. Or maybe I should join a dating agency. I haven't actually ruled that one out in all seriousness, but it's a very last shot, and hopefully a long way down the road."

"If you give yourself a chance you might meet someone naturally."

"I did, I met Joshua."

"He'll never leave that wife and kids for you."

"I know he won't."

Her phone bleeped and she reached into her pocket and read the text.

"Is that Joshua?" he asked.

"It is actually and I'm running late." She looked embarrassed. "I don't mean to rush you, but you wanted to see me about something?"

"Ah, yes," he said and looked down at the envelope containing her dismissal letter. "Actually, it's not very important. I don't want to hold you up any longer."

"Oh, right," she nodded and stood up.

She stopped at the door and turned, full of concern. "You won't say I admitted to the affair to anyone, will you?"

"I'll make a deal with you. If you don't tell Joshua that I know, then I'll say nothing to anyone else."

She nodded and left.

He reached in for the dismissal letter and tore it up.

Brooke was shaken as she left the television studios. As she sat into her car, her mobile rang.

"Yes?"

"Brooke, it's Aidan Doyle here."

"Hi, Aidan, how's Donna?"

"She's not very well. She was in a bad way last night, and we had to bring her to see a doctor who admitted her into a clinic."

"Oh no! I'm sorry to hear that!" Brooke closed her eyes in dread.

"She was alright before she appeared on your show. She went to pieces after."

"Aidan – it was she who approached us. Nobody forced her to come on the show."

Aidan hung up the phone.

8

Brooke sat distracted in the boardroom as Kim ranted on at the top of the table. She had been completely taken aback by Guy Burton revealing he knew about her and Joshua. In a strange kind of way their affair hadn't seemed real up to that point. She had felt herself and Joshua were like naughty kids with a secret. Knowing someone else knew made it suddenly feel very real. And even though she had put on an uncharacteristically defiant show, she felt bad about the situation. For a while she had felt sure he was going to fire her.

As she stared at Joshua, she wondered if he ever felt guilty.

"Brooke!" shouted Kim from the top of the table, jolting her out of her thoughts.

Brooke sat up quickly. "Sorry?"

Kim threw her hands in the air in exasperation and adopted a sarcastic tone. "Sorry for distracting you, but have you got any guests lined up for the coming month?"

"Yes – sorry, of course." Brooke started riffling through her paperwork and grabbed the first one that came to hand. "But first . . . I have something of concern to report. Do you remember Donna Doyle who was on the programme recently?"

"What about her?"

"Her brother rang me last night. She's been taken into a clinic."

"Good, she needed to be there. As soon as she's out again, grab her," said Kim. "Now, can we get on with the meeting?"

"She's a heartless bitch!" spat Brooke that night as she and Joshua had a takeaway in her apartment. "She didn't give a damn about Donna."

"She doesn't allow herself to get caught up in the guests' stories. It's about the show to her, and that's where it stops."

Brooke reached out for her glass of wine and took a drink. "I wish I could tune off as quickly."

She continued eating and saw he was looking distracted.

"What's wrong?" she asked.

He snapped out of the trance he was in and looked at her. "I was thinking of terminating my website for a while."

"You can't do that. It's a wonderful medium for you."

"It's just I'm having trouble with somebody who keeps posting vicious messages on it."

"Threatening stuff?"

"Not threats, no. Just nasty comments. I just wish they'd piss off. Now their comments are attracting more negative response from other people and the 'Number One Fan' is encouraging them! I don't operate my blog for other people to attack me on it."

"Look, why don't we just contact the website supplier tomorrow and block them from posting any more stuff?" she suggested.

"I was going to do that, but I didn't want them to think they were getting to me and I gave a shit."

"Well, you obviously do give a shit! And they'll know it if you terminate your website! So let's ban them from your site and move on, and we can concentrate on you getting *The Tonight Show*. Leave it to me. I'll sort it for you first thing in the morning."

He reached over and kissed her "Thanks."

Joshua and Soraya were on the couch at home. Soraya was watching his television show while Joshua was on his website.

"Don't look on the message board," advised Soraya. "You'll only get irritated by whatever your 'Number One Fan' says."

"No, I won't, because he or she is no more."

"Huh?"

"I spoke to Brooke about it and she contacted the website supplier today and banned Number One Fan and other abusers from posting on the site any more."

"Excellent. That's the end of that then," smiled Soraya.

"It's a bit of a relief, to be honest. He, or she, was really beginning to bug me."

Soraya went back to watching the show.

"For fuck's sake!" Joshua suddenly cried, giving her a start.

"What on earth is the matter?"

"The Number One Fan put a posting on last night before they were blocked today. Listen to what he wrote – *This is my last posting on Joshua Green's site. Due to the success of my comments on this message board I have decided to expand and have opened my own website aptly entitled – The We Hate Joshua Green Website. Join me there where I continue to campaign and expose this shallow man and his tacky show for what they are.*'"

Joshua quickly did a Google search and within seconds he had clicked into the new website.

"Who would be bothered doing all that?" asked Soraya incredulously as she looked down at the elaborately designed website.

"I don't know!" said Joshua, shaking his head.

9

Guy had noticed that Brooke looked awkward when she saw him again after their exchange in his office. They passed each other in the canteen and she nodded to him before quickly making her way down to some friends with her tray of food.

A few days later he was down at the Joshua Green studio and he sought her out.

"Brooke, do you have a copy of the schedule of guests for the next couple of months?" he asked her.

"Eh, sure," she said, quickly searching through her file and presenting him with it.

"Thank you," he said and studied her for a few moments.

She nodded and quickly scurried off.

Guy went through the schedule later on. The majority of the guests were the usual 'he said/she said' roll call of marriage infidelity and family disharmony, desperate to hang the dirty laundry that was their lives out for public inspection. However, one line-up worried him. There was a girl called Donna Doyle who he read from the notes had been admitted into a psychiatric hospital after a previous appearance on the show.

Guy left his office and headed down to the studio, where he found Brooke looking after some audience members.

"Brooke – a word?" he called over to her.

Brooke approached in what she hoped was a confident manner, but she really didn't want any more to do with Guy Burton. She was still recovering from the encounter in his office. And he unnerved her. Why was he bothering with a lowly researcher like her to ask for schedules and things, instead of talking to Kim, the producer?

"Yes, Guy?"

"This schedule you gave me, I've been going through it, and I'm a bit concerned about the girl Donna Doyle who has already appeared on the show."

"Really?" She hoped she had managed to conceal her dismay. She knew there was a problem about Donna.

"Is it true she has been in a clinic having . . ." he read from the script, ". . . *suffered nervous exhaustion*?"

"Well, she was being treated in there, yes."

"And who has assessed Donna to check her state of mind and whether she is strong enough to re-appear on national television?"

Brooke looked confused. "Assessed?"

"Yes, which counsellors have spoken to her?"

"Well, nobody – except for me."

"*You!*"

Brooke went bright red. "Yes."

"But you're not a trained counsellor, are you?"

"No, I'm not," Brooke said, going redder.

"And where is the show's counsellor?" asked Guy.

"There isn't one at the moment. We had a counsellor called Richard, but he left, and he wasn't replaced . . . he was only ever part-time anyway."

Guy looked at her incredulously. "But you can't just put a woman in such a fragile state of mind on television. It's not right, is it?"

Brooke said nothing, but looked at the floor.

"Well, is it?" Guy pushed.

She looked up at him helplessly.

"And was she assessed before her first appearance?" he pressed her.

"No. We didn't know at the time how bad she was."

"But she should have been properly assessed, as should all guests who appear on such a show."

"It's not for me to say."

"But I'm asking for your opinion. Do you think it's acceptable?"

"Look, I'm only the researcher. I don't make the decisions about who goes on and who doesn't. I just compile a list of the people who have contacted the show."

"But you've met the woman, you've talked to her?"

"Well, I haven't actually met her since she was in the clinic. I've spoken to her on the phone."

"The *phone*." Guy's tone was loaded.

"Yes."

Guy sighed in exasperation. "Then, in your opinion, having assessed her over the *phone*, do you think it's acceptable to put this woman on the show again?"

Brooke felt stressed and didn't know what to say. She decided to tell the truth. "No – no, I don't think she should be put on."

"Thank you." Guy turned and walked off.

Brooke watched him, feeling even more stressed. Why had she said that? Would he say it back to Kim? Kim would fire her on the spot surely.

Kim was marching down the corridor when Guy stopped her.

"Sorry, Guy, can we meet up for a drink later or something. I'm in an awful hurry, we're just about to start filming."

"No, look, I really need to talk to you now," insisted Guy.

"About what?" Kim stopped and looked at him irritably.

"It's about a guest you're planning on using."

"What about her?" she asked, looking at the paperwork in his hand, and wondering how he got hold of it.

"You're putting a woman on the show who has just been released from a clinic. Donna Doyle."

"So?"

"I don't think you've thought this through, Kim. You're leaving yourself, and the station, wide open to accusations of exploiting a vulnerable person. We can't be seen to put somebody who is mentally unwell in a potentially manipulative situation. We have a duty of care to everybody we feature on all our programmes . . ."

As Guy continued to speak about his misgivings, Kim's face glazed over and his sentences just became a mumble of words.

"Guy!" she said, interrupting his monologue. "Do you know what I say to all that?"

"What?"

"Pants!"

Guy's face dropped. "Sorry?" he asked, not sure he'd heard what he thought he'd heard.

Kim looked around and saw the boardroom was free.

"I think you and I need to have a woman-to-man chat," said Kim, taking his arm and leading him over to the boardroom.

They entered and she closed the door firmly behind her.

"Guy – can I ask you a question?"

"Eh – I suppose."

"How many affairs do you think I've had?"

He was taken aback. "I'm sorry?"

"How many times do you think I've been unfaithful to my husband?"

"I haven't a clue, I'm sure!"

"Never! Not once! Since I married Tom Davenport I've remained resolutely faithful to him. It's not because I haven't had the inclination, I can tell you. Or the opportunity, let's face it." She flicked her hair back in a confident manner. "No, the reason I have maintained my marriage vows is because I believe in the sanctity of marriage. I believe in the sanctity of family. I would never do that to my Jasmine, I would never betray the family. And that is what separates me from the folks out there that we feature on our show. *Comprende?* These people on *The Joshua Green Show*, they have a different set of values from the likes of you and me, Guy. Having an affair, or the many other misdemeanours they enjoy, is nothing to them. They thrive on the drama. They'd make going down to the supermarket a drama. They *love* the drama of it all. And we facilitate the drama. We're providing a public service to them. You don't understand them, Guy. I do. And I don't think you ever will.

You must understand it takes more than looking good in a suit, a fine quality in itself I'm sure, to be a true television professional. So why don't you leave the programme-making to me, and I'll leave the . . . whatever you do best . . . to you."

She smiled at him, patted him on the shoulder and walked out.

The day's filming complete, Jasmine came on set to find her mother. They had planned to hit the town for the night.

"Everything alright?" asked Jasmine, seeing her mother looking slightly anxious as she put on some lipstick in her office.

"It's just that Boy Scout of a new station boss sticking his oar in where it's not wanted or needed," said Kim, throwing her lipstick in her handbag.

"Guy Burton? I thought you got on great with him in our house that time?"

"So did I. But there was something about him I just couldn't get through to, and today he started to lecture me about a guest on a show. *He* lecturing *me!*"

"The cheek of him!"

"I had to put him back in his box this afternoon, and you know I hate when I'm forced to be pushy with people! It's goes against the grain for me."

"I know."

"And what about Brooke?" questioned Jasmine coyly.

"She's still here! He hasn't given her the heave-ho yet. I'll give him until the end of the week, and if he hasn't sacked her by then . . . well, I'm just going to get very angry with Mr Guy Burton. Very angry indeed . . . Now, there's a bottle of champagne with my name on it somewhere, let's find it."

10

Soraya looked around their house the morning of the photo shoot and thought it looked like it had been transformed into a photographer's studio. There was lighting everywhere and cameras. Then there were make-up assistants and people from the PR department at RTV.

"The house looks gorgeous," said Valerie Hunter, an editor from *Privilege* who was in charge of the feature, in a sugar-sweet voice.

"Thanks, Valerie."

"The readers are going to love-love-*love* seeing where Joshua lives!"

"Yes, we all like to have a nosy at other people's gaffs, don't we? I'm guilty of it anyway," chuckled Soraya.

Soraya would have liked to have had a say about what to wear during the photo shoot, but the fashion editor from the magazine had descended on them the previous week, riffled through their wardrobes and dictated the pace.

"What time is kick-off?" asked Joshua as he came in, dressed in an Armani suit and fiddling with his cufflinks.

"The photographer wants to start as soon as possible. It shouldn't take more than three or four hours."

"Well, we're ready whenever you are, Valerie," said Joshua, going to the mirror over the fireplace and starting to smooth down his hair.

"Em, can we hold on for another while?" asked Soraya awkwardly.

"What's the problem?" said Valerie, concerned.

"It's just that we're waiting for Lee."

"*What?*" shouted Joshua, swinging around. "Where is he?"

"I don't know!" said Soraya.

"What do you mean – you don't know? He's upstairs getting ready. I saw him there half an hour ago."

"He's not there now – he must have slipped out."

"Slipped out!" Joshua was incredulous as he pulled out his mobile and started to phone Lee.

"Oh dear – will he be long, does any one know?" asked Valerie, looking stressed, but her voice still sugary-sweet.

"It's rung through to voice mail," said Joshua before speaking into the phone. "Lee, this is your father. Where are you? Get back here immediately."

One hour passed and there was still no sign of Lee.

"I'm going to kill him! I will just plain kill him!" declared Joshua, trying to ring Lee's mobile for the twentieth time.

"Did you try Helen?" Soraya suggested.

"She'll be at work," Joshua dismissed the idea.

"It's worth a try," urged Soraya.

Joshua dialled Lee's aunt's work number and got through to her.

"Mrs Green, the children, they will get hungry soon if we don't feed them," said Ulrika who was trying to keep Daniel and Danielle, dressed in identical clothes, occupied on the floor.

"I'm afraid we can't wait much longer to start the shoot," said Valerie who had become very stressed. "We're wasting time."

"Please, can we give him just ten more minutes?" pleaded Soraya.

"Ten minutes maximum, but then we are going to have to start the shoot without him, I'm afraid."

"No, Helen hasn't heard from him," said Joshua, closing over his phone. "The bloody little fool – what does he think he's playing at?"

"We can't do the photo shoot without him, we just can't!" said Soraya. "All these family photos! It wouldn't be right!"

"Well, what choice do we have?" asked Joshua.

"We'll just have to reschedule the shoot," said Soraya.

"Out of the question!" snapped Valerie whose previously sugar-sweet voice had suddenly adopted a steely no-nonsense tone. "It would cost too much time and money to set up again just because a teenager has sulked off."

"Well, I'm not doing it without Lee!" Soraya insisted.

"I hate to mention the word 'contract' at this point," Valerie said, her voice becoming menacing, as she shot a warning look at the equally stressed RTV Public Relations Manager.

"I'm sorry!" snapped Soraya. "I'm not going to be bullied into this shoot when one of our family can't be here for it."

"The onus was on you to ensure he was here," Valerie pointed out. She had given up pussyfooting around so-called celebrities when the going got tough years ago.

"Well, we're sorry to have wasted your time, and we'll pay you back any money that today's cancellation has cost you," said Soraya.

"You cannot be fucking serious!" Valerie's voice went up several octaves.

"And please don't swear in front of my children!" said Soraya.

"Can everyone calm down!" said Joshua, wishing that Kim was there to take control. "Soraya – a word, please!" He took her by the arm and led her out to the hall and into the kitchen where he closed the door.

"I mean, who do these people think they are?" said Soraya. "Coming into my home and taking over and then trying to force us to go ahead with the shoot when Lee is not here!"

"Soraya!" Joshua put his hands on her shoulders and looked at her seriously. "We can't cancel today's shoot. Too much organisation went into it."

"But –"

"No buts! Valerie is just doing her job and she can't cancel today. This is Lee's fault. He did this on purpose to try and upset the day for everyone. He is being his usual selfish self, not giving a thought to anybody else."

"I don't want to have a family photo shoot without him, Joshua!"

He pulled her close. "And neither do I. But he's given us no choice. We have to get on with it, okay?"

She looked at him, her expression a mixture of angry and frustrated.

"Okay?" he pushed.

"Alright!" she conceded.

He took her by the hand and led her back into the lounge.

"Right, let's get started!" said Joshua.

"Great! Let's start with the whole family on the sofa," suggested Valerie, her sugar-sweet voice reinstated.

Guy pulled into Joshua's driveway and took in the house as he got out of his car. The public relations manager had suggested that he drop by the Greens' house the day of the photo shoot in order to see how they did things. Guy wouldn't normally be bothered with such nonsense, but given the intrigue that had been fed to him concerning Joshua, his programme, his wife, his mistress and his mad producer's ambitions, he thought it might be interesting to examine him in his natural habitat.

As he headed to the front door, a youth entered the driveway. The youth scowled at him and nearly pushed him aside to get up the steps to the front door ahead of him.

"Hello!" said Guy.

The youth ignored him, pushed open the door and went in. As Guy entered the house after him, he saw that the shoot must have come to an end as the photographer and others were trooping through the hall.

Joshua and Soraya were in the kitchen with Valerie.

"I can't wait to see the photos! They're going to be amazing," said Valerie.

"Let's hope so! And sorry for the delay at the beginning of the shoot," apologised Joshua.

"No need to apologise. I've got two teenagers myself at home. I know what you're going through," Valerie sympathised with a sigh.

"Lee is very considerate as a rule," said Soraya defensively, who had gone right off Valerie since she had witnessed the other side of her.

"I'm sure," smiled Valerie. "Anyway I'd better be off!"

She collected her bag and, with a last sugary-sweet smile, left the kitchen. As she left Lee came in.

"And here he is!" Joshua's voice was raised. "The wanderer returns!"

Valerie swept onward regardless and met Guy in the hall.

"Hi there, I'm looking for Joshua," said Guy.

"They're all in the kitchen," said Valerie, pulling an amused face as the voices in the kitchen rose.

She left the house and Guy hovered in the hall.

"What's the problem?" asked Lee, taking a can of Coke out of the fridge and opening it.

"Don't come the innocent with me! Where the fuck were you?" demanded Joshua.

"Out."

"But you *knew* the photo shoot was on today."

"Oh, was that today? I forgot." He took a drink from the can.

"*You forgot!*" Joshua went marching over to him. "Don't insult my intelligence. You were upstairs until shortly before the shoot and you knew we were all getting ready for it! You just couldn't bother your arse doing it. Today was very important for me, for this family, and you just waltzed out."

"I said I forgot, and if I forgot how could I show up?" Lee looked nonchalant.

"So when you left this morning and you passed the photographers and their cameras all coming into the house, you didn't remember about the shoot?"

"I'm bored with this now."

"*You're bored!*"

"Joshua, it's been a long day. Let's just leave it," urged Soraya.

"No, not this time. That's what he's banking on. You are grounded, my laddo! Grounded until further notice."

"What do you mean – grounded?"

67

"You're not going out anywhere until you learn some responsibility and respect."

"You can't do that, I'm eighteen."

"My house, my rules!"

"You can shove your fucking rules!"

"Who do you think you're speaking to?"

"I don't know what you're complaining about. You didn't want me in your perfect family photos for your crappy magazine. Because you don't want me to be part of your perfect family."

"Lee, how can you say that?" cried Soraya.

"Because it's the truth. *He* wanted just you and Danielle and Daniel in the photos, not me! I'm just a bad reminder of his past and where's he's from. You want to airbrush me out of your perfect life, so I did you a favour and didn't show up to your stupid shoot. And don't pretend it's otherwise."

"You are some kid!" Joshua shook his head in despair.

"Oh and get rid of that patronising look, Dad. Keep it for your freaks on your freak show!"

"How fucking dare you!" shouted Joshua.

"Will you keep your voices down, you're going to upset the children!" pleaded Soraya, turning to go and check on them.

With a shock, she saw Guy Burton standing in the doorway.

"Guy!" she exclaimed in surprise.

"I'm sorry . . . I should have knocked," said Guy.

Soraya and Joshua shot each other embarrassed looks.

"Saved by the geeky stranger!" said Lee, pushing past his father, walking quickly out of the room and marching up the stairs.

"Lee! You get back here and apologise!" demanded Joshua.

"Piss off!" came the response from up the stairs.

"Guy, I'm so sorry about that," said Joshua.

"No need to be. I'm the one who should be sorry. As I said, I should have rung the doorbell. It just looked like it was open house."

"It has been open house, all day long," smiled Soraya. "Never have a photo shoot in your home, Guy – they take over."

"I don't think there's much chance of anyone wanting to photo-shoot me in my home," smiled Guy.

"Throw a spoilt teenager into the bargain and you've got bedlam," sighed Joshua.

"He's seems a spirited chap," remarked Guy, walking further into the kitchen.

"That's one adjective for him," giggled Soraya. "Have you any children, Guy?"

"No."

"Then you're lucky, mate, believe you me," Joshua threw his eyes heavenwards.

"He doesn't mean that, ignore him," said Soraya. "Coffee? Tea?"

Soraya took the remote and turned off the television in the drawing room. Joshua was sitting beside her on the couch surfing the internet on his laptop.

"That was all excruciatingly embarrassing today – your new boss walking in on the Third World War in the kitchen," sighed Soraya.

"The kid's got no manners. He insulted my boss – geeky stranger, indeed!"

Soraya giggled. "Guy seemed to take it in good spirit."

"That's not the point. Just because Guy is a nice easy-going person he won't take offence. But what if he wasn't? Lee could have caused serious trouble."

"When you're that age, you don't think."

"That's no excuse."

"I think we might have been wrong in trying to force him to sit for those photos, Joshua," said Soraya.

"I can't do right from doing wrong! If I didn't include him he'd accuse me of not wanting him to participate, which he did anyway. And when I tried to include him, I'm accused of bullying him."

"I'll have a word with him, and try and smooth things over."

"Thanks, love," Joshua said, leaning over and kissing her. "You know, I may be coming across as hard on him at times, but it's only because I care what happens to him. I don't want him going down the same road as his mother, and sometimes he just reminds me so much of her."

"I know," Soraya nodded.

Joshua returned his attention to his computer screen.

"The bloody bastards!" he said all of a sudden.

"What's wrong?"

" I'm reading the 'We Hate Joshua Green' website."

"What's on it now?"

"A load of rubbish. A load of comments about guests on the show. Here's some stuff about me. It describes me here as vain, condescending, unpleasant and I think I'm superior."

"What else is there?"

"It pulls my blog page apart as well. They wrote that my review of last Saturday's Manchester United match was the worst review they ever read! They say I know fuck-all about football and should stick to exploiting people's misery for my own profit!"

"Why are you torturing yourself reading that stuff?" Soraya was getting annoyed.

Seeing Soraya was getting upset, he turned off the computer and smiled at her. He tried to make light of it. "I should feel complimented that I irritate somebody so much they've gone to the bother of setting all this up."

"Anyway, nobody's going to bother reading an obscure website. You're getting huge ratings every week, so you're getting the last laugh."

11

"Brooke! Phone call!" shouted one of the production runners across the studio.

Brooke excused herself from the cameraman she was talking to, went to the phone on the wall and picked up the receiver.

"Brooke, this is Guy Burton's secretary. He wishes to see you this afternoon at four."

"Why?" Brooke was disconcerted.

"I don't know, I'm sure. And if I did I wouldn't be at liberty to discuss," said the woman with marble-sounding vowels. "Is there a problem?"

"No, four is just fine." Brooke hung up the receiver and leaned against the wall deep in thought. What did he want with her this time? She was just a researcher, there was no need for the Director of Programmes to be summoning her up to his office not once but twice. It must have something to do with her sleeping with Joshua. She sighed loudly as it occurred to her that they were probably going to get rid of her because of it. It was too much of a risk if it was ever exposed.

Most people sleep their way up the ladder, she thought. Only *I* could sleep my way out of a job! She sighed to herself as she walked back to the studio. "Oh well . . . it looks like it's going to be back to the typing pool tomorrow."

71

That afternoon Brooke was kept waiting half an hour outside Guy's office. She ignored his secretary's occasional condescending looks. It was obvious the last time she had been summoned to Guy's office it had been meant as a warning not to continue her affair with Joshua. She was supposed to have looked suitably disgusted with herself, hung her head in shame, and apologised profusely for being such a bad girl. Instead, the shock of someone knowing about her and Joshua had thrown her so much she had been uncharacteristically defiant, defensive and cheeky. It's a wonder she hadn't been fired on the spot. And ever since then Kim had not even bothered being rude to her any more. She had heard Guy Burton had spent an evening at Kim's house. They were now obviously best buddies and Kim was getting what she wanted: her out. And there was nothing she could do. She had played with fire, and now she was to be roasted. She supposed she could go to Joshua, cause a scene, kick up a fuss. Part of her was sure Joshua would insist she stayed, that he would defy Kim. But there was another part of her that wasn't so sure he would, and she wasn't in the mood to test him. Wasn't in the mood to find out her lovely romance was in actual fact about her just being an available bit of ass. Besides, if she did cause ructions, people would start to talk, and maybe even guess about her and Joshua, and that could end up destroying them all. No, she would go quietly.

"You can go in now," said the secretary.

Brooke stood up and went into Guy's office.

"Take a seat, Brooke," said Guy, who didn't even look up from his paperwork.

She sat down and waited as he continued to scribble his signature on a mountain of paper. After a while, she found her nerves reaching breaking point and she blurted out: "You could at least have the manners to look me in the face while you fire me!" She immediately regretted saying it as he looked up at her in surprise.

"I'm sorry?" he asked.

"Well, this is what all this is about, isn't it? You're getting rid of me for sleeping with Joshua. I would prefer if you just came out and said it, and stopped playing with me!"

He sat back and looked at her, amused. "I'm not sure if I'm more surprised by your strength of character or your bizarre paranoia," he said.

"Well, why else would I be sitting in the Director of Programme's office, for the second time?"

"I'm not saying I approve of you shagging our star. I'm not sure you realise the consequences of your affair being exposed, not only to Joshua and his family, but to both your careers and the station. But the reason why I called you to my office today is because I want to promote you to assistant producer on Joshua's show."

Brooke blinked several times.

"Starting beginning of next week."

"Assistant producer?" she repeated the words as incredulously as if he told her she was about to become prime minister.

"Yes, your salary will reflect the new position. To be honest, observing the show, your role extends much beyond the role of researcher as it stands, ignoring the fetching of dry-cleaning and take-out food for Joshua and Kim."

"Does Kim know?"

"Not yet. I'll inform her tomorrow."

Brooke laughed cynically. "But Kim will never let it happen! She hates me, she wants me out!"

"I'm sure she doesn't. I'm sure that's just another example of that bizarre paranoia you seem to suffer from," he smirked at her.

"But why? Why are you giving me a promotion?"

"Because I think you deserve it."

She sat there in shock, the excitement growing all the time. "Thank you. Thank you for this. You don't know what it means to me."

"I think I do. Don't fuck it up."

"Are you joking me? I'll work twenty-four hours a day, seven days a week, three hundred and sixty-five days a year with this new job." She jumped up out of her seat. "Is there anything else?"

"No. Just keep it under your hat till I get a chance to inform Kim tomorrow."

"Yes, anything you want. And thank you again!" She turned and nearly fell over the chair in her haste to get out of the office.

12

Kim walked past Guy's secretary. "I've a meeting with Guy for three o'clock, love."

"Please wait here – he's on the phone," demanded the secretary, but Kim ignored her, rapped on Guy's door and entered.

Guy looked up in surprise at the unannounced entry into his office, but on seeing it was Kim Davenport he wasn't surprised at all.

"Hello, Guy!" she said, closing the door behind her.

The phone rang on his desk and he picked it up. "It's alright. Jane, I'll see Mrs Davenport now," he reassured the secretary and hung up the phone.

Kim pulled up a chair and sat down. "I hate waiting around, don't you? Time's too short to be sitting in a reception waiting. If a person says three o'clock for a meeting, I always assume they meant what they said and come straight in at three o'clock on the dot. You know I hate these people, usually men, who keep you waiting out in their reception for ages. It's all psychology. They're trying to give the impression they're so busy. I know you would be a far too straightforward type of lad to be bothered with all that . . . Anyway, you wanted to see me?"

"Yes, it's about Brooke Radcliffe."

"I'm glad you've brought that one up. I noticed she's still hanging around, after our little agreement to bin her."

"That's the problem, you see. I can't let her go."

"You what?" Kim's face turned red.

"I broached the subject with HR, and I'm afraid there's nothing in her contract that gives us grounds to dismiss her."

"Oh come on, Guy, there's always something in the contract you can use to ditch a bitch!"

"I'm afraid not in Brooke's. We've gone through it with a fine-tooth comb. If we tried to get rid of her, we'd only end up in the Labour Court and we'd end up losing."

Kim stood up and started to pace up and down angrily. "You see, this is what you get when you send a boy to do a man's job. I should have taken care of the little scrubber myself! Contract indeed!"

"I know this is a frustration to you."

"You can say that again! I thought I made it clear the danger she is to our future!"

"You're talking about the alleged affair with Joshua?"

"No, I'm talking about her predisposition for wearing yellow!" Kim spat sarcastically. "Of course I'm talking about the affair!"

"Well, I can see no evidence of an affair. And, to be honest, even if there was, they are both over eighteen. It's none of our business."

She looked at him incredulously. "Are you kidding me? If this got out it would be the equivalent of a nuclear bomb hitting this tatty television station!"

"Besides, I think you're wrong. I don't think they are having an affair."

"Let me tell you something, I am *never* wrong about these things. I've a nose for what's sordid . . . What has you convinced they are *not* having an affair?"

"I asked her outright."

"*You did what?*"

"Don't worry, I didn't mention you, or bring you into the equation. I just said I heard a rumour she was sleeping with Joshua Green and wanted to check if it was true. She said she wasn't."

"Well, to quote a famous English lady – she would say that, wouldn't she?"

"Well, I'm inclined to accept her denial."

Kim threw her hands into the air in despair. "Men!"

"Another thing. When Brooke joined the station it was expected she would be promoted into production at some stage. It's written into her contract that she would be given this opportunity. We have to honour that contract. She starts as the assistant producer on *The Joshua Green Show* from next Monday."

Kim's mouth dropped open. "Are you on heroin?"

"My hands are tied, there's nothing I can do."

She stood there, arms folded, studying him intensely "I see . . . And I suppose I'm expected to train her?"

He held out his hand to her. "Could she have a better teacher?"

"A teacher can only teach a student who's able to learn. Not a retard, with some kind of Amazing Technicolour Dreamcoat of a contract!"

"I'm sure you'll do your best."

"In the meantime, the researcher position is vacant now Brooke has been promoted to better things. I will tell Jasmine she starts as a researcher on the show on Monday."

Guy looked concerned. "Oh no, don't do that yet. HR says the position has to be advertised openly. We can't be accused of nepotism."

"Only insanity?"

"You can tell Jasmine the researcher position will be advertised on the website and she can apply along with everyone else. I'm sure a girl with her talent and connections will get the job no problem."

She looked at him squarely. "You can bet your bottom dollar on it."

Joshua was seated with a gang in the RTV canteen having lunch when he spotted Guy come in and join the queue for food. He watched as Guy was served and then as he walked across the canteen to a quiet corner where he sat down on his own.

Joshua decided to take the opportunity and left his laughing crowd. As he walked through the canteen he passed two girls giggling as they sat in front of a laptop screen. When they saw him, they stopped laughing and snapped the laptop shut. But not quick enough that he didn't see that they were reading the 'We Hate Joshua Green' website. His blood began to boil. He had been keeping an eye on that website and it was becoming increasingly cruel about him and took the piss out of him all the time. And there was nothing he could do about it.

He reached Guy. "Hello there," he said, smiling broadly.

"Oh, hi." Guy looked surprised to see him.

"Do you mind if I join you?"

"Be my guest." Guy nodded to the spare seat in front of him.

Joshua sat down. "I just wanted to apologise again for the other day. My son's behaviour," he said.

"It's forgotten. There's nothing to apologise for."

"Soraya is mortified. You must think we're like one of those dysfunctional families on my show," smiled Joshua.

"Nonsense."

"I'm not saying we're the Waltons either," Joshua smirked. "But Lee isn't usually as rude and argumentative as you saw him that day."

"I'm sure he's not."

"He can be a bit of a handful, but we try our best with him."

Guy nodded.

"Anyway – will you come round to ours for dinner one night? Soraya suggested it. You can get to meet the real us and we can get to know you better."

"Oh – that's very nice of you. I'd be delighted to."

Kim marched into the kitchen at home, opened a bottle of white wine and filled a glass to the brim, before taking a big gulp. Tom came meandering in.

"Oh, you're home. I wasn't expecting you." He put on the kettle. "I thought you'd be out painting the town red."

"I've had a shit day and wasn't in the mood," she said, taking another mouthful of wine.

"Maybe just as well. It would have been your fourth night out in a row. Everyone needs their beauty sleep," he said, emptying some digestive biscuits onto a plate.

"That bastard of a new Director of Programmes is making my life difficult."

"That nice chap you spent the afternoon drinking gin here with?"

"It was whiskey, not gin, and he's not nice at all!"

Tom yawned while he put the tea bag in a cup and poured the water from the boiling kettle in. "Looks can be deceiving, I suppose. There's a good programme on at ten about the Orient Express. I'm quite looking forward to it."

"As if I fell for all that crap about Brooke Radcliffe's contract being watertight! And that there was a provision that she should become a producer! Does he think I'm stupid or something that I'd fall for that shit?"

"I'm sure nobody could ever think that, my dear," Tom said, stirring the tea.

"What's the bastard playing at?" she asked.

"The tangled webs we weave!"

"He's messing with the wrong girl if he thinks he can outsmart me!"

"Anyway, I'm off into the living room. I might just catch the end of the news."

He picked up his tea and biscuits.

"I feel like doing something dramatic," she said, looking around the kitchen. "I think we should get a new kitchen."

He started chuckling.

"What's so funny?" she asked.

"You! The country is gone to the IMF and you're off to MFI! Whatever you think, my dear. The gardens have always been my domain, and the house . . ." he took a rueful look around at the seventies-style interior, ". . . has always been yours."

She watched him amble out of the kitchen and finished her glass of wine.

Brooke pulled up outside a small terraced house in a rough part of Dublin. She got out, locked her door and walked up the small garden path to the door.

Aidan Doyle opened to her knock.

"Oh, it's you!" he said, unimpressed. "Donna said you were coming over."

"How is she?" asked Brooke, stepping into the hall.

"How do you think?" he asked.

She wished he wouldn't be so hostile to her, but she understood he was just being concerned about his sister. Donna had been released from the clinic the previous week and she had rung Brooke and asked her to visit.

Brooke walked into the small sitting room and found Donna there.

"Hello!" Brooke smiled at her and gave her a kiss on the cheek. "You look well."

Aidan looked on protectively as they chatted away about everyday stuff. Eventually his phone rang and he went to the other room to answer it. Donna sat forward quickly.

"I have to get back on your show!" she whispered. "I need to see Glen again. He won't talk to me. If we get on to the show, I can see him again. Is it all arranged?"

Brooke didn't know what to say. She wasn't at all sure whether it would be Guy or Kim who would win on this one. "We're discussing the line-up at the moment . . . I'll be letting you know. But, Donna, you need to concentrate on getting better now and –"

"But you told me Kim Davenport had said yes!" Donna wailed. Then her expression changed and she glared at Brooke. "I want to see Glen again, Brooke, and I *am* getting back on your show," she said threateningly, then quickly changed the subject as Aidan came back into the room.

13

"Well!" said Kim with a big false smile as she positioned herself in front of Brooke. They had just finished recording a show and the studio was busy as the audience made their way out. "I believe congratulations are in order."

Brooke went red. "You mean my promotion? I know. I was so surprised when Guy told me."

"Not as surprised as I was when he told *me*!" Kim's smile didn't falter. "I'd love to take a read through this magical bullet-proof contract you apparently have. I thought you were on a bog-standard RTV contract."

Brooke ignored this. "I'm thrilled," she said.

"And I'm thrilled for you. But I wouldn't let it go to your head, love." Kim's smile dropped. "All it means in my book is that you've gone from washer-upper and bottle-opener to chief washer-up and bottle-opener."

Brooke sighed. "Look, Kim. This is a fantastic opportunity for me and I'm giving it my very best shot. I want this to be a success for me."

"As far as I'm concerned it's a waste of an opportunity. You weren't a good researcher and you won't be a good assistant producer."

"Well, I won't be if you won't back me! I'm counting on you to train me. I want to learn from you."

"Oh, I think a girl like you has learned all the tricks she needs to get on in life already."

"Look, I don't know what you're talking about, Kim. I just want to do my job and do it as best I can. I don't think you know me at all."

Kim moved a little closer and lowered her voice. "Oh, I think I know you very well . . . the trouble is, I don't like what I know."

"But why?" Brooke was exasperated.

"Oh a number of reasons, but mainly . . ." Kim leaned towards Brooke's ear and whispered, "I don't like girls who mess around with married men."

Kim pulled back, smiled falsely at her and walked off.

Walking across the car park at RTV, Guy pressed the zapper of his BMW and went to open his car door.

"How could you do it?" came a cry from behind him. He turned around to see a visibly upset Brooke, with a tearstained face, standing there.

"I'm sorry?" he asked, confused.

"You told Kim about me sleeping with Joshua! How could you do it? How could you tell her that? I told you in confidence and you then went and told my boss."

"Brooke . . ."

"We made an agreement that we wouldn't tell anybody and you broke it!" Brooke turned and ran away.

That evening Brooke and Joshua were having dinner in Tribecca. They were sitting at a corner table. Joshua was retelling the whole situation of the photo shoot while Brooke listened attentively.

"Lee did it on purpose. It's going to look odd now with him not in the photos."

"Just mention in the interview he's away on holiday after his exams."

"I suppose I could," Joshua looked pensive. "Hmm, that's not a bad idea."

Brooke took up the bottle of red wine and began to refill their glasses.

"And then when Lee finally showed up," Joshua went on, "we had this shouting match in front of the new Director of Programmes, of all people."

"Guy Burton?" Brooke looked up sharply in surprise.

"Yes," Joshua nodded and then suddenly snapped, "Watch it!"

Brooke had stopped concentrating on pouring the wine, missed the glass, and spilled some on the tablecloth.

"Fuck it!" muttered Brooke, cleaning up the spillage with a linen napkin. "What was Guy Burton doing there?" She handed the napkin to an attentive waiter who had come hurrying to the table.

"The PR department suggested he come by for the photo shoot," said Joshua. "Goodness knows what he makes of us after witnessing the row between me and Lee."

"You should have been more discreet."

"You know our house, take us as you find us."

"Did he have anything to say for himself?"

"Guy? Not really, he seems like a good bloke."

Brooke sat back and watched Joshua eat his lamb. Things had become so complicated since Guy had arrived on the scene. Indeed, what did he make of them all? Watching Joshua and Soraya play happy families while he was aware of the truth.

She looked around at the other diners. They were in a discreet corner, but everywhere Joshua went people recognised him.

"Joshua . . . doesn't it ever worry you people might think there is something going on between us?"

"What do you mean?"

"I mean being seen together like this, eating out."

He started laughing and sat back. "No! Don't be daft. Why would anyone ever suspect anything? I'm having a business discussion over dinner with my show's researcher."

Assistant producer, Brooke corrected mentally. Joshua had made no mention of her promotion, let alone offer congratulations.

"It's the perfect guise – nobody would read anything in it. The thought would be ludicrous to them!" He chuckled again as he continued to eat.

She watched him and reached forward for her wineglass.

Brooke stirred in the dark and opened her eyes. She leaned forward and turned on the bedside light to see the time.

"Joshua, wake up. It's time for you to go home."

Joshua mumbled in his sleep and turned over.

"Joshua!" She nudged him.

"I'll get up in half an hour," he mumbled.

"No, Joshua, it's three in the morning. Soraya will wonder where you've got to."

He struggled up and yawned.

"Do you want me to make you coffee or anything?" she asked.

"No, don't bother." He yawned again, swung out of bed and started to get dressed. "You know that idea for the show we discussed yesterday?"

"Idea?"

"Yeah, the one about the girl who keeps dumping the grooms at the altar?"

"Yes, we were going to call it 'Never the Bride'."

"Yeah, cancel the idea. It's a bit boring really."

She nodded, and wondered how his mind worked, to think of the show at such a time.

He leaned over and kissed her forehead. "See you tomorrow."

"Will I call you a taxi?"

"No, I'll get one in the street." She watched as he left the room and heard the front door bang after him. She turned off the light and went back to sleep.

14

"I've got kick-off on my show in twenty minutes, so we need to make this snappy," warned Kim as she sat down in Guy's office. She was beginning to dread these summonses, which inevitably resulted in his meddling in affairs that didn't concern him.

"I was just thinking about the time slot for Joshua's programme."

"It's always had the ten o'clock night slot," said Kim.

"But most of these confessional talk shows have afternoon slots."

"A-f-t-e-r-n-o-o-n?" Kim repeated the word slowly as if it was a fatal disease.

"I think it's worth considering. Let's face it, you have more of a captive audience for this kind of show in the afternoon. It's either watch a talk show, a second-rate cookery programme or a repeat of a 1950s movie."

It took a lot to make Kim cry but, in spite of herself, her eyes started welling up at the thought of afternoon television.

"Guy, I have come too far for too long to end up on afternoon television," she said, her voice low and menacing.

"It's only a suggestion," he said. "We'd have to run it by advertisers, sponsors, audience think tanks . . ." His voice had adopted a sing-song carefree tone. "I think it might be a good idea."

Kim stood up slowly and just stared at him, before she turned and walked out of the room.

He watched her go and smiled to himself.

Kim had driven home in zombie mode.

"Tom!" she shouted as she entered the house.

"In here!" said Tom from their bedroom.

"I have had the day from hell," she declared, marching into their room and over to the drinks tray. She poured herself a drink. "I don't know what to do! I don't know what his problem is! It's like he doesn't like me or something. It's like he's trying to undermine me and the show. But why? It's a cash cow. It's keeping the channel afloat."

"Hmmm. Where has that navy tie of mine gone to?"

"I can only imagine he's a very stupid man. Thick as shit!" She gulped down her drink.

"Ah well, I'll have to make do with the black tie."

She looked around and saw that Tom was packing a suitcase. "Why are you packing? Where are you going?" she demanded.

"I've got the bridge competition in Rome. I told you about it – at least twice."

"Bridge competition? How long will you be gone?"

"A week. You didn't see my new Marks and Spencer jacket anywhere, did you?"

"I don't remember you saying about being gone for a week."

"Probably too tied up in that high-flying media career for it to even register, my dear." He continued packing.

She took another gulp from her drink. "If that bastard thinks he can get the better of me, he's got another think coming. I've tried to be nice to him. I tried to be friends."

"I do hope there's a good film on the flight over. I do wonder why airlines seem to think that all their passengers share the film tastes of eighteen-year-old girls. I remember going to New York once when I had to sit through the same Richard Geer smaltz four times. Twice going over and twice coming back!"

"Guy Burton is obviously one of these people who think they

can just arrive in and take over without a thought to the power structure that exists. I've noticed him trying to smarm up to Joshua all the time. I've seen them have lunch in the canteen and he's going to theirs for dinner. So what's his plan? He wants to keep Joshua and get rid of me? That's like trying to have Cagney without Lacey, Morecambe without Wise. Starsky without Hutch!"

"Anyway, I'd better run or I'll miss my flight! I'll see you in a week, my dear!" He blew her a kiss and walked out.

She watched him walk unconcerned out of the room, and a couple of minutes later heard his car rev up and drive away. Tears stung her eyes as she took another gulp from her drink and turned and looked out the window at the extensive back gardens, beautifully tended by Tom. The prize-winning roses he was so proud of. As he always said the inside of the house was her domain and the outside was his. It was an un-negotiated compromise, like everything else in their marriage.

You could get anybody's attention. You only had to find what button to press.

Kim was showing the swimming-pool contractor around the back garden.

"I want a huge heart-shaped seventies-style swimming pool, just here, taking in as much of the garden as you possibly can. Anything the pool doesn't take up, I want you to just patio over."

"That shouldn't be a problem, Mrs Davenport. You don't want to keep any of the flowers or shrubs?"

"No, the whole thing is much too high maintenance. I can't be bothered with it any more."

"Right. I'll give you a quote within the day."

"Good! And just one more thing – I want it all done within a week."

Kim drove through the lavish gateway and up the drive through the gardens that resembled a golf course in their expanse and pulled up in front of the large period house. This was the home of Henry King, who was the Director General of RTV. The ultimate power at the station. He was now in his mid-sixties and had been with the channel for forty years, working his way up from tea boy to Director General. He had adopted a hands-off approach over the last few years, keeping a fatherly eye on everything, but not getting overly involved in the nitty gritty.

Kim and Henry went back a long way, and as she pressed the bell on the front door, she looked forward to seeing him. The maid answered the door and showed her through the ornate hallway and a double door to the lavish drawing room.

A big smile on his face, Henry stood up and held out his hands to her. Kim, grinning broadly, walked towards him and took both his hands in hers and kissed him on both cheeks.

"You're a bold girl, Kim. You don't come and see me as much as you used to," he chastised mockingly.

"That's because I'm so busy keeping your Number One show on the road," she answered back.

He sat down and patted the seat on the couch beside him.

She sat down. "Why is it that whenever I see you, Henry, I feel as if I'm a young girl again?"

He roared with laughter. "You don't look much older than a young filly to me, Kim. I tell you something, if it wasn't for me being married to my Bess and you being married to your Tom, you'd have to fight me off!"

She leaned forward to him and smiled wickedly. "Oh, but how I'd enjoy the fight!"

He leaned forward to her conspiratorially. "Tell me – do you still sleep with Tom?"

"Yes – but only out of spite!"

Henry roared with laughter. "You're a bad bitch, Kim, a bad bitch!"

"You bring it out in me, Henry. Anyway, enough of this foreplay, let's get down to business."

"Yes, to what do I owe the pleasure?"

"I wanted to have a word with you about the new Director of Programmes."

"Guy Burton?"

"Yes."

"What about him?"

"Can we fire him?"

Henry sat back, surprised. "Fire him! But why?"

"Because I don't like him and I don't think he's much good."

Henry stood up and went over to the drinks cabinet. "Well, no, I can't fire him, Kim. He's just signed a contract with us. He'd sue us for a fortune. Besides, he comes highly recommended. He's supposed to be the best there is around. And we need the best, Kim. The station is in a terrible mess. Ratings down, advertising revenue down." He took a bottle of wine and plunged a corkscrew into it. "And I have the politicians breathing down my neck all the time. Going on about being answerable to licence-fee payers, and cuttings costs and stopping the waste of money . . ." He filled two glasses. "You'll love this wine, Kim. I bought a casket in the Loire Valley last summer. Two hundred and fifty euros a bottle." He handed her one of the glasses and sat down beside her again. "What has Guy done to upset you, Kim?"

"He keeps interfering on my patch, Henry. Messing with my schedules, messing with staff, and now messing with my time slot!"

"Your time slot?"

"He's suggesting moving my show to the afternoon."

"Oh, surely you're mistaken, Kim, he'd never do that."

"He told me he was thinking of it."

"Well, he probably is confused. Why don't you leave him to me, Kim, and I'll have a little chat with him."

"Would you, Henry?"

Henry leaned over, patted Kim's knee and winked at her. "Leave him to me. Some of these boys can be a bit over-ambitious . . .They try too hard in my opinion. If it's for you, it won't pass you, that's always been my motto."

"Thank you, Henry. He's shit anyway. Mark my words, he'll be gone in a year . . . Which brings me to my next point. Did he say anything to you about considering our Joshua for *The Tonight Show*?"

"Well, no, he didn't."

Kim raised her eyes. "Why does that not surprise me? That will teach me to speak to the monkey instead of the organ-grinder . . . I think our Joshua would be perfect for it."

"Really? Tell me more," said Henry, all interested and sitting nearer to her.

"Mind if I disturb you for a minute?" asked Henry King as he tapped on Guy's door and entered his office.

"Oh, hello, Henry. Of course not, have a seat."

Henry sat down and smiled warmly. Guy liked Henry. He was a kindly fatherly man, who commanded great respect from everybody. He was unfortunately not really up to the job of running a modern television station, but had a job for life anyway.

"How are you fitting in, Guy?"

"Very well, thank you, Henry. There's so much potential here. We just need to get everything moving in the right direction."

"And no better man to do it than you. Just wanted a quick word with you about *The Joshua Green Show*."

"Oh?"

"I commissioned that programme myself. Kim Davenport came to me with the idea and I loved it. She's a wonderful woman, Kim, a wonderful woman. You'll find her a great asset to work with."

"Yes?"

"So the show is my pet project, so to speak." Henry got up and walked around the desk. He stood beside Guy, looking out the window. "I don't think we should mess around with something that's not broken, Guy. The show is our success story, so I think it would be daft to move schedules around, don't you?"

Okay, the bloody bitch went over my head to the top, thought Guy.

"Well, it was just a suggestion, Henry. I thought a bit of experimentation might help the ratings."

"Keep your experimentation for elsewhere, Guy. Best left alone, don't you agree?"

"Perhaps, if you think so."

"You're a good lad, Guy, a good lad!" Henry leaned down.

"And what's this little secret you've been keeping from me about you considering Joshua Green for *The Tonight Show*? I think it could be a splendid idea!"

Guy looked up at Henry with concern.

Guy marched through the television studio. That Kim Davenport knew how to get what she wanted, he conceded that. With her manoeuvres, he imagined she was a wonderful chess player. He had been invited to Joshua and Soraya's for dinner that night and he wasn't in the mood for them after Henry's visit.

Just then he came face to face with Jasmine, dressed in a pin-striped suit and carrying a clipboard.

"Hi, Guy!" She smiled flirtatiously at him.

He stopped and smiled cynically at her. "Jasmine – do you know, I see you more in this building than most of the people who are actually on the payroll here."

"I know – Mum says enthusiasm is the best way to get ahead."

"Indeed."

"Anyway – I *am* working here now."

"Are you?" He was surprised.

"Yes. Well, not officially yet. But I soon will be when I get the researcher job, so Mum said that I may as well come in now and start working on the show."

"Did she indeed? I didn't think the position had stopped being advertised yet let alone interviewed."

"It's not, but it's a done deal, isn't it? According to Mum." She grinned at him and walked off.

15

Unlike the previous time Guy had been at the Greens' home, he was presented with a perfect picture of domestic bliss as he was led into the drawing room and handed a glass of vintage red wine. The Scandinavian au pair brought Danielle and Daniel in to say goodnight to 'uncle' Guy. Soraya was putting the finishing touches to the dining table and was the perfect charming hostess. Joshua of course took centre stage with jokes and stories and behaved as if he and Guy were old friends. Even Lee, although still managing to look somewhat surly, was civil.

Guy was led into the dining room and they all sat down to a traditional roast beef dinner, complete with Yorkshire pudding and gravy.

Guy sat at one end of the table, Joshua at the other, Soraya to one side and Lee and the Scandinavian au pair on the other. Ulrika's only contribution to the conversation was to say 'It's okay' in a bored voice when Guy asked if she enjoyed different aspects of life in Ireland.

Guy imagined Lee had been severely blackmailed to be on the best of behaviour all night. But despite this it was glaringly obvious there was a huge and unpleasant issue between Joshua and his eldest son.

"More gravy, Guy?" smiled Soraya as she moved the silver gravy jug closer to him.

"Thank you," nodded Guy.

"Ulrika, do you want more food?" urged Soraya.

"No, it's okay," said Ulrika.

"Poor Ulrika. She's still getting used to our food. I don't think you're a big fan so far, are you, Ulrika?"

"It's okay," sing-songed Ulrika.

Joshua gave her a knowing look. "She's sneaking off to McDonald's all the time, that's why she's not hungry."

"Leave Ulrika alone, Joshua, she's a treasure with the children and I'd be lost without her," admonished Soraya.

"Thank you, Soraya," Ulrika smiled over appreciatively.

"Are the children in a crèche?" asked Guy.

"They spend Monday and Tuesday mornings during the week in a crèche in town. It's good for them to mix with other children and it's good for me to have 'me time'. I can do some shopping in Grafton Street and we usually have lunch all together in Stephen's Green if the weather is fine."

Guy nodded, thinking how Soraya's life seemed very together and organised. Very normal yet privileged. If only she knew how the whole thing was a sham what with Joshua's affair.

"What about you, Lee? More beef?" asked Soraya.

"I'm fine," said Lee, not looking up.

"Lee's just finished his exams, so he's a bit uptight at the moment, anxiously awaiting his results," explained Soraya.

"Really?" said Guy. "What do you hope to do now you've left school, Lee?"

"Don't know," said Lee, and sat back, folding his arms.

"Maybe you might follow your father into television presenting some day," said Guy.

Joshua choked on his wine. "Lee is not cut out for television presenting, I can assure you."

Lee shot his father a dirty look.

"Well, there are lots of other things he could do in television," said Guy.

"I don't think the world of television is waiting for the arrival of Lee Green," said Joshua, "if you don't mind me saying so, son."

Lee gritted his teeth.

"Lee is going on to do an Arts degree," said Soraya. "Which will give him plenty of time to decide what he then wants to do with the rest of his life."

"If I get the right points to get into university!" snapped Lee.

"Well, if you don't get them, you've nobody to blame but yourself," said Joshua. "And you can just repeat until you do get the right points. In fact, you can repeat until you're thirty if it takes that long to get you into a college course. That should keep you out of trouble."

"*You –*" started Lee.

"Em – where are you actually from, Guy?" Soraya cut in quickly.

"London. Born and bred."

"You've picked up a bit of a mid-Atlantic accent," observed Soraya.

"Well, I was a very long time in New York."

"It must be hard coming to a new city and not knowing people," she said. "If you need anything, just give us a call."

"Thank you, I will," Guy smiled back at her.

Guy walked down the upstairs corridor from the bathroom. It was after eleven and Ulrika had gone to bed as had Lee. He passed an open door and saw Lee at a desk on his computer.

"Everything alright?" asked Guy, stopping at the doorway.

Lee looked up in surprise and nodded, before concentrating on the computer screen again.

"I know what that feels like, incidentally," said Guy.

"Sorry?" Lee looked up at him, confused.

"Being pushed into something you don't want to do."

"I don't know what you're talking about." Lee shook his head and looked at the screen again.

Guy walked into the room.

"Being forced to do an Arts degree that you don't want to do. It's not fair. Have you told them you don't want to do it?"

"Have you ever tried telling my father something when he's not listening . . . Anyway, I have to do something, so I might as well do that."

"Well, why don't you get a job somewhere?"

Lee looked at him frostily. "I don't fancy working in a fast-food joint for the rest of my life, thanks."

"No, but there's lots of other jobs out there. Think about it. Then you'd be earning your own money. You'd be independent – you could do what you wanted to do. If you go to university, you'll be under your dad's thumb for the next three or four years. Answering to him about everything."

"I know but what else can I do?" Lee looked horrified at the thought.

"You know, there's a researcher job going at the station at the moment that you might be right for. Why don't you apply for that?"

"A researcher job? I'd never get a job like that."

"You just need to be lucky in life, that's all. Why don't you apply? You never know, you might get it. That would show your father."

Lee looked at him curiously. "Where can I find out about the job?"

Guy walked over to the desk. "Let me sit down there."

Lee stood up and Guy sat down and started to tap away on the keyboard, bringing up the job application on the RTV website.

Lee stared at the detailed job application in confusion and apprehension.

"These applications are just all about knowing the right things to say. They are looking for certain answers and if you give them you'll get an interview. And if you get to that stage, I'm sure you'd be in with a good chance to get the job. I'll fill out this application for you. I'll have it done for you in five minutes. I can fill these things with my eyes closed."

Lee watched in amazement as Guy started to type in the online application with frightening speed, asking him only a few brief questions such as his date of birth. Guy had the application emailed off before Lee knew what was happening.

Guy sat in the big armchair, playing with his glass of cognac as he chatted away to Soraya and Joshua.

"So – seemingly your name is being thrown in the hat for *The Tonight Show*," said Guy.

Joshua sat up, surprised. "Em – Kim had mentioned it. But I didn't realise it had gone any further than that."

"It's gone further. Henry King thinks you should be considered – and so do I. But the competition is obviously very strong and nothing is promised."

Soraya laughed, embarrassed. "I feel a bit awkward now. I hope you don't think we invited you over to dinner to canvas you in any way."

Guy studied Soraya who appeared to be the most genuine person you could meet.

"No, I know that didn't even enter your head."

Joshua sat back, looking a bit shocked. "I didn't think Kim was serious when she mentioned me for the job."

"Oh, she was very serious. I don't think she's a woman who jokes around too much. And she's certainly got you in the line-up."

"It would be such a massive step for me."

"I'm sure you could manage it – if the opportunity comes your way," Guy assured him. "I'm going to brief the PR department to release a statement saying you're being considered for the job. Get the public used to the idea."

16

Kim sat in the living room, reading a schedule for the following week's programme.

The front door slammed.

"Tom?"

"Yes, it's me, I'm back. I'm just going up to change and unpack and will be down in a few minutes."

She continued working away until Tom came back down ten minutes later.

"Good trip?" she asked.

"Yes. Very good. We came second in the bridge competition."

"Congratulations."

"Thank you . . . Anyway, I'll just go out and check on the garden. I see there hasn't been much rain. The roses probably need watering."

He walked over to the patio window and went out.

Kim looked up from her paperwork and began to count. "One . . . two . . . three . . . four . . ."

There was suddenly a loud scream from the garden followed by a splash.

". . . and five!" said Kim and began to read her paperwork again.

A minute later Tom walked back through the patio doors, drenched in water and holding a garden shears.

"Somebody has put a swimming pool in the garden!" he declared.

"Really?" asked Kim, not even looking up from her paperwork.

Tom walked across the living room and out to the hall, leaving a trail of water behind him.

Kim put down the paperwork and chuckled.

"See, you can get anybody's attention," she said aloud. "You just have to know what button to press."

Kim came through the patio windows and found Jasmine floating on an inflatable chair in the new pool.

"Enjoying the pool?" she asked.

Jasmine took off her sunglasses and shaded her eyes with her hand as she looked at her mother. "Very much so. I'm feeling guilty enjoying it though when it's at the expense of Dad's beautiful rose garden."

"Don't be. Has he said anything about it?"

"No. He never would, would he? But he must be upset, he loved this garden."

"I still left him the front garden . . . for now!" Kim smirked.

"Mum!"

"I'm joking!"

"Lee Green is here to see you," said Guy's secretary.

Guy sat back. "Right . . . send him in."

A few seconds later Lee came awkwardly into the office.

"Hello there. This is a pleasant surprise," said Guy.

"I hope you don't mind me dropping in. It's just I was called for an interview for that researcher job you filled out for me and I just had it now."

"Good for you."

"I wouldn't say I have a chance in hell of getting it. I was shocked to be called. I was only called because you filled out the application form for me and they were impressed by it."

"Don't put yourself down. You never know how you did."

"But I didn't realise that the job was on Dad's show."

"Oh, is it?" Guy looked surprised.

"Maybe I should tell him I've gone for the job. I don't think he'd be too happy about it."

"Well, the way I look at it is, if you get the job tell him then, if you don't then there's no need for him to know, and no harm done."

Lee started to bite on a nail. "I suppose. I don't want to get him all worked up if nothing will come of it."

"Exactly."

"Em . . . I thought Dad's friend Kim would be involved in the interview if it's for their show but she wasn't."

"We're trying to change recruiting practices here at the station, and centralise everything through HR. There was far too much nepotism going on."

"Sorry?" He looked confused.

"Em, people giving jobs to their relatives and friends."

"Oh!"

"At least if you get the job nobody could accuse anyone of pulling tricks, as it all went through HR."

"I guess. Anyway –" Lee stood up, "I just thought I'd let you know."

"Thanks, Lee. And the best of luck with it."

Guy waited until Lee had left he room, and then he picked up his phone.

"Hi, everything went alright with Joshua Green's kid today?" He listened. "Yes . . . yes, he is bright . . . never mind that, he'll learn quickly . . . it's good to get them at that age – they can be shaped properly into what you want them to do."

The next day when Lee got a call from HR saying he'd got the job, he could hardly believe it. He kept thinking there must be a mistake. He rang the station and asked to speak to Guy.

"Congratulations! That's wonderful news!"

"I never thought I'd get it. I don't know if I'll even be able to do the job." Lee sounded very nervous.

"You'll be provided with the proper training. It's time for you to start having confidence in yourself."

"I guess."

"Have you told your father?"

"No. I'm frightened to. He'll hit the roof when he finds out. He won't want me under his feet at his work. I don't think he'll even let me start."

"When are you due to start?"

"Next Monday."

"Well, why don't you tell him nothing for now? Just show up at the studio on Monday morning and let HR take care of it all. If you've signed your contract and everything by the time he finds out, there's nothing he can do, is there?"

17

Kim was in the studio, preparing for the filming of a show.

"Somebody here to see you, Kim!" a production assistant shouted across the studio.

Kim looked over and was surprised to see Donna Doyle there with her brother Aidan. She hurried over to her.

"Hi, Kim, you remember me – I'm Donna Doyle. I was on your show a while back."

"Yes, Donna, how are you? I hear you were not very well."

"I'm fine now. It's just I want to get back on your show. I need to see Glen again so we can sort out our relationship."

Ten out of ten for perseverance, thought Kim as she raised her eyes to heaven.

"Why didn't you contact Brooke rather than just show up, Donna?"

"I tried to. And Brooke first told me you wanted me back on the show but now she keeps saying it isn't a good idea because of my breakdown."

"Does she indeed!" Kim scowled.

"And she's right!" snapped Aidan. "I don't want her back on the show either."

Kim studied the hostile-looking brother, as uncooperative as ever.

"Okay, Donna, why don't you tell me how things have developed with – what was his name again?"

"Glen," confirmed Donna with a nod.

Kim liked nothing better than a good follow-up story, and Donna Doyle's obsession with her brother's friend was showing no sign of abating.

"Okay, Donna, I can give you a few minutes. Let's sit down here. Now fill me in on what's been happening."

Kim was taking a few notes when she saw Lee Green saunter in and look curiously around.

"Sorry, Donna, one second," Kim interrupted Donna's flow. She shouted over to Lee. "You're father's in his dressing room if you're looking for him!"

"Eh," Lee shifted awkwardly, "I'm not looking for him. I'm starting work here today. As a researcher."

Guy checked with HR to see if everything had gone smoothly on Lee Green's first morning of work. They informed him Lee had signed his contract and been sent down to Joshua Green's studio to start work. Guy sat back and waited for the nuclear fallout. It happened when he was having his lunch in the canteen.

Kim came storming in and sat down opposite him.

"Joshua Green's sulky, socially backward son showed up in my studio this morning under the impression that he is my show's new researcher."

"I'd heard he got the job alright."

"Tell me this is a joke."

"I don't think it is. According to HR he won out against pretty fierce competition."

"Including my Jasmine!"

"I know. Is she taking it hard?"

"*What do you think?* She was assured of that job."

"By you, not by the station."

"And what experience does Lee Green have for that job?"

"Well, what experience did Jasmine have really?"

"I'll have you know that Jasmine is a graduate in media studies from the DCB."

"DCB?"

"The Dublin College of Business."

"Oh! I thought it stood for the Dublin College for Bimbos!"

Kim sat back in horror. "How dare you!"

"Sorry, Kim, I shouldn't have said that. But, listen, I don't make the decisions on researcher jobs for programmes. That's what we have a HR department for."

"It was never their decision before you arrived. It was the producer's decision."

"Oh look, Kim, I'm far too busy to be bothered with all this. If you have a problem take it up with HR."

"I would if I could get a straight answer out of the bastards!"

"Well, that's your problem."

"First Brooke! Then Lee! What's going on, Guy?"

"How would I know? You'd swear it was my son and my mistress getting jobs and promotions. Why would I be bothered trying to get them these positions? Maybe it's Joshua pulling strings behind your back."

"No, he wouldn't do that. He'd never go behind my back."

"You seem very confident of his loyalty."

"I am. Besides, the last thing Joshua wants is that son of his working on the show. He'll hit the roof when he finds out."

Brooke looked nervously at Lee. They were just offstage in the studio, ready to start shooting the programme.

Lee had turned up that morning announcing he was the new researcher. Kim had marched off with steam coming from her ears to confront HR and Guy Burton about it and hadn't been seen since.

"Your father must be pleased?" probed Brooke who had been left to mind him.

"Um, he doesn't know yet. I thought I might surprise him."

Some surprise, thought Brooke. If she knew Joshua, and she did, he'd be horrified. She realised Lee had probably just kept putting off telling his father, full sure how he'd react. She was irritated to now be in the thick of this domestic conflict herself. Lee was a touchy point for Joshua at the best of times, but she was frightened of his reaction when he found out that he did this behind his back. As she looked at him, she wondered what on earth use he would be as a researcher. But then she guessed, when Joshua found out, he would be gone so quickly they'd never have a chance to find out.

She stepped out onto the stage and saw that the audience were taking their seats as the floor manager and the cameramen went to their places.

Then, as she walked back offstage she saw Joshua arrive, fresh from Make-up.

"Joshua, can I have a word with you?" said Brooke, rushing up to him.

"Not now, Brooke, we're due to start filming." He suddenly spotted Lee and did a double take. "What are *you* doing here?"

"Em – I'm working here now."

"Working? Sorry?"

"Yeah. Working."

"As what exactly?" Joshua looked at him, bemused.

"He's the new researcher, Joshua," said Brooke. "He applied for the job and got it."

Joshua looked at her, startled, then marched over to Lee.

"What's been going on?"

"I got the job, that's all."

"*You* got the job!"

"Yeah – it might surprise you, that somebody believed in me."

Joshua's face went red and his voice rose. "More like they gave you the job because they thought they had to – because you're my son! You didn't tell them I knew nothing about it, did you?"

"They didn't even ask me about you."

"How fucking dare you do this behind my back? Apply for a job on my show, use my name to get it and just show up like Little Lord Fauntleroy!"

"You're always telling me to show ambition, so I did."

"You're a sneaky little fuck is what you are, and you can think again if you think you're going to work here. You're going straight home."

"No, I'm not. I signed my contract this morning and I'm staying."

"You signed a contract? And what about university?"

"I don't want to go. I don't want to waste three or four years on subjects I don't like."

"Well, you can get used to it, because that's exactly what you're going to do. Now go out to reception and get them to call you a taxi to take you home and we'll talk about this later."

"I'm not leaving. I'm staying to do my job."

"Lee, I'm not messing here! Go home."

"No!"

"Right! I'll just put you in the taxi myself!" Joshua grabbed his arm and started marching him away.

"Let me fucking go!" shouted Lee as he struggled against him.

Brooke was conscious that all the show's staff were looking on by this time.

"I think we'd better all calm down," she advised.

"Shut the fuck up, Brooke, and stay out of it! If you hadn't gone running off to get your promotion, the job vacancy wouldn't have come up in the first place!"

Brooke stepped back, startled at his words.

Kim suddenly arrived. "What's going on?"

"Did you know he was applying for the job?" demanded Joshua.

"I only found out this morning. I've been up in HR trying to sort it out. He got the job alright."

"Yeah, well, easy come, easy go. He's tendering his notice. He's going straight home."

"I'm not and get your fucking hands off me!" shouted Lee, pulling free of his grip.

"Okay, everyone, just shut the fuck up and calm down!" Kim's stern voice restored order. "Now we've got a show to shoot so everyone to their places and we'll discuss this later."

Joshua shot Lee a filthy look and walked onto the stage.

Brooke looked after Joshua, in shock at how he had spoken to her. She saw Lee looking dejected and went over to him.

"You alright?" she asked.

"Yeah – I'm used to it."

18

Joshua marched into their home followed by Lee. He went into the drawing room and poured himself a big glass of whiskey.

"Everything alright?" asked Soraya, looking up.

"No, it's not!" snapped Joshua as Lee walked into the room. "Congratulate your stepson on his new job!"

"Job?" asked Soraya, confused.

"He applied for the researcher job on my show, without telling me, and somehow managed to wangle it! They obviously gave it to him because they thought they had to as he is my son!"

"Lee, why didn't you tell us?" demanded Soraya.

"Because I didn't think I'd get the job," explained Lee.

"And what about university?" asked Soraya.

"Oh, what about it indeed!" Joshua's voice dripped sarcasm.

"I don't want to go. I've been saying it and you weren't listening. Now I've got a choice."

"Oh, well, I don't know!" Soraya was exasperated.

"Well, I do. He's not going back there," said Joshua.

"I'll have you in the Labour Court if you try and get rid of me!" warned Lee.

Joshua laughed loudly and viciously "Oh, you're some kid. Sue your own father!"

"Well, maybe it might be for the best if he stays," suggested

Soraya hastily. "If he's not cut out for further education and can get a break at the television studio –"

"Don't you start!" Joshua raised his voice.

"I'm just saying!" said Soraya.

"I have a very stressful job where I have to concentrate. I'm not playing baby-sitter for *him*!"

"See! He doesn't want me. He never has!" shouted Lee.

"Oh, I need some space from you!" shouted Joshua.

"Well, you can have it. I'll go and stay with Aunt Helen tonight!" said Lee as he stormed off.

"Lee!" Joshua called after him.

"Oh, let him go!" said Soraya. "With the mood you're both in he's better off staying with Helen tonight."

"Maybe you're right. She always manages to calm him down. But who's going to calm me down?"

Brooke opened a bottle of red wine, poured herself a large glass and went and sat on the sofa. She needed a drink after the day. The tension on the set had been unbearable after Lee arrived in. But what she couldn't get over was the way that Joshua had spoken to her, and in front of the whole crew. He had just flipped out at her and talked to her as if she was – well, as if she was nothing to him. He had really embarrassed her and she felt humiliated. Guy's words of warning had been ringing in her ears all day.

Speaking of Guy, she really wished she hadn't attacked him in the car park that day. She had forgotten herself, talking to her superior like that. She had been seriously pissed off to find out Kim knew about her and Joshua and lashed out. She had passed Guy a few times since, and he had just blanked her. He was a tough man. He didn't seem to feel any need to sort the situation out with her. But then, why should he? She meant nothing to him. He had done her a kindness promoting her and she had shot her mouth off in return.

To her surprise, the intercom rang. She got up and answered it.

"Brooke, it's Joshua."

She wondered what was he doing here. Maybe he felt bad about his outburst and was coming over to apologise?

"Brooke?"

"Yes, hi, Joshua," she said and buzzed him in.

She opened her front door and he came in a minute later. He looked flushed and stressed.

"I'm glad you have a bottle open," he said. He went and got himself a glass from the kitchen and poured himself a drink.

"I wasn't expecting you," she said, sitting down on the sofa.

"I just had to get out of the house. Get this – Soraya started defending him! Started saying him getting the job might be a good thing."

"Oh!" said Brooke, realising the last thing on his mind was an apology for the way he had spoken to her.

He paced up and down, ranting about Lee's appointment.

"Joshua!" she said eventually, interrupting his tirade.

"What?" he snapped.

"I was a bit taken aback today at how you spoke to me," she said nervously.

"What are you talking about?"

"When I tried to calm the situation between you and Lee down. You spoke quite aggressively to me."

"What's your point? You could see how much stress I was under."

"I know that. But I think you were out of order."

"Look, don't pull this shit with me, darling. Just because we're going out together doesn't mean you're not still the researcher on the programme. I can't pussyfoot around you just because of our personal life. That wouldn't be fair on me."

"I'm actually the assistant producer."

"Yeah, whatever. Look, I'm really going through enough at the moment without you getting hormonal on me. What with me now being nominated to take over *The Tonight Show*. And this new nasty and personal *'We Hate Joshua Green'* website! And now, on top of it all, it looks like I'm stuck with Lee at the studio. He won't go. He's the most stubborn person you could meet."

"If he does stay – aren't you worried?"

"Of course I'm worried! His capacity to fuck up –"

"No, I mean – worried about us? That he'll find out about us seeing each other?"

Joshua looked bemused. "Well, no! Why would he suspect anything? Nobody in their right mind would ever think we were seeing each other."

Brooke felt herself get annoyed. "Why? Why is that beyond the realm of possibility in people's minds?"

He shrugged. "Because I've got somebody like Soraya at home."

His words were like a blow to her.

"Do you know, I haven't eaten all day with everything going on. Come on, let's go out for something to eat," he suggested.

She looked at the open bottle of wine and the quiet evening of television she had planned for herself, and realised she didn't fancy going out and listening to Joshua's woes.

She got up, sighing to herself. She reminded herself that it was likely the only offer she would get all week.

Jasmine sat in the lounge with a box of Kleenex on her lap, stifling her sobs.

"I always found rejection hard to take. But this! Rejected from my own mother's show!" She wiped away another tear.

"I know, darling. It stinks of shit!" Kim gulped down her gin.

"I loved doing that job. I was made for it!"

"I know. I was the one who made you for it! Joshua is furious. I mean, he comes to work to get away from his family, not to see them!"

"I think it's the worst thing that has ever happened to me!"

"I don't buy Guy Burton's 'nothing to do with me' act for one second. And he just sits there, taking it all in, and giving nothing away. I don't know what he's up to but I sense trouble. And everyone has their weak spot."

She looked out at the swimming pool covering her husband's former garden.

"Do you know what you're going to do, Jasmine? You're going to spend the next week following Guy Burton around to see what he gets up to."

"Following him? But what if he spots me?"

"He won't. You can borrow your father's car. And do you still have that big blonde wig that you wore to that fancy-dress party last year, when you went as Dolly Parton?"

"Yes."

"Well, you can wear that and he'll never spot you. See it as training for being a researcher!"

"He totally overreacted!" said Lee to Soraya in the kitchen. "You should have seen him in the studio. He physically attacked me, trying to throw me out!"

"Don't try and paint yourself whiter than white, Lee. You had no right going behind our backs and doing something like that. Whatever possessed you?"

"I just want a chance of working there."

"This isn't a game, Lee. It's your father's career. And you've never shown enough responsibility in the past to let him think he can trust you. I mean, if you speak to him in the studio in the abusive way you speak to him here at home, you'll be fired on the spot. You have to show him some respect."

"But he has to show me some too!"

The front door opened and slammed shut.

"Soraya?"

"In here!" she called.

Joshua came into the kitchen and glared at Lee.

"Oh, what a surprise to see you! I thought you'd be out being the next Rupert Murdoch!"

Lee rolled his eyes and got up. "I'll see you later."

He walked out, leaving Joshua fuming.

"What's he been saying for himself?" he asked Soraya.

"He seems serious about the job."

"He hasn't been serious about anything in his life!"

"I'd hoped you would have calmed down about it."

"Not a chance!"

"Look, Joshua. We've no choice in this. He's got the job and that's the end of it. You're just going to cause more hassle by not going along with it, for yourself and everybody else."

Joshua gave her a filthy look and walked out of the room.

19

"Anything to report?" asked Kim.

It was the seventh day of Jasmine following Guy around and so far he seemed to be living the most boring life imaginable. The most exciting thing he did was pay a parking fine.

It was seven o'clock and Jasmine was sitting in her father's car in her Dolly Parton wig on the phone to Kim.

"He's just pulled into this secondary-school car park."

"What's he's doing there?" Kim was confused.

"There are people going into the building – I think there are evening classes in there."

"Typical! He's learning origami for kicks!"

"Will I come home?"

"No, follow him in and see what class he's signed up to."

"Okay."

Jasmine fixed her wig and walked into the building.

"Can I help you, love?" asked a woman in the corridor who looked like someone in authority.

"Em, yes, I'm looking for the origami class."

The woman looked confused "There is no origami class."

"Oh. The French lessons then?"

"Upstairs on the right."

Jasmine hurried up the stairs and spotted Guy going into a

TALK SHOW

classroom. She hurried down and was about to go in when she heard the same woman calling her.

"No, love. The French class is here," said the woman, pointing to a door near the top of the stairs.

"Thanks!" Jasmine walked back to her. "Could you tell me what's going on in that classroom down there on the right?" She pointed to the one she saw Guy go into.

"That's the Alcoholics Anonymous meeting, love." The woman looked pointedly at her Dolly Parton hair. "You know, we run a class on hairdressing as well – you might be interested."

"So, he's an alky!" stated Kim in glee. "You know, I thought he was nursing his drinks a long time when he was over here. And my indoor palm tree hasn't been the same since. He was obviously throwing his drink into the plant pot when I wasn't looking!"

"What are you going to do now?" asked Jasmine.

"You know something, I've been worried myself about my drink intake recently. Maybe it's time I tackled the problem myself." She smiled at Jasmine and knocked back her gin.

It was Monday lunch-time and town was busy. Guy walked across the street and into the park on Stephen's Green. He started scouring the small park looking for Soraya. But couldn't spot her. He walked round and round, willing for her to be there but there was no sign of her. She did say she took lunch in the park on Mondays and Tuesdays if it was fine and it was a nice summer's day. He knew he was grasping at straws hoping that she might be there. She was probably having lunch with friends, or maybe one of the children was ill and hadn't gone to the crèche that morning.

Just as he was about to give up he saw Soraya stroll into the park, carrying a few shopping bags, the sun bouncing off her blonde hair. She walked over to a free bench and sat down. He walked towards her at a quick pace, his briefcase swinging.

As he passed her he heard her call out.

"Guy?"

"Oh – hello there!" He stopped and looked surprised to see her.

"How are you?" She smiled broadly at him.

"Good. I was just at a meeting with a production company on Harcourt Street, taking a shortcut through the park."

"On your way back to the station?" she asked.

"I was going to grab a taxi at the rank," he said.

"I'm waiting for Ulrika to bring the children from the crèche. Would you like some lunch? I've got loads!" She opened her Marks and Spencer shopping bag.

He sat down beside her. "I'm not really hungry – thanks anyway."

"I insist," she said, handing him a sandwich and a soda. Then she began to unwrap her own sandwich.

"All I seem to do is be fed by you! I'll have to take you and Joshua out to dinner soon."

"That would be nice," she smiled.

"You look like you've been busy," he said, nodding at her shopping bags.

"Yes, I needed to get a few things."

He took a bite of his sandwich and a drink from the soda before speaking again. "I hear Lee's come to work for the station!"

Soraya raised her eyes. "Don't mention the war, please!"

"Joshua's not too happy about it?"

"That's an understatement. I just don't know how Lee managed to land the job! He's never shown any initiative with anything in the past. He has to be pushed to do everything."

"You might have been underestimating him."

"Obviously we were. Joshua reckons HR gave it to him because they thought Joshua wanted him to have it. But I thought, if that was so, they would have called Joshua to check it out first."

Guy shrugged. "I don't know how HR do things. Oh, well, Joshua will get used to it."

"He can be very stubborn. He likes things his way. At least I'm not working there any more! I think I'd crack up with the tension!"

"Do you ever miss work?"

"Gosh, no! To be honest, I never really enjoyed work. I never got that much out of it. I just fell into my job as a researcher in television. I never really knew what I wanted to be. We're not supposed to be like that, are we? My generation of women. We were the ones who were given all the opportunities and were supposed to seize them. We were supposed to go boldly from the womb and do excellently at school and college and then go on and carve brilliant careers as media darlings, or captains of industry or concert pianists. But that was never really me, you see. I was average at school, even more average at university once I discovered boys and parties. I floundered around not knowing what to do with my life. A family friend eventually took pity on me and sorted me out with a researcher job on television. I felt terribly guilty doing that job, feeling I was robbing somebody else, who would love doing it and be really good at it, of the opportunity. Whereas I was just filling in time around my social life. Then I met Joshua and he wasn't like anybody I had met before. I was amazed at him – he swept me off my feet. The things he would say and do! So we married. I knew I wanted children quickly. I felt I needed them to even things up. He had Lee, and I felt the family needed balancing out. Now I'm deliriously happy just being a wife and mother. I'd be appalled if I had to go back to work."

He listened intently and nodded. "If you want – I could have a word with Joshua to try and make him see that having Lee there might be a good thing?"

"That's not fair on you. I don't want to get you involved. You've enough to be doing running RTV."

"If I can be of any help, I'd only be too pleased."

She smiled at him. "You know, when you're dealing with Joshua you have to realise there's more to him than meets the eye. He's not this brash arrogant talk-show host everyone thinks he is. I mean, there's this new website set up against him recently and it's upset him. He struggled for years with Lee on his own. He struggled away in radio broadcasting for years. Money was tight, he was on his own, it wasn't easy. But he always had dreams to get to where he is now, so why shouldn't he enjoy the fruits a bit?"

"Indeed, why not?" nodded Guy, thinking about Brooke.

He was just going to ask about Lee's mother when Soraya sat forward and waved across the park.

"There's Ulrika now with the children."

He looked over and saw Ulrika pushing a double buggy. He sat back to finish his sandwich.

20

It was the day that the *Privilege* magazine featuring Joshua and his family came out and Joshua had spent the morning in his dressing room at HTV studying the photos and interview which showed them in the best possible light. And yet here he was feeling agitated and stressed. He had been itching to find out what that website had said about the *Privilege* spread and couldn't resist checking it on his laptop.

The website had copied the photo on the front of the magazine and reprinted it on the screen. He read the accompanying article.

'Joshua Green has sunk to a new low. Not content to exploit the luckless guests on his show, he has now decided to prostitute his family. Yes, in a vomit-inducing photo shoot Green shows off his 'stunning' wife Soraya and their 'adorable' two sprogs, Daniel and Danielle. (Why do your two kids have practically the same name, Joshua? You obviously had as little imagination when naming your brats as you do for ideas for your show!) Joshua sold his family to the highest magazine bidder in a cynical ploy for more publicity. As part of this circus he also allows the readers to take a look at most of the rooms in his gaudy, oversized house. It's obvious from his home that he is well compensated for exploiting his guests' misery. As his guests return to their council flats and their meagre existence, Green surrounds himself with valuable antiques and a trophy wife.

His wife is exploited in a number of revealing dresses for the benefit of Green's career. She ends up looking like a high-class hooker lounging in her boudoir. But he doesn't stop there – he allows his kids to be photographed as well. It's all about the money for this mercenary pair . . .'

Joshua quickly clicked off the screen as the door of his dressing room opened and Brooke came in to talk about the show's schedule.

Joshua came into the kitchen and handed Soraya a copy of *Privilege*.

"Here it is," he smiled, handing it over to her.

Across the front page was a glossy photo of Joshua, Soraya, Daniel and Danielle, smiling in their drawing room. The headline across the bottom of the photo read *'Talk Show King Joshua Green and his beautiful wife Soraya invite us into their stunning home as he tells us about his bid to be Chat Show King with* The Tonight Show'.

"Well, it's out there now. Everyone knows you're going for *The Tonight Show*," said Soraya as she riffled through the magazine, looking at the photos.

"Can I help you, love?" asked the woman in the secondary school as Kim entered.

"Yes, I'm looking for the class for the lushes," said Kim.

"Sorry?"

"AA?"

"Ah, upstairs, down the corridor, last room on the right. You've missed the first fifteen minutes."

"I know. I got delayed in the pub!" Kim winked at her and headed upstairs.

Kim opened the door slightly and peered in. They were all sitting in a group and sure enough there was Guy. She pushed the door open quietly, crept in and sat discreetly at the back, making sure Guy didn't spot her. She listened as they all gave their stories, until it was Guy's turn.

"I'm finding it very difficult since I started at the television channel. There seems to be such a big drinking culture there. And if you're not drinking you won't be one of them. There always

115

seems to be a drink being put into my hand. Like it's an expectation that I should drink."

"And have you been tempted?" asked the team leader.

"There's always the temptation," said Guy.

"Maybe you should make it clear you don't drink," suggested the leader.

"I'd be ostracised even more in that place. The whole place revolves around the pub, and I don't want to draw attention to myself by making statements."

"That's understandable," said a woman in the group.

"And I'm worried because there are functions where I need to circulate and mix and it's hard to do that without the crutch of a drink."

"So you have to be extra vigilant," advised the leader. "Anyone else feeling particular pressure through work at the moment?" He looked around group and spotted Kim. "Hello there. You're a new face. Would you like to introduce yourself?"

All eyes turned and looked at Kim, including Guy's.

"Em . . . my name is Kim." She looked over at Guy and smiled. "And I'm an alcoholic!"

The group was disbanding and Guy walked straight over to Kim.

"What are you doing here?" he demanded.

"Same as yourself, Guy. Facing up to my demons."

"But you drink like a fish."

"Precisely! I've been worried about my drinking for a while now and thought I'd better do something about it."

He looked at her cynically. "And why this meeting? It's not anywhere near where you live."

"I can't imagine it's anywhere near where you live either," she pointed out. "But it's a happy coincidence, isn't it, Guy? It's nice to have somebody you know here."

"What part of the 'anonymous' bit don't you get?" he asked, annoyed.

"Well, I suppose if you would prefer me to attend another meeting, I could. But the trouble is we'll always have that knowledge about each other now, won't we? We'll always know each other's weakness."

He stared at her.

"And I want to ask something from you, Guy. Can I rely on your discretion, in the same way you can be assured you can rely on mine?"

He cleared his throat. "Of course."

"Oh, I am glad! Because something like this can ruin a reputation, can't it? I mean we're all such hypocrites, aren't we? I mean somebody can drink until they keel over and vomit on the floor and everyone just thinks he's great craic. And yet as soon as people hear there's an actual problem, he gets a label, and you can never get away from that, can you, Guy?"

Kim sat up on the stool beside Jasmine at the bar in The Shelbourne.

"Well, I think that's the last time we'll have any trouble with him," she announced.

"What happened?" demanded Jasmine anxiously.

"A double gin and tonic, love," Kim said to the barman before turning back to Jasmine. "You know, listening to all those stories about how drink ruined their lives has given me quite a thirst."

"Was he there?" asked Jasmine impatiently.

"Of course he was there. Spilling out how he was craving drink to give him confidence to do his new job."

"That doesn't sound like Guy Burton."

"Well, I managed to see him without his suit of armour on tonight, and it's a pretty sorry sight, I can tell you." Kim took a large drink of her gin and tonic.

"And?" asked Jasmine.

"And we chatted afterwards. I told him his secret was safe with me. As long as he plays by my rules. So tomorrow you can go to HR and tell them you're my new PA."

"PA?" Jasmine was confused.

"Well, you don't want to be a researcher now Bart Simpson has just become one. You'll end up carrying him."

"Good thinking. And what will I be doing when I'm your PA?"

"Well, more or less what you do for me anyway, except the station will pay you a salary for doing it from now on."

"Mum – did I ever tell you that you were my hero?"

"There's no need to, love. I tell myself I'm a hero every day."

21

Guy picked up his ringing phone.

"Guy, it's Celeste in HR. Jasmine Davenport arrived in this morning saying you were employing her as Kim's new personal assistant. It's the first I've heard of it. Is it true?"

Guy sat thinking, twisting the phone cord into a knot.

"Guy?" pushed Celeste.

"Yes, it's true. Give her a year's contract." He put down the phone and stared ahead.

Brooke sat at her desk going through her work. She looked over at Lee who looked lost and out of his depth. She could see Kim through the glass panel in her office, high-heel-clad feet stretched out across her desk, as she laughed down the phone.

This new position of assistant producer hadn't really changed Brooke's role any. She seemed to be doing the same job as before, albeit she did feel more confident in the meetings about speaking her mind. And now it looked like Lee was to be trained by her, which was a pain. She had passed Guy that morning and he had blanked her as usual, cool blue eyes staring ahead. She felt she needed to take control of the situation and apologise for shouting at him. A copy of *Privilege* magazine was on her desk, an incredibly glossy photo of Joshua and Soraya mocking her from the front cover. She took up the magazine and flung it in the bin, then walked over to Lee and handed him some paperwork.

"Lee, can you go through all these, please? Ring the people up and ask them to come in and see me. If they can't come in, make an arrangement for me to see them in their homes."

He grabbed the papers, grateful for something to do. "Okay . . . Who are they?"

"Potential guests for the show. I need to see them to estimate how they'd come across on television and to see if they are authentic."

"Oh! Are they all not real?"

"No. Some people will do and say anything to get on TV, but they can be easily weeded out."

He nodded. "I'll ring them now."

"Thanks," said Brooke.

"Eh, Brooke?" he asked.

"Yes?"

"Where's my father's office? It's just I never see him up here?" His father, after his outburst, was now studiously avoiding him.

"These are the offices for the production staff. He doesn't have an office up here. He has a dressing room in the studio, and attends the meetings in the boardroom."

Lee nodded and started reading through the paperwork.

Brooke had turned to walk back to her desk when she saw Jasmine arrive in a miniskirt, high-heeled thigh-high boots, black leather jacket, black beret and oversized sunglasses. Brooke thought she looked a cross between a dominatrix and a member of the Baader Meinhof group.

"Hi there. Where's my desk?" asked Jasmine.

"Your desk?" questioned Brooke.

"Yes, I'm starting work here today as Mum's PA." She smiled broadly.

"What?" Brooke didn't hide her shock.

Kim came swinging out of her office. "Jasmine, this is your desk outside my office." She pointed at a desk that had arrived that morning.

"Yippee!" said Jasmine, sitting down at it and turning on her computer.

"No time for that now, Jasmine – we're late for lunch," said Kim as she threw on her coat. She handed Brooke a pile of paperwork. "Brooke, all these potential guests you gave me are shit! Tear them up and start again. I want pure drama! Not second-hand drivel! You know who called in to see me? Donna Doyle. Fresh out of that clinic she was in and anxious to meet the love of her life on our show again. I thought we had agreed to have her. Sign her up."

"Donna! I don't think that's a good idea!"

"So she was telling me. Just phone her and get her back on the show with the brother and her ex-boyfriend. We won't be back this afternoon. Come on, Jasmine!" Kim marched off.

"Ta ta!" waved Jasmine as she followed her mother out.

Brooke waited for her moment to approach Guy. It was after work and he was in the car park heading towards his car.

"Guy?" she said, coming up behind him.

He seemed startled and jumped slightly. He probably thought she was going to attack him again, Brooke thought.

"I just wanted to say sorry for shouting at you before," she said. "I had no right to do that."

"No, you hadn't," agreed Guy, looking at her coolly.

They stood in an awkward silence. She had thought he might take the opportunity to explain why he had told Kim about her sleeping with Joshua. Obviously he didn't feel the need to explain himself.

"It's just . . . It's just I was really annoyed that you broke our agreement not to tell anybody about me and Joshua. And I was angry that you told Kim of all people."

"I didn't tell Kim about you and Joshua. She was the one who told me."

"What?" Brooke was shocked.

Guy looked down at his watch. "Look, I'm supposed to be at a function in The Clarence. I have to rush. If you want to continue this conversation you'll have to come with me." He walked around his car, opened it and got in.

A. O'CONNOR

"I can't go to a function with you!"

"Why not?"

"Because I'm not dressed correctly."

"It's an after-work affair. Everyone will be in their work clothes. Are you coming?" He started up the engine.

"I've something on. I can't."

"Meeting with Joshua?" he asked with a smirk.

She sighed and nodded.

"It's actually a function for documentary makers," he said. "There would be a lot of people that it would be good for you to meet there."

She thought for five seconds, then suddenly she jumped into his passenger seat, glancing at him nervously. As he revved up and sped off, she took out her phone and texted Joshua saying she couldn't make it that night.

Brooke found the function very interesting. There were a lot of producers there whose work she had long admired. And being with Guy for the night meant she was introduced to them. Some of them even handed her their cards. She noticed they all wanted to befriend Guy, aware he could commission their documentaries at the stroke of a pen. He accepted their attention in the same cool manner he seemed to take everything.

By nine o'clock nearly everyone had gone home.

"Did you enjoy the evening?" asked Guy, as he and Brooke walked through the hotel reception.

"Very much so. Thank you for inviting me."

"I didn't invite you. We were having a conversation that I had to cut short – the idea was, if you came with me, we could continue."

"But we didn't get back to that conversation."

"Yes – where were we?"

"You were telling me that Kim told you about me sleeping with Joshua."

"That's correct."

"But how does she know?"

"She said it was down to woman's intuition."

122

"Nothing gets past her. But why didn't you explain that to me when I accused you of telling her?"

"I didn't feel the need to. I thought, if you wanted to believe I broke our agreement, then so be it."

She studied him, trying to fathom him. "Well, then I owe you a double apology. Firstly for attacking you. And secondly for attacking you in the wrong."

"Double apology accepted," he said, and managed to smile at her as they stepped out on to the street. "Where to now?"

"Well, home, I guess."

"You haven't eaten."

"No."

"Well, how about dinner?"

22

Shanahan's on the Green wasn't so busy that night and they were seated fairly quickly at a corner table.

"Have you been here before?" asked Guy after they both ordered steak.

"A couple of times," said Brooke.

He looked at her, guessing she'd been there with Joshua.

"How's Joshua's son working out?" he asked.

"Well, as good as an eighteen-year-old straight from school can be, I suppose," said Brooke.

"I'd like you to do me a favour."

"Yes?"

"I want you to look after him. Be kind to him. Teach him what he needs, to do the job properly."

"Why should I play Mary Poppins?" she said, looking irritated.

"Because everyone wants and expects him to fail. And you are the only person who can stop that from happening."

"You're asking me to cover for him?"

"I'm asking you to train him adequately."

The steak arrived and they began to eat.

"I've annoyed you?" he asked.

"Well, yes, you have. It's taken me years to get where I am, and Lee just gets this job handed to him. I had to learn the very hard way, and yet you expect me to make it easy for Lee. That's not fair."

"No, it's not, is it? But I'm sure people helped you along the way as well?"

"Very few!" She almost spat the words.

"I helped you. I promoted you," he pointed out.

"True," she conceded.

They ate in silence for a while before she spoke again. "Alright, I'll help him as best I can."

"Thank you," he said and smiled at her.

She watched him eat. "I wouldn't have made life difficult for Lee anyway. That's not my style."

"I never suspected you would. But I'm asking you to just go the extra mile with him."

"Why do you care?" She was curious.

"I don't really. I just like everyone to be given a fair chance in life."

"Aren't you wonderful?" she said and smiled sarcastically.

"One day somebody might be looking for a producer for a programme and they might give *you* a chance."

Brooke took a drink from her red wine and looked sceptical. "I don't think I'll ever have the ability to carry a whole programme on my own."

"Why not?"

"I'm great at doing the back-up stuff. Organising everything and making sure things run smoothly. But I wouldn't have the confidence to be in charge."

"Let me tell you something. Everybody, and I mean everybody, doubts themselves. Nobody is born thinking they can do everything. We all fear the same things: rejection, failure, being laughed at, not loved. But it's how we manage to project ourselves that counts."

"I can't imagine Kim ever fears anything."

"I can assure you she does. She's got her own insecurities. Things in her life upset and bother her. But some of us are just better at showing confidence than others. Once you learn to show confidence, Brooke, then you'll be able to run your own show and everything else in your life."

She stared at him, her eyes widening as she took another drink.

Guy pulled up in front of Brooke's apartment block.

"Well, eh, thanks for the evening and everything," she smiled at him.

"No problem," he nodded at her.

She went to open her door but it was jammed.

"Here, let me, there's a knack to it," he said and he reached over and pulled the lever, unlocking the door.

She felt uncomfortable as he leant across her and as he pulled back his face stopped opposite hers and they stared at each other.

"If I make the first move, you could accuse me of harassment," he said. "But if *you* make the first move . . ."

She leaned forward and kissed him, then drew back and looked at him.

"Now there could never be any accusation of harassment," she said.

He smiled at her and then leaned in to kiss her.

Brooke opened her front door and turned on the light. Guy walked in behind her.

"Welcome to my home," she said, taking off her coat. "It's small, it's completely in negative equity – but it's mine." She smiled at him and walked through to the kitchen.

"It's very nice," he said, as he walked around taking it all in.

She came back in with an open bottle of wine and poured two drinks, then lit herself a cigarette. She drew heavily on it.

"You smoke a lot?" he asked, sitting down and raising his glass of wine, then smelling it before returning it to the coaster.

"Probably. Who's counting?"

"How long have you lived here?"

"Four years. I bought at the height of the market. Typical! My luck!"

"And is this where Joshua comes?" he asked, sitting back.

Her face clouded over and she walked over to the windows and looked out.

"Well, we hardly go around to his, do we?" she snapped. "Not with his wife and children there."

"No. I just thought that you might book into hotels or something."

"Ohh, that would be lovely and sordid, wouldn't it? We only book into hotels when we're away for business weekends. Otherwise we come here." She turned around and smiled falsely. "The scene of the crime!"

"It's none of my business," he said.

"I'm just wondering what you think of me. Making a pass at you in the car, sleeping with married men – you must think I'm a right slapper!"

"You didn't make a pass at me. I invited you."

"You're probably wondering who made the first move between me and Joshua. It was him actually, for the record. It was late in the studio. There had been a Christmas party. Yes, it was as clichéd as that. We were the last ones to leave and he made a move. I was shocked. I hadn't even thought of him in that way before. I thought he was happily married with children. I thought he hadn't even noticed me. I was flattered. He was everything I dreamed of and I was more than willing . . ." She drew from her cigarette and rubbed her forehead. "I was . . . I am repulsive."

"No, you're not."

"I am. I'm revolting. I happily got involved with a married man without giving a second thought to his wife or family. I told myself that his marriage was of no concern to me. The truth is, I was delighted he was cheating on Soraya with me. It was my way of getting one up on her. Now if that doesn't make me revolting, then what does?"

"And what has she ever done to you?"

She started laughing. "Nothing of course! Nothing directly. In fact she's always gone out of her way to be extra nice to me . . . but everything indirectly. Everything is a struggle for me, nothing is for her. She gets everything handed to her, including Joshua. But now he was choosing to leave her at home and go out for the evening with me!"

"And was that enough to satisfy you?"

She drew on her cigarette. "I thought it was. Until recently."

"What changed?"

"You – fuck you! Questioning me! Questioning my attitude to life and Joshua. Pointing out I was getting the raw end of the deal with Joshua. Promoting me – making me realise that my talent and hard work wasn't going unspotted. That maybe I deserved more in life."

He got up and walked over to her.

"You do deserve much more than him." He took the cigarette out of her hand and stubbed it out in the ashtray.

"Do I deserve you?" she asked.

He stared at her before pulling her close.

23

Brooke had a hectic day lined up in work and she was finding it very hard to concentrate after her night with Guy. If she had begun to think having an affair with Joshua was one of the biggest mistakes of her life, then sleeping with the Director of Programmes was fairly high up there in her faux-pas league as well.

That afternoon she had met Donna Doyle, as directed by Kim who reminded her that her favourite kind of story involved stalking, rehab or nervous breakdowns and this one had all three. Donna had been accompanied by her brother Aidan who was also to appear on the show. Despite his hostile attitude, she felt sorry for him. He seemed stuck between his concern for his sister and trying to make her see sense. Later, and separately, Brooke had met the object of Donna's interest, Aidan's friend Glen. As Brooke listened to him, it did appear that Donna's behaviour was reaching worrying levels. He was just at his wit's end as she continually showed up at his house and work. He was hoping the show would make her see sense and move on.

Brooke wondered how this show would go ahead considering Guy's strong opposition to Donna appearing but Kim had breezily told her to fire ahead and not to worry about that.

Joshua was reading the website in his dressing room.

'So Green now thinks he's capable of hosting The Tonight Show and has thrown his hat into the ring of candidates being considered.

129

He actually must not watch his own shows for him to even think that he could host a serious talk show. He'll be laughed off the screen the first night the show goes out. Nobody is going to watch him interviewing stars and politicians. The man has the IQ of a gorilla. Stick with what you know, mate – Gutter TV!'

Brooke came into Joshua's dressing room and he snapped his laptop shut.

"The publicity department asked you to autograph these for your fan club," she said, handing him a pile of photographs.

He took out a pen and started scribbling his signature.

"I suppose we'd better keep the fans happy. Especially as I'm going for *The Tonight Show*. I need as much support as I can get."

"True," said Brooke.

After he'd handed her back the signed photographs, he yawned and said, "Come on, let's go get some lunch."

"Oh, I can't today, Joshua. I said I'd do lunch with some friends."

"Oh!" He looked surprised but not too bothered. "Can't you put them off? I wanted to have a chat about Lee?"

"Sorry, Joshua. I can't."

Joshua headed into the canteen on his own and came face to face with Guy.

"Hi there," said Joshua.

"Hey! Going for lunch?"

"I am," said Joshua as they joined the queue.

"Everything alright? You look a bit glum?"

"Oh, it's nothing!"

"You're shooting a show this afternoon, aren't you?" said Guy.

"Yeah."

"Well, I can't have you going in front of the camera when there's something bothering you. So talk to me!"

Joshua looked around the canteen and saw the same two girls he'd seen before looking at a laptop and sniggering over at him.

"The walls have ears here. Let's go get lunch somewhere else," he suggested.

They walked down to a quiet pub nearby and ordered lunch.

"So – go on," urged Guy.

"My son Lee has got a job on my show."

"I heard about that. You're not happy about it?"

"No, I'm not! You don't know what Lee is like. I've had terrible problems with him in the past."

"Like what?"

"He bunked off school more times than I can recall. Disruptive behaviour in school. I had to beg the headmaster not to expel him. If he wasn't bullying he was being bullied. He went between gangs of friends. He kept terrible company. I mean, I sent him to a fee-paying school so he could find decent friends. And he ended up with this gang who drink cider like it's 7Up, and I know they do drugs. I've found marijuana in his room."

"I see," Guy nodded. "So – he wasn't a grade A student. Which of us were? I hated school. But as soon as I started work, I loved it. It might be the same for Lee. It might be the making of him."

"Yeah, and he fucks up my programme in the meantime."

"Kim Davenport isn't going to let anybody fuck up your programme. She'll kill him first."

"That's true," nodded Joshua.

"And there's Brooke," said Guy.

"Brooke?" asked Joshua, concerned.

"Yes. She's a true professional and she'll make sure he gets just enough responsibility but not enough where he can do harm."

"She does seem to be watching over him a lot," said Joshua. "But you don't know what he's like. He gets bored and distracted in a second."

"So what's the worst that can happen? He gets bored within a couple of months, gives it up and goes on to his university course?"

"I suppose."

"Look, let's face it – you push any eighteen-year-old in one direction and they storm off into the other. You're playing this all wrong, Joshua. You need to have a neutral stance on this. He'll dig his heels in if he knows you want him out."

"You're right," Joshua nodded slowly. "I guess that's just what Soraya has been trying to tell me at home as well."

"Has she?"

"Yeah, she thinks I'm getting worked up about nothing. We've even been rowing about it, and we never row."

"Well, I think you owe her an apology."

"Yeah. I mean, she's fantastic. I think me and Lee would have killed each other ages ago if it wasn't for her acting as peacemaker all the time."

"You've got a gem in her. So – do you feel better about the situation now?"

"I do – thanks, Guy. I just needed to get it off my chest."

"There's something else, isn't there?" asked Guy as their lunch arrived.

"It's silly really."

"Look, Joshua, if it worries you then let me know."

"It's just there's this really vicious website set up about me."

"What kind of stuff is on it?"

"Well, it's been going on for a while. It started off as banal enough. Saying my show was crap and I was rubbish. And every time I wrote on my webpage they would attack what I was saying. But it's getting really venomous now."

"I see. And have there been any threats?"

"No threats. But it just makes me worried that somebody hates me so much out there. And they've started attacking Soraya and my family."

"To be honest, celebrity always attracts this kind of thing in my experience. If you feel threatened then we should get the police involved. However, if it's just a bit of star-hating then that's an occupational hazard unfortunately."

"Yeah – you're right. I shouldn't let it get to me."

"The trouble is there's no control of what goes on the internet really. It's the sewerage of the publishing world."

Joshua walked into the kitchen with a big bunch of flowers.

"What are these for?" Soraya asked as he kissed her.

"For being a jerk with you over the past few days . . . You're right, of course, about Lee. I was handling it wrongly."

"Well, I'm glad you've seen sense. He was wrong to go behind our backs, but we're only making him more stubborn by objecting at this point."

"That's what Guy was saying as well."

"Guy?"

"Yes, I ended up going to lunch with him and spilling out my problems. He said the same as you about it all."

"Nice to have an ally for a change."

Lee sat in Guy's office.

"So – how are you getting on with the new job?" asked Guy with a smile.

Lee sighed loudly. "I don't know! I've just been trying to stay out of my dad's way to be honest."

"Has he calmed down any?"

"He's just ignoring me most of the time."

"And Kim?"

"Well, she obviously doesn't want me there, but she's just ignoring me too. I think she's afraid to say anything to me in case she sets my father off and adds fuel to the fire."

Her programme comes first, thought Guy. Even though she doesn't want Lee there, she won't rock the boat and upset her star.

"Brooke is being cool with me. She explains things to me and takes time to show me what to do."

"Good. Well, just follow her lead."

"I'm worried about tomorrow as there's a production meeting, and I don't know how to handle it."

Guy sat forward. "Nobody likes when the new person pretends they know everything, so take a bit of a back seat tomorrow. Also, you'll set your father off if you say too much."

"But I don't want to come across like a geek either," said Lee.

"Just look attentive and write notes during the meeting and look interested. If somebody asks you a question then answer it as best you can. Brooke will step in if she feels you can't answer something."

Lee nodded.

24

As the show was being recorded in the studio, Joshua's groomed appearance was in stark contract to that of his guests, who were a particularly unsavoury line-up that day. There was Barry, a man in his early thirties, dressed in jeans and an oversized shirt not tucked in, the glimpse of a tattoo on his arm. Beside him sat his wife Janet, a woman who looked defeated by life, unfit and dowdy. And in a chair positioned away from them was Bella, a younger woman dressed sexily in cheap clothes, a defiant and mischievous look on her over-made-up face. Joshua had just explained to the audience that Bella was Janet's sister and Barry's sister-in-law. Bella was also heavily pregnant.

"Before I reveal the result of the lie detector test you previously took," Joshua interrupted them loudly, "Barry, do you still deny having slept with your wife's sister Bella, and being the father of her unborn child?"

"Bella's a mad bitch, Joshua," said Barry dismissively and angrily. "Always was and always will be. I didn't go near her."

Bella sat forward and shouted, pointing her finger accusingly at Barry: "Right – so you're trying to tell me that you never gave me a lift back to mine after our Janet's birthday party this last year? That you never invited yourself in for a cup of tea? And that you never did what we ended up doing and got me the way I am, carrying my sister's husband's child?"

"As I said, Josh, she's a mad bitch. She might have come on to me, more than once. Many times more than once, I can tell you. But I love our Janet to pieces and I'd never do that to her. I'd say I'm the only fella on our estate who hasn't been with Bella, but the kid's not mine. I swear it on our Janet's life."

"That's an easy to thing to swear on, since her life means all of that to you!" Bella clicked her fingers.

Joshua turned to Janet. "Janet, you've been married to Barry for eight years, and you have three children with him. Am I correct?"

Janet was sniffling slightly. "That's right, Joshua."

"And what do you make of your sister's accusation she slept with your husband?"

Janet sat up and looked angrily at Bella. "Our Bella was always making things up, Josh – she was lying before she could talk, that one. She broke my mother's heart with the things that came out of her mouth."

"So you believe Barry one hundred per cent?" pushed Joshua.

"One hundred per cent, Josh!" Janet nodded vigorously.

"And has Barry always been faithful to you, Janet?" asked Joshua.

"Not always, Josh, no," Janet accepted, looking uncomfortable and nervous.

The audience, which had been transfixed and silent up to now, started booing.

Joshua's voice became loud and accusing. "Isn't it true that your husband Barry had an affair with a neighbour of yours, two doors down, two years ago?"

The audience were now shouting abuse.

"It's wasn't Barry's fault," Janet said defensively. "That one who lives two doors down is the biggest slut on the estate!"

"Except for your Bella," Barry interjected.

"Even the postman won't go to her door, in case she pounces, and the milkman used to leave the milk at the end of the road for her to collect! We used to call her Elevator Knickers!" said Janet.

The audience burst into loud guffaws.

Joshua looked at Barry sternly. "And where is that neighbour now?"

"I don't know – she went off to Limerick, last we heard," shrugged Barry, unfazed.

Joshua approached Barry. "Listen, let's face it, you don't have the best reputation around. We have lots of other examples of your cheating. But if Bella is carrying your child, that is your responsibility. You owe it to the child. Because one day that child is going to come knocking on your door and demand to know where you were all its life. Do you understand me?"

Barry sat looking bored as the audience started to roar their disapproval.

Joshua became angry. "Hey – don't you come on my show with that attitude! You came on here to sort out the mess that is your life. Now we can help you. We've got trained counsellors waiting out back to talk to you and Janet and Bella to help you find a way forward. But you have to take responsibility for the mistakes you've made in your life. Because, I tell you, I go home every night to my kids and I can look them in the eye and tell them they are the most important thing to me. Will you be able to do that?"

The audience broke into applause and cheers while Barry managed to look suitably ashamed.

Joshua turned and walked away from them, then swung around and tore open an envelope he had suddenly produced. "Right," he proclaimed. "Bella claimed that on the 14th of December last year you, Barry, came to her house and slept with her. Barry, you denied this. And our lie detector test shows . . . *that you did in fact lie!* You *did* spend the night with her."

Bella jumped to her feet and started pointing her finger in Barry's face. "I told you that you wouldn't get away with it!"

Joshua walked up and down in front of them like a teacher in a classroom. "Barry – anything to say?"

Barry shook his head and looked embarrassed.

"What about you, Janet?" asked Joshua. "Have you anything to say? What do you think of your husband sleeping with your sister? You still look as if you're in denial, Janet. Let me ask you something . . . why do you believe everything he says?"

Janet shook her head and looked confused. "I don't know, Josh . . .
I guess love is blind."

"Yes – but it seems brain-damaged as well in your case!" said
Joshua to the immense glee of the audience.

The production team were sitting around the table in the boardroom.
Lee was right at the end of the table, as far away from his father as
possible. Brooke's mobile bleeped and she opened the text which
read: *Are you free to meet up tonight? Guy*.

Kim was standing at the top of the table.

"Right. Great show today, everybody. Everyone loves a reunion.
Even if they are going back to a bad marriage. Bastard husband,
put-upon wife and slut sister-in-law. A perfect combination for our
show. Now, as you all know by now, Joshua is being considered for
The Tonight Show. And if Joshua gets it, then that means most of
us will be going with him. So we all need to work doubly hard from
now on to demonstrate that we are the best. We have to produce
excellent television to prove to the powers that be at RTV that
we've got what it takes. Can I count on everyone?"

She looked around the table and they all nodded their heads
enthusiastically.

"So Brooke – and Lee," she glanced down at him at the end of
the table, raising an eyebrow, "what line-up of guests have you got?"

"Okay," said Brooke, "I was speaking to Donna Doyle during
the week, her brother and ex. They are all set to come into the
studio for filming on Thursday."

"Good. If it's anything like the last time they were on, it will
make an excellent show," said Kim.

This line-up was giving Kim extra joy because Guy Burton had
objected to it. And what could Guy do to stop her in her tracks,
now that she knew his deepest darkest secret? The fact that he
allowed Jasmine to join the RTV workforce without so much as a
whimper showed the new-found power she had over him.

Kim's mobile started to ring. "I'll just take this, continue without
me," she said and went off into a corner of the room to answer it.

As Brooke continued discussing the future line-up, she was distracted by Kim's voice which was rising with temper as she spoke into her phone.

"I don't believe it!" shouted Kim, returning to the head of the table and slamming her mobile down.

"What's wrong?" asked Joshua, looking concerned.

"Your son! That's what's wrong!" snapped Kim.

Everyone else stared down at Lee who went bright red.

"That was HR. They said they have been inundated by complaints that your son got the job on the programme. The others who had applied for the job were particularly irate!"

"But how did that get out?" Joshua was even more concerned.

"Ahh – and here comes the science bit!" Kim spoke sarcastically. "Seemingly it was revealed on the 'We Hate Joshua Green' website!"

"For fuck's sake!" Joshua sighed loudly and rubbed his face in annoyance.

Brooke reached into her bag, took out her laptop and opened it up.

"This looks very bad for us," Kim said. "In these days of high unemployment, pulling strings to get your son a job in a public body, which RTV is – well, it's just bad public relations."

"And how did they find out about Lee getting the job?"

"Come on, Joshua, if somebody is going to the bother of having a website dedicated to hating you they are bound to find out information like this."

"But it must be somebody connected with RTV," Joshua pointed out.

"Hundreds of people work at RTV," said Kim. "And how many people do those hundreds know? Things get around quickly. As a friend of mine once said – it's a big city but a small town."

"Here it is!" Brooke had logged on to the website and started to read. "'Joshua Green's son has got the new job of researcher on his show. Congratulations to Lee, who beat off stiff competition from four hundred applicants. Yes – four hundred.

"'We wonder what special qualifications Lee has for the post. Well, he's sat his school finals. However, that was only a short while *ago and he hasn't received the results yet as they come out at the end of summer. Okay, so officially he hasn't even got the Leaving Cert yet. He must then have got amazing work experience in that case, working in television. He must be a real prodigy with an amazing track record. No, he has never worked in television before. In fact the kid has never worked before full stop. In that case he must have a great personality. All-singing, all-dancing, bursting with enthusiasm – so much so that RTV just had to have him. We're afraid that's not the case either. Not only does Lee not have an amazing personality, but he has no personality at all (like father, like son). So that leaves us with the only qualification Lee has – he's Joshua's son! Surely this would not have been the basis of him getting the job, would it?'"*

Lee got up and stormed out of the room, slamming the door after him.

"You should have stopped reading when it started getting personal about him," snapped Joshua.

"He's going to read it himself anyway," Brooke defended herself.

"Yes, but not in front of an audience," Joshua pointed out.

"Oh, who cares if his feelings are hurt?" interrupted Kim. "This looks terrible for us. What the bloody website is saying is true. And everyone is going to think you arranged it for him to get the job, Joshua."

"Great!" Joshua threw his hands into the air. "I didn't want him here and now I get accused of fixing it!"

"We are a public service, we can't be seen to pull strings like this," Kim said.

"Or like Jasmine getting a job as your PA," Brooke pointed out.

Kim glared at Brooke. "Thin ice, Brooke. You're sailing close to the wind and on very thin ice."

Brooke forced herself to be quiet and sat back as they all started to argue, and thought about the text from Guy.

25

Brooke had texted Guy back saying she was available to meet that evening and they decided on Canal Bank restaurant as a rendezvous.

As she made her way there she felt herself becoming quite nervous. She hadn't expected Guy to want to meet up again. She wasn't sure if she wanted to meet up with him either. He was way outside her comfort zone. He already knew too much about her. She didn't like how she owed him too much with her promotion already. And he was so probing, in a subtle way, and worse still she ended up telling him stuff she really didn't want to. He seemed to have a knack of getting her to open up.

She pushed the restaurant door open, looked around for him and saw he was seated down at the back. He smiled broadly at her as she approached the table and she managed to smile back as she sat down.

He started talking straight away about work. And as they ordered pâté for starters and lamb for main course, she felt herself being drawn into his conversation. He was being very open about new programmes he was commissioning and she was intrigued to hear about the direction he was planning on moving the station – so intrigued that they were halfway through their dinner before she realised they hadn't spoken about anything else. She stared at him as he described the production needs for a new series.

He suddenly stopped speaking and smiled at her. "What's wrong?" he asked.

"Sorry?" She shook her head out of the trance she was in.

"I'm sorry, I think I've lost you. I've been going on a bit, haven't I? I didn't mean to bore you."

"Oh no! You're not boring me in the least. I'm listening, honestly I am."

"Anyway, enough about me." He leaned forward and nodded. "How was your day?"

"Oh, more of the same. Same shit different day," she smiled.

"How is Lee working out?" he asked, as he continued to eat.

"Fine, he . . ." she trailed off as she remembered the pandemonium his appointment had caused that day, but decided not to say anything about it.

"I hear there was a bit of problem with HR. It somehow got out that Joshua's son got the job."

She looked at him guardedly and sat back. "I don't really want to tell tales out of work, Guy."

He sat back himself and put both hands into the air in a defensive fashion. "I'm not asking you to! In fact, I didn't think you knew anything about it. I thought it was me telling tales."

She relaxed and smiled. "Oh!"

"Yes, there's some website that attacks Joshua and they revealed that Joshua's son got the job and now everyone thinks the bloody thing was fixed."

"Yes?" said Brooke.

"I can see how it might be thought, can't you? I mean somebody with an MA in Communications was turned down in favour of Lee."

"Well, Joshua didn't fix it. He was furious when he found out."

"So I believe."

"He would have fixed it for Lee *not* to have got the job."

"And how did Joshua take it when he found out that he was been accused of nepotism?"

"He hit the roof of course. Started swearing."

"Understandable. What about Kim?"

141

"She was really angry. She was furious that Lee got the job in the first place so she went on the attack."

"What did Lee do?"

"He just stormed off."

"Trouble in paradise," he smiled at her as he finished his lamb, and listened to Brooke continuing to talk about the incident.

Guy drank his coffee as Brooke came back into the restaurant from a cigarette break and poured herself another glass of wine.

"I was surprised to hear from you again," she commented.

"Why? We work in the same place. You were bound to hear from me again."

"You know what I mean. That you would want to see me again – just the two of us."

"I enjoyed our time together. I thought it might be good to see each other again."

"But I'm seeing somebody else."

"Who happens to be married."

"Precisely. Why would you want to see somebody already involved in such a messy situation?"

"You're wasted on that messy situation," he said, leaning forward and stroking her hand.

She looked down at his hand. "I'm quite comfortable with that messy situation, bizarre as that may sound. I know where I am with it. I don't know where I'd be with someone like you."

"I'm quite straightforward really."

"I doubt that."

"Anyway," he sat back quickly and folded his arms, "aren't you jumping the gun a bit here? All I said was I enjoyed the last time we were together. I'm not suggesting you give up your messy situation, since you enjoy it so much."

She smirked at him. "So what are you suggesting – exactly?"

He began to stroke her hand again. "What's sauce for the goose is sauce for the gander. Joshua does what he pleases, so why shouldn't you?"

"Joshua?" asked Soraya, coming out into the hall as he arrived home.

"Is Lee here?"

"Yes, he came home in a terrible mood. He told me what happened and then went and shut himself into his room."

"You see, this is what I was frightened of. The whole day was disrupted. His appointment caused chaos and put everyone into a bad mood for the day."

He marched over to the stairs and shouted up, "Lee! Down here – now!"

He strode into the lounge and poured himself a strong drink.

"The whole afternoon wasted! As we all squabbled about what to do, and whose fault it was."

Lee came into the room, scowling.

"Really mature, Lee!" snapped Joshua. "Storming out of the meeting like that like a spoiled child! Oh, I forgot – you *are* a spoiled child."

"Well, I wasn't going to stick around listening to that shit from that fucking website."

"Why not? That's what grown-ups do. We put up with the shit and try and sort it out. You're in a workplace there, not here at home where you can just swan off when the going gets rough."

"And you loved it, didn't you? You loved what they were saying about me on that website."

"I didn't actually, for the record. Like everything else on that bloody website it pissed me off. But this is not all about you, Lee. Can't you see that you getting that job has left me wide open to attack, and caused me nothing but hassle, as I told you it would. You caused so much waste of time today as we tried to sort this out."

"Well, you don't have to worry any more. Because I'm not going back to your stupid job with your stupid show in your stupid station. I quit!" Lee turned and stormed out of the house.

"Lee!" Joshua shouted after him but he didn't respond. He threw back his drink and said, "Oh, well, that's that then, if he's not going back. We can start getting back to normal again."

"You don't have to look so pleased about it," warned Soraya.

The mobile phone ringing cut into the night's silence.

"Joshua, your phone is ringing. It's time to go home," mumbled Brooke as she turned over in the bed.

143

Guy turned on the light and sat up. "It's Guy here beside you, incidentally."

Brooke's eyes shot open and she cringed with embarrassment. "Sorry – I –"

He looked at her warily. "No need to explain."

She started cursing to herself as Guy jumped out of bed, got the mobile out of his blazer pocket and answered it. "Hello?"

Brooke looked at her watch and saw it was one in the morning.

Guy walked into the next room to continue his conversation on the phone. A couple of minutes later he came back in and started to get dressed.

"I'm afraid I have to go," he said.

"*What?*" Brooke was incredulous.

"That was a friend in need."

"Is a friend indeed! What do they want at this time of the night?"

"That's what I have to go and find out."

"For goodness' sake!"

"Sorry!" He bent over and kissed her forehead. "I'll let myself out."

He turned to walk out of the room.

"Oh, and Guy?"

"Yeah?"

"Apologies for the name mix-up." She looked suitably embarrassed.

"Easily done!" He smirked at her and left the apartment.

As she heard the door slam she called out loud, "Will I ever get anybody to stay the whole night with me!"

She then turned off the light and went back to sleep.

Guy drove slowly down O'Connell Street looking out for his caller. There weren't too many people around but the ones that were looked drunk or dodgy. He spotted Lee standing on the side of the road and pulled over. He reached over and opened the passenger door.

"Lee, get in!"

Lee sauntered over, got into the car and Guy drove off.

Guy immediately spotted that Lee was quite drunk and looked in a bad way.

"Sorry for ringing you at this time," slurred Lee. "It's just my wallet was stolen and I couldn't get through to my friends."

"That's all right. But you shouldn't be around there at this time of night, Lee, especially in the state you're in. How much have you had to drink?"

"Too much."

"That's obvious." As Guy glanced over at him he suspected he had taken something else as well.

"Pull over!" Lee suddenly shouted.

"What?"

"Just pull over!" Lee demanded.

Guy did as he was asked and Lee opened the door, stuck his head out and was sick.

"Okay, your father will kill you if you go home in that condition. Let's get you sobered up."

The Millennium Building was one of Dublin's few skyscrapers and Guy lived on one of the upper floors. It was a habit he had picked up in Manhattan. He liked living far above ground. Guy came out of the kitchen and placed another cup of coffee in front of Lee, who was managing to sober up.

"So what happened?" asked Guy, sitting down opposite him.

"I've quit the job," said Lee.

"But why? I thought you were getting on well there and enjoying it."

Lee shrugged.

"Lee, I know about the website and what it said about you."

"Well, then you know why I quit."

"Lee, whoever is writing that website doesn't know the facts. Your father didn't fix the job for you, and everyone at the station knows that because they know how pissed off Joshua is that you're working there. Correct?"

"Well, he hasn't hidden the fact he doesn't want me there, no," Lee nodded.

145

"So who that matters is going to believe that he fixed for you to get the job?"

"I didn't think of it that way . . . But Kim started kicking off saying it would cause trouble for everyone."

"Kim kicks off over everything. It's what she does. You haven't officially handed in your notice, have you?"

"No. But I stormed out and told Dad I wasn't going back."

"So you're playing right into your father's hands here, aren't you? He doesn't want you working there and now you're gone. You've made his day."

"He always gets what he wants anyway, so nothing new there."

"So let this time be different. Show him this time that you aren't going to let him get his way, by showing up tomorrow morning bright and early and eager to do your job."

"It would really piss him off," agreed Lee.

"I know what I'd do, if I was you. I wouldn't give in."

"Okay, you might be right," Lee said, nodding slowly.

"What does Soraya say about it all?" asked Guy.

"Soraya never really takes sides on anything."

"No?"

"She always plays Devil's Advocate. She tries to get my father to see my point of view and for me to see my father's."

"That's very – noble – of her."

"Yeah, I trust her. She's never let me down."

"And what about your mother? Your real mum?"

Lee looked up from his coffee, startled.

"She's not around," he said.

"Has she passed away?"

"No, she hasn't." Lee began to look very uncomfortable.

"But you don't see much of her?"

Lee's phone started to ring. "It's home," he said.

"You'd better answer it – they'll be wondering where you are. Best not say you're here either."

Lee answered the phone. "Yeah . . . I'm just over at Colin's . . . Nothing, we went out to a nightclub. I'll be back soon." He turned off his phone. "I'd better be going." He stood up and put on his jacket.

"I'll give you a lift home," said Guy, standing up.

"There's no need. I can get a taxi . . . if you could lend me some cash."

"It's no problem. It's not that far . . . As I was saying, best not say you were here tonight. I have to work with your dad and I'm good friends with him, so I don't want anything I say going back to him."

"I wouldn't dream of saying anything. You've been very good to me."

Guy nodded and smiled and headed towards the door.

26

Joshua drove into RTV's car park with "Lovely Day" blasting from the radio. It was going to be a lovely day, he thought. Lee had arrived in at all hours the night before, and hadn't even got up by the time he had left the house that morning. Obviously sleeping off his hangover. Lee's foray into the world of show business had obviously come to an end and things could now get back to normal. He might even go out with Brooke that night to celebrate. His mobile rang and seeing it was Soraya he answered it, putting it on loudspeaker.

"Hi, hon."

"Joshua, my mother was just on."

He raised his eyes to heaven. "Yes?"

"She was just checking numbers for the summer vacation."

Soraya's parents had a stunning villa in the South of France. Every summer Soraya and Joshua headed out there for a couple of weeks and usually invited some friends to join them.

"I imagine Kim and Tom will be coming again," said Joshua.

"And Jasmine?"

"Baby always comes too."

"Did you ask Tony and his wife?"

"They can't make it, I already checked with them. I was thinking of asking Fiona and Mike Fallon?"

"Oh, I don't know, Joshua. She can be over the top and intrusive. I found her a bit irritating at Guy Burton's party in The Shelbourne."

"Exactly, she can distract your parents," he pointed out. He felt he was always under a microscope when he was with Soraya's parents. They were pleasant enough to him, but they could never quite hide their disapproval of Soraya's choice of husband. "We could ask Helen along? She might be handy with Lee – he always behaves himself a little better when she's around."

"Much as I like her, I don't think so. It's awkward between her and my parents . . . Actually, what about Guy?"

"Guy. I don't know . . ."

"He's lovely company, and it might be nice to invite him along?"

"I don't know if it would be putting him in a compromising position with *The Tonight Show* coming up."

"Darling, you work in show business. Everyone in it gets into compromising positions all the time and thinks nothing of it."

"That's true. Well, I'll mention it to him then."

"Good. Daniel is calling for me, I'd better go."

"See you later, love."

Joshua was humming happily to himself as he came out of the lift and walked through the huge open-plan office. He stopped in his tracks when he saw Lee sitting at his desk, looking busy working.

"What are you doing here?" demanded Joshua.

"Last time I checked, I worked here," answered Lee.

"But I thought –"

"You thought wrong," answered Lee and he continued working.

Joshua stormed off to Kim's office, only to find Guy already there and the two engaged in a heated exchange.

Kim was talking nineteen to the dozen, her arms flailing as she spoke.

"I just think it looks very bad for the show employing Joshua's son and now it's got out –"

"This is all a storm in a teacup. Who cares if Joshua's son works for the station?"

"The four hundred people who applied for the job for a start!" snapped Kim.

"So what are you suggesting we do? Sack him? That wouldn't be fair, would it? I've checked with HR, and everything is bona fide, all employment procedures carried out by the book. We'll just release a quick statement to that effect and that's an end of the matter."

"But –"

"But nothing, Kim. I'd be far more worried if it got out that your daughter had suddenly got a job at the station when there wasn't one even advertised."

Kim stood up abruptly. "I'm going for a drink, I need one. Care to join me for a vodka, Guy?" She smirked at him knowingly.

"Thank you, but I'll pass." He looked at her coldly and she marched out.

He turned to Joshua. "She's making a mountain out of a molehill," he assured him. "Nothing irregular was done. In fact, it makes a good story. The PR department should get behind it and do a photo of the two of you together. The public will love it. How your son got a job on your show without you knowing. Turn it around to your advantage. And it will be a nice story with you going after *The Tonight Show*."

"I can't see Lee agreeing to that," said Joshua.

"Of course he will," Guy assured him.

"Eh – Guy – me and the family and a few friends are heading to the South of France to Soraya's parents' place for the summer break. We were just wondering if you wanted to come along too? Even if it's just for a long weekend."

"Oh!" Guy looked surprised.

"It's usually relaxed. We just hang out by the pool, play golf, nice restaurants at night. Ulrika comes as well, so the kids are well occupied. But – no pressure – if you've something on . . ."

"Thank you, I think I'd enjoy that very much."

27

Guy had tickets for the theatre and invited Brooke to go along. She was unable to concentrate on the play as she was preoccupied with the man who sat beside her. Guy was a polar opposite to Joshua. All Joshua really did was talk about himself, she had realised. Guy never seemed to talk about himself. He did talk about work and his plans for RTV but, apart from that, he was more interested in her and questioning her about everything. She wasn't used to this kind of attention and it unnerved her. And yet she loved it.

Afterwards they walked towards Grafton Street while she listened to him minutely dissect and analyse the characters in the play.

"Did you ever work as a reviewer?" she questioned.

"No – why?"

"I think you'd make a very good one. You really were paying attention to that play, weren't you?"

"It's what I do for a living – pay attention. I have to understand what people want, what makes them tick so I can give them the programmes they want to see. I have to analyse things to see if they'll work for an audience."

"Doesn't that stop you from enjoying a programme or play or a film for its own sake then? Can't you just switch off and watch something without all that analysis?"

"I enjoy it – in my own way." He smiled at her. "So what are you up to for the summer holidays?"

"Holidays! I haven't really even thought about that yet."

"Now who doesn't switch off and enjoy themselves?" he teased her.

"I find holidays a bit head-wrecking to be honest. All that packing, all that security at airports, and then when you get there it's too hot and you break out in hives and everyone complains or it rains and everyone keeps saying 'we were unlucky with the weather'."

He started laughing.

She laughed too, glad she had amused him. "And then everyone starts getting cantankerous after a couple of days. The fights start over which restaurant to go to, which beach to go to, whose turn it is to wash up. Nope! I think I'll stay at home with a good book."

"You can't do that. Everyone needs a break."

She wondered for a second if he was hinting that she should go away with him.

"Where are you going to go yourself?" she probed.

"Joshua and Soraya have asked me to join them at her parents' place in France."

She got such a surprise she nearly stopped walking, but forced herself to act normally. "Really? You're honoured. Those invitations are like gold dust. Everyone wants to get invited by them."

"Yes, Joshua said it's quite spectacular."

"Of course it is! Would you expect anything less? Of course, the squawking sprogs will be there. I can't imagine anything worse."

"Actually Ulrika, their au pair, is going, so she takes care of them apparently."

"Whatever you do, be careful with the food. Joshua got terrible food poisoning there last summer."

Guy looked at her sceptically.

"Soraya's parents are supposed to be terrible snobs," she went on. "They make a lot of people feel uncomfortable. Joshua told me that himself."

Guy stopped abruptly and looked at her. "Why are you doing this?"

"Doing what?"

"Trying to put me off going."

"I'm not! I'm just trying to prepare you for the worst."

"You're jealous."

"I am not."

"You are."

"Of what?"

"Of everything. Of Soraya and Joshua, and their life. And the holiday. And how you're not invited by them."

"How would I be invited? They only invite the top brass."

"Well, jealous that you're not the top brass then, and you think you never will be."

"I think I'll go home."

She started to walk off quickly, but he followed her.

"And most of all you're jealous because everyone else is doing something for the summer except you!" he went on. "Everyone else has plans, but you are so afraid to live a fulfilling life that you'd prefer to bury yourself in work and arrange your life around a man who will always put you in second place. He goes off with his wife, and his children and his friends and has a great time, and you wait patiently at home, hoping that he might remember to text you while he's away. But he won't even be bothered to do that!"

She stopped, turned around and slapped him across the face.

He looked at her, stunned, and rubbed his cheek.

"I'm sorry!" She covered her mouth with her hand. "I didn't mean that!"

"It felt like you did."

"Well, I did then! You shouldn't have provoked me."

"Since when was telling the truth a provocation?"

"I hate any kind of violence," she said, removing his hand from his cheek and inspecting her handprint emblazoned across it. She leaned forward and kissed the offended cheek.

"Kissing it better?" he asked with a smirk.

She sighed and smiled back.

"Come on," he said.

He put his arm around her and they walked slowly off.

28

Joshua's show was due to start recording in an hour. Brooke and Lee made their way to meet the guests who were due to appear that day.

"This is Donna Doyle?" checked Lee. "The girl stalker?"

"Don't call her that," urged Brooke.

She glanced at Lee, who seemed a bit pale that day. She, like everyone else, had assumed he wouldn't show up again after storming out. But he had and kept his head down and got on with his work. She had expected the worst from Lee when he'd arrived at RTV. She'd expected him to be a right royal pain in the ass, petulant, spoiled and unreliable. In short everything Joshua had told her about him. But although he was never going to win Personality of the Year, he certainly tried to do his best, and was extremely annoyed with himself when he didn't get things right.

"We separate the guests prior to the show and put them in different rooms," explained Brooke to Lee. "We give them a pep talk and try and make them feel comfortable. Most of them are nervous at appearing on television."

Lee nodded.

"Kim usually comes in as well for a talk with them before we start filming." Brooke thought that Kim's version of a pep talk was designed to inflame the guests' anger in order to make better television but she couldn't say that to Lee.

She opened the door to one of the hospitality rooms and they walked in.

Donna Doyle was there, sitting beside her brother Aidan. Brooke thought Donna had lost weight since she'd last seen her and she looked very pale. Aidan looked extremely unhappy.

"Hello again, Donna," said Brooke, smiling, and she kissed her cheek before turning and smiling at Aidan. "This is Lee who is a new researcher on the show."

Lee managed to smile at them.

"How are you feeling today?" asked Brooke as she sat down on the couch opposite them.

"I'm okay, Brooke," said Donna. "I just want to get this sorted out with Glen. He still refuses to talk to me –"

"And you refuse to let go!" snapped Aidan.

"I just want a chance to sit down with him and discuss where things went wrong between us," said Donna.

Aidan shook his head in disbelief. "That's the problem, Donna. There *is* no you and him! There never was!"

"And that's what *we're* here for, to act as go-between," said Brooke. "Look, everyone wants closure on this. So this gives you your opportunity to say what you want to Glen, and for him to say back what he wants to say to you. Feel relaxed and confident and don't be distracted by the cameras or the audience. The most important thing is that you realise where you stand with Glen and accept it, and he in turn understands what you've been going through."

The door suddenly swung open and in walked a beaming Kim.

"Donna!" declared Kim, her arms outstretched. "Good to see you!" She bent and hugged Donna. "I'm so glad you've decided to come back on the show to discuss your relationship with . . ." Kim glanced down at the notes, "Glen. Now I just wanted to have a word with you before we go on air. Joshua can be a complete bastard, as you know. So don't let him bully you! If he shouts at you, then you shout back! Between ourselves, I think he's a misogynist and he'll try and portray you as a bunny-boiler or something. So you need to fight dirty here, Donna."

Lee looked on, shocked at what Kim was saying.

"And as for this Glen, don't let him get away with anything, darling. You might think you're in love with him, but he's going to try and portray you as a stalker again, so you need to let him know that he gave you mixed messages. Anything you can think of. Think hard, Donna. He's used you and now he wants to throw you away like an empty Coke can. You need to show him for what he is and this is your chance to put the record straight."

Aidan buried his head in his hands. "Donna, let's get the fuck out of here. It's not too late. Let's go home and forget about all this."

Kim was alarmed. "Of course it's too late! Everything is arranged, the audience are arriving now. You aren't going anywhere, I'm afraid."

"I don't want to go anywhere," said Donna. "I want to sort this out. This is the only place that he'll talk to me."

Aidan shook his head in despair.

Lee and Brooke walked down the corridor after Kim.

"Does Dad know what she says about him?" Lee whispered to Brooke.

"She does it to get them prepared so they get worked up and are in fighting form."

"But do you agree with that?"

"It's show business, Lee. You might as well get used to it."

Kim reached the door of the other guest room where Glen was and turned around and looked at Lee.

"Are you still here?" she asked.

"Yeah," he nodded. "Where else would I be?"

"Well, there's no need for three of us going in here. You toddle on back to Donna and Aidan and keep them company until the show starts."

He nodded and left. Kim raised her eyes heavenward, opened the door and walked into the room.

Glen was on the sofa. He really was a cool-looking guy. Brooke imagined he would be the big catch in his area. She imagined how a girl like Donna would fall for somebody like him, and not have the experience to realise she would mean nothing to him.

"Glen, thanks for coming in today," said Kim, smiling sympathetically and sitting down beside him.

Brooke sat opposite him.

"I just want this nightmare over!" he said. "It was either come in here today or go to the police. And I couldn't do that, not with her brother being my best mate."

"You know the old saying – a woman scorned!" said Kim. "I can see you've had a tough time with her since you were last on our show."

"I'm at my wit's end. She's a psycho!"

"Well, Glen, today is your opportunity to get closure on this once and for all. You need to tell her straight so she never bothers you again. Don't hold back – you've probably just been too nice too her. The days of letting her down gently are over."

"Yes!"

"And Glen, take none of Joshua's bullshit! He always seems to take the woman's side in these situations. Maybe he feels sorry for them or something. But stand up to him, don't let him portray you as having done anything wrong."

Brooke sighed quietly at the way Kim wore different hats for different audiences. She would say anything to whip up the guests for dramatic effect.

At that moment the door opened and a beautiful girl with big hair and lots of make-up walked in. She was carrying two cups of coffee. She handed one to Glen and sat down next to him.

"And who might you be?" asked Kim.

"This is my girlfriend, Rain."

"Rain?"

"Yes," said the girl.

"Rain? As in – pissing down?" said Kim, getting all excited. "Why weren't we informed about you before?"

"I didn't want to get her involved," said Glen.

"Why not? She *is* involved! I take it Donna knows nothing of Rain?"

"We didn't want to provoke her further," said Rain.

"Honey, the girl is in treatment, you couldn't provoke her any more if you tried. I think it's vital that we put you on the show today as well, Rain."

"I don't know about that –" began Glen.

"This could be the answer! If you really want to show Donna that there's no future between you, then show her you have somebody important in your life – Rain!" Kim took out her pen, grabbed a notebook and started to write furiously. "What's your surname, Rain?"

"Lamb."

"As in – Mary had a little . . . ?" Kim smiled broadly at her.

"Eh, Kim, may I speak to you for a minute?" asked Brooke, concerned. She got up and walked out to the corridor.

Kim looked irritably after her before getting up and following her.

"What is it?" asked Kim impatiently.

"Kim – you can't put that girl Rain on the show."

"And why not?"

"Because it will destroy Donna!"

"You're being ridiculous, Brooke. Rain's appearance will rescue this from being a run-of-the-mill puppy-love story and make it interesting. Another woman involved claiming her man! Brilliant!"

"I strongly advise against this, Kim. Donna is too fragile to learn on a television show that the love of her life is with somebody else."

"Fragile my ass! Have you read your own notes about Donna? She parks outside his house all night long. Rings his work incessantly. Now we're putting Rain on, and that's an end of it."

"In that case, I'm going to warn Donna about Rain, and tell her she's coming on the show."

Kim became very agitated and angry and leaned towards Brooke. "You'll do no such thing, Brooke. I do not want Donna prepared for this. I want a close-up on her reaction when Rain comes on stage and it is revealed Glen is seeing her. I want that reaction to be natural and unrehearsed. You are *not* going to ruin that moment for our viewers. Don't you understand what makes good television at all?"

"You're setting Donna up for public humiliation, and I don't think she can handle it."

"Can I remind you, it is *she* who wants this. You are not a social worker, Brooke, and if you can't handle what is expected of you, then you should get the fuck out of the industry! And if you disobey me, I'll make sure you get kicked out of it anyway, golden contract or not! Do I make myself clear?"

"Crystal!" Brooke glared at her.

"Now you run along and join Boy Wonder back with Donna, and I'll continue with Glen and Rain." Kim went back into the room and slammed the door.

Brooke went marching up to Guy's office.

"Is Guy free?" she asked Guy's PA, her face flustered.

"Have you an appointment?" asked the PA haughtily.

"Just tell him Brooke is here and it's urgent."

The PA lifted the phone and delivered the message. She then hung up the phone, looking surprised. "You can go in."

Brooke gave her a triumphant look and strode into Guy's office.

"Hello! This is a surprise," said Guy, leaning back and putting his hands behind his head.

"Guy – it's Kim! You have to stop today's show! That girl Donna Doyle, the one released from the clinic, she's on today and Kim is planning on revealing that Glen, the man she's obsessed with, has a girlfriend. Actually bringing the girlfriend on! She won't be able to take it, Guy. You have to stop the show."

Guy stared at her for a while.

"Don't you understand me? Kim is playing games with a fragile mind and it's not right. You asked me before did I think this girl should be allowed on the show. And I'm now saying loud and clear that she shouldn't, Guy."

Guy sat forward and said briskly. "I'm afraid there is nothing I can do, Brooke."

"What?" She looked at him in surprise.

"It's Kim's show, and she has the power over what does and does not go on."

"But I thought you were standing up to her. I thought you were the only one who could stand up to her."

"My hands are tied," he said and folded his arms.

"I see." She stood up straight. "I obviously have been getting a few things wrong then, in that case." She turned and walked out.

Joshua looked directly at the camera as he spoke from the stage.

"Our next guests are returning to our show from a previous appearance. You might remember Glen briefly dated his best friend's sister, Donna. He subsequently tried to break up with her but she refused to let go. Since that last appearance Donna has been seeking professional help. In fact she has spent some time in a clinic. She has been receiving help from psychiatrists. She's back living at home, but Glen claims that she has been stalking him again. Ladies and gentlemen, please give a warm welcome to Glen!"

The audience began to clap and cheer enthusiastically as Glen walked onto the stage and sat on one of the four chairs positioned there.

Joshua walked to the side of the stage and sat down on it, looking up at Glen.

"Glen, things haven't improved with Donna since you last appeared on the show?"

"That was only the beginning, Josh. It's become a complete nightmare. Since then she's been ringing me up all the time. Sometimes from her own phone, other times from private numbers, saying nothing. If I go out, she's following me in her car. If I go out to a pub or restaurant, I look around and see her sitting there nearby looking over. She sits opposite my house at night in her car. She's driven herself to a breakdown, and she's driven me close to one too. She's a psychopath, and a sociopath."

"That's a lot of paths for one person," said Joshua, standing up quickly. "Okay, let's bring on Donna and her brother Aidan, who is Glen's best friend."

Donna and Aidan walked onto the stage. Donna looked distressed and Aidan reluctant as they sat down.

"You're only telling one side of the story, Glen," Donna accused loudly.

"Donna, you haven't been that well since you were last on the show?" asked Joshua.

"It's been all Glen's fault," said Donna. "Making promises to me and then treating me so bad."

"Glen claims you sit across from his house at night in a car, Donna. And that you follow him when he's out. Is that true?"

"I've approached him a few times to try and talk to him. To try and sort all this out. But he's exaggerating. He's got such a big head he wants everyone to think that women chase him all the time."

"Well, let's see if we can bring on somebody to verify Glen's sequence of events. Ladies and gentlemen, please give a warm welcome to Rain, Glen's new girlfriend!"

Kim was standing beside the cameraman. "*Now*! Give me a close-up on Donna's face. As close up as you can get!"

As Donna's face showed her shock, devastation and bewilderment, Rain walked on to the stage and kissed Glen. She sat down beside him and they held hands.

"Rain, how long have you being going out with Glen?" asked Joshua.

"Two months."

"I can see from Donna and Aidan's reaction that this is the first time they've heard about you," said Joshua.

"I work with Glen, that's how we met. He told me from the beginning he was having trouble with an ex who kept threatening suicide and following him. So we agreed to keep our relationship very quiet. It was daft, but I would enter his house through the back, things like that, so I wouldn't be spotted."

"And have you witnessed Donna's behaviour?"

"Oh yes. I've seen her sitting across from the house all night in her car. I've been there for the phone calls. I've seen the emails. I got frightened for him and urged him to go to the police. He wouldn't because of Aidan. But I've been frightened by the whole situation."

"Well – you shouldn't go stealing other women's men then, should you?" shouted Donna.

"I am not your man!" Glen shouted back. "I am not your boyfriend! We dated briefly. Whatever we had was not important to me. I don't love you, I never have. I don't even like you any more. Now leave me alone!"

Rain was suddenly shouting. "He's the first man that ever gave you a bit of attention and you couldn't let go and you thought you wouldn't meet anybody else! And you won't now everyone has seen what a nut you are!"

Donna put her face in her hands as she began to shudder and sob.

Brooke was waiting offstage for the guests as Kim came over to her smiling.

"Excellent show! See how a little creativity can turn a mediocre story into riveting television? Rain's appearance was as refreshing as a downpour on a desert, if you'll pardon the pun."

Aidan led a fragile-looking Donna over to them. "Donna really needs to talk to somebody professional."

Kim looked at Brooke and said, "That's your department."

Brooke rolled her eyes as Kim walked off.

As the audience began to depart, Guy, who had watched the show from the back row, headed back to his office.

29

Joshua was at Brooke's apartment and was stretched out on the sofa, talking away. Brooke sat on the couch across from him smoking a cigarette as she drank her wine. She was thinking about the show that day. Donna had been in a terrible state after the show and she had tried to comfort her. She had been so worried about her that she had rung her that evening and spent another hour on the phone counselling her as best she could. Her brother Aidan was furious about the whole thing, but particularly that they hadn't been told Rain was going to appear on the show. And she had been left to deal with it all as Kim waltzed off, no doubt to a late and extended lunch with Jasmine. She was angry about the whole situation. Angry at always being left to clear up the mess. Angry that Kim and Joshua got all the credit and the perks and she got all the abuse from the jerks.

"Brooke?" Joshua suddenly snapped, jolting her out of her thoughts. "Are you even listening to me?" he demanded.

"Of course I am."

"What was I talking about then?" he checked.

She stared at him blankly.

"I knew you weren't listening!" he accused.

"Oh Joshua!" she said, feeling annoyed. "You're not a teacher in school checking if a pupil is paying attention!"

"Well, just as well, because you'd just have failed your test! I was talking about the summer holiday – that we're all going to Soraya's family villa in France."

"Right."

"I'm really looking forward to it. Can't wait to just chill out and relax."

"Sounds divine." Her voice was heavy with sarcasm, but he didn't notice.

He got up and headed out to the hall and into the bathroom.

Her phone started to ring and she picked it up. She saw it was Guy.

She paused for a second before answering it. "Hi, Guy."

"Hi there. Just checking if you had calmed down any since you stormed out of my office?"

"I'm sorry. I just thought you gave a shit about the quality of television we were making when you asked me before did I think it right to put somebody with a psychiatric problem on air."

"I do care."

"Well, why didn't you stop it then?"

"That's not my job. It's your job."

"*My* job?"

"Yes, I appointed you assistant producer so that you could provide a moral compass for the show."

"I try to, but have you ever tried to go against Kim?"

Guy remained silent.

"She threatened to fire me if I interfered in today's show," Brooke went on indignantly.

"So what use are you as an assistant producer if you just get railroaded all the time?"

"I don't get railroaded –"

"Well, that's what it sounds like, which means I made a mistake appointing you."

Brooke was taken aback. She heard Joshua come out of the bathroom.

"Look, I can't talk right now," she said, lowering her voice.

"Sorry, I didn't realise you were in company. Where are you?"

"At home."

"Oh – I see!" said Guy knowingly. "Night in with Joshua?"

"Well, yes – if you must know."

"I was ringing you because I left my cufflinks in the bathroom on the sink last night. I hope Joshua doesn't find them," said Guy.

"*What?*"

Guy started laughing and said, "Only joking!" before hanging up.

Brooke looked in irritation at the phone and lit up a cigarette, taking a deep drag.

Joshua walked in and made a face. "Do you ever not have a cigarette in your hand?"

He went over and opened the window.

"Sorry for smoking in my own home, I'm sure!" she snapped.

"What's wrong with you tonight?" asked Joshua.

"Nothing."

"There is. You've been not yourself for a while."

"I'm fine, I said," she said irritably.

He came and sat down and they didn't speak for a while.

"It looks like Lee isn't going anywhere," he said at last.

"He seems to be settling in," she answered, hoping she wouldn't have to listen to an hour of Joshua giving out about his son again.

"We're probably going to have to be a bit more careful from now on in that case," Joshua said.

"Careful?"

"Me and you . . . With Lee around all the time, we should be extra careful."

"And how do you propose we do that?"

"Well, things like going away for weekends are out for a while. I can't explain a weekend away as a business trip at home when Lee will be aware there is no business trip."

"What else?"

"We probably shouldn't leave work together any more for an evening out. He might get suspicious."

"Anything else?"

"Perhaps we shouldn't be seen out having dinner alone. Word might get back to Lee."

"So what then *do* you suggest we do?"

"I guess I can come around here and we can spend time together."

"*Here!*"

"Yes."

"Joshua, I don't need company to stay in my own home. I've got a television to stop me feeling lonely."

"But what can we do? I have to protect my family."

"And what about me? I want a life, Joshua. I want to go out to restaurants and bars occasionally and enjoy myself."

"But you have friends for that."

"Joshua . . . what am I actually going to be getting out of this relationship?"

"What you always have, the time we spend together."

"And what do you get out of this relationship?"

"Same answer – the time we spend together."

"Do you love me?" she asked.

He started laughing, embarrassed. "Brooke! What kind of a question is that?"

"A fairly straightforward one, I'd have thought."

"Brooke – what is going on?"

"Don't worry, Josh, I know you don't love me. I know you've never loved me and I know there isn't a chance you ever would. I know what this affair has been about – just a bit of fun – for both of us. We get on, we love our work, and this sexual relationship is just an extension of that. Nobody gets hurt as long as nobody finds out. But I want more."

"From me?" He looked alarmed.

"No, not from you. You're not capable of giving any more. You can go home to your perfect family and have me as a bit of fun. But I don't have anything else in my personal life but this. And this affair is stopping me from getting something for myself."

"You don't want something for yourself. You're a career girl, married to your job and happy to be fucking the boss."

"Is that a fact?" She blew a cloud of smoke into his face to his irritation. "And how do you know that?"

"Because I know you." He started laughing "Come on, Brooke, take a look inside your fridge. I bet there's four bottles of chardonnay, two ready-made meals and precious little else." He went into the kitchen and opened the fridge and laughed loudly. "Nearly right! There's only three bottle of chardonnay. You must have had a heavy night last night!"

"And since when did the contents of a fridge indicate what a person was like?"

"I'm just saying that this is you. You like quick, you like non-commitment. You live life on the go. And our relationship fits into that. Our relationship is like one of those ready-made meals. Doesn't take long to warm up, not too time-consuming, and fills the gap."

"You say the most romantic things!" She glared at him.

He pointed to the opened bottle of wine. "You've even started getting screw-cap wine bottles because it's less hassle than a corkscrew. Even a corkscrew is too much commitment for you! I know you, Brooke!"

"Actually – no, you don't. And do you know why you don't? Because we never talk about me, we only talk about you! You never ask me how I feel or what I think or anything about me. I can tell you what you had for breakfast this morning. In fact, I could probably tell you what sainted Soraya had for breakfast while I was at it."

"There's no need to speak ill of Soraya. She thinks very highly of you."

"Well, she wouldn't if she knew I was fucking her husband. The fact is, Joshua, I'm sick of being an extra in somebody else's life. I want to be the star of my own show."

He looked at her condescendingly. "Darling, you ain't ever going to be a star of anything."

"That's because you haven't left any room in my life for me to be."

"So I guess this is it, then?" he asked. "We're through?"

"I think we're better off calling it a day."

"And what will you do then, Brooke? Stay in on your own

preparing work for the next day, with one eye on the soaps while knocking back your screw-cap wine? Heading out with your mates at the weekend trying to pull?"

She looked at his sneering face and blurted out, "I've already met somebody actually."

He laughed. "Who? A mechanic you picked up in a club in Temple Bar at the weekend? Good luck with that one!"

She so wanted to tell him about Guy, but he had sworn her to secrecy. "No, actually. He works in our business. He's handsome, successful, charming and intelligent."

"He sounds wonderful, Brooke! In fact, he sounds so wonderful that if he didn't exist you'd have to make him up!" Joshua winked at her knowingly and stood up. "Anyway, I'm going to go back to my lovely wife, home and family. And I'll leave you with your microwave meal, screw-cap bottle of wine, and fantasy boyfriend."

He turned and walked out of the apartment.

She stared at the door as he closed it behind him. Then she took up her glass of wine and hurled it at the door, smashing it into smithereens.

30

Brooke was hardly able to sleep that night. So many emotions were going through her head from anger, to sadness, to being happy it was all over with Joshua. She headed into work very early and found herself in the RTV canteen at seven thirty with just a few of the night workers finishing their shift and having breakfast there. She sat down and had a coffee. She was surprised to see Guy walk in and get some toast, scrambled eggs and tea. She thought about creeping out but realised he would spot her so she sat still.

He took his tray and turned and saw her. He walked over to her.

"You're in early," he commented, sitting down.

"So are you."

"I'm in early most mornings."

"It's tough at the top."

He poured his tea and took a mouthful and started eating his breakfast.

"So – how was last night?" he asked.

"Huh?"

"Your romantic night in with Joshua?" He looked at her mockingly.

"Oh, don't start, Guy. I'm not in the mood this morning." She shot him a warning look.

"What's wrong?" He pushed his tray aside and reached out to her hand, concerned.

"And don't be nice to me! That's even worse!" she snapped.

"What happened?" he sighed.

"I finished with Joshua."

"Oh!" He looked very taken aback. "How did he take it?"

"He got very bitchy actually."

"A blow to his ego, I'd say. How do you feel?"

"Confused and upset. But I'm glad I did it."

"What made you?"

She looked at him, perplexed. "The words were coming out of my mouth, but it was like you were putting them there for me."

Joshua drove to work, thinking about his confrontation with Brooke the previous night. He wished he hadn't been so cutting. That wasn't fair and she didn't deserve it. He couldn't help himself. All those years doing his show meant he had to be always on the offensive, always have a clever remark, always put somebody down when they put it up to him. He was in character and his whole being, his livelihood, his life depended on being that person. But he'd gone over the top with Brooke. She was a good kid. She had been loyal and supportive of him. She'd been the only person he'd been unfaithful with since being with Soraya. Although there had been plenty of women before Soraya, he hadn't looked at anyone since. Himself and Brooke had hit it off instantly and their affair seemed to just naturally progress. It was difficult for him. He was under tremendous pressure with the show, having to perform all the time. And then there was all the trouble with Lee. And Kim saying Number 5 in the national ratings wasn't good enough and they needed to get to Number 1. And then there was the aiming to take over *The Tonight Show*. And then that fucking idiot on the internet writing all sorts about him. And then being famous brought its own pressures. People always expected you to be a certain way. People always thought they knew you even if they'd never met you before. And you were always trying not to disappoint them, trying to live up to their expectations. And with home being so busy with the au pair, and the toddlers, and Lee, and her parents and the comings and goings – well, Brooke was just a lovely oasis of calm where he could just get everything off his chest. It was like therapy. He pulled his car into his parking space in the RTV car park. He reached over to the glove compartment and took out a bottle of pills. He checked the label. His doctor had prescribed them for the anxiety attacks he'd been having. He always checked the label so as not to mix them up with the other pills he had for migraine. He grabbed a couple and swallowed them down.

Brooke had decided to avoid Joshua for the day, and she cringed as she saw him come walking straight at her in the studio.

"Hi there," he said and smiled warmly at her.

"Hello, Joshua," she said, looking coolly at him.

He glanced around to make sure nobody was in earshot.

"Listen – about last night. I'm sorry."

"About which part exactly?"

"I didn't mean to say those things. I think you're a great girl!"

"Don't patronise me, Joshua."

"I'm not! I've really enjoyed our time together, and I suppose all things must come to an end. So . . ." he held his hand out to her, "no hard feelings?"

She viewed his hand coolly before saying, "Piss off – and you can get your own McDonald's in future. Asshole!" She turned her back on him and walked away.

Joshua stormed into his dressing room and slammed the door behind him. He opened a drawer with a key and took out a bottle, unscrewed the lid and shook out a couple of his anxiety pills. He knocked them back before locking the jar away again. He sat down and looked in the mirror. He looked like shit, he thought. His sleeping patterns were getting worse. He needed this forthcoming holiday, he couldn't wait to get away.

He needed to get away from this situation that had developed with Brooke. Her challenging him, attacking him. He didn't want to be her enemy. In spite of himself, he opened up the laptop and went on to the website dedicated to hating him.

It was like a strange obsession he couldn't stop. It irked, him, annoyed him and upset him. And yet he needed to know what the person was thinking about him and writing about him every day. See if they had discovered anything new about him.

He started to read: *"The Joshua Green Show has sunk to an even lower low. All those promises made to guests on the show that they will be seen by trained counsellors are false. There are no counsellors working on that show. Usually the guests are shoved out the door as soon as the show is over with no further offers of help. All Joshua's promises that his team will keep in touch with their guests and help them work out their problems are false. They never make contact with guests again, unless they think they can make a follow-up programme and abuse them further. If guests insist on seeing a counsellor after the show, they are fobbed off with a researcher who has no training in this field and probably does more damage than good. The show and RTV won't pay for a counsellor. The guests are thrown out with the rubbish regardless of how damaged they have been by being exposed on national television.'*

Joshua stared at the screen in shock.

An emergency meeting was called in the boardroom and attended by Kim, Guy, Joshua and Brooke.

Joshua was pacing up and down frantically.

"What the fuck are we going to do?" he asked.

"It's very damaging for this to get out," said Guy. "It displays the show in the worst possible light. We should have trained counsellors dealing with people who have such emotional problems."

"Alright!" snapped Kim. "Coulda shoulda woulda! But we didn't so what do we do now?"

"Maybe it will be contained on the website and won't get any further," suggested Brooke.

"No, it's already been picked up by other websites according to PR. And they have already been asked by a newspaper to comment on whether it's true."

Kim stood up. "Okay, let's try and put a lid on this. We used to have a trained counsellor on the show, but he left abruptly and we didn't have time to find somebody suitable."

"Oh Kim, counsellors are two a penny," said Brooke.

"Whose side are you on?" snapped Kim.

"I'm just trying to cover every angle."

"Well, don't! Let's just find a solution. And Joshua – will you stop pacing! You're making me dizzy!"

Joshua returned to the table. "But who wrote this? This narrows the net. This is somebody within RTV."

"Not necessarily," said Brooke. "Look at the amount of people who work here, and how many people they know, and who they talk to. To say nothing of the guests themselves! These kinds of things can spread."

"Brooke is right," said Guy. "It was probably an open fact there was no counsellor on the show. But now it's reached a whole new level of communication and will rapidly become common knowledge. I think it will very much damage the show. I don't think Henry King or the directors will be too impressed."

"They don't have to be told, do they?" asked Joshua.

"I'm afraid they do," said Guy.

As Guy left Brooke caught up with him.

"I was just wondering if you were up to anything tonight? And if you wanted to come over to mine for dinner?"

He smiled at her. "I'd be delighted to."

31

Brooke came into her apartment, laden down with shopping bags, and went into the kitchen, putting all the bags down on the kitchen top. She then opened up her fridge freezer and took out any ready-made meals there and threw them in the bin. She took out the screw-top wine bottles and stashed them under the sink, before replacing them with fine French wines which had corks.

She then took out all the fresh food from the bags and unwrapped the cookery book she had bought.

As she began to chop the vegetables, she poured herself a glass of wine.

Two hours later a beautiful lamb dish was bubbling away in the oven, and she had changed into an elegant dress. The intercom rang and she answered it.

"Guy?"

"Yeah!"

She pressed the buzzer, unlatched the door and waited for him. He walked in and got a start when he saw her.

"You look very – groomed," he said.

"Thanks." She leaned forward and kissed him, then led him into the sitting room. She uncorked a bottle of wine and poured him a glass, saying, "Make yourself comfortable. I must check something in the oven."

"Don't fuss," he said and followed her into the kitchen. "Something smells good. I never had you down as a domestic goddess." He looked through the oven window.

"There's a lot of things about me you don't know."

"Really?" He nodded, amused. "Eh, can I have a Coke or something for now? I'm a bit thirsty."

"Sure, help yourself."

He reached into the fridge and took a can, before following her back into the main room.

The door to the balcony was open.

"I thought we could eat outside – it's such a beautiful evening," she suggested and he followed her out.

She had the small table out there elegantly laid. They sat down.

"Well, I'm guessing you're in a much better mood than you were this morning. You're obviously not taking the end of your relationship with Joshua too hard?"

She smiled falsely. "Joshua who?"

An hour later, Brooke was engrossed in a story Guy was telling her about the last television station he worked for.

She took a long drink as he finished his tale and asked, "And did she ever work in television again?"

"No – that was the last that was seen of her."

"Shocking!"

Guy suddenly looked around and started smelling the air. "What's that burning smell?"

A look of alarm spread across Brooke's face and she jumped up and ran inside. The apartment was smoky and when she opened the oven a cloud of smoke engulfed her and set off the smoke alarm.

Guy came in behind her, coughing.

"I can't believe it!" she gasped as she managed to get a glimpse of the cremated dinner through the smoke.

Guy turned off the oven and disconnected the alarm. Then he threw open the windows and started to wave the smoke around to disperse it.

Brooke turned around, stressed, leaving the oven open.

"A simple fucking dinner! And it's destroyed! I followed the blasted cookery book to the detail."

"You forgot to put on the timer," said Guy, coughing again.

Brooke's eyes suddenly welled up. Seeing she was upset, he came over and held her.

"It's no big deal!" He was laughing.

"It is! I wanted to cook a wonderful meal!"

"Look, I never had you down as Martha Stewart, so there's no need to pretend you are. We can just send out for fast food."

"Fast food!" She thumped his shoulder in horror. "I didn't want fast food! I wanted slow, laboriously cooked food that took hours to prepare but would be appreciated, respected and loved!"

"I don't know what you're talking about!" he said, as he continued laughing.

"Stop laughing!" she warned.

"Come on!" He took her hand and led her out on to the balcony. "At least we can breathe out here."

He lifted her glass of wine and handed it to her.

"Sorry!" she said. "It's just been a bit stressful lately."

"There is no need to apologise. You haven't done anything to apologise for." He took out his mobile. "What do you want – Chinese, Indian, pizza?"

"Pizza," she said, annoyed with the whole metaphor Joshua had created about how she ate reflecting how she lived.

Guy phoned a pizzeria and gave an order.

"Now – sorted! So relax!" he said. "You know what you need – a holiday."

"Probably."

"Why don't you come with me?"

She looked at him, perplexed. "But you're going off to Soraya's palace by the sea."

"I know – come with me."

She looked at him in horror. "Are you for real?"

"We'll have a great time."

"I can't even believe you're suggesting that."

"Why not? I'm just bringing my new girlfriend along."

She was thrown and flattered by his description of her, but not enough to overlook the insanity of what he was suggesting.

"It's out of the question, Guy. I'm not going on holiday to a man

I've been having an affair with and his wife and children. It would be – immoral!"

"It was never moral in the first place, so no point in trying to get sanctimonious now. What's the big deal? It would show Joshua that you've moved on."

"How exactly? By showing up on his holiday with him? Uninvited! You've a funny sense of what moving on entails. I have some pride, you know . . . And what about you? You insisted Joshua shouldn't know that we were seeing each other."

"That was when you were seeing him as well! It doesn't matter now you're finished with him. As long as he doesn't ever find out I knew about you and him. That could make things awkward for our professional relationship."

"You're all heart! The answer is no, Guy. Thanks for the offer – but no!"

"But –"

"It's not going to happen. I'm going to change my clothes. This dress reeks of smoke." She walked into the apartment.

Soraya was brushing her hair at her dressing table while Joshua lay out on the bed staring at the ceiling.

"The others reckon it was an open secret that there was no counsellor and anyone could have heard it and wrote it on the internet."

"That's very plausible," agreed Soraya.

"But I don't buy it. I think it's somebody who works in RTV or somebody who has been on the show."

"One of the guests?"

"Yes, or their family. It makes sense to me. The website is too full of personal attacks – and now for them to know this about my show! I think it's some kind of insider, or connected to an insider."

Soraya put the brush down and came and sat down by him.

"Joshua. You don't know that. I think you're being a bit paranoid."

He sat up. "Really? Are you sure?"

"I'm not sure about anything with this website but I think you should try and relax and just forget about it. Worrying yourself to death won't help. Alright?"

32

Trying to avoid Joshua was trickier than Brooke had hoped. Unfortunately they were consistently forced to be together. Gone was the easy and relaxed relationship they used to have, and it was replaced by a cool and distant one.

It was the day before the last programme before the summer break and there was a production meeting in the boardroom. Brooke sat down near Kim, who as ever sat at the top of the table. Brooke remembered how she would go out of her way to avoid sitting near Kim at these meetings. But now she went out of her way to get the seat next to her. Guy had suggested it, and said the seating around the table was important and she needed to sit beside Kim to demonstrate to everybody that she was next in charge. Guy was so clever and shrewd that way. He seemed an expert in behaviourism. He had advised so much on small things that she wouldn't have even thought about before but now realised were so important in projecting the right image for herself.

"So – we are all set for tomorrow's show," said Kim, glancing down at her notes and starting to read. "The O'Briens. The couple are living on the breadline, and yet the wife cannot stop spending on credit cards. Her obsessive shopping has brought the couple to the edge of bankruptcy and –"

"Actually, I've received some disturbing news about this couple

178

this morning and I think we should cancel them," interrupted Brooke.

"What?" asked Kim, looking up in surprise.

"I got a call this morning from a woman who says she is a friend of the O'Briens. She told me their story was totally made up and they haven't any financial difficulties."

"And why would they make this up?" demanded Kim.

"Seemingly Mrs O'Brien is obsessed with the idea of having a television career. She's applied to every reality show going and came up with this idea for our show to kick-start her hoped-for career."

"And have you contacted the O'Briens about this accusation?"

"Of course, straight away. They deny it, but I don't believe them. My heart tells me they are lying."

"I told you to leave your heart at the door when you come into this place. We've no reason not to believe them, and so we'll go on with the filming of the show as planned." Kim turned back to her notes.

Brooke sat back, fuming. She had been dismissed again. She remembered all the stuff Guy had been saying to her. About being assertive, and that he had promoted her to be the show's moral compass.

She suddenly sat forward. "I'm sorry. The O'Briens are frauds in my opinion and I think we have a duty to cancel their appearance."

Even though there wasn't a sound, Brooke could sense the sharp intake of breath around the table.

"I beg your pardon?" Kim spoke slowly while she stared at Brooke.

Brooke nearly lost her nerve for a moment but then thought of Guy and cleared her throat. "As the assistant producer, I veto the O'Briens' appearance on the show."

"Veto?" Kim's voice raised. "Where do you think you are? The United Nations Security Council?"

"If they are frauds and it ever got out, our credibility would be in tatters, especially after it has been recently revealed there is no counsellor on the show."

"If – and the word is '*if*' – they are frauds, you should have

179

smelled it out before and not at the last minute when it's too late to reorganise. Now, you're forgetting your place, Brooke."

Brooke raised her voice. "My place is assistant producer. And when I say that certain guests are not acceptable, then I should be listened to."

Joshua sat forward. "It's actually my name on the show. And I trust Kim impeccably. She has years of experience in this industry and when she makes a judgement call on *my* show, it is never to be questioned."

"I'm trying to save us from a potential huge embarrassment," Brooke said, taken aback by Joshua openly confronting her.

"No – you're trying to stamp your authority for the sake of it," said Joshua, "and cause disruption as a consequence."

"Brooke is right!" Lee suddenly called from the bottom of the board table. Everyone stared down at him.

"I met the O'Briens last week with Brooke and they are complete liars."

Kim threw her hands into the air in despair. "Now – now we are going by a teenager's opinions!"

"Be quiet, Lee," warned Joshua.

"No! Brooke is right. If the husband was so upset with his wife's spending, like he claimed to be, why was he wearing a Rolex himself? And he was dripping in designer clothes and jewellery. They are attention-seekers."

Joshua looked at Lee, surprised by his attention to detail.

Kim's eyes darted from Brooke to Lee. "Now listen, Batman and Robin, I want to hear no more on this. The O'Briens will appear on the show as scheduled. Now, I've better things to be doing than listening to your shit, so this meeting is over."

Kim stood up and marched out. Everyone else hurried from the room quickly as Joshua packed his briefcase. Brooke waited until everyone had left before going over and slamming the door shut.

Joshua looked up in surprise and saw Brooke standing with her arms folded.

"Well, thank you!" Brooke said. "Thank you very much for your support."

"You shouldn't have challenged Kim in that way, undermining her authority."

"And what about her undermining me? My authority!"

He started laughing. "Darling, you don't have any authority to be undermined."

"I know you and Kim hate the fact," she said, "but I am the assistant producer and I insist on the respect that entitles me to."

He started laughing dismissively.

"Of course this has nothing to do with the show, or my position, or the O'Briens," she went on. "You decided to put me down just now because I dumped you, and your ego just can't take it."

"*You* dumped *me*! I think you'll find it was the other way around. I told you that we should call it a day."

"No, you *asked* me was I calling it a day!"

"Look, if you want to reinvent it in your head that way to make you feel better, then do that," he said condescendingly.

He went to walk out the door and stopped beside her. "I don't care what fancy title you're giving yourself, try not to get ahead of yourself. Kim won't tolerate it for long, I can assure you. I'm doing you a favour telling you this. I don't want to see you out of a job, and having to rely on your mechanic boyfriend to support you – if he exists."

"Is Guy with anyone?" asked Brooke as she marched past his PA's desk.

"No, he's on his own," said the PA who made no attempt to stop her as she opened his door and walked into his office.

"Hi!" he said, looking up and smiling at her.

"I just wanted to ask – is that invitation to go on holiday with you to Soraya's still standing?"

He looked at her, surprised, before answering. "Yes."

"Then I accept. I would love to go with you."

"Great. I'll text Joshua and tell him to expect one more. But let's not tell them it's you I'm bringing just yet. Let's surprise them when we arrive down – what do you say to that?"

"I think that's a great idea."

181

33

The plane touched down at the Côte d'Azur airport outside Nice at noon. Soraya was relieved that Daniel and Danielle had not been too much trouble on the plane – she and Ulrika had managed to distract them most of the time. Joshua slept most of the way over, catching up on lost sleep. He had been demonstrating insomniac behaviour of late and Soraya hoped the rest at her parents' villa would relax him and help him switch off from his worries.

They emerged into the arrivals lounge, Soraya carrying Daniel and Ulrika Danielle, while Joshua pushed the trolley with the mountain of luggage piled high on it. Lee had grabbed his own luggage and disappeared.

"*Soraya!*" shrieked the familiar voice of her mother, Annabel.

A woman in her mid-sixties raced across to them and embraced Soraya.

"Hi, Mum!" Soraya hugged her back.

Soraya's father, Laurence, pushed Annabel aside and embraced his daughter.

"You look fabulous, darling," said Annabel to Soraya as she hugged the children in excitement. "And Joshua! Mustn't forget Joshua!" Annabel reached forward and gave him a quick peck on the cheek. "Where's Lee?"

"Oh, he's around somewhere," said Soraya, looking about.

"So all landed safe and sound," said Laurence as he looked at Ulrika curiously.

"This is our new au pair, Ulrika," said Soraya.

"Lovely to meet you. How was your flight?" enquired Laurence.

"Okay," Ulrika said and shrugged.

"What happened to the Lithuanian you had last time?" asked Annabel.

"She got homesick. Ulrika is from Stockholm."

"You did well to stay away from a Polish one," Laurence whispered to Soraya. "You wouldn't believe the amount of marriages that have broken down out here over Polish au pairs."

"Joshua! You are looking so young!" declared Annabel.

"Am I?" asked Joshua, looking chuffed with himself.

Annabel squinted at him. "Oh, no. It was just the way you were standing in the light."

Joshua's face dropped.

"Anyway. Let's get back to the villa!" said Laurence. "Let me help with you with the luggage, Joshua."

"Oh thanks!" said Joshua who had been struggling with the trolley.

Laurence reached forward and took a briefcase that was resting on top of the other suitcases. He then linked his daughter's arm and they all headed off quickly, except for Joshua who was left struggling with the overloaded trolley.

The packed people-carrier, Lee having been at last located, made its way along the twisting roads rising high above the shimmering blue Mediterranean until they drove into the forecourt of the sprawling villa.

Annabel and Laurence showed everyone to their rooms and left Joshua to bring all the luggage in.

"I wonder if we should help Joshua with the rest of those cases," said Soraya as she began to unpack the first of her cases in their room. Their bedroom was expansive, with open patio windows that led out to a balcony overlooking the sea.

"No, he's quite alright managing on his own," said Annabel who was sitting on the bed watching her daughter hang up clothes in one of the wardrobes.

"The exercise will do him good. Is he putting on weight?" asked Laurence, who was smoking a cigar at the balcony door.

"No, he's not! And don't say that to him!" warned Soraya.

"I wouldn't dream of it. He just looks a little peaky, I thought," suggested Laurence.

"He's fine. He just needs a bit of a rest. He's been under tremendous pressure at work."

"When you've negotiated a ceasefire between Arabs and Israelis in a tent under gunfire in the blazing heat like your father has, then what Joshua calls pressure doesn't figure!" Annabel pointed out, referring to Laurence's illustrious diplomatic career.

"Joshua has had his own pressures at work. His show has reached Number 5 in the national ratings."

"Really?" said Laurence. "There's no accounting for people's tastes."

"You can watch the show abroad now on the internet if you want to," said Soraya.

"Darling, if I feel the need to look at rubbish, I'll just look into our bin," said Annabel matter of factly.

"Mum!" snapped Soraya. "He's also been put forward to host *The Tonight Show*."

"*The Tonight Show*?" Annabel looked unconvinced. "I can't see him managing that. Can you, Laurence?"

"No, frankly, I can't."

"He seems to be in with a very good chance to get the job. The new boss at RTV, Guy Burton, is backing him. That's the man who's joining us out here."

"The American? I do like Americans. You always know where you are with them," said Laurence.

"So I would appreciate it if we could all be nice to Joshua. And no nasty barbs or comments," said Soraya.

"But we're always nice to Joshua! He's the father of our grandchildren!" said Annabel.

"And on top of all that he's had to contend with this nasty internet site called 'We Hate Joshua Green'."

"Imagine having a website dedicated to hating you! What an accolade!" said Laurence.

"I might look it up later on the internet," said Annabel. "Can anyone put a posting on it?"

"Mum!" warned Soraya.

34

Joshua and Soraya strolled hand in hand down the beach near her parents' villa. It was nearly noon, the sun was high in the sky and only a few tourists interrupted their solitude. They had only been there a couple of days but Soraya felt Joshua already seemed relaxed. Luckily, he was only having to put up with the occasional quip from her parents. Guy and his lady friend were due to arrive later that day, so she felt that would relax him further. Guy was always such nice company and it would diffuse an often uneasy family situation.

Joshua's mobile bleeped in his pocket and he took it out and opened the text.

"Who is it?" asked Soraya.

"Just Guy. They're at Dublin Airport now so should be over here in a couple of hours. He said not to bother collecting them, he's hiring a car."

"Will he find the way here alright?"

"I imagine Guy could find his way to anywhere. Don't you?" Joshua smirked.

"You're probably right," she nodded and smiled. "I'm intrigued to see what his partner looks like, aren't you?"

"I think I can guess. Pleasant, successful, attractive. Everybody's friend but nobody's fool kind of woman."

Brooke looked out the window of the plane at the runway and had to do a reality check. She was actually sitting on a plane with the

A. O'CONNOR

Director of Programmes of RTV, about to set off to spend a few days with her ex, his wife, her parents, kids and au pair. Was she insane?

"Penny for them?" Guy interrupted her thoughts.

"It's nothing. Just wondering if this was the wisest move."

He took her hand and squeezed it. "Whatever you have – had – with Joshua is in the past. So just forget about it and enjoy your holiday. Okay?"

"I'll try! When do they start serving drink on this flight?" She looked around for a stewardess.

"Dutch courage? Just think of Joshua's face when you arrive with me," Guy said with a smirk.

"That's what I'm thinking of! Maybe I should get off the plane."

The plane's engine suddenly started growling.

"Too late now!" Guy smiled.

"This is going to be the holiday –"

"Of a lifetime," he changed the ending of her sentence.

"And if the Greens weren't bad enough, I'll also have to put up with Kim Davenport."

"*Kim?*" Guy's smiled dropped in disbelief.

"Yes, Kim and her husband will be there as well. They always go."

"Why didn't you tell me before?" demanded Guy, frowning.

"I thought you knew."

Maybe it was the Riviera sunshine. Maybe it was the azure blue of the Mediterranean. Maybe it was the chic people they drove by. Maybe it was the open-topped red sports car Guy had insisted on renting and she now found herself seated in as he manoeuvred the hilly roads. Whatever it was, she was filled with a sense of excitement that overshadowed her nerves as they approached the villa.

"It looks more like a hotel," commented Brooke as the car swerved to a halt in front of it.

"Impressive alright," agreed Guy as he took off his sunglasses and took in the house.

186

They stepped out of the car as a couple in their sixties sauntered around of the side of the house.

"Hello there! Welcome to the South of France! I'm Laurence. You must be Guy?" He put out his hand and Guy shook it. Laurence then turned to Brooke. "And you are?"

"Brooke Radcliffe," she introduced herself and shook his hand.

"Please make yourselves at home. Treat our home like your own during your stay here," urged Annabel with a big smile as she shook their hands.

"Thank you. And thank you for having us."

"Any friends of Soraya's are friends of ours," said Laurence.

"And Joshua's," Annabel reminded her husband with a smile.

Brooke liked the look of this couple immediately. They seemed quite young for their age. Laurence was a distinguished man, and must have been very handsome in his day. Whereas Annabel was very glamorous and still very beautiful.

"You found the place alright then?" called a voice from the house and Guy swung around to see the speaker was Joshua who was coming out of the main entrance holding Soraya's hand.

"Yes, I just set the sat nav," said Guy.

Brooke held her breath as she turned around and faced Joshua and Soraya.

"And I think you both know Brooke," said Guy, smiling broadly and putting his arm around her.

Soraya's face was startled but Joshua looked astounded.

"Did you know they were seeing each other?" questioned Soraya as they dressed for dinner that evening.

"Of course I didn't know!" snapped Joshua angrily. "I'd hardly keep that a secret. Why didn't he warn me?"

"Warn? That's a bit too strong a word, isn't it?" said Soraya, putting on her earrings.

"I just can't believe it. *I can't believe it!*"

"What's not to believe?"

"But she's . . . *Brooke!*"

"I've always thought Brooke a very charming and gorgeous girl. I'm not surprised he asked her out."

"Oh, he didn't ask her out, I can assure you. *She* did all the chasing, I'm sure. Kim was right about her, she's a gold-digging social-climber!"

Soraya looked at Joshua, confounded and confused. "What is your problem, Joshua? Your friend isn't allowed to go out with your programme's staff? I never had you down as a snob."

No, but my boss isn't allowed out with my ex-mistress, he thought furiously. He forced himself to relax, realising his reaction was unsettling Soraya.

"I'm delighted," said Soraya, turning to put on her lipstick. "I would much prefer to spend a holiday with Brooke than some high-powered bitch – which was what I was expecting."

"Looks can be deceiving, you know," said Joshua.

Soraya stood up and gave him a warning look. "Come on, we'll be late for dinner."

Dinner was roast chicken and salad and it was served at a large round table on the veranda, which looked down the hills to the sea. Ulrika had just returned from putting the children to bed and joined them. Lee, true to form, was missing. Brooke observed them all at the table. Soraya as pleasant as ever. Laurence, the perfect host, going round and filling everyone's glasses. Annabel, looking as glamorous and bejewelled as a blonde Shirley Bassey. And Joshua giving her, his ex-mistress, a disbelieving nasty look.

"You're a dark horse, Brooke. When did you two start seeing each other?" asked Soraya with a smile.

"Oh! Eh . . ."

"We've been seeing each other a few weeks now," said Guy, taking her hand and smiling lovingly at her.

Joshua's evil stare became more pronounced as he started doing the arithmetic in his head.

"Well, I think you make a very charming couple," smiled Annabel as she leaned toward them and nodded.

"Thank you," said Brooke, embarrassed.

"You work on Joshua's show, is that right?" asked Laurence.

"That's right. I'm a producer on it," Brooke informed him.

"A recent promotion," Joshua pointed out, looking knowingly at her. "Only a matter of – weeks – in fact!"

"Can I ask you – whatever drew you to work on such a show?" asked Annabel, looking displeased, before quickly looking at Joshua. "No offence, Joshua."

"Well, em, television is a hugely competitive area. I was lucky to get the break to be honest," explained Brooke. "But I would like to move on one day. I'd really like to produce documentaries."

Joshua's expression turned to astonishment and he mouthed "*Oh please!*" to her.

"How fascinating," said Annabel.

"You really are a dark horse," said Soraya, smiling.

"*Do* tell – what kind of documentaries do you see yourself making? Wildlife?" Joshua's voice dripped sarcasm.

"In fact, I would like to produce documentaries about public figures. Biographies."

"*Really?*" said Joshua, eyes wide in exaggerated amazement. "For example – Mata Hari?"

"I've actually been meeting some interesting documentary-makers recently through Guy."

"I bet you have!" Joshua nodded.

"It's lovely to meet an ambitious girl who knows what to do with her life," said Annabel. "Don't go letting some man distract you and ruin your career, darling!" And she gave Joshua a contemptuous glance.

"I can assure you, Annabel, I have great faith in Brooke and aim to push her in her career to her full potential," smiled Guy.

"Oh, what a lovely man you are! Did you always want to work in television, Guy?"

"I studied film at university. I wanted to be a film director. But I ended up commissioning programmes instead."

"What did *you* study at university, Joshua?" asked Laurence. "Oh, that's right, you didn't *go*, did you?"

Joshua chewed on his chicken.

"I'm sure you went to the university of life, isn't that right, Joshua? That's what they all say to get out of an embarrassing question." Annabel beamed a false smile at him.

"In fact, from what I hear your diplomatic career would make a wonderful documentary, Laurence," said Guy.

"Me?" Laurence's face lit up.

"You know, you are actually right, Guy," agreed Annabel. "I always said you should write your autobiography, Laurence, but perhaps a television documentary would be better."

"I thought you didn't approve of television," Joshua pointed out.

Annabel's red-taloned finger pointed across the table at Joshua and, with a gleefully nasty look, she said, "*Wrong, Joshua. Wrong!* I don't disapprove of television per se – it's just certain types of television I disapprove of. *Yours* – for example."

"Mother!" said Soraya, with a warning look.

"No offence meant, Joshua." Annabel failed to look contrite.

"Let's have a talk about it over the next couple of days, the documentary," said Laurence. "Say, do you play golf, Guy?"

"I do actually."

"Excellent. Then you can join myself and Joshua on the golf course tomorrow for a game. It will be nice to have some proper competition for a change."

Brooke was walking through a corridor towards the bathroom when someone grabbed her and pulled her into the library. Joshua stared at her as he slammed the door shut.

"Joshua! What are you doing?" she demanded.

"What the *fuck* are *you* doing?"

"Trying to get to the bathroom!"

"How dare you come to my wife's family home uninvited!"

"I was invited actually. Guy invited me."

"And what the fuck are you doing going out with him?"

"Last checked it's a free country. I can see whoever I want. *I'm* not the one screwing around while married."

"I want you to pack your bags first thing tomorrow morning and get yourself back to Dublin."

"Not a chance, Joshua. I'm out here with my boyfriend on holiday with his friends, and I'm going to stay."

"I just cannot get over the brass neck of you! I thought you were a nice girl."

"No, Joshua, you don't know anything about me. You just assumed I was a nice, easy – in every sense of the word – girl without much ambition or talent who was delighted to be fucking a big star like you."

"That you should come here and eat with my wife, and chat away to her parents and avail of their hospitality without a thought of the deception or any guilt!"

"You know, Lee is right about you. You do talk to everyone like a guest on your show."

"And what about you and Guy?"

"What about him?"

"From what you were saying out there you were seeing both of us at the same time."

"There might have been a brief overlap period. But guess what? There was a long overlap period when you were seeing me and married to Soraya. Also, I had to compare and contrast you and Guy to see who was the better lover so I could choose who to continue seeing . . . he won."

"Bitch!"

"Hands down!"

"Cow!"

"If the cap fits!"

"And does Guy know about me and you?"

She thought of the pact she had with Guy. "No, not a thing."

"Well, maybe he should. I don't know if I can let a friend continue seeing someone like you."

"Tell him away! And I'll tell Soraya about us two. And I might as well tell her lovely parents while I'm at it. Not that you could go down any further in their estimation, by the sound of things. They have the measure of you. They know their daughter is too good for you. And now I know I'm too good for you too."

She reached for the door handle and opened it and marched out.

Joshua slammed the door after her and paced up and down. Outside the open patio window, Guy waited for a while before heading back to the dining table.

35

The next morning, Soraya came out onto the patio where she found her mother at the table on the laptop.

"Hello, darling. Sleep all right?" asked Annabel, not looking up from the screen.

Soraya sat down opposite her and poured herself a strong coffee. She would have slept all right if Joshua hadn't had such a restless night. If he wasn't tossing and turning, he was pacing the floors.

"Fine," she said, sipping her coffee. "Have they all gone off to the golf course?"

"Yes, your father, Joshua, Guy and Lee headed off about an hour ago . . . You know, this website about Joshua is fascinating."

"Mother! What are you doing reading that garbage?"

"I was intrigued when you mentioned it. It doesn't hold back, does it? It's quite witty in places though, if somewhat cruel."

"Mother, switch that off now!" Soraya demanded, her eyes wide with anger.

"Dear me! It's quite unflattering about you as well, my dear." Annabel looked her up and down curiously. "*Do* you dress too young for your age, do you think?"

Soraya reached forward and slammed the laptop shut. "If I do, it's because I learned how to from you!"

"Don't be so touchy, darling."

"That bloody person is causing my husband a great deal of

stress. You don't know what it's like to be a television star and be attacked in such a fashion."

"Star! Is that what we're calling him now? Joshua Green is hardly up there with Elvis, Marilyn and Liz Taylor, is he?"

"I'm warning you!"

"Alright! Sorry I mentioned it . . . Having said that, I've a feeling that website is going to become my guilty pleasure!"

"Is Brooke up yet?" Soraya changed the subject.

"No sign of her. She's probably tired from the travel yesterday. I have to say Guy is a most charming man, don't you think?"

"Yes, I like him."

"Good-looking, in control, authoritative, powerful. It's no wonder Brooke is swooning over him . . . In fact, he's the kind of man I always imagined you would end up with."

Soraya sighed loudly. "Well, Joshua suits me just fine. More than fine."

"Your problem is you didn't play the field enough when you were younger. If you play the field enough, you make your mistakes and move on, so that then you are fully aware of what you need when you're searching for *the one*."

Soraya looked at her incredulously. "Well, sorry I wasn't a bigger slut before Joshua, Mother!"

"You're twisting what I'm saying."

"It's very obvious what you're saying – it's what you've always said. You don't like Joshua and you wish I'd married someone else. Well, I haven't and you'll have to get used to it." Soraya drank off her coffee and walked inside.

Laurence swung his golf club and hit the ball far into the distance. He watched it as it landed on a green.

"That's what I call the son-in-law shot. Started off not expecting much, and it still manages to disappoint you."

He had been partnered with Joshua. Not that he had wanted to be. But Lee had insisted on playing with Guy.

"Has Lee had a bit of a personality transplant or something?" said Laurence as he observed Guy teach Lee a golf move.

"Why?" asked Joshua, looking over at his son in time to see him erupt in laughter as Guy cracked some joke.

"Well, I've never seen him laugh before," said Laurence. "He almost looks as if he's enjoying his holiday, for once."

As Joshua looked on he had to admit Lee did seem to be in a very good mood, despite still being rude and surly to Joshua himself. Maybe it was as Guy had said and the kid didn't suit school and was blossoming in the workplace.

As the morning's golf dragged on, he found himself getting irritated by Guy and Lee getting on so well. And mainly because he was used to having grown-up conversations with Guy where he could talk about himself and get sound advice back. No chance of that with Lee around. And as for Laurence, he wasn't far behind in trying to get Guy's attention all the time. With Brooke now seeing Guy, he felt this was another example of his life being invaded, taken over. There was no room left over for him.

Guy swung his club and teed off.

"Brilliant shot!" complimented Lee.

"Do you think so? I think I could have done better," said Guy as they began to walk across the green.

Guy stopped, reached into his pocket and gave Lee ten euros. "Actually, do me a favour, will you? Run up to the club house and get cigarettes for Brooke. I'll forget later."

"Sure thing," said Lee, taking the money. "What does she smoke?"

"Marlboro should be okay," said Guy as he continued across the green.

Brooke glanced at her watch and saw it was after one. She hadn't been out of their room all morning, and Guy had been off playing golf for four hours.

She hadn't fancied venturing down alone to Soraya and her mother, and so had stayed holed up in the bedroom, admiring the stunning scenery and trying to fathom how she had got herself into this situation. She was starving, so she reached into her handbag and took out a Mars bar which she began to devour. She reran the confrontation she'd had with Joshua the previous night. He'd seemed so angry and venomous, and yet she'd stood up to him and given as good as she'd got. She was quite proud of herself. But she still had to contend with the arrival of Kim later on.

"*Brooke? Brooke!*"

She suddenly heard her name being called by Soraya from outside. She quickly swallowed the mouthful of chocolate, threw the rest of the bar on the locker and walked through the patio doors to the balcony. She looked down from the balcony and saw Soraya standing there, a vision in a long white summer dress, sunglasses and sunhat, looking up at her from the patio.

"I hope I didn't wake you," apologised Soraya.

"No, I was about to come down," said Brooke with a smile.

"Oh good. We're about to have lunch if you want to join us? We can have a proper catch-up?"

Cringe, thought Brooke. "Lovely!"

"I was just discussing with Mum about tonight. We're thinking of booking a restaurant in Nice. Would you be on for it?"

"Oh sure! Whatever you think. I'm easy." Unfortunately – thought Brooke.

"Excellent. I'll get Mum to book it then!" Soraya disappeared inside the house.

"So – eh, that was a surprise, you turning up with Brooke," said Joshua. The morning's golf had now stretched into the afternoon and Joshua and Guy were partnering each other.

"I guess I should have said something. I'm sorry. I've had a lot on my mind recently, and I thought I'd said it to you."

"Oh, it's no problem. She's a great girl, Brooke. I've always found her a great girl," Joshua said, then he stopped talking while he teed off and watched the ball fly through the air.

The two men strolled across the green.

"You've been seeing each other a few weeks then?" Joshua asked.

"Yeah, I don't keep count of these things, do you?"

Joshua laughed loudly. "Sure there's nothing for me to keep count of. Boring married husband and father that I am."

"Do you ever miss it?"

"Miss what?"

"Well, you know, the fun of going out with somebody new? The excitement of a new relationship?"

"No. I mean, I've got Soraya. Why make do with a takeaway beefburger, when you have steak at home? Not that I'm calling Brooke a takeaway beefburger or anything."

36

Brooke stepped back from the mirror and looked at herself. She had spent a couple of hours in the afternoon chatting to Soraya and her mother, pleasant to a fault. Then she had returned upstairs, had a long bath and started preparing for their evening out. If she had been allowed through the doors of Versailles, she wanted to look the part. But she wasn't sure who she was going to the effort to impress – Guy, Soraya and her family, or Joshua.

The door opened and in walked Guy. "Sorry I'm so late back. It's hard to get that Laurence off the golf course and, since he was driving, we were stuck."

Guy stopped in his tracks as he took one look at Brooke and his mouth fell open.

"You look really well. Your hair really suits you like that. Makes you look like Cheryl Cole."

She had arranged it to one side, cascading over one shoulder. She came over and kissed him. "Thank you."

"For the compliment?" he checked, raising an eyebrow.

"For everything. For me being here, and having the confidence to be here, instead of being at home with one eye on a soap and another on work, waiting for that call from a married lover."

"Looking like that, you'll never have to wait for a call again," he said with a smirk. "They've booked a restaurant in Nice for tonight."

He pulled off his T-shirt and walked into the bathroom. "I need a shower," he said.

Brooke glanced at her watch and saw it was after seven. "But they said to meet downstairs at seven."

Guy turned on the shower. "Go on downstairs and I'll join you soon."

Brooke hesitated for a second, about to say something, but then caught her reflection in the mirror and smiled at herself. "Alright. See you down there."

Guy combed his hair in the mirror in the bedroom and put on his blazer. The television was on and a news programme was showing. Guy, who could speak fluent French, vaguely listened as the newscaster warned there was a drought in the South of France and spoke about there being an appeal from the local government to conserve water. As Guy listened he suddenly remembered being eight years old and sitting in a classroom at school. He remembered listening to the teacher.

"Water is a very precious commodity," she had said. "Big parts of the world hardly have any water at all. That's why we should always use water carefully and try and conserve it as much as we can."

Guy turned the television off with the remote. Then he walked into the bathroom and turned on all the taps full blast as well as the shower. Leaving all the taps and shower running he walked out of the room, closed the door and joined the others downstairs.

Later that night Joshua drove Soraya home through the hills to the villa in silence. On the radio "You've Been My Baby for So Long" was playing loudly. They had left the others in the restaurant. Joshua had complained of a headache and so they had left early.

He seemed so deep in thought as he drove, it was as if she wasn't there.

"Joshua, is everything alright?" she asked eventually.

He snapped out of his trance and glanced at her. "Yes. Why wouldn't it be?"

"You're not enjoying this holiday at all, are you?"

He looked irritated. "How could I? With your parents getting their quip in whenever they get the opportunity!"

She sighed. "Is that the problem?"

"I mean, who do they think they are? And who do they think they're talking to? They're the only people I know who do not give me the respect I deserve."

"It never has bothered you so much before," she pointed out.

"Well, even I have a limit! *Especially* when it's in front of my friends. In front of my boss and my bloody researcher! Who was not invited here in the first place, may I add."

"It really seems to be bothering you that Brooke is here." Soraya looked at him, puzzled.

"Look, I don't care who Guy brings along for his holiday fuck. But I would rather it wasn't somebody who I associate with a clipboard and pen on my show. I want to get away from work for a week or two."

"I think it might be more than just a holiday . . . romance . . . between those two. They only have eyes for each other."

"She only has eyes for anybody who can further her career, that one. You know, if I was a good friend to Guy, I would warn him."

"Warn him about what exactly?" Soraya's voice rose in anger.

"Warn him that she's a user."

"And what evidence do you have for that exactly?"

"I just know. You don't do the kind of shows I do without getting a sixth sense for people."

"Speaks the new Freud!" she mocked. "Anyway, so what if it furthers her career? She's going out with a handsome, intelligent, charming man, who just happens to be powerful as well. Good luck to her. I've always said she has potential."

"Bah!" he dismissed.

She looked at him and then suddenly said, "You're jealous!"

"*What?*" He swerved the car slightly.

"Jealous! You thought that you were going to invite your friend, the head of RTV, over to France and you would have him totally focused on you, your career. You thought he would talk to you about *The Tonight Show* all the time. And now you're battling for his attention with Brooke."

"You're nuts."

"And you're jealous."

Guy sat at the table in the restaurant, Brooke to one side of him, Lee to the other and Soraya's parents opposite.

"It's a pity Joshua and Soraya had to go home early," said Guy.

"Oh, he's always getting headaches! If he's not getting headaches, he's getting sunstroke," said Laurence.

"Or food poisoning. Remember last summer?" Annabel pulled a face at the memory.

"Try living with him all the time!" Lee said, grimacing.

"Now, Lee, show your father a bit of respect?" Guy said lightly.

"Sorry," apologised Lee with a smile.

"Here!" Guy pulled out his wallet and threw Lee a hundred-euro note. "Go up to the bar and order another bottle of champagne."

"Guy! That's the third you ordered tonight!" Annabel squealed with delight.

"Who's counting?" said Guy, smiling at Brooke. "Come on, let's have a dance."

Brooke let him lead her up to the dance floor where they slow-danced to the music flowing from the live band.

"Enjoying yourself?" he asked.

"Now Joshua has gone home, yes, I am," she said, smiling back.

"By the sound of it, I think *everyone* is enjoying themselves now he's gone home!"

"Tell me something. Why are you friends with him?"

"What do you mean?" he asked.

"Well, you seem to be good friends but I don't think you have that much in common with him."

"Don't we?"

"No. You're so together, and in control, you don't need things from people. He's . . . well, he's Joshua. Temperamental, dramatic, demanding, and needy."

"Sounds like you're over him?"

"It does sound like that, doesn't it?"

"Anyway, we *have* something in common."

"What?"

"You!"

Guy stroked Brooke's hair as they lay in bed.

"It's some place her parents have here, isn't it?" he said.

"It certainly is. It's exactly as I imagined it would be."

"Yeah?"

"Uh huh. She stinks of wealth and privilege."

"I guess she does. She's a lady, alright."

Brooke started laughing mockingly. "A *laydee*."

"Do you not like her?"

Brooke sighed. "What's not to like? I guess I was jealous of her, if I'm to be honest. She's everything I thought I wanted to be."

"But not any more?"

"No. I'm waking up to how good my own life can be. Not envying others. Besides, regardless of her fifteen-bedroomed villa and doting parents, I don't think it made her childhood as happy as I thought it was."

"What makes you say that?"

"She told me."

Guy sat up and looked at her. "What did she tell you exactly?"

"Well, you know when you go into their house, it's children screaming, and au pairs sulking, and stepsons marching off, and television-host husbands tweeting all the time."

"Yeah."

"She told me she loved the pandemonium. From what she said, she was lonely growing up, being an only child in these embassies with busy parents. I think what she has now is really different from what she had when she was growing up. I think she's terrified of being on her own. I think she's terrified of things being quiet."

37

Joshua came downstairs the next morning rubbing his head. He'd had a blinding headache the previous night which no amount of pills managed to rid him of. This was, without doubt, turning into the worst holiday of his life. It was bad enough seeing Brooke going out with his friend. But to be confronted with it every minute of the day while trapped in this mausoleum of a house was driving him to the edge. And he was taking the whole situation out on Soraya, who was demanding to know what was wrong with him. And how could he tell her?

Then Brooke seemed different from the Brooke he knew back in Dublin. The Brooke he knew would never have put him in this situation. The Brooke he knew cared about him and wouldn't want him to be uncomfortable and embarrassed. He walked into the kitchen and found her alone there, helping herself to an apple from a lavish display of fruit.

"Making yourself at home?" he asked, his voice hostile.

She glanced up at him defiantly. "Yes. Annabel and Laurence told us to."

"Did they really? Annabel and Laurence!" He went to the door and glanced outside. The others were eating breakfast on the patio. He walked close to Brooke and lowered his voice. "Don't think for a moment that Annabel and Laurence are friends of yours or anything near it. You wouldn't even be allowed in the South of France only you're with Guy."

"I think you're talking about yourself, Joshua. It's you they wouldn't have near the place only you're married to Soraya. And I'd say they regret that little fact every day of their lives."

"Why are you still here? I told you to pack your bags and get the fuck back to Dublin!"

"Well, I suppose I could go up to Guy and tell him you've asked us to leave, if that's what you want." She started to walk away. "We'll be gone by noon."

"Wait! I didn't mean Guy to go. Just you."

She turned and smiled and shook her head in a confused fashion. "You obviously don't know how this works, Joshua, so I'll try and explain it to you. Me and Guy are a couple now. So where he goes, I go. And when I leave, he leaves. Understand?"

"What will it cost me to get you out of my life? Name your price and I'll write you a cheque."

Her face creased with anger and she walked up to him. "You can't buy me off, Joshua? What do you think *I am*?"

"Look, I know the salary you're on. You could do with the money – name your price and I'll pay it."

Her hand reached out and slapped him across the face. "Out of all the times you've failed to give me the respect I deserve, this is the very worst! I'm not some cheap tart to be bought off for services rendered!"

Joshua rubbed his face which had her handprint emblazoned across it. "I hope you know there's no job for you back on my show when you get back to Dublin," he hissed.

"Oh yes, there is."

"I don't want you on my show any more. Kim's been dying to get rid of you for months, you know that. Once I give her the nod, you'll be thrown out in the gutter where you belong."

"Joshua, last time I checked I was still sleeping with the boss. Try and get rid of me and I'll bring you and Kim and your shitty show down."

"Guy would never do that to me."

"Guy will do what the woman he's sleeping with asks him to do. You and he might be great friends, but I wouldn't ask him to choose between the two of us, if I were you. You might just lose."

Brooke walked out of the kitchen with as much control as she could muster. But inwardly she was seething with rage.

Damn Joshua Green! How dare he think he could offer her money and she would disappear! Did he think she was that cheap? Obviously!

He always made her feel second best. Always made her feel as if she should be delighted to be on his show, in his bed, in his life. While Guy made her feel as if she could do better in life, and deserved more, and could achieve more, Joshua had always put her down. And now she was unsure what was stronger, her growing love for Guy or her growing hatred for Joshua.

Everyone had finished breakfast on the patio and Soraya was clearing away the dishes.

"Let me help you with that," said Guy, standing up.

"There's no need," smiled Soraya.

"No, I want to help," he said, gathering up some plates and following her inside.

They walked into the kitchen and found Joshua there, his hands grasping the kitchen top, lost in thought.

"Joshua? Are you alright?" asked Soraya.

Joshua was quickly jolted back to reality and smiled. "Yeah, course I am."

Soraya put down the dishes and felt his forehead. "How's your headache?"

Joshua quickly pushed her hand away. "It's fine, don't fuss, Soraya."

"He was up half the night with a headache," she explained to Guy.

"No, I wasn't, stop exaggerating," Joshua said, and forced a smile at Guy.

"If you're not feeling well, Joshua, maybe you should take some more time off after the holidays and not rush back to the studio?" suggested Guy, his face filled with concern.

"No!" Joshua said, full of alarm.

"It might be an idea, Joshua —" began Soraya.

"*I said no!*" Joshua said sharply. He then started laughing. "Will you stop fussing, Soraya, I'm not one of the bloody kids!"

Soraya and Joshua sat on the veranda watching the others as they played tennis down the lawns.

"Don't ever do that to me again," snapped Joshua.

"Do what?" asked Soraya.

"Make me out to be some kind of hypochondriac nut-job!"

"What are you talking about? I just mentioned you had a headache."

"No, you said I was up half the night with a headache, giving the impression I was stressed out or something."

"Well, it's the truth, you are stressed out, and you won't tell me what's wrong. I thought Guy was very good to offer you time off."

"Soraya! Have you the brain you were born with? When the Director of Programmes offers a television star time off, it's time that television star got worried about his position."

"Oh for good sake, Joshua, now you are being absolutely paranoid. Guy is our friend."

"He's our friend, but he's also my boss. Can you bear that I mind next time you say I was pacing the floors all night?"

"You are just impossible these days."

"And you are beginning to bore me."

Raising her tennis racket, Brooke hit the ball and fired it across the net where Lee swiped it back at her. She and Guy were playing Laurence and Lee in a doubles tennis match. As Guy raced across the court to hit the ball, he was keeping one eye on the patio, not too far away, where Soraya and Joshua seemed to be in the middle of a heated argument.

"Out!" shouted Lee.

"Guy!" Brooke admonished. "You didn't even look at where you were hitting that ball!"

"Sorry!" said Guy.

Just then Soraya stood up from the table on the patio and went marching off towards the beach.

"You know something. I've still got a hangover from last night," said Guy, smiling. "I am going to suffer from dehydration if I continue playing any longer."

"You can't just walk out in the middle of a match!" said Lee.

"It's either that or be carried off in half an hour when I collapse!"

"That's because you're old!" accused Lee.

"And less of your cheek, please," warned Guy with a smile.

"If he's old, what does that make me?" asked Laurence.

"Ancient!" said Lee, laughing.

"You know, I think I preferred you when you said nothing at all!" said Laurence, heading off the court at the same time as Guy.

"Come on, Brooke, we'll let those two old fogeys have a cigar, and we'll have another match," said Lee.

"Alright, but I'll be retiring soon myself," warned Brooke.

As Laurence headed into the house, Guy slipped off and walked down the path that led to the nearby beach.

As he walked along the sand he spotted Soraya sitting on some rocks gazing out to sea.

When he drew level with her, he started climbing up the rocks to her. "Mind if I join you?"

She got a start, and snapped out of her trance. "Oh hi, Guy!"

He reached her and sat down beside her.

"I had to come for a walk. Lee was bullying me into playing more tennis and I had to escape."

Soraya laughed. "Yes, Lee is proving to be quite a headstrong character these days." She glanced at him. "He seems very fond of you. I didn't realise you knew each other so well."

"Well, the people at RTV think it's a big place. But it's not really, not compared to the networks I've worked for. You get to know people very quickly."

"Not that Lee is causing any problems on this holiday. He's actually been a dream."

"He's seems happy enough, alright."

She sighed. "I wish his mood would rub off on his father."

207

"Joshua isn't enjoying the holiday?"

She looked nervously at Guy and closed her mouth.

"Soraya?"

"It's nothing, Guy. Just ignore me."

"It obviously is something. You can trust me, Soraya. I like to think we're friends."

"Guy, I don't want to be disloyal to Joshua."

"You're not being disloyal. You're confiding in a friend. And if I can help Joshua in any way, I will. You know that . . . Has he not been happy?"

"No, he's been miserable, Guy. And I don't know why. We were so looking forward to having this time off, getting away from all the troubles at home. But he's worse since coming over here. He's in this surly mood. Everything I say is wrong."

"You've been arguing?"

"Quite a bit. Which is not like us at all. I mean, Joshua is usually rowing with somebody, but never me. I hate it. I hate arguing with him."

"Has he said what the problem is?"

"I guess it's work, and the problems he's had with Lee and that damned website. To be honest, my parents aren't helping either."

"I notice they don't hold back when they talk to him," Guy said with a sympathetic smile.

"That's an understatement. He isn't used to people talking to him like they do."

"And what's the problem? Is it that they just don't like him?"

"I suppose, yes. He's not what they expected for me. And then they never warmed to him. They find him arrogant and hate his show and . . . oh, it just goes on and on."

"Poor Soraya!" He looked at her sympathetically.

"Oh, there's nothing poor about me. I'm very lucky and happy with my life."

He looked at her for a long while. "You work very hard at trying to make everyone happy, don't you?"

She looked at him in surprise.

"And tell me, Soraya, whose job is it to try and make you happy?"

She smiled slightly out of embarrassment and looked away, staring at the sea.

"Do you know what I think?" he said in a kindly voice.

"What?"

"I think Soraya puts everyone's happiness before her own . . . I think Soraya has been lonely in her life, growing up in these big houses. I think Soraya is so happy just to have her family that she doesn't think she has the right to have off-days like everyone else. I think that she doesn't want to risk her marriage and her family by ever showing that she might not be happy about something. I think Soraya doesn't allow herself to show how she really feels."

Soraya turned from looking at the sea and stared at Guy and he saw her eyes were beginning to well up.

"*Soraya! Soraya!*"

The shouting from the distance tore into their private world.

Soraya wiped her eyes and stood up quickly. "It's Ulrika." She pointed to the au pair walking down the beach with the children, carrying buckets and spades.

"Come on," said Guy, smiling and standing up. "Let's go make sandcastles."

"Sandcastles! I imagined you would prefer to spend the afternoon in a casino somewhere," remarked Soraya.

"Ah, you see, you don't know me at all," said Guy as the two of them began to climb down the rocks to the beach.

38

Guy and Brooke strolled down an avenue in Cannes and stopped as they saw a mannequin in a boutique window showing off a stunning sheer cream dress.

"That would look great on you," said Guy.

"I don't think so. I don't have the figure to wear that."

"You do have the figure. Come on in and try it on."

"No!" she objected as he dragged her into the shop.

Ten minutes later she was modelling the dress for him and looking at herself in the mirror.

"It's practically see-through!" she said.

"Come on, I'm buying it for you."

"No, it's far too expensive and I'd never wear it."

"Yes, you will. You'll wear it when Kim arrives over tomorrow."

"No way!"

But he had gone to the cashier and paid for it before she could stop him.

Kim perused the bottles of champagne in the Duty Free at Dublin airport.

"Hmmm, this one should be nice." She put another bottle into her already full basket.

"Don't you think we've got enough?" said Tom.

"No, too much is never enough," snapped Kim.

Tom sighed. He wasn't looking forward to spending time with Kim in this mood. "I thought you might have cancelled our visit when you found out Guy Burton was going to be there," he said cautiously.

"Why would I do that?"

"Because I thought you said you hated him, and he was making your life hell," he reminded her.

"Ahh, but that was before."

"Before what?"

"Before I discovered his weak point. Everyone has their weak point, Tom," Kim said.

"Don't I just know it," Tom said bitterly as he remembered his former rose garden.

"In actual fact – I think I'll even buy Guy a present," she said as she chose a bottle of vodka and put it in the basket.

Jasmine came rushing over, holding up two different pairs of sunglasses for her mother's opinion. "Mum – Gucci or Chanel?"

"Chanel, darling – every time."

39

Guy was relaxing on the bed watching television. A film by the great director Clement Lagarde was showing and Guy watched it intently. He loved watching movies. He loved nothing more than getting lost in a great drama. Even though it pained him as it reminded him of what could have been in his life. What very nearly was but was robbed from him.

Growing up in London, Guy's passion was film. When a film came on the television or in the cinema, it was like the rest of the world wasn't real and he got lost in what was happening on the screen. There was no connection in his family with film, and it was expected that he would follow in his father's footsteps and become an airline pilot. So when he applied to go to film school, everyone got a shock. But for him it was what he had always wanted to do. He dreamed of one day directing great films.

He was recognised in college as being extremely gifted and graduated top of his class. However, he realised after college that his chosen profession was overcrowded, with any kind of opportunities thin on the ground. Despite his talent, it seemed to be a world where connections were everything, and he had none.

He managed to pick up stints working on soap operas as a production runner. Which generally meant making yourself as useful as possible, no job too small. These were the only opportunities open to him, and he managed to string enough gigs together build a résumé. When he applied for a job as production runner on the new Clement Lagarde film he didn't even expect to hear back, despite his excellent qualifications and emerging CV. Lagarde was a legend, a French film director with an often dark and disturbing vision, whose films had crossed successfully into the English-speaking world. When Guy was called for an interview, he was amazed. He was even more amazed when he got the job. And to his delight and astonishment he was off to the heart of the English countryside for five months to work on the new Lagarde film.

The setting of the film was an old castle. The star was a very beautiful, golden-haired, French, twenty-five-year-old actress called Marie-Louise. She wasn't well known outside her native France, and even there she was a soap actress. People were amazed that Lagarde had chosen her for his new film. But then Lagarde was known for making unknowns into stars. But it wasn't Marie-Louise that mesmerised Guy, it was Lagarde. He worshipped his films and to be in his presence, even though he never even acknowledged Guy or any other of the lower staff, was a dream come true.

As ever Guy made himself as useful as possible, always had a ready smile and no job was too small or menial. During filming he could hear his own heart beating he was so taken away with it all.

All the production staff were put up in a local hotel. Marie-Louise stayed in a luxury suite in a five-star hotel, and Lagarde himself had rented a local manor house for the duration of the filming.

It soon became clear that Marie-Louise was not the most focused of actresses, particularly for a film as dark as this which needed all her attention. She would totter onto the film set, the epitome of a French movie star, swathed in glamour, her bouffant strawberry-blonde hair like a halo of candyfloss framing her angelic features, cuddling the love of her life, a little poodle called Poppet. And there would ensue a series of blazing arguments between Lagarde and her, as Poppet yelped incessantly.

Eventually Lagarde had shouted: "Get that bitch off my film set!"

For a moment everyone was unsure whether he was referring to the actress or the dog before he clarified the issue by pointing to Poppet and declaring, "I don't want to see that fucking mutt on my set again!"

"*Non!*" screeched Marie-Louise. "Don't swear in front of my baby!"

None of it bothered Guy, he just loved being there. As the other members went back to the hotel after a day's filming to drink, eat and party, Guy would stay on the set working on what was needed the next day or looking through the stills that had been discarded.

One night he was working late, tidying up the set, when Lagarde suddenly appeared.

Lagarde looked as surprised as Guy to see somebody there.

"Who are you?" he asked.

"I'm a production assistant," said Guy, smiling.

"What are you still doing here?"

"I'm just getting the set ready for tomorrow."

"Such commitment," said the director as he sat in his chair. "So you're not back getting drunk with the others at the hotel?"

"No, I prefer it here."

"What is your name?"

"Guy Burton."

"So you like working on my film then?"

"I love it."

Lagarde laughed and studied him, bemused. "You have, no doubt, big dreams for yourself? To be big in the film world."

"Film is everything to me," said Guy with a shrug.

"You should be careful about making one thing everything to you. Because if you lose it, you have nothing."

Guy shrugged again. "I can't help how I feel."

"No, you can't." Lagarde sighed and fell silent, brooding.

Guy waited quietly, wondering what he was thinking.

"I don't know if I can continue with this film, Guy Burton," he said at last.

"*What?*" Guy approached him in horror. "Why?"

"Because I chose the wrong actress. This role is too big for her. I misjudged. I usually think I can spot a great talent and nurture it.

TALK SHOW

But not with Marie-Louise. You see this scene we are trying to shoot every day? It is pivotal to the story, and she's needs to give me real emotion. She needs to show she is distraught, inconsolable. How does she act instead? Like she just broke a fingernail. It is no use." Lagarde seemed resigned to it, as he fell into a silence again.

Eventually Guy moved forward. "Can I make a suggestion?"

Lagarde looked at him in surprise. "If it amuses you."

"When Marie-Louise comes on set tomorrow after make-up, just before you start filming tell her that her dog escaped from her hotel and was run over by a car."

Guy immediately regretted saying it as Lagarde's face became a mask of disgust.

"What kind of a mind even thinks of such a thing?" demanded Lagarde.

"I'm sorry –"

"But it might just work."

The next morning Marie-Louise teetered onto the film set, her face beautiful but blank as the filming began. After ten minutes of filming, Lagarde interrupted and broke the news to Marie-Louise of Poppet's unfortunate demise. Marie-Louise's screaming and wailing could nearly be heard in the next county. She cried, she roared, she begged to go home. Lagarde refused to let her go as the cameras continued to film her despair. And he made her say all the lines in her distressed state over and over again. By the end of the day's filming Lagarde declared it was the best day's work he had ever done. That evening a very live and excited Poppet was brought onto the set to an ecstatic and incensed Marie-Louise.

"You bastard! You *bastard!*" Marie-Louise screamed at Lagarde as she kissed her dog a thousand times.

"You should thank me, my dear – today you have become a great actress!"

Later Lagarde found Guy on the set and said, "Thank you, you saved my film."

From that moment Guy's life changed as he was taken under Lagarde's wing.

He kept Guy near during the filming, elevating him to being his own assistant. Guy couldn't believe his luck – an opportunity to learn at his hero's side – as he paid minute attention to everything Lagarde did.

Lagarde even took him back to the manor house he was renting. He was married to a Shakespearean actress called Pippa. Now nearing fifty, she had been married to Lagarde for twenty-five years. It was in fact he who had given her her big break. Pippa stayed in London while the filming was in progress but made the journey down to the film set and the manor house for regular visits.

"This is Guy Burton," Lagarde introduced him to her. "My new discovery."

"Pleased to meet you," smiled Pippa. "I'm his old discovery."

As the months rolled on, the filming continued at a smooth pace. One night after Guy had driven Lagarde back to his manor house he went in for a drink. He loved listening to Lagarde's stories of all the films he had made, and Lagarde loved telling his war stories from the movie sets.

"They say art is based on life and they say life imitates art," said Lagarde. "But the truth is life *is* art. We are all directors of life. We can make our lives good films or bad films, interesting films or boring films. It is all there for us to manipulate whatever way we want."

Guy listened, fascinated.

When the filming was drawing to a close Lagarde said he wanted Guy to work on his next movie, the filming of which was scheduled to start in Spain the following month.

"You could be a great director," Lagarde told him. "You have the eye for it. If you do what I say and watch me. I always can spot great talent. And that is what you have."

Guy was working late on the film set one evening, going through the stills, when Lagarde came in to say goodbye.

"How is that going?" he asked.

"I'm not too sure if I'm getting this right," confessed Guy.

"Well, I won't be at the house tonight. If you need me, phone for me at The Clarington Hotel."

"Will do," nodded Guy as he went back to concentrate on his work.

A couple of hours later Pippa Lagarde arrived unexpectedly from London.

"Oh hello, Guy, I'm looking for Clement. I just went to the house. He's not there."

"He's at the Clarington Hotel."

"Oh, I see, thanks. Don't work too hard," she said, smiling, and left.

Later Guy was able to reconstruct what happened next . . .

Pippa went out to her sports car and drove away towards the Clarington Hotel. She pulled up outside the building, handed her car keys to the doorman and walked into the grand reception area.

She glanced around the restaurant but couldn't see Lagarde.

"Has Clement Lagarde been in here tonight?" she asked the head waiter.

"No, madam, he hasn't been in all evening."

"I see."

She turned and walked back to reception.

"Is Clement Lagarde booked in here tonight?" she asked.

The reception looked up the computer. "No, I'm afraid he isn't."

"I see, there must be a mistake." She smiled at the receptionist and went to leave the hotel. Then she suddenly stopped and slowly turned. She walked back to reception.

Ten minutes later she was walking towards Marie-Louise's suite armed with a key.

She had easily got Marie-Louise's room number from the star-struck receptionist and nabbed the spare key when she briefly left her desk.

Pippa unlocked the door and walked into the darkened room. She reached for the light switch and turned it on, flooding the room with the chandelier's glow.

Lagarde and Marie-Louise were rolling around the bed.

"Merde! What the fuck?" shouted Lagarde.

"Is this a private party or can anyone join in?" asked Pippa.

The next day Lagarde came screaming at Guy and fired him off the set, telling him to leave immediately. Shocked, Guy tried to reason with him, but Lagarde wouldn't listen. Guy left, trying to understand what had happened. He tried to make contact with Lagarde again, but unsuccessfully.

He eventually managed to contact Pippa and heard from her the details of what had happened that night. He begged her to speak to Lagarde for him. She pointed out that there was no point as Lagarde's reaction was completely irrational, that indeed it might do more harm than good as he might accuse *her* of having a liaison with Guy. In any case, she wasn't speaking to her husband.

Guy eventually tried to get other jobs in the film industry, but Lagarde had blacklisted him. As far as Lagarde was concerned Guy was associated with a bad memory. Somebody he didn't want to run the risk of bumping into again. Guy never worked on another film.

40

Brooke was full of nerves about Kim's arrival that evening. Now Joshua had made it clear he wanted her off the show, Kim would take great pleasure in being the one to give her the boot. She had spoken the truth to Joshua when she said that it would be a risk for them to try and get rid of her when she was seeing Guy. But it didn't make her feel secure or good to know the only thing keeping her from the streets was her relationship with him. If Guy knew he had this power over her, it would certainly give him the upper hand in the relationship. Having said that, she was used to somebody else being the upper hand in relationships. The difference was Joshua took advantage of that, and she believed Guy never would.

She stood in front of the mirror, looking at herself in the dress Guy had bought her in Cannes. She had to admit she looked fantastic in it. She was wearing her hair to one side and falling over one shoulder as Guy had advised her to. She didn't believe his compliment that the style made her look like Cheryl Cole. But, as she scrutinised herself, she had to admit there was a passing resemblance that night.

She sighed loudly. Kim and Co were due to arrive any minute. Soraya's parents had arranged a drinks party that night in the villa, inviting some of their neighbours and friends along. Brooke took a final look at herself in the mirror before steadying her nerves and going down to meet everyone.

She hovered at the top of the circular staircase, looking down at the small crowd of people chatting, laughing and enjoying a drink in the lounge.

"Ah, there you are!" said Laurence, spotting her.

She walked down the stairs.

"You look amazing, Brooke!" Soraya complimented loudly, smiling broadly. "I hardly recognised you."

Joshua was deep in conversation with Guy when he turned his head and saw Brooke. He was startled at how glamorous and beautiful she looked and his mouth dropped.

Guy placed his hand on Joshua's back and winked at him as he said, "A bit better than a takeaway beefburger, eh?"

Guy then went over, kissed Brooke and placed an arm around her.

"What do you want to drink?" asked Laurence.

"A white wine, please?" said Brooke, feeling embarrassed by all the attention.

"Kim phoned a little while ago. They're on their way from the airport now. Their flight was delayed," said Soraya.

At that moment the front door was flung open and in walked Kim with her arms in the air. "Here we are! Large as life and twice as natural!"

Tom and Jasmine walked in behind her. Kim marched down the steps into the main lounge where everyone was.

"Sorry we're so late! It was a nightmare. Delays at Dublin Airport. Then they circled around Nice for what seemed like an eternity. But don't worry, we're raring to go and looking forward to this party you've organised for me." Kim smiled broadly at everyone.

Soraya and her parents moved forward to greet the new arrivals but just then Kim spotted Brooke. She didn't quite recognise her for a few seconds, then she roared, "What the fuck are *you* doing here?"

"Are you sure you don't want to pop up to your room and freshen up?" said Annabel to Kim.

"Honey, the only freshen-up I need is another Martini," said Kim, handing over her empty glass. She had sent Tom and Jasmine up with the suitcases. She turned to Joshua and demanded, "Why didn't you warn me that little scrubber was going to be here?"

"I only found out myself when they arrived. And, to be honest, I'm as shocked as you are."

Even more, I imagine, thought Kim, thinking of their affair. Her mind was working overtime as she tried to fathom what was going on, what Guy Burton was up to. Everyone else might have fallen for his 'couldn't be nicer' approach, but she hadn't.

Tom and Jasmine came back downstairs and joined them.

"The room is beautiful, thank you," Tom said to Annabel as he took a glass of wine from her.

"Glad you like it," smiled Annabel.

Guy sauntered over to Kim, Tom, Joshua and Annabel.

"Greetings," he said and bowed his head in a slightly mocking salute. "Good to see you again, Tom."

"You too," Tom smiled amiably.

"I do love when Tom Davenport visits – he insists on doing all our gardens for us," said Laurence and everyone laughed.

"Well, you're just full of surprises, Mr Director of Programmes," said Kim to Guy with a big smile.

"Am I?"

"There I was thinking your avid interest in our programme was down to ratings, whereas you actually had a personal interest."

"I've a personal interest in all my programmes," said Guy.

"You're hardly riding the researchers on every RTV programme, are you?" Kim laughed. "Oh, I nearly forgot, I bought you all some presents."

Kim went to some carrier bags, took out the presents and started handing them out.

"Soraya – perfume for you. Joshua – aftershave. Annabel and Laurence – champagne. Teddies for the children. Cigarettes for Lee – yes, I'm afraid I have seen him smoking outside the RTV building, Joshua. And I even bought you something, Guy."

"Really? You shouldn't have bothered." Guy was surprised.

Kim handed a plastic bag over to Guy.

"Kim, you're too good," said Soraya.

Guy reached into the bag and took out a bottle of vodka.

"I hope you like that brand," Kim said with a smug smile.

He looked at her coolly and put it down on the coffee table. "I can see a lot of thought went into that," he said coldly.

"And Brooke! I'm sorry, I didn't get you anything because I didn't know you'd be here," said Kim, pulling a face.

Brooke sat down and glanced around the small crowd. Apart from the people from Ireland, the other guests all seemed a well-heeled Riviera set. Soraya was mingling with everyone, making sure everyone's glass was constantly filled, charming people, her soft voice effortlessly gliding from English to French depending on who she was speaking to. Brooke remembered that when she was Joshua's mistress the sight of Soraya playing perfect hostess used to send her into a crisis of self-doubt and negativity. But now it didn't seem to bother her to such an extent. She was ignoring Kim's constant glares which held a mixture of disbelief and contempt. Kim was in a group talking to Guy, Annabel and Joshua. Brooke braced herself and went to join them. Guy smiled at her and put an arm around her.

"So tell me," said Kim as she ate an oyster, "when did love start blossoming for you two? Was it all eyes across the crowded RTV canteen? I love a good romance, don't you?"

"I think some things are best left private, don't you think, Kim?" said Guy with an enigmatic smile.

"Well, actually, no, I don't. I've made my career by getting people to open up. I don't like secrets and covering things up. I think that's one of the great changes in society over the past twenty years. We wear our hearts on our sleeves now. No more cover-ups and dirty little secrets."

"And do you think your brand of television programme has encouraged that?" enquired Laurence.

"I certainly do. When historians look back on the last thirty years Oprah Winfrey will be up there as one of the great social changers of our time."

"I don't think we'll see Joshua Green up there as one of the great social changers though. No offence meant, Joshua," smiled Annabel.

"Mark my words," said Kim, "we've only seen a fraction of what Joshua can do. Once he gets the opportunity to front *The Tonight Show*, we'll see just what he's made of!"

"Oh, we live in hope," said Laurence.

"Eh, hello, I *am* here, everybody," said Joshua.

"As if we could forget," said Annabel.

Lee went up to the drinks cabinet and poured himself another drink.

"Lee, that's the last drink you're having tonight. I don't want a repeat of last summer where you chucked up all night," said Joshua.

Lee sniggered. "Forget it. I'm drinking what I want tonight and you're not stopping me. If I have to listen to you all night, I'll need some alcohol to deaden the senses."

"Right, just for that bit of cheek," said Joshua, reaching forward and grabbing the drink from Lee, "you're not even having that drink."

"I'm over eighteen and you can't stop me from drinking what I want!" Lee pointed out angrily.

"That's where you're wrong, mate," insisted Joshua.

Soraya spotted the burgeoning row and excused herself from the French couple she had been speaking to and marched over.

"Oh, for fuck's sake!" she suddenly snapped loudly, giving everyone a start. "Do we really have to play out this same old charade in front of everybody? Nobody wants to see you two squabble."

Everyone looked at Soraya, shocked.

"Joshua, if Lee wants a couple of drinks then bloody well just let him have them – he's on his holidays like everyone else!"

"Well, thanks for your support," snapped Joshua. "You can clean up the vomit later."

"It inevitably would be left to me to do anyway," said Soraya.

"Trouble in paradise," Annabel whispered to Laurence with a satisfied smile.

Guy suddenly said in a soft voice, "Actually, Lee, you should listen to your father and go easy on the drink. Why don't you finish the one you have now and go on to soft drinks then, eh?"

Lee looked at Guy and then calmed down and shrugged. "Okay."

Joshua mouthed over "Thank you!" to Guy.

"Well, thank goodness for that," said Kim with an amused smirk. "It's always a problem to know where to draw the line with teenage children. Although luckily my Jasmine never gave me any trouble."

"That's because you were too busy encouraging her to keep up with you!" said Tom.

Jasmine was putting on her lipstick. "Mum taught me how to mix the perfect Manhattan on my fifteenth birthday. It's stood to me ever since."

"These things are important as you go through life," said Kim.

Brooke had ventured out on the patio and was having a cigarette as she looked out at the sun setting over the Mediterranean. Kim came out and stood beside her.

"Have you a spare cigarette?" she asked with a smile.

"Oh, yes!" Brooke opened her packet and offered it.

Kim took one and lit it with a lighter that was resting on the wall. She inhaled and turned to face Brooke.

"You know, Brooke, I owe you an apology," she said.

"Why?" asked Brooke guardedly.

"Because I completely underestimated you. I just thought you were a slut knocking off the married star of the show. Now I see you're a much more calculating and dangerous creature than that."

"And what makes you say that?"

"Joshua was only a step up the ladder. You had your sights on much higher things."

"I'm not going out with Guy because of who he is."

"Of course you're not! But it's wonderful that he is who he is all the same, isn't it?"

"I don't really care what you think, Kim."

"Well, that's obvious. I mean you don't care what anyone thinks, do you? You can just show up at Soraya's family home, without a thought of how many times you fucked her husband. That takes some doing. You know, I'd love to put you on our show. Examine what makes you tick. But you'd be too clever to give anything away, wouldn't you?"

Guy walked out onto the patio. "Brooke, fancy a dance?"

Brooke turned quickly and smiled. "Oh yeah!"

The Beatles' "Michelle" was playing inside as Brooke and Guy took to the floor.

"Everything alright?" asked Guy.

"Not really. I could just about take it here until Kim arrived. But she's getting great delight in telling me what a slut I am."

"So what?"

"Guy, why are we putting ourselves through this? Okay, I might have wanted to make a point and give Joshua the two fingers and that's why I came here. But I'm actually not enjoying this any more. We could set off tomorrow and drive down the coast, just the two of us, and actually enjoy ourselves. You're the only person I want to be with out here. Joshua is in the past."

He smirked at her. "You'll be telling me you're falling for me next."

"Maybe I am," she said as she rested her head on his shoulder.

Kim wandered back inside and sat down on a couch beside Joshua who was staring at Guy and Brooke.

"They make a beautiful couple, don't they?" said Kim as she dragged on her cigarette.

"I want her off the show as soon as we get back," said Joshua in a determined voice.

Kim glanced at him and dragged on her cigarette. "Darling boy, I have tried everything in my power to bin the girl already. It was impossible to get rid of her before, but now with her screwing the boss, well . . ."

Joshua looked at her. "Are you serious?"

"We might even have to start listening to what she says in board meetings from now on."

"For fuck's sake, Kim, I thought you could do anything!"

"Most things, Joshua, but even I have limitations. Guy Burton is a tricky individual who I have just managed to enter into an entente cordiale with. A little upset might shake the applecart. And if I

225

sacked his girlfriend, well, I just think that would upset the applecart quite a lot."

"Well, what can we do?"

"Not much, I'm afraid." She studied Joshua's angry face. He wasn't aware she knew about his relationship with Brooke. He wasn't aware she had sniffed it out months ago and had it confirmed by Brooke. More importantly, she was aware that Guy Burton did know about Joshua's relationship with Brooke. And yet it hadn't put him off starting a relationship with his friend and colleague's ex. Maybe it was just a fact that Brooke Radcliffe's womanly wiles made every man want to be with her but Kim guessed Guy was a much more complex creature than that. And the whole situation was screaming 'danger' at her. Kim contemplated telling Joshua that she knew about him and Brooke. She was aware that he would feel very exposed if she did but maybe it was necessary.

"Joshua, maybe it might be an idea not to look so pissed off about Brooke being here. It's giving off strange signals," she warned and discreetly nodded over in Soraya's direction.

Joshua saw that Soraya was studying him in confusion from the other end of the room. He quickly sat back and started eating some canapés that were on a table beside them.

"Unless they are the correct signals?" Kim asked, studying him intently.

"What are you talking about?" Joshua snapped.

"Were you sleeping with Brooke?"

Joshua's face went bright red in a mixed look of anger and embarrassment.

"How can you say such a thing?" he demanded.

"Because it's true?"

"Of course it's not true! There was nothing between me and Brooke."

Kim sighed and sat back before saying, "Don't kid a kidder, Joshua. I've always known about you and Brooke, I've known it from the beginning. And if I ever doubted you were sleeping with her, you have certainly confirmed it by your reaction to her going out with Guy. Men don't react the way you have over their researcher's new boyfriend. But they do act that way with ex-girlfriends." Kim paused while she considered the situation and took a drink. "And in fact only with ex-girlfriends they have feelings for."

"Why didn't you say anything to me? If you knew?"

"I didn't think it any of my business. I didn't want to embarrass you. Lots of reasons. I hoped it would just fizzle out and that would be the end of it. What were you thinking of, Joshua? A man in your position poking the payroll?"

It was Joshua's turn to sigh loudly. He felt relieved that somebody at last knew and that he could actually confide in somebody. "It just started as a bit of fun. Brooke was so pleasant and accommodating, and I knew she fancied me. And I obviously fancied her. It was an ego boost."

"Somebody who gets your viewership shouldn't need any extra ego boosts."

"Well, I obviously did . . . I felt I could be myself with Brooke. Tell her my problems. Talk openly. Not have to pretend to be a star all the time."

"Can't you do that with Soraya?" Kim glanced down the room at Soraya who was now pleasantly chatting to Guy.

"All we seem to talk about is the children. Or the next party we're going to. Or Lee. Or where to find the next au pair. Or her parents."

"Am I supposed to feel sorry for you?"

"I'm just trying to explain."

Kim turned and faced Joshua, narrowing her eyes. "Now you listen to me, Joshua. You've had a very lucky escape with Brooke. She's moved on to bigger and better things. But what if she hadn't? What if she'd gone to the papers? Your career would have been over. Not to mention your marriage. Not to mention *my* career!"

"I knew she would never do that."

"You never know anybody, Joshua. I thought the guests on your talk show would have shown you that. You push the wrong buttons with anybody and they will eventually bite you back."

"So I'm just supposed to ignore the fact she's over here in my wife's villa and going out with my friend?"

"What choice do you have? She is here and she is!"

"Do you think I should warn Guy about her? That's she's using him."

Kim realised she was in a quandary. She couldn't tell Joshua that Guy already knew about his relationship with Brooke as it would entail exposing herself as having been the one who told him. She could never let Joshua know she had gone to the boss of RTV to reveal his affair. He would never forgive her.

"No, of course say nothing," she snapped. "Guy Burton is big enough and ugly enough to take care of himself, I can assure you. Anyway, what makes you think Brooke hasn't already told him?"

"Because I asked her and she said she hadn't. Anyway, I know by Guy. He's acting totally normally with me. I mean, even bringing her over on holiday here. He would never have dreamed of doing that if he knew the truth. It's Brooke who has no morals."

"She's not your problem any more. Anyway, I wouldn't worry too much. By the way she's bed-hopping up the ladder, she probably has her sights on the President of France now!"

Guy was watching Kim and Joshua deep in conversation as he feigned interest in what Jasmine was twittering on about.

"Mum says the position of PA is the best place to start in a television company, because you're learning at the knee of someone who knows what they're doing," said Jasmine as she twirled her hair.

"Yeah?" said Guy as he unsuccessfully strained to hear Kim and Joshua's conversation.

"And let's face it, you can't learn from a better knee than Mum's."

"Uh huh."

"I was initially disappointed not getting the researcher job but as Mum says – my miss is my mercy, and I'm learning much more in my role of PA."

"Sure."

"As Mum says, if I was a researcher I would be stuck on the phone all day bogged down in detail, whereas now my day is much more varied."

Guy nodded and smiled, thinking about the three-hour lunches he had heard Kim and Jasmine had taken to enjoying regularly.

The drink continued to flow. By ten o'clock Laurence and Annabel were having a game of poker with Guy and some of their French friends at the large table in the room.

Kim and Jasmine were dancing wildly with each other out on the balcony.

Guy spotted Soraya sitting on a couch on her own and excused himself from the game and went to join her.

"Are you winning?"

"I always win at poker," he said. He looked at Kim and Jasmine dancing.

"They certainly know how to enjoy themselves, don't they?" said Soraya with a smile.

"They are certainly party girls. Where's Tom gone?" Guy looked around the room and didn't see him.

"Oh, he slipped off an hour ago when the music started becoming too loud," explained Soraya.

"You'd never put them together, Kim and Tom, would you?"

"I guess not. I've known them a long time, so I'm used to them. I couldn't see them with anybody else at this stage. I think Kim needs someone like Tom to balance her. If he wasn't around to ground, she'd probably self-combust or something!"

Guy looked into her eyes. "In the same way that Joshua needs someone like you to balance him?"

Soraya was surprised and looked away quickly, studying the dance floor. "The other day on the beach, Guy, I shouldn't have said those things about Joshua."

"What things? All you said was that he wasn't enjoying the holiday as much as you had hoped," he said, looking kindly at her.

She looked at him cynically. "I said more than that, Guy. There's no need to pretend you can't remember to spare my embarrassment."

"It won't go any further, if that's what you're worried about."

"Well, I know you're going out with Brooke, but she does work on Joshua's show and I'd rather she didn't know that me and Joshua have been fighting like cat and dog."

He reached over, put his hand on hers and smiled kindly at her. "Anything you said to me was in the strictest confidence and I wouldn't dream of uttering a word. I know I haven't known you and Joshua that long, but you've been really good to me since I started at RTV, and I'd like to think we've become good friends."

"You are a good friend, Guy. You've been a tower of strength for Joshua, and Lee as well for that matter."

"And I hope I'm a friend of yours as well," he said and squeezed her hand before releasing it.

Kim watched Guy put down his glass on a table as he and Brooke went out for a dance on the patio. She then glanced around the room and saw everyone was busy talking. Discreetly she took her glass containing straight vodka and leaned over to Guy's glass of coke and tipped the contents into it.

She then went over to the music and suddenly turned it off. She took up a fork and clinked it loudly against her glass to get everyone's attention. Brooke and Guy came in and reclaimed their drinks from the table.

"Ladies and gentlemen, if I could just have your attention for a moment. I just want to thank Annabel and Laurence for having us all over here tonight. And as you all know Joshua has been given the opportunity to host *The Tonight Show* at RTV in the capacity of guest-presenter. Obviously this is, in effect, a trial run where Joshua can impress the powers that be and demonstrate that he, and only he, has the talent to become the permanent presenter of *The Tonight Show*! So can I ask you all to raise your glasses and toast Joshua!"

Kim raised her glass and looked happily around. Glasses were raised.

"To Joshua and his new show!" cried Kim.

"To Joshua!" everyone except Annabel, Laurence and Brooke responded.

Kim studied Guy as he chinked his glass against Brooke's and then put it to his lips and took a large mouthful. She watched his face became confused as he swallowed his drink. His face became panicked and he looked down at his glass. He quickly picked up his glass and smelt the contents, and realisation dawned on him that he had drunk alcohol.

"Are you alright, Guy?" Kim called over to him.

He looked up at her.

"Maybe you want another drink?" she asked and picked up the vodka bottle.

His eyes clouded over as he stared at her.

He walked up to her and, leaning forward, whispered to her. "Don't fuck with me."

She held his look. "I don't know what you're talking about."

Kim found Tom in his pyjamas, reading a book, sitting up in bed.

"Why have you gone to bed so early?" she asked.

"Quite simply – I was tired!"

"But don't you want to be downstairs enjoying the party?"

"Not really. I'll leave all you media types alone."

"It's not just media people down there. There's Annabel and Laurence and their friends. I'm sure you could find somebody you have something in common with."

"As I said – I'm tired."

"You're always tired! Well, when it comes to doing anything I want to do anyway. You never get tired of gardening, or bridge, or watching programmes about the worldwide financial crisis!"

"Well, when you spend tomorrow doing Annabel's rose gardens with me, I'll spend tomorrow night doing whatever you want to do. Deal?"

"Rose gardens! I've got the antithesis of green fingers. I only have to pass by a plant and it withers up and dies."

"Exactly. Our marriage is like a comfy old slipper matched with a sharp-heeled stiletto. There's no point in us trying to find common ground at this stage – there simply is none."

"Well, there must be more to life than this."

"There is for you, my dear. There's your work, and your parties, and your drink and your friends. That's why we're here, isn't it?"

"Right! Well then – enjoy your read!"

"I aim to!" said Tom as he concentrated on his book again.

She left, slamming the door behind her. She walked down the corridor, her face creased in agitation. As she passed Guy and Brooke's room, she heard the sound of water running. She stopped and knocked on the door. There was no answer, so she let herself in.

Guy made his way upstairs and down the corridor to the bedroom to use the bathroom. He entered, closing the door behind him, then jumped as he turned and saw Kim sitting in a chair over by the window, legs crossed and a large drink in her hand.

"What the fuck are you doing here?" he demanded.

"Oh, I was just passing by your room and I heard all this water flowing, so I came in. Someone had left all the taps running."

He glanced at the en suite where everything had now been turned off.

"The maid must have left them on – second time she's done that," he said, walking further into the room and looking at her warily. "So you just decided to sit down and have a drink while you were here?"

"Well, any time any place anywhere, you know me!"

"Yes, I do."

"I saw you paying poker earlier. I bet you're a very good poker player, aren't you?"

"I'm not bad."

"I'd say you're brilliant. Never giving anything away. Never letting anyone in past that mask you wear. It would be impossible to win at poker against you because you'd never reveal your hand. The other players could never guess what you're playing with. Or playing at."

"We must have a game some day, and you can find out for yourself."

"I'm already wondering what you're playing at, Guy."

"Playing at?"

"Everyone else might be fooled by you. Everyone else thinks

you're the best thing ever. But all the arithmetic doesn't add up with you, as far as I'm concerned."

"You make me sound like a mathematical equation."

"Oh, everyone is a mathematical equation, Guy. Just some are harder to figure out than others. And I can't figure you out at all."

He sat down on the bed and stared at her. "What's there to figure?"

"Why would you show up at Joshua's holiday villa with Brooke?"

"Eh – because I'm seeing Brooke," he said, making a face to indicate she was stupid.

"But you know Brooke was seeing Joshua."

"I don't know anything of the sort. I know you tried to say they were seeing each other. I told you before I asked Brooke straight out, and she denied it."

Kim sat forward and abruptly put her glass down. "Okay, Guy, let's cut the bullshit here and talk straight. I don't believe for one minute that you don't know that they were seeing each other. I think you did ask her when I told you and I think Brooke admitted it."

His eyes narrowed. "And so what if I did know?"

"Now we're getting somewhere!" she exclaimed, picking up her drink and taking a gulp. "So – was that why you didn't fire her when I asked you to? And why you promoted her? Because you fancied her? You wanted to bonk her? Have a relationship with her? Whatever took your fancy?"

"Perhaps. That would all make sense, wouldn't it?" he said. "She wouldn't be the first person to get a promotion because the boss fancied her."

"Hmmm, that would tidy up everything and explain things. A simple case of lust."

"There you have it." Guy smiled at her falsely.

"Apart from the fact I don't buy it. Not for a second. As gorgeous as she looks tonight, and you truly have done a wonderful Eliza Doolittle on her, something doesn't seem right about that relationship."

"And why?"

233

"Why did you bring her out here? To Soraya's family villa. Knowing the situation. Why would you do that? If you did have genuine feelings for Brooke, then the last thing you would do is expose her to her married lover and his family. And since you knew about Brooke and Joshua, and the Greens being such good buddies of yours, then why would you put *them* in that situation? You can plainly see how upset Joshua is from having her here. The strain he is under. I know he did wrong riding Brooke, but if you are the good friend you claim to be, then why make him suffer in this way? As you know he is blissfully unaware that you know about him and Brooke. He just thinks she's a manipulative bitch."

"You've got all the questions and none of the answers, Kim."

"Well, I don't know what you're playing at, but I'm going to put a stop to it. Tonight. I care too much about Joshua and Soraya to let you continue with this little game you're playing. I'm telling Joshua you know about him and Brooke, that you've known all along. We'll see how long your friendship lasts then."

Guy started laughing. "You don't care about them. Joshua is your meal ticket, that's all. You were flailing around television for years trying to get your big break. And you finally got it when you discovered Joshua."

"That's where you're wrong. I do care about them."

"You only care about yourself, and Jasmine. You're not going to say one word to Joshua and I'm going to tell you why. Because he will find out that the reason I do know is because you are the one who told me. That you, his best friend and confidante, came up to the new boss at RTV and exposed his affair to me."

Kim's face turned anxious. "I only did that out of concern for him. So that you would get rid of Brooke and get him away from her."

"Well, he might believe that. And then again he might believe you were trying to discredit him to his new boss. Many things might run through his mind, especially as he seems to be in a bit of a paranoid and fragile mood. He will see it as you going behind his back and putting him into a vulnerable position. One thing for sure, he'll lose that trust he has in you. And look at it from the show's point of view: once the producer loses her star's trust, everything is gone. So, no, you won't say anything to Joshua about me knowing." He stood up. "Shall we join the others?"

She stared at him for a while before standing up and sauntering over to him. She stood very close to him, staring into his eyes.

"What's going on in there?" she asked, tapping the tip of her finger against his temple. "Who are you?"

He held her stare. She raised the glass of vodka she was holding so it was just between their faces.

"You enjoyed that vodka I slipped into your Coke earlier, didn't you?"

She took a sip of the drink and put the glass close to his mouth.

"Why don't you have another sip?"

"I don't want it, thanks all the same."

"Oh, you want it alright. You're dying for it. You want to grab that glass and knock it back. Go on, I won't tell anybody. One little sip won't harm you. You can confess it in your therapy meeting next week."

He stared at her, smelling the alcohol.

The door opened and Brooke walked in.

"Oh!" she said, startled at seeing them so close together.

Guy quickly turned and walked away.

"Kim was just leaving. She was giving me a warning on water conservation, weren't you, Kim?"

"Of course I was. I'd better join the party." She turned and smiled at Brooke as she walked past her and closed the door behind her.

Brooke walked slowly into the room, her face confused.

"What was going on there?" she asked.

"Nothing. Just an argument about Joshua hosting *The Tonight* show."

She nodded slowly. "If I didn't know better, I'd swear it looked like you were being intimate there."

He started to laugh. "We were having an intimate moment alright, but it was far from romantic, if that's what you're insinuating."

She laughed as well as he headed into the bathroom. She went to the wardrobe, opened it and took out her suitcase.

He came out of the bathroom to see her putting a dress in.

"What are you doing ?" he asked.

"Packing." She looked at him and spoke slowly as if she had to explain something he already knew. "Because we're leaving in the morning."

"Leaving! Where to?"

"What we agreed downstairs. That we would drive down the coast to Monte Carlo or St Tropez or something. To get away from here."

"Hold on! You mentioned it would be nice to head away, but I didn't think you were serious."

"Of course I was serious! You can cut the atmosphere down there with a knife!"

"No, Brooke, I'm sorry but we can't go off tomorrow."

Brooke's face dropped in surprise and disappointment. "But we said –"

"No, *you* said it would be nice for the two of us to drive away. In the same way it would be nice to give up work and live on a beach in the Caribbean. But practicalities stop us from carrying out these fantasies. We work with Joshua, and he and his family were good enough to invite us here on holiday. We can't just take off. It would be rude."

"But I'm beginning to find this whole situation horribly awkward, Guy."

He smiled at her broadly. "Then you should have kept your knickers on, and not slept with Joshua, darling."

Brooke's face dropped.

"Oh, come on, stop taking it all so seriously!" He enveloped her in a big hug and kissed her. "Come on, let's go back downstairs." He walked to the door and waited for her there.

When she didn't move he smiled at her and walked out.

Jasmine was talking to Soraya. "Well, I now have my typing up to twenty words a minute."

"Very good."

"It's really far more interesting than being a researcher, and I'm learning far more."

236

Soraya nodded and looked for an opportunity to be rescued. She spotted one when she saw that a guest's glass was empty. She excused herself from Jasmine and went to get more wine.

"So you're enjoying the new job a lot by the sound of it," said Guy as he sidled up beside Jasmine.

Jasmine smiled at him and twirled her hair. "Loving it!"

"Between you and me I'm hearing pretty good reports back about you as well."

Jasmine's eyes widened. "From Mum?"

"Not just from your mother. Others at RTV have been singing your praises to me."

Jasmine's eyes widened further. "Really? Who?"

"Ah, that would be breaking confidentiality. But you obviously have a big future ahead of you at RTV."

"That's my life's dream!"

"The only thing, Jasmine, is I feel you might be limiting yourself where you are."

"On Joshua's show?"

"Yes. You see, the trouble is, you're always going to be in your mother's shadow there."

"That's the way it's always been. I'm very comfortable there."

"But I think it's time for you to expand a bit, if you are truly going to have the big television career you're made for."

"But expand where? It was bloody difficult to get the job I have now without Mum pulling strings left right and centre."

"When we get back, why don't you drop up to my office and we can have a chat. I've a few things in mind for you."

Jasmine's mouth dropped open in delight. "I'd love to!"

"Let's keep it between ourselves until then. Heh?"

"You bet!"

41

Guy walked out on to the patio where he found Joshua sitting at a table on his own.

"What are you doing out here? You're missing the party!"

"Some fucking party! Annabel and Laurence's snobby friends playing poker and comparing the sizes of each other's yachts!"

Guy nodded and smiled.

"Where's Brooke?" asked Joshua.

"She was up in the bedroom. I don't think she's come back down yet."

Joshua looked at his watch and saw it was nearly eleven. "You know, if I have to endure another couple of hours of this, I'll go mad. Why don't we creep off down to the town and have a few drinks there?"

"Ahhh, won't we be missed?" Guy was hesitant.

"No. They're too busy listening to The Rolling Stones." Joshua pulled a face *"The Rolling Stones!"*

"I hear you!" Guy laughed. "Yeah, okay, let's slip off for a couple of drinks then."

"Quick, before Lee realises we're going and insists on coming too!"

The two men stood up and walked around to the front of the villa. They began to walk down the wooded road that twisted down the hill to the town.

"You're God in Lee's book, by the way," said Joshua.

"No, I'm not," said Guy.

"Yes, you are."

"He's a nice kid. I don't mean to tread on your territory with him or anything."

Joshua raised his hands. "Hey, you're welcome to that particular territory. Lee is a right royal pain in the ass. And if he stops being that for even an hour because he wants to impress his boss, you, then I'm delighted."

Guy laughed.

"You were totally right about him incidentally," said Joshua. "College obviously wasn't for him. He has blossomed since he started at RTV."

"See – I told ya!" Guy smiled at him.

They reached the bottom of the hill and walked towards the town which was spread out around a port. That night the port was hopping with nightlife. The bars and restaurants along the harbour were full and the cobbled streets crowded. The prostitutes came up to them in the street and started speaking in French.

"No, thanks," said Joshua as they walked quickly ahead.

They went into a small bar, ordered two beers and sat down at a table.

"This is brilliant!" said Joshua. "Getting away from that villa for a couple of hours. I couldn't breathe up there, it's so claustrophobic at times."

"I'm not sure how you are equating a ten-bedroomed villa with being claustrophobic."

"Wherever Soraya's parents are is claustrophobic."

"Annabel and Laurence seem very nice to me."

"That's because you're not married to their princess."

"They do seem to give you a hard time."

"You don't know the half of it, mate. They have another pile in Ballsbridge, but luckily they spend a lot of time out here in France and I don't have to see them all the time."

"It does sound like Laurence has had a very interesting career. I would be interested in looking into doing a documentary on his life

– if you don't mind? I wouldn't want to do anything that makes you feel uncomfortable."

"Eh – I thought that was all just guff?"

"No, it's the kind of programme that wins awards."

"Programmes that win awards do not bring in the ratings or the advertising revenue. That's what Kim always says."

"Well, she would say that, wouldn't she? She's never won any awards. Look, if making a programme about Laurence makes you uncomfortable, then I'll knock the idea on the head."

"It's just I've already got Lee in RTV, the last thing I need is Laurence in the canteen every time I go in."

"It would be a documentary. He wouldn't even be in RTV."

"I won't object as long as he doesn't come anywhere near me."

"It's only an idea. Nothing might come of it. But if we do go ahead, I might let Brooke work on it."

"Brooke!" Joshua looked alarmed.

"Don't worry. I won't take her away from your show or anything."

More's the pity, thought Joshua.

"It's just something she could work on around your show. She's got so much talent, that girl."

Joshua sat back. "She's a competent researcher but she doesn't have that much experience in producing. She won't thank you for throwing her in at the deep end."

"Brooke is gagging for it. You should know that," said Guy with an innocent smile, causing Joshua to cough loudly. "She's dying to get her teeth into something challenging."

"I thought dealing with the clowns that come on our show was challenge enough."

"There's so much more she can do than that. You must have spotted her potential over the years?"

Joshua shifted uncomfortably. "When you have somebody as large as life as Kim, everyone else slips into the background."

Guy smiled. "Come on! Don't tell me you didn't spot her and know she was going places."

"As I said, she was always good at her job."

"Can I ask you a question? She's very private and coy about her life before she met me. I'm curious. If you could fill in any gaps for me?"

"Me?"

"Yes. I know you two are close friends . . . Who was she seeing before me?"

Joshua reached forward, grabbed his drink and took a large gulp. "I don't know, Guy. As you said, Brooke is a very private person. She doesn't go into details like that."

Guy sighed loudly. "Pity. I know she was seeing somebody right before me."

"How do you know that?"

"She more or less said."

"Did she give any details?"

Guy took a drink from his beer and shook his head. "Nah! Only he sounds like an absolute arsehole."

Joshua smiled tightly. "Really?"

"Yep. A total idiot is how she described him. Vain, self-obsessed, shallow, not very bright."

Joshua moved around in his chair. "Why did she bother going out with him so?"

"He got her in a weak moment, and then by the sounds of it she couldn't get rid of him. Kept showing up uninvited. She was just being kind by continuing to see him."

"Charming."

"And lousy in the sack as well by all accounts!" Guy started laughing.

"Well, women can say these things when a relationship has ended. It makes them feel better about themselves if they put down the bloke."

"Nah – not Brooke. She's too honest. She says it as it is. That's what I love about her."

Joshua leaned forward. "Love?"

"Did I just say that word? I did say that word, didn't I?" Guy was looking surprised. "The thing is, Joshua, I think I've fallen for her."

"*What?* But you've only been seeing her a wet weekend."

"I know. But sometimes you just know, don't you? I'm sure it was the same for you and Soraya. I can't imagine what things were like before I met Brooke. I've got so used to her being around so quickly. I feel stupid saying this, but I can't stop thinking about her."

"Whoa! Guy! You need to slow down here."

"Slow down?"

"I always thought you were a sensible in-control guy. You're the person I look to for good advice. Those aren't the words of a sensible man."

Guy sighed. "I guess she's just swept me off my feet."

"For fuck's sake! If Lee said something like that, I'd slap him across the face! Pull yourself together, man! You've just said you don't know anything about her past or anything!"

"I know enough."

"You don't know anything." Joshua looked around the bar and then leaned forward conspiringly. "If I tell you something, will you promise me . . . *promise me* . . . you won't tell anybody? Not even Brooke. *Especially* Brooke."

Guy nodded enthusiastically. "Go on."

"That fella you said she was seeing before you. I heard a rumour, well, that he was married."

Guy's eyes widened in horror. "Married?"

Joshua nodded sadly. "I'm sorry to be the one to break it to you. But you're one of my best friends. And I think you need to know all the facts."

Guy sat back, looking dazed. "Maybe he was separated."

"Married, period . . . with kids."

"Fuck!"

"I know."

"I never guessed that."

"Just go in with your eyes open, that's all I'm saying . . . I'll order us another beer."

Guy pointed to his still full pint. "No, just get yourself one. I'm alright."

Joshua went up to the bar and left Guy sitting at the table, looking stunned.

Guy and Joshua left the bar and walked down the busy street by the port.

"Do you fancy going to another bar?" asked Joshua.

"I guess we'd better be getting back to the villa before they miss us," advised Guy.

"They're too busy playing poker and getting drunk to even notice we're gone yet," said Joshua with a laugh.

"I tell you one thing, I don't fancy that trek back up that hill. Let's try and get a taxi."

"There's always taxis waiting outside the hotel, let's head for there."

As they walked down the street Guy spotted a group of three men standing to the right-hand side. He noticed them because they seemed to be staring at him and Joshua. He suddenly felt danger as one of the men left the group and quickly ducked between the crowd towards them. Guy held back and distanced himself from his companion as he realised the man was focusing on Joshua, who was walking on and chatting away.

As Guy stood back he observed the man come up to Joshua and start trying to talk to him.

Joshua saw the smiling man in front of him, speaking French.

"No, no, I don't speak French," he said in a dismissive fashion and continued walking.

Suddenly the man kicked the legs from under him, causing him to go flying to the ground.

"What the fuck . . .?" shouted Joshua, as he lay sprawled on the ground.

Swiftly the other two men moved over to him. As Joshua attempted to get up, one of them punched him in the face, while another reached into his jacket, grabbed his wallet and ripped the Rolex from his wrist.

"*Hey!*" Guy suddenly roared as he ran towards them.

The men ran off and disappeared into the crowd. Guy gave

chase but then turned and ran back to Joshua who was attempting to get up off the ground.

"Are you alright?" asked Guy, crouching down.

"For fuck's sake. They came from nowhere. Did you see them?" Joshua managed to scramble to his feet with Guy's help.

"No, a bunch of guys pushed ahead of me and we got separated. All I saw was you falling to the ground and then I couldn't see what was going on."

"Bloody bastards!" cursed Joshua as he wiped away the blood from his face.

"Come on, let's find the police," said Guy.

"No, I just want to go home."

"Okay. You've had a shock. Let's get you back to the villa."

Most of the guests had gone home by the time Joshua and Guy got back but they found that the residents, except for Tom, were all up chatting and laughing.

Soraya let out a scream when she saw Joshua and rushed over to him.

"What happened?"

"He was mugged. Down in the town. In a crowded street, what's more."

"Mugged? The town? What were you doing down there?" demanded Soraya as Joshua sank down on the couch.

"We crept out for a drink or two," said Joshua.

"Without even bothering to tell anybody?" Soraya was angry and upset as she inspected his wound.

"I'm sorry. It was my fault. It was my suggestion. We only planned to be gone for an hour," said Guy.

As Soraya cleaned away the blood, she said, "Was there not enough booze here that you had to go off to some seedy bar?"

"It wasn't a seedy bar!" snapped Joshua.

"You know, the town has become so rough these days," said Laurence, shaking his head in regret. "There's been nothing but muggings of tourists down there recently."

"Well, thanks for bloody warning me!" snapped Joshua.

"Well, how were we to know you were going to creep off in the dark of night?" said Annabel.

Kim was inspecting the wound, looking anxious. "What if it's not healed in time for his guest presentation of *The Tonight Show*? You can't go on television looking like you've done ten rounds with Rocky!"

Soraya gave her an irritated look and pushed her away.

Brooke went over to Guy, kissed him and put her arms around him. "Are you alright?"

"Yes, they didn't come near me. They just targeted Joshua for some reason."

Laurence raised his eyes. "It would be you, of course, Joshua. Drama seems to follow you around like flies to pony pooh!"

"What did you say?" said Joshua, standing up and pushing Soraya out of the way.

"Well, I mean, every time you come out here something happens. If it's not food poisoning, it's sunburn, if it's not sunburn, it's sprained ankles, if it's not sprained ankles now it's muggings!"

Joshua pointed to his bruised face. "So this is my fault, is it?"

"No, of course it's not your fault, Joshua. But you have to admit you are rather unlucky when holidaying here. Maybe you should be more careful. I mean, if you go wandering around the port area after midnight, you're looking for trouble."

Joshua's voice rose. "You know, I've had just about enough of you and your fucking ignorant remarks!"

"And at last we see the true Joshua," remarked Laurence with a sigh.

"Don't fucking sigh at me, in that patronising way you always do!"

"Joshua!" begged Soraya.

"No, Soraya, I'm sorry. I've put up with enough shit from your parents over the years and I'm not taking it any more." Joshua was shaking with anger. "Food poisoning! I got food poisoning because I ate that disgusting paella you both forced me to order in the restaurant last summer. Sunburn! You told me the fucking sun lotion you gave me was Factor 25, when it was only Factor 5!"

"It's not our fault you can't read French on the bottle," said Annabel.

"Sprained ankle! You hit the fucking tennis ball down the hill, and insisted I retrieve it as you said it was the only one left! And later I discovered a mountain of them in the garage!"

"So it's all our fault, is it?" asked Laurence, half annoyed and half amused.

"I suppose we hired the mugger to get you down in the town tonight as well, did we?" asked Annabel with an arched eyebrow.

"I wouldn't be fucking surprised!"

"Well, you can just add rampant paranoia to your other many faults," said Laurence.

"And you can add snobbishness, vindictiveness, bitchiness –" began Joshua.

"*Joshua!*" cried Soraya.

"– and nastiness to yours! Diplomats! I don't know how you have the cheek to call yourself diplomats. You're the least diplomatic people I know!"

Jasmine burst into a fit of giggles as she looked on.

"Soraya, how, oh how did you end up with this for a husband?" said Annabel. "You who were given every opportunity and privilege in life, and you present us with this as a son-in-law!"

Joshua's voice rose to a screech. "Because it's not all about you two! You self-centred miserable gits! It's about who *she* wanted to marry!"

"Easily known he would turn our family into one of those awful peepshow families he features on his show," said Laurence. "It was only a matter of time. He knows nothing else!"

"The bump to his head has obviously sent him over the edge," sighed Annabel. "Let's face it, he was teetering there for long enough!"

"Stop talking about me as if I'm not here!" demanded Joshua.

"I put it down to bad breeding," said Laurence.

Tears started to spill down Soraya's face.

Guy left Brooke and went over to Joshua. "Come on, everybody, calm down. You're upsetting Soraya."

"I don't want this, Guy," explained Joshua. "They are driving me to it. Picking on me all the time."

"Poor defenceless Joshua!" smirked Annabel.

"He's made a career out of victims, so why shouldn't he play at being one himself?" said Laurence.

"Come on, Joshua, you've had a shock in the town. Just calm down," advised Guy.

Kim's mobile started to ring and she took it out of her pocket, surprised.

"Who can it be at this time?" she said, viewing the number. "It's Ben Pearson's number."

"Who's that?" said Laurence.

"The head of PR at RTV," Guy told him.

Kim went off to the balcony as she answered the phone.

Annabel and Laurence were giving Joshua withering looks which he was returning.

"Maybe everyone should head to bed," suggested Guy.

"I think that's a very good idea before anything else is said," agreed Soraya as she quickly wiped her tearstained face.

Kim walked slowly back into the room, looking grim.

"What did Ben want?" asked Guy.

"He was saying that Donna Doyle, the girl we had on the show . . . that Donna Doyle has committed suicide."

42

The next day the holidaymakers all boarded a plane for Dublin.

Soraya sat stony-faced, looking out at the runway, steadfastly not interacting with Joshua who sat beside her.

"I wonder how all this is going to impact on the show," Joshua said to her for the fiftieth time. "What kind of backlash there's going to be. They can't hang the girl's suicide on us, can they?"

Soraya turned around and looked at him angrily. "I don't know anything about the suicide, but I tell you one thing – if we weren't going back to Dublin today, I think there would have been a murder in France!"

Kim and Tom were sitting behind Joshua and Soraya.

Kim was on her mobile, anxiously talking to Ben Pearson. "Ben, we're on the plane now. We'll head straight into RTV for a meeting with you when we land . . . Yep, Guy and Joshua are here with me. And we'll see how we can deal with this mess."

She ended the phone conversation and began to dial another number.

"They've given the signal to turn off mobile phones," Tom informed her.

"Have they indeed?" said Kim sarcastically.

"You're back at work already, I see. That's the shortest holiday I've ever been on. I never even got a chance to look at Annabel's roses."

Kim raised her eyes to heaven and made her next phone call.

Behind Kim and Tom, Brooke was sitting with her head resting on Guy's shoulder, sobbing quietly. "She was a nice girl, but just so troubled. I can't believe she would take her own life."

"I know," soothed Guy as he stroked her hair.

"She used to ring me on the mobile and I used to try and deal with her as best I could."

"Look, even the psychiatrists who were dealing with her couldn't do anything. You couldn't have done anything to save her."

"I just feel so bad."

Behind Brooke and Guy sat Lee and Jasmine. Jasmine was busily putting on her make-up while Lee read his book.

"Lee, if I ask you a question, will you answer me truthfully?"

Lee looked up from his book. "I'll try to."

She turned around and he saw she had one eye done in green eye-shadow and the other in blue.

"Which of these matches my eye colour the best? Green or blue?"

Lee shook his head in exasperation and started reading his book, again.

If anyone was under any illusions about the serious impact of Donna Doyle's death, one look at the newspaper headlines dispelled that. All the tabloids were leading with Donna's suicide with headlines like *'Joshua Green's Reality Guest Kills Herself'*.

As Kim, Guy, Joshua and Brooke met for an urgent meeting in Guy's office with Ben Pearson, the station was being bombarded with queries from the media.

Kim had never taken to Ben Pearson. He had been Director of Public Relations and Corporate Affairs at RTV for ten years. A man in his fifties who was an old-style corporate public-relations man, he had no time or tolerance for the way his profession had been bastardised over recent years. He saw the media as an enemy to be controlled and not trusted.

"It's every reality show's worst nightmare come true," stated Ben. "A guest commits suicide."

"A guest with a long history of mental illness who we were trying to help," Kim said quickly.

"By not providing the proper counselling that we promised her."
Guy looked at her pointedly.

"It looks very bad," said Ben. "This poor girl appeared on the
show twice, I understand?"

Brooke had gone to the bathroom and had a good cry before the
meeting and now had managed to pull herself together.

"That's right," she answered. "Donna developed an unhealthy
obsession with her friend's brother. They all came on a few months
ago to discuss it. But she continued to stalk, for want of a better word,
the lad and so they came back on a couple of weeks ago."

"That's it in a nutshell," said Joshua.

"I watched a re-run of the show this morning," said Ben. "You
weren't exactly kind to the girl, were you, Joshua?"

"I'm not paid to be kind to my guests. I'm paid to try and get
them to see sense, which is what I tried to do with Donna."

"To be fair, I've seen the show as well," said Guy, "and Joshua
was soft enough on her compared to normal."

"Thankfully," said Kim.

"We should never have put her on a second time," Brooke
stated. "I said she shouldn't be put on because she had been in a
psychiatric clinic."

"Oh lovely!" said Kim angrily. "And the rat jumps from the
ship, and sticks the knife into the rest of us. Is that how it is?"

"I'm just stating the facts. I warned you she was vulnerable."

"Everyone is vulnerable who appears on our show, Brooke. That's
the essence of the show."

"Well, then the whole thing stinks!"

"Of course it stinks! Television stinks! Everything stinks, you twit!"
shouted Kim.

"If we could all calm down," said Guy. "Ben, what do you suggest
we do?"

"We can't hold the media off any longer," said Ben. "We release
a statement offering our sincere regret for what has happened and
sympathy for the family. We say Donna was a wonderful person
who we tried to help as best we could. We don't admit any liability
and we make no further comments on the future of the show."

A typical Ben Pearson 'tell the bastards nothing' approach, thought Kim. However, she had to admit it was probably the best approach on this occasion.

"What do you mean – the show's future?" asked Joshua, his face clouded in concern.

Ben and Guy swapped worried looks.

"We're going to have to see how all this pans out, Joshua," said Guy. "This is major and we don't know how the public might backlash."

"Oh come *on*, don't try and tell me the show is at risk from this!" said Kim.

"The revelation on the website that there was no counsellor is very damaging," said Ben. "And all the press have picked up on that. As I said, we'll have to see how this pans out. What we need to do now is come across as being as contrite and concerned as possible."

"Which is what we should be anyway!" insisted Brooke.

"Will you stop trying to play the martyr!" demanded Kim. "We're all as upset about Donna as you are, we're just trying to deal with it as adults. You wanted to be a producer – then start acting like one. Producers have to deal with things. They have to deal with very bad things. So start dealing with it!"

"I think Joshua needs to visit Donna's family as quickly as possible," suggested Ben.

"Of course. I was planning to do that today in any case," said Joshua.

"What the fuck happened to you anyway?" asked Ben, looking at Joshua's black eye.

Joshua glanced at Guy. "Long story."

"It's fortunate the show is on its recess until we can figure out how to move forward," said Guy.

"And what about testing Joshua with *The Tonight Show*?" asked Kim.

Guy gave Ben a fleeting look. "I don't know if we can go ahead with that, at this time."

"*What?*" shouted Joshua, standing up.

"You can't do that!" insisted Kim.

"I just don't know if the timing is right – I'm sorry," said Guy.

43

The chauffeur-driven Mercedes drove through the streets of the rundown area. People watched as they drove by. Joshua and Kim sat in the back seat, while Brooke sat in the front beside the driver.

"It might have been an idea to come in a more discreet form of transport," said Brooke.

"You know, you've become such an expert on everything since you started screwing the boss!" snapped Kim.

"It's just a bit of common sense, that's all," said Brooke.

"Can we just try and get through this," suggested Joshua who was dreading the visit to the Doyle family. Funny, he could cope with horrible family situations on a daily basis on his show. But this was different. Maybe it was because it wasn't on a stage, with floodlights and cameras and a live audience. He never went into his guests' homes and saw their lives close up. And they never – as far as he knew – ended up in such tragic circumstances.

"Here we are," said the driver as he pulled up outside a row of houses.

Joshua took a deep breath and stepped out of the car with Kim and Brooke.

He looked up at the modest little house and opened the small gate. They trooped up the short pathway to the front door and Brooke rang the doorbell.

"I'll go in first," volunteered Brooke. "I dealt with them the most."

The door opened and a man in his fifties stood there.

"Hi – Mr Doyle?"

"Yeah?"

"Mr Doyle, we're –" began Brooke.

The man saw Joshua. "I know who you are, come on in."

The three of them walked in and he closed the door after them. They followed him into the front room. There were a few people there, all grief-stricken.

"This is Donna's mother, Eileen, and you know her brother, Aidan."

Eileen was stifling sobs as Joshua stepped forward and began to speak. "I just wanted to say on behalf of the show that we are very sorry to hear what happened to Donna. She was a wonderful girl who –"

"She was nothing to you!" Aidan shouted, suddenly leaping to his feet. "She was just somebody that you could use for your fucking show!"

"Aidan!" his father said softly.

"I know you're very upset, and I can't imagine what you're going through," continued Joshua.

"You're just spinning the same old lines you use for your show! There's no meaning in those words you're saying. You don't give a shit about Donna!"

"That's not true, Aidan," Brooke said, as the tears she was trying to hold back began to spill down her face.

Aidan looked at Brooke. "I know you spoke to her a few times and tried to help her. *But him!*" He pointed to Joshua. "*And her!*" He pointed at Kim. "She meant nothing to them! She was just somebody they could use to make money out of!"

Kim's face was a mixture of sympathy and no-nonsense. "Come on, Aidan, we didn't come here and beg Donna to come on the show. She contacted us. Again and again. Now it's just not fair laying all the blame at our door. She had problems. Ask the doctor who was dealing with her."

"So you didn't encourage her before the show to get angry? I saw you goading her, missus. And you didn't spring Glen's girlfriend on her on the show without any warning? You knew what that would do to her, and you did it anyway."

"We were trying to give her a quick sharp shock," said Kim.

"Well, congratulations, you gave it to her!" Aidan spat. "And you never even gave her the counselling you promised her!"

"Look, I think we'd better go. We're just making a bad situation worse," said Brooke.

"Alright," said Joshua and he turned to Donna's parents. "Again, I'm so sorry. I –"

"*Just go!*" yelled Aidan. "And don't come near us again!"

Joshua, Kim and Brooke left the house and walked quickly down the pathway and into the waiting car.

"Get the fuck out of here – *quickly*!" Joshua said to the chauffeur.

They sat in silence as the car drove from the estate.

"Well, that was quite traumatic," Kim said eventually.

Joshua was pale as a ghost as he stared out the window. "Maybe they're right. Maybe we are responsible."

"That's ridiculous!" snapped Kim. "It's like blaming the publican for serving drink to somebody who then goes out and drink-drives."

"Well, there is a certain duty of care there," snapped Brooke.

"Okay, Brooke! What do you want me to say? You were right and I was wrong. You said she was too fragile to be put on the show and I overruled you. Does that make you feel better?"

Brooke stared ahead, not saying anything.

"When you've been producing programmes as long as I have, then maybe you might make a bad judgement-call one day as well," Kim went on. "We shouldn't have put her on the damned show. There. I've said it! As it stands, I refuse to accept any further guilt for Donna's suicide. The programme did not make her kill herself. The girl could not cope with rejection and it wasn't the show that made her like that. In my opinion she would have killed herself regardless of the show. If you two want to tear yourself up with guilt, then you do it. Count me out."

"Ahem," said the driver. "Where to?"

"It's been a long and exhausting day," said Kim. "Can you drop us all home, please. Me first."

44

After Kim was left off home, Joshua and Brooke sat in silence as the chauffeur drove on to Brooke's apartment. When he pulled up outside her block, Brooke got silently out of the car without saying goodbye to Joshua. The driver then drove on to Sandymount to drop Joshua off.

"Oh dear, I'm afraid we have a little bit of trouble ahead, Mr Green," warned the driver as he neared Joshua's house.

Joshua looked ahead and saw a group of journalists gathered outside his house.

"Oh shit! That's all I need!"

"What do you want me to do?"

"What can you do? They're waiting for their photos of me and won't go away until they get them. Just pull into the drive and drop me off just outside the house."

Joshua braced himself as the car turned into the driveway. Cameras were stuck up to the window of the car, snapping away. Joshua quickly opened the car door and got out. He was immediately surrounded by journalists and photographers.

"Joshua, can you make a comment about Donna Doyle's death?"

"Is it true you cut your holiday in France short?"

"How do you think this will affect the future of your show?"

"Are you still being considered for *The Tonight Show*?"

"Did you know Donna was suffering from mental illness?"

"Why do you have a black eye?"

Joshua ignored the questions as he struggled up to the front door. He let himself in with his key and closed the door behind him with some difficulty as the media crowd was pushing in. He closed his eyes and leaned against the door, while he sank down to the ground.

Soraya came out into the hallway, holding a glass of cognac.

"I thought I heard the door bang," she said, viewing him. "They've been out there all day."

He looked up at her. "Where're the children?"

"I sent them and Ulrika to go and stay with Jessica and Jack for the night. I didn't want them here with the press out there. Ulrika was getting agitated and she was unsettling Daniel and Danielle."

"Lee?"

"He hasn't been home. He said not to wait up."

Joshua got up from the floor and walked into the lounge where he poured himself a large cognac. He went to the window and pulled the cord, drawing the curtains over.

"It's getting dark, I don't want them taking any photos through the windows with the lights on."

He knocked back the cognac and then poured himself another one.

She viewed him, pale, stressed, with a black eye to boot. If it was a normal situation she would have already enveloped him in compassion, sympathy, subtle questions and encouragement. But she found it hard to be like that to him after the holiday. She was too angry with him.

"So," she said at last in a matter-of-fact voice. "What's going on?"

"It's just all a bloody nightmare. We had a meeting with Guy and Ben Pearson. Then we visited Donna's family."

"How did that go?"

"Nightmare. The brother kicked off at us and we had to leave."

"He's angry, it's understandable."

"Kim says it's not our fault. That Donna wasn't well."

"Well, I imagine Kim was going to absolve herself of any responsibility quick enough anyway."

"Ben said it's every reality show's worst nightmare."

"He's right."

"This might be it, Soraya, this might be the end for me."

As she looked at him she realised she had never seen him look so scared and uncertain. "Why do you say that?"

"Because Ben and Guy said it. They said it might affect the future of the show. And they said they might have to cancel my guest-presenter slot on *The Tonight Show*."

"I see." She took a swig from her drink.

"Is that all you can say?"

"Well, what do you want me to say, Joshua?" she said, her voice raised. "Do you want me to be the strong and supportive wife? To hold you in my arms and whisper that everything is going to be alright?"

"Well – yes!"

"And you know I'd like nothing more than to do that. But I'm not feeling that warm to you at the moment, Joshua. Not after your appalling behaviour in France."

"Okay! So I might have gone a little overboard with your parents last night. I had, if you remember, just been attacked down at the port, mugged, punched. And I come back and your parents start lording it over me again. Cut me a little slack here."

"It's not just last night though, Joshua, is it? Even though your antics were unforgivable. To talk to my parents like that in their own home! And in front of our friends! Have you lost your mind?"

"I just couldn't take any more of their put-downs."

"So you acted like a spoilt, pampered, self-obsessed star. Which is exactly what you are! But, as I said, it's not just that. It's your other behaviour. The way you were surly and rude to Brooke all the time. I mean, the poor girl is just out to have a few days' holidays, and you go out of your way to make her feel ill at ease and unwelcome."

"You don't know anything about it!"

"I don't care. You were Brooke's host and you acted abominably towards her."

"So I was rotten to your parents and Brooke. What other crime am I guilty of?"

"The way you treated me."

"You?"

"Yes. You've never behaved like that to me before. Spoken to me in that way. Been rude to me. Dismissed what I was saying. I couldn't do anything right."

"I behaved to you the way I always do."

"No, you didn't. You behaved to me – well, the way you usually behave with Lee. All we did was row. We never row. Can't you see how you were?"

"I didn't realise –"

"It was as if – as if I didn't know you any more."

"Soraya –"

"And I didn't want to know you either. Not that person you were over there."

He put down his drink and came and sat beside her. "I've never seen you like this before. So angry."

"You've driven me to it. I can put up with a lot, Joshua. I'm a coper. But I'm not putting up with the way you have been."

He buried his face in his hands. "I never meant to hurt you. It's the last thing I want to do, Soraya. I don't care about anybody else. I only care about you. If I don't have you, I have nothing. Please forgive me. It's just, and I know it's no excuse, but everything has been building up on me. And I'm so frightened that I'll lose everything, and I'll be back to the way I was before. Before I became famous. Before I got the show. Before I got you and the life I have. And I've risked it all."

"You haven't risked it all."

"I have. By the way I've been. And now with Donna's suicide I might lose it all. And I don't think I can cope with that, Soraya. I just don't think I could cope."

Soraya put her arms around him. "You're not going to lose everything. And you're certainly not going to lose me." She pulled his hands from his face and smiled at him. "You're not getting rid of me that easily, Joshua. This awful thing with Donna, it will blow over. And your guest-hosting of *The Tonight Show* will happen. And you'll go from strength to strength with me there beside you."

"If I could just believe that, Soraya."

"Believe it, because it's true." She held him tightly.

Brooke curled up on her couch hugging her knees as she thought about Donna and her family. She wished she hadn't gone to the Doyle house with Joshua and Kim. To the Doyle family, Joshua and Kim were from a world that had exploited Donna for its own greed. But she had developed a relationship with Donna. She was different from them. Or was she? Wasn't she just another cog in the machine that used people and spat them out?

Her mobile rang and, seeing Guy's number come on the screen, she answered it.

"How was it?" he asked.

"Terrible. They're in bits. And the brother was openly hostile. Yelled at us to get out."

"What are you doing now?"

"Just sitting here feeling shit."

"Well, come over to mine and let me look after you."

She managed to smile. "Who invented you?"

Myself, he thought, as he hung up the phone.

45

Carrying a large file, Kim came marching into the sitting room where she found Jasmine reading a magazine.

"How did it go?" asked Jasmine.

"Shit, how else? Come on, we've got work to do."

"Oh!" said Jasmine, jumping up.

Kim threw her a phone. "Get me Doctor Donald Collins at the Brookfield Clinic. Then get me the number for Dr Patricia O'Reilly at the Whitelodge Psychiatric Hospital."

"Consider it done!" said Jasmine as she quickly began to dial directory enquiries.

"And then get me Henry King on the phone at his home. If those bastards think this is going to bring me down, they can think again." Kim poured herself a drink, sat down and opened the file.

"What's that?" asked Jasmine.

"It's Brooke's file on Donna Doyle. I robbed it from her office. I'm going to scrutinise every inch of it. If you're ever looking for something, Jasmine, then keep scratching away until you find it. You'll get there eventually."

Brooke waited for the front door of Guy's apartment to open, then fell into his arms.

He stroked her hair. "Come on," he said, leading her inside. "It's all over now."

"Well, it is for Donna," said Brooke, sighing.

She hadn't been to Guy's home before. They always seemed to end back at hers. He had told her he was renting an apartment in the Millennium Tower, but she hadn't expected anything like this. It was a penthouse, with a huge living area and floor-to-ceiling windows that offered magnificent views across Dublin. As she wandered over to a window and looked down at the water of the docks below, her own apartment seemed very meagre in comparison. She wondered why he seemed always to want to go back there instead of suggesting this place.

"Some place," she complimented.

"Yeah, an estate agent showed me a few and I liked this one best."

"I can understand why," she said, turning and sitting on one of the white sofas.

"How did Joshua take the visit?" he asked.

"Just said how sorry he was to them. He seemed in bits really," said Brooke.

"And Kim?"

"She acted as you would expect her to act. In control and trying to defend the show when things got rough. I suppose what she was saying was right – it just sounded wrong when she said it."

"Well, the show always comes first for Kim."

"True . . . and what *of* the show, Guy? Where does this leave us all?"

"Well, a dead body is never a good image for a television show to be associated with, Brooke." He studied her carefully, deciding what to say. "I don't know, to be honest. It all depends on how the next few days pan out. What the public thinks."

"So Joshua's survival is not guaranteed."

"It's far from guaranteed."

"*Aha!*" shouted Kim at the top of her voice at three in the morning.

Her shout jolted Jasmine out of her sleep where she was stretched out on the couch.

"Get me Henry King again on the phone, Jasmine," Kim ordered as she waved a piece of paper around in the air.

"What? But it's the middle of the night!" Jasmine protested.

"It doesn't matter. He's going to want to know what I have."

46

Guy drove out to Henry King's house. He had been summoned for a meeting with there with Henry and Kim. Easily known Kim would go straight to the top to protect her patch.

On arrival, the butler showed him through to the drawing room where Henry was sitting in regal grandeur, with Kim already there on a couch.

"Ah, there you are, Guy. Kim was here early and so we started without you."

"I'm sure you did," said Guy, looking coolly at Kim.

He sat down in a chair opposite them.

"This is all a terrible business," said Henry, gesturing to that day's newspapers, their headlines still dominated by Donna Doyle's death, scattered across the coffee table. That morning's papers carried photos of Joshua arriving back at his house the previous evening.

"So – what to do?" asked Henry, throwing his hands in the air.

Guy sat forward and spoke confidently. "I think we have to cancel *The Joshua Green Show*. A situation like this is irrecoverable in my view and the station needs to distance itself from it as soon as possible."

Kim leaned forward and seethed at him. "Four words for you – *over my dead body!*"

"Well, no, over Donna Doyle's dead body, if the truth be told."

"This is no time for your sick humour," warned Kim. "Tell me, do you hold Joshua's show responsible for Donna's death?"

"It's impossible to say. But I think it's certainly a contributing factor. And the most important thing is it will be perceived by the public as a contributing factor."

Kim waved a file in the air. "Well, I have something here that says otherwise! It's a doctor's report from the *previous* clinic she was in. She gave a copy of it to Brooke. Donna Doyle tried to kill herself two years ago. Long before she ever appeared on Joshua's show."

"Show me that!" said Guy.

Kim flung the report over at him. "Brooke probably didn't even read the report. I always said she was a crap researcher. It will all come out in the inquest which will exonerate the show."

"But that will be some time off," said Guy. "And in the meantime, we can't release this information. We don't have permission from the family to release it and I don't think they'll be too willing to help us out of a corner, from what I hear."

She looked at him smugly. "Oh, little boy, watch a master at work and you might just learn something. I was speaking to Glen, the unfortunate object of Donna Doyle's attentions this morning, the guy who Donna was stalking. He is obviously feeling as bad about this situation as we are. I mean, people are unfairly pointing the finger of blame at him as well as our show. I asked him was he aware of Donna's previous suicide attempt. Being a close friend of her brother's, he obviously was. I just explained to him that if he revealed to the press about her previous bid, which incidentally was prior to her starting to stalk him, then it would absolve him, and us into the bargain, of any wrongdoing."

"And did he agree to do it?" asked Guy.

"Not only has he agreed to do it, he is giving an interview to a newspaper right now, organised by myself with a little help from Ben in PR."

"And that will definitely all be backed up at the inquest?" checked Henry.

"I've spoken with some people who know the doctor who treated Donna and it is confirmed," said Kim.

"Are you sure?" Henry asked.

"Are my sources ever wrong?"

"Well, this does shed a whole new light on the situation," said Henry.

"I don't think it does. Mud sticks," said Guy.

"So what are you suggesting in that case?" Kim was becoming exasperated.

"I still think we have to axe the show," Guy insisted.

Kim threw her arms in the air. "Our show will be exonerated in the paper tomorrow and by the following inquest. And you want to axe one of our biggest stars – Joshua?"

"I think it's bad for the station's reputation."

"Oh grow up, Guy!" Kim picked up the newspapers on the coffee table and flung them at him. "Joshua Green is on the front of every newspaper in the country. Everyone is talking about him and his show today." She stood up and started pacing up and down. "This could be the biggest revenue opportunity RTV has ever seen. If we go ahead and put Joshua fronting *The Tonight Show* as a guest presenter as planned, I can guarantee you we're looking at one of the biggest television audiences of the year. And you want to cancel all that?"

"The channel is nearly broke, Guy. Imagine the revenue we would get from the advertising?" Henry urged.

"So, you're going to exploit Donna and her family further?" Guy shook his head in shock and bewilderment.

"Stop being so melodramatic," dismissed Kim. "Television is about real life. Audiences want to see real life reflected. And that's what we have here with Donna Doyle. I'm saying what happened to Donna has nothing to do with Joshua – his show just showed the audience what was going on in her life. And if you cancel him now, one of the other channels will snap him up quicker than an ice cream on a hot day. RTV's loss will be somebody else's gain. And this channel will go further down the toilet while you make documentaries about diplomats that nobody wants to watch."

"Well, I'm afraid Kim makes a very convincing argument, Guy. Let's make no decision as of yet concerning Joshua's regular show. Let's see how all this pans out with the public and the press. But, as

A. O'CONNOR

Kim said, we are sitting on a massive opportunity with Joshua to launch him as the presenter of *The Tonight Show*. It wouldn't be the first new career born out of scandal. I say let's continue with Joshua fronting a trial *Tonight Show* as planned. Nobody could accuse him of exploiting anybody hosting a serious chat show, except maybe the odd fading actress and corrupt politician or whoever else is being interviewed."

Guy nodded and smiled. "As you wish."

As Kim drove frantically away from Henry King's house, her heart was palpitating. She reached for a cigarette and lit it.

Guy was back in his office when his mobile rang.

"Guy?"

"Yeah?"

"Hi, it's Soraya. I'm so sorry for disturbing you. I was just wondering if you're free to meet?"

Guy waited anxiously in Roly's restaurant in Ballsbridge. Soraya arrived, dressed casually in jeans, T-shirt and blazer, her long blonde hair cascading down her back. She reached the table, bent down and kissed his cheek.

"Thanks for meeting me, Guy."

"No problem. I was delighted to get your call. How are you?"

"I'd like to say fine. But I'm not."

"Okay. What's the problem?"

"It's this whole business with Joshua. He's not been taking it too well, Guy."

"I can imagine. It's a terrible thing to happen."

"The press were in siege outside the house."

"Are they still there?"

"No, most have gone now. The statement from RTV gave them something to print."

"At least that's something."

"But he's sitting inside, really stressed and worried. He thinks this might be the end of his career. Is it true?"

266

"There have been rumours, Soraya. I can't deny it."

Soraya put her hand to her forehead and sighed.

"I mean, there are some people who want to axe Joshua's show because of this."

"That would kill him. His career is everything to him."

"I know. I'm sorry."

She looked up at him. "Look, I know Joshua was a right royal pain in the ass in France. I know he was unpleasant to Brooke. And as for the last night when he kicked off with my parents – well, let's not even go there. But he knows he was in the wrong and he really regrets it."

"As you said before, he was under a lot of pressure."

"But if you saw him now, your heart would go out to him, Guy. He just sits there, not saying much, with that black eye which makes me feel even more sorry for him!"

"Do you want me to talk to him?"

"Well, that would be helpful – he listens to you. But what he really needs now is reassurance. That his career will not suffer. That his trial run at presenting *The Tonight Show* will go ahead. Can you give him that assurance?"

Guy looked at her and folded his arms. "I think you credit me with more power than I have, Soraya."

"You're the Director of Programmes. I know you can push for it."

"But there are other people at RTV to consider."

"I'm just asking for *your* support, Guy. Can we rely on it?"

He studied her beautiful face for a long while. He nodded. "Of course you have my support. Joshua's a close friend and I'll push as much as I can to have his guest presentation aired as scheduled."

Soraya's hand reached for his arm and she squeezed it appreciatively "Oh, thank you, Guy! You'll never know how much this means to me, to us."

He rubbed her hand. "Anything I can do to help you, I'll do." He paused. "But what about you and him?"

"Us?" She looked surprised.

"Are you getting on any better since France?"

"Yes, thankfully. He's apologised for the way he was. And he

267

just seems so lost since Donna's death that everything else doesn't seem to matter at the moment."

She glanced at her watch. "I'd better go, I have to collect the kids."

He walked her down the street to her Range Rover.

"I'll let you know what's happening," he promised as they reached her vehicle.

"Thanks, Guy, for everything," she said and she reached out and kissed him on the cheek.

47

Guy was sitting in his office back in RTV, swinging from side to side, thinking about his meeting with Soraya. He picked up his phone and spoke to his secretary.

"Ring down to Jasmine Davenport on *The Joshua Green Show* and ask her to come up and see me."

Twenty minutes later Jasmine came walking into his office, smiling, her hair in a beehive and wearing an outfit with the midriff cut out of it. Guy thought she looked like Ivana Trump mixed with Mata Hari.

"Hi there," she said, sitting down opposite him.

"Hi, Jasmine," he smiled at her. "How's everything down on the show?"

"Well, it's all a bit subdued after what happened to poor Donna," she said sadly.

"Yeah, I know. It's tragic."

"Tragic," she nodded.

"Anyway, I wanted to have a word about you."

"Me?" She looked surprised but delighted.

"Remember I was saying I was hearing great things about you."

"Yes, I do."

"Well, I've been giving you a lot of thought."

"Have you?" Her eyes widened as she started twirling her hair.

269

"I've worked in television a long time, Jasmine, and I like to think I've developed a sixth sense."

"For what?"

"For people who I think will have a big future in television. And I think you're one of those people."

"Well, I was brought up in the industry with Mum. It's like second nature to me." She nodded enthusiastically.

"That's why I want to help your career. I want to make you one of my PAs."

Her mouth dropped open. "You mean work up here in the Director of Programmes office?"

"Exactly. Out there with Jane." He pointed to the door. "I think a girl with your brains and talent and future needs to be given the best opportunity to realise her potential. Up here with me you'll be at the very heart of everything. My Girl Friday. What do you say?"

"I say yes!"

"Hello?" shouted Kim as she came home and walked through the hall.

"In here!" called Tom from the living room.

On entering the room she found Tom and Jasmine at the coffee table with an open bottle of champagne in an ice bucket.

"What's all this about?" asked Kim, amazed at seeing Tom drinking a glass of champagne instead of his usual cup of tea.

Tom poured Kim a glass and handed it to her. "We're celebrating Jasmine's good news."

"What good news?" Kim asked, smiling but perplexed.

"Brace yourself for this, Mum, you will not believe it!" squealed Jasmine excitedly.

"I'm bracing!" said Kim, now really curious.

"You just happen to be looking at the Director of Programmes of RTV's new PA!"

Kim's face was confused. "Director of Programmes . . . you mean Guy Burton?"

"Yes! Can you believe it!" Jasmine was nearly exploding with pleasure.

"Hold on," said Kim, putting down her glass quickly. "Start at the beginning and tell me exactly what has been going on."

"Well, just that! Guy Burton rang for me to come up today. He said he was totally impressed by me, that I was fabulously talented – he had said that already in France – and offered me a job as his new PA!"

"And you accepted?"

"Of course I did."

"The dirty, conniving, manipulative bastard!" spat Kim.

"Kim?" Tom was shocked.

"Well, you can just go in to Mr Guy Burton tomorrow morning and tell him you're not accepting his generous offer!"

"What are you talking about, Mum?" Jasmine's face dropped. "This is the kind of opportunity we dream of in media school!"

"Well, you can keep on dreaming, because it's not going to become a reality."

"But why?" Jasmine was disbelieving.

"Because I say so, that's why!"

"Dad!" pleaded Jasmine to Tom.

"Kim, you can't be serious. This is a brilliant opportunity for Jasmine."

"Yes, too brilliant to be true." Kim stood her ground.

"Unless you can give clear and concise reasons why our daughter should not take this job then I think she should take it," said Tom.

"Oh piss off, Tom, you don't know anything about it!" Kim picked up her glass of champagne and knocked it back in one.

"I'm waiting," pushed Tom.

"So am I!" pouted Jasmine.

"Because Guy Burton is a manipulative user who is up to something and I'm not going to let him use you to get it."

"That's not a clear and concise reason. It's you insisting you get your own way without backing it up, as usual," stated Tom.

"I'm sorry, darling, you're just going to have to trust me on this one," said Kim as she looked at Jasmine.

"Trust! I wouldn't trust you with anything," said Tom, as he glanced out the window at the swimming pool. "You just don't want Jasmine to take this job, because it will be giving her independence away from you!"

"That's not true!" Kim was horrified.

"It is. You want her there as your best friend and confidante and you don't want her having any independence!"

"Bullshit!"

"Like the time she wanted to move in with friends at college and you wouldn't let her."

"That was totally different. She was too young and she has a beautiful home and she's allowed to do anything she wants here! It's not one of those homes where she is in any way restricted, let's face it!"

"Oh no – if she took out a load of cocaine and did it in front of you on the kitchen table you'd think it was a laugh. And that's precisely why she needs to stand on her own two feet away from you. And this job with Guy, a perfectly nice man in my opinion, is a wonderful way for her to do it."

"You don't know anything about him! You don't know what he's capable of," said Kim.

"Tell me then! What has he actually done?"

"It's impossible to put in words . . . He's . . . he's just lying to everyone!"

"A media person lying! Surely not? Call the guards, get the police!" Tom's voice dripped sarcasm. He turned to Jasmine. "Jasmine, in my opinion you should take this job and make a go of it, away from your mother for a change."

Jasmine stood up and through her sniffles said, "I'm sorry, Mum, but Dad is right. I'm taking the job, and that's the end of it." She flounced out of the room.

Tom looked triumphantly at Kim.

"You stupid man, you don't know what you're pushing her into!"

"I know what I'm pushing her away from," retorted Tom.

"You've always been jealous of the bond between me and Jasmine."

"Me and Jasmine have our own perfectly fine bond, one that isn't continually forged over a bottle of champagne," said Tom.

Kim looked out at the swimming pool. "This is your revenge for your damned rose garden, isn't it?"

"No, it's just trying to do what's best for our daughter instead of you, for a change." Tom stood up and walked to the door. "Now, if you'll excuse me, I have a bridge class."

48

Kim called in a favour from somebody who worked in HR and managed to get Guy's address, and that night she drove over to the Millennium Tower. She waited until the door was opened by somebody coming out of the building, slipped in and got the lift to the upper floor where he lived. Experience had told her the element of surprise was always best in these situations. Give him no indication of her arrival till she was at his front door.

She knocked loudly on the door and waited a while, before knocking again. The door opened and Kim was surprised to see Brooke there, looking twice as surprised to see her.

"Is he in?" asked Kim straight out.

"Eh," Brooke looked over her shoulder. "Guy, it's Kim Davenport."

"What?" came Guy's surprised answer from somewhere in the apartment.

Kim pushed the door open and walked in past Brooke.

"Do you mind?" said Brooke irritably.

"No, not really," Kim answered in a blasé voice as she took in the spacious apartment with the breathtaking views across the city.

Behind an island in the kitchen Guy had stopped cooking and was viewing her suspiciously.

"I never had you down as a cook. But then you're really full of surprises, aren't you?" said Kim.

274

"What are you doing here?" he asked, turning off the cooker and coming into the living room.

"I think you know why I'm here." Kim turned and looked at Brooke. "Do you want to have this conversation in front of the children or will we have it privately?"

Guy looked at Brooke. "Brooke, could you give us a few minutes on our own, please?"

"Sure – I have to go and get cigarettes anyway," said Brooke as she grabbed her blazer. Giving Kim a suspicious look, she left the apartment.

"What a nice scene of domestic bliss you paint," said Kim. "I never had either of you down for that role, but there you go, looks can be deceiving. For every old sock there's an old shoe."

"Kim, she won't be that long, what do you want?"

Kim sat down and stared at him. "Why did you offer my daughter that job? And don't feed me that bullshit you gave her about being magnificently talented."

"Well, no I won't, because let's face it," he allowed himself a small laugh, "she isn't!"

"So what's the story? What with Brooke's promotion, and Lee's job, and now Jasmine's offer you're handing out titles quicker than a Tudor King! I've heard about encouraging youth, but this is ridiculous."

"I think Jasmine will be very useful to me."

"For answering your phones and opening your mail?"

"I figured I just needed a little insurance against you, and she was the only thing I could think of."

"I want you to tell her tomorrow that you made a mistake and send her back down to my department."

"No can do . . . Have you told Joshua that I recommended his show to be axed yet?"

"No, I haven't spoken to him. He's holed up in his house and I've been busy trying to keep this show on the road."

"Good, and you're not going to tell him either. In that meeting with Henry King I was simply making a business recommendation that I was overruled on. I wouldn't want Joshua to know about my recommendation. He is one of our biggest stars, and I don't want anything to get in the way of our professional relationship by you shit-stirring."

Kim nodded. "And so you've brought Jasmine up to work with you as a kind of – what – threat? To make sure I don't say anything? Is that the best you can do?"

"Yes, it was."

"And what will you do if I tell Joshua you were gunning for him to be fired?"

"I don't know. But I'll have plenty of time to decide. And you won't say anything to Joshua because you won't risk Jasmine's career . . . and, you know, I think she has a bit of a crush on me . . ."

She viewed him contemptuously before saying, "I'm sorry."

"For what?"

She took up a glass of water and tipped it over his head. "For that!"

"What the fuck do you think you're doing?" he roared.

The key turned in the front door and Brooke walked in.

Kim leaned forward and whispered to him. "If you do anything to my daughter, I'll finish you off."

He hissed back. "I won't do a thing. And you won't tell Joshua . . . I think we understand each other."

Kim turned and walked past Brooke out of the apartment.

"What was all that about?" asked Brooke uneasily, closing the front door.

"I don't know what she goes on about half the time. I think she's half mad. Anyway, the dinner's burning."

Guy walked back into the kitchen and, picking up a towel, began to dry the water off his head.

49

Pulling into the drive of the Greens' home in Sandymount, Guy noticed the blinds downstairs were all pulled down even though there were no longer any journalists hanging around outside the house. The house didn't have its usual hustle and bustle look. Lee had told him that Ulrika and the kids were staying with close friends of theirs as Joshua needed some peace and quiet. Even Lee hadn't bothered going home for the last couple of nights, staying with friends the first night and Guy last night. Joshua was in a morbid mood, seemingly, and Soraya was concentrating on trying to lift his spirits.

Soraya opened the door to him.

"Hi there, thanks for coming over," she said as she leaned forward and kissed his cheek.

"How is he?" asked Guy.

"A little better today, but a long way from being back to normal. I just think if people could see him now, they would realise he's not the cold tough cookie he portrays on television. He's really feeling Donna's death."

"He's lucky to have you."

"And you. You know, you're the only person from the station who has bothered to keep in contact since all this blew up. Even Kim hasn't phoned."

Too busy working behind the scenes saving Joshua's ass, not to mention her own, thought Guy.

"Are people at RTV blaming him for all this?" asked Soraya.

Guy gave her a sympathetic look. "Maybe it's best you don't know what they're saying."

"No, don't hide the truth from me, Guy, whatever about Joshua. What are people saying?"

"Well, people are calling for the show to be axed to be honest. They're saying Joshua is finished."

"Oh no!" Soraya rubbed her temples.

"Anyway," Guy put his arm around her back, "that's what people are saying, but it's not what's going to happen. Not if I've anything to do with it."

She smiled sadly at him.

"Where is he?" he said. "I've a few things to talk to him about."

"He's out the back. Come on."

He followed her through to the kitchen and out through the patio doors to the back garden. Joshua was sitting on a garden chair by a table on the patio.

"Hiya, pal! How are you?" said Guy cheerfully as he slapped him on the back.

"Hey, Guy, thanks for dropping over," said Joshua and he managed to smile. Guy and Soraya sat at the other chairs at the table.

Guy had to admit he had seen Joshua look better. Pale, drawn, he obviously hadn't been eating or sleeping well. Soraya reached over to the large jug of orange juice and poured herself and Guy a glass.

"So how's everything in television land?" asked Joshua with a wry smile.

"Same as ever, pal, same as ever. And how are you?"

"I've been better, Guy," sighed Joshua. "I just keep thinking that she was just another sad-luck story on the conveyor belt of sad-luck stories we dish out every day. There was nothing remarkable about her. Nothing that made her stand out from the rest of the guests. If only I'd known."

"I keep telling him it wasn't his fault," said Soraya.

"Of course it wasn't," agreed Guy.

"The headlines of those papers are screaming that it was."

"They're just trying to sensationalise it. Isn't that right, Guy?"

"Sure."

"In fact they are exploiting this far more for their sales than your show ever did," said Soraya.

"You know what they say – today's news tomorrow's fish-and-chip paper," said Guy.

"They don't serve fish and chips in newspaper any more," said Joshua.

"Well, then, tomorrow's recycling bin," said Guy.

"You know that fucking website that I was obsessed with? All those headlines in the papers are like that, but magnified by a thousand. People writing negative things about me, and I've no control over what they're saying."

"I just think of all the people I've been friends with. And so few of them have called me up, asked how I was. Is that how fickle the whole thing is?"

"When you're up, you're up, and when you're down, you're down," said Guy with a shake of the head.

"When I'd go to parties they'd flock to me, wouldn't they, Soraya?"

"Yes."

"But now they're keeping their distance. Not wanting to be, I don't know, contaminated or connected with the bad story."

"As you said, people are fickle."

"This fucking business is fickle." He turned and looked Guy straight in the eyes. "Tell me straight – am I through? I can take it, Guy. But you have to be straight with me. I need to know where I stand so I can see what my future is."

Soraya held her breath.

Guy shook his head. "No – you're not through, Joshua. Not yet, anyway."

Soraya let go of her breath and began to breathe normally. "So what's going on?" she asked.

"I won't lie to you. This has shaken the station and there were a lot of calls for you to go. But I tried my best to stick up for you, and I think people finally started to listen to what I was saying."

"Thank you, Guy." Joshua nodded his appreciation.

"So the show isn't about to be cancelled?" said Soraya.

"There's no decision made on your regular show yet. But you've been given the go-ahead to guest-present *The Tonight Show*."

Soraya clapped her hands together. "But that's wonderful!"

Joshua looked a mixture of surprised, relieved and terrified. "Is it?"

"Of course it is!" Soraya hugged him.

"But come on, let's face it, am I able to do it at the moment?"

"Will you stop with this self-doubt, Joshua!" said Soraya.

"Why not self-doubt? Maybe everyone's right. Your parents, the person behind the website," and Brooke, he added mentally. "Even the press now. I'm just a guy who got lucky when Kim Davenport was looking for somebody to host her tacky show. I'm a one-trick pony who won't be able to pull off a mainstream chat show."

"I much preferred you when you were an arrogant so-and-so!" said Soraya despairing. She grabbed his face and turned it to her. "Look at me! You've had an anxious couple of months. You've been under a bit of pressure. And now you've had a terrible and unexpected shock. But you'll come through this – *we'll* come through this. And we'll be better and stronger after it. Do you understand me? Now I want you to get back to yourself. And become that arrogant, self-obsessed cocky bastard I fell in love with. Do I make myself clear?"

He nodded and, leaning forward, kissed her tenderly on the lips.

Guy sat observing the whole scene with interest.

The phone rang inside the kitchen.

"Let it go through to the answering machine," said Soraya.

The answering machine bleeped and instructed the caller to leave a message.

"Joshua? This is Kim." Her voice was loud and clear. "Get your ass in to the station tomorrow. You've been given the go-ahead to guest-present *The Tonight Show* and we've no time to waste. I'm calling a meeting of the team for ten in the morning sharp. We need to line up guests, ideas and strategies. It's no time to sit around thinking about what's happened. If you're not in the studio by ten, I'll come over and drag you in myself." She hung up.

"She doesn't wait around, does she?" said Guy.

"She never does," said Joshua as he sat up straight. "Okay, we've been given another chance here. Thanks to you, Guy. And I can't mess it up. I can't fail at this. I have to prove to everyone I'm more than a one-trick pony."

"That's right, Joshua," encouraged Soraya.

"Do you know something? Now more than ever I have to make this show work," said Joshua.

"Why?" asked Guy.

"Well before, if I proved to be no good on *The Tonight Show*, I could have slipped back to my normal show and thought I'd given it my best shot. But now, after what has happened, everyone will be watching me, waiting for me to fail. I can't let that happen. And, you know, after what's happened with Donna, I don't want to go back to my old show. I'm sick of dealing with people's dirty laundry. I'm sick of the fights and arguments on that show. I want to do something else. I want to do a regular talk show."

"Well, at least you're thinking along the right track," said Guy as he rose to his feet. "I'd better be off. I'm meeting Brooke for dinner."

"I'll see you out," said Soraya.

"See you in work tomorrow," said Guy and he clapped Joshua on the back.

"And thanks, Guy, thanks for everything," said Joshua.

Soraya and Guy walked to the front door and she opened it for him.

"I don't know how I'll ever thank you," she said, smiling at him.

"There's really no need."

"There's every need. You just saved his career."

"Well, he's the one who has to save it yet, by making the show a success."

She leaned forward, enveloped him in a big hug and held him for a while before pulling away and kissing him on the cheek.

"Thanks," she whispered.

He walked down the steps and got into his car. He looked up at the house, feeling unnerved, agitated and stressed. He put the key in the ignition, revved up and tore out of the drive, speeding down the road.

Guy opened the door to his apartment and walked in, throwing his keys on a side table.

"Hello?" he called.

"Hi," said the voice from the spare bedroom.

A second later Lee came out.

"Your father is an absolute prat, do you know that?"

"Tell me about it. Try living with it."

"He's sitting there in the garden feeling sorry for himself over that girl's suicide."

"It's all about him, don't ya know," said Lee.

"Leaving it to Soraya to pull him out of his self-induced depression."

"I think he does it just to get her attention."

"Anyway, it's full steam ahead with this guest-presentation show by the looks of it."

"Yeah, I got a call from Brooke to say the team has to meet at ten tomorrow."

"Speaking of which, she's coming over here tonight, so you better get off home and make yourself scarce."

"Fuck, the atmosphere is shit at home," grumbled Lee.

"Not when last seen. Your father was doing a good impression of The Show Must Go On."

"Martyr to the cause."

"Martyr to himself, more like."

Lee got his bag and headed to the door.

"Thanks for putting me up," he said.

"Any time. Keep me informed on how the new show is going."

"Will do. I'll phone you with all the news tomorrow."

"Good kid."

"And where have you been?" demanded Joshua as Lee came in the door.

"Staying with Aunt Helen," Lee lied.

"Well, thanks for being around and giving your support," said Joshua.

"Whatever!" said Lee, going upstairs.

50

Brooke sat in the canteen early the next morning with a copy of a newspaper in front of her. The headline read *'Exclusive – Interview With the Man Stalked by Joshua Green Suicide Girl'*.

What a headline, thought Brooke. All the right ingredients – stalker, suicide and a celebrity name. If that wasn't a big seller then nothing would be. She looked at the photo of Glen and his girlfriend Rain on the front page. They looked as if they'd had a make-over for the photo, and she sincerely hoped they hadn't been paid for giving the interview. Not that it really mattered if they had, she supposed. She guessed she just didn't want anyone else exploiting the situation. Seemingly it was Kim who had organised the whole interview to deflect the blame from the show. It remained to be seen if the ploy had worked. Seeing it was nearly ten, she got up and headed towards the boardroom.

As Kim looked around the show's team, a subdued mood seemed to be prevalent.

"Right, everybody. I'm not even going to mention the last few days and what's been happening. But I will tell you this. It is imperative, and I mean *imperative* that we don't fuck up our shot with the *Tonight Show*. We've got one chance to do it, so we'd better get it right. And our normal show might not be there any

284

more. So unless any of you want to be looking for a new job in this climate, I suggest you put your all into getting this right."

There was a general nodding of heads in agreement.

"So I want concepts, I want ideas. I want lists of guest who we think would make this show go a bomb. I want lists of guests who we all think are shit. I want innovation and I want it now. Brooke, get on to the agencies and see which stars are available. Forget grubby little scrubbers looking for their fifteen seconds of fame and prostituting their lives for a bit of television exposure. I want proper stars. Get going."

Everyone got up and began to leave except for Joshua and Kim.

As Brooke gathered her paperwork, Kim said, "Not, so fast, Nancy Drew. Sit down a minute."

Brooke sat back down and waited for everyone else to leave the room. She had given it much thought. She'd known they'd both round on her as soon as she got back to the station, and she wasn't going to take it from them. Both of them had attacked her viciously in France. She was the partner of the station's boss. She was a producer on the show. And they would give her the respect she deserved.

Kim reached into her briefcase and flung a file at Brooke.

"That's your file on Donna Doyle. I'm just giving it back to you."

Brooke was annoyed. "I wish you'd ask if you want anything from my files, rather than riffling through them yourself."

"I would have if I could trust you. But experience has told me if you want anything done around here then you have to do it yourself. Did you know that Donna Doyle had tried to commit suicide previously?"

"I knew she had suicidal tendencies, but I didn't know she had actually tried to kill herself, no."

"Well, if you had taken the time to read the doctor's report she had given you, you would have seen that she had."

Brooke saw red. "First of all, I am not a trained counsellor, Kim, something you seem to constantly forget. Doctors' reports and stuff like that were usually left to the counsellor on the show to go through. But, if you remember, we didn't have a counsellor working on the show at the time because Richard had walked off set the previous month, mainly because you had called him an ill-informed windbag. Actually if my memory serves me correct you said he blew more hot air than St George's dragon. Ring any bells?"

"That's beside the point. This doctor's report had come into your hands and you failed to spot she had tried to kill herself previously."

Brooke held her hands up. "I refuse to take responsibility for that. I was a researcher whose responsibility it was to garner the guest's story and point of view. Any medical was beyond my remit. But in actual fact, besides all that, I did strongly recommend she shouldn't appear on the show. You overruled me."

"Even if we had known she'd tried to kill herself, would it have stopped us from putting her on the show?" asked Joshua as he stared down at the table.

"Well, probably not, but I think everyone is missing the point here," said Kim in an exasperated voice. "This could have cost us the show. The fact that I discovered she had form with suicide might just, and I stress the word – *just* – save our bacon. Only for me scouring the file and spotting that fact, we'd have been hung out to dry, no questions asked."

"It would have come out in the inquest anyway," Brooke pointed out.

"It would have been too late by then. Joshua's career, mine and everyone else's on the show would be over. Maybe your new boyfriend might have found a new role for you producing dull documentaries, but the rest of us would be screwed!"

"We were understaffed," said Joshua. "I suppose what Brooke is saying is true. It shouldn't have all been left to her. We should have had a full-time counsellor dealing with a show like ours."

Brooke looked at him in surprise, and then gave him a grateful nod.

"Anyway, I've things to do if we want this *Tonight Show* guest presentation to be a success," said Brooke as she stood up and walked out.

"I don't know why you're bothering to defend her," said Kim. "After she pulled that stunt and showed up in France, putting you into such an awkward position."

"I said it because it's true. There's no point in trying to put all the blame on her."

"I wasn't trying to blame her. I was just trying to point out that oversights can cost careers."

"And lives." He looked at her pointedly, and then studied her intently. "Do you never feel guilty about things, Kim. About anything?"

"No, I don't. I think guilt is a waste of human emotion. What good does it do or achieve? What's done is done and over-analysing things that are past isn't going to change things."

"You really think that?"

"Yes. Everybody is responsible for themselves and only themselves. You aren't responsible for other people's actions or reactions. You just do what you have to do to get through."

"It sounds cold."

"It's not cold. I'm not cold in the least. I'm passionate, and temperamental and full of enthusiasm for life and I love what I do. If other people have a problem with that, it's not my fault. And it's not my problem. Cold? Someone like Guy Burton, now he's cold."

Joshua looked at her, shocked. "Guy's not cold. He's one of the nicest people I've ever met. He's so helpful. He was over at my house only last night trying to cheer me up. We owe him so much."

"We?"

"With him arranging me to guest-present *The Tonight Show*. Only for him, we'd be out on the street."

Kim's face creased in frustration "He –" She stopped herself from continuing as she thought about Jasmine sitting outside his office, in his domain, at his mercy.

"Just be careful, Joshua, okay?" she said, standing up. "I'd better get on. We've got a show to put together."

Brooke didn't move from her desk for the rest of the day, compiling lists of guests and seeing who might be available and, more importantly, who would be interested in appearing on the show.

"I've finally managed to get someone who works at Tom Cruise's agency on the line," Lee shouted over at her.

"Put them through!" demanded Brooke excitedly.

"Hello," said the deep American accent on the other end of the phone.

"Hi there!" Brooke said. "I'm just enquiring about whether Tom would like to appear on our new chat show here in Ireland."

"What's the details?"

"Well, it's for Joshua Green who is Ireland's chat-show king and he is guest-presenting Ireland's premier chat show next month. It's a live show."

"*Next month!* Are you for real? Do you know Mr Cruise's schedule for the next two years?"

"I'm sure it's unbelievable. But it would be a very quick interview."

The agent sighed loudly. "Give me the details anyway?"

"Details?"

"Expenses, travel costs etc."

"Oh, of course. Well, RTV would of course pay for Tom's flights and accommodation."

"Naturally. Expenses?"

"Expenses?"

"Let's talk dollars, pounds, euros."

"I see. And we could – would," she glanced down at the meagre budgets she had been handed, "provide him with, say, €500 expenses."

She heard a 'click' sound on the other send of the phone.

"Hello? . . . Hello?" she said, before realising the agent had hung up.

"Will he appear?" asked Lee excitedly.

"No, I don't think so," she sighed heavily. "Any luck getting me Madonna's agent on the phone?"

Brooke was still making calls to America at nine in the evening and everyone else had gone home.

Joshua came out of the lift and walked through the open-plan office, getting a start when he saw Brooke.

She looked up at him and felt very uncomfortable.

"Sorry – I'm looking for Lee. He wanted a lift home," said Joshua.

"You just missed him. He's headed down to the car park."

"Right." He hovered awkwardly. "Burning the candle at both ends?"

"Trying to get us a big star for the guest presentation."

"Any luck so far?"

"Unfortunately not with our budget. Em, thank you for sticking up for me today with Kim." She spoke coolly.

"No problem. She was being a bit irrational."

"Nothing new there."

He turned to go and then stopped and turned around. "I'm sorry too – for being so rude and aggressive in France."

"Soraya put you up to saying that?"

"No . . . I was out of order."

"Yes, you were."

"I just got a terrible shock when you arrived in with Guy."

She sighed and sat back. "I guess that was very out of order of me. I'm sorry too I did that. I was just angry with the way you had treated me and wanted to show you that I could not be dismissed."

"Well, you certainly showed that!" He smiled at her. He held out his hand. "Friends?"

She viewed his hand. "No, not friends . . . but work colleagues." She shook his hand tightly and smiled cautiously at him.

He nodded at her and walked out.

She waited until the lift doors closed and then picked up the phone and dialled Los Angeles again.

51

Brooke had spent days trying to build up a guest list for the show, but was finding it very difficult.

"Why is our budget so small?" she demanded of Guy.

"The station's on its uppers last checked," he pointed out.

"I know but this is *The Tonight Show* – it's the station's flagship programme."

"Yes, but it's only a trial run, and they never get big budgets."

"But it's live!"

"Look, it's a test drive for Joshua, no more. If he passes and is awarded *The Tonight Show* then he'll get a normal budget."

"But how are we supposed to produce a good show on this lousy budget?"

"Welcome to the world of being a producer!"

She felt nervous going to the next meeting. She had not secured any major-league name. In fact she hadn't even secured a flicker of interest.

Kim looked at Brooke as the production team gathered. "Who have you got for me?"

"I have Audrey Driver interested in appearing on the show," said Brooke.

"Of course she is, she'll do anything to promote that model agency of hers. Every time you turn on the television she's there promoting herself. She's hardly out of the ordinary. I'll pass. Next?"

"Cathal Fitzgerald said he'll make an appearance."

"He's so 2006. All he'll want to do is promote whatever new band he's just signed. Forget it. Who else?"

"Fiona Fallon said she'll do it."

"Oh please!" begged Kim in despair.

"Fiona's always good for ratings," said Joshua. "Amusing, attractive –"

"Oh come on, if we have to rely on her jaded old tits for our show, then we're well and truly fucked!"

"I'm not saying for our main attraction. I'm saying for a second guest."

"So who is our main attraction going to be? That's what I want to know."

"We don't have the budget for anyone major league." Brooke said it as it was.

Kim closed her eyes and tapped her long red fingernails on the table. "Isn't it funny, Brooke, that you can only deliver excuses and never results? It was the same when I asked for better guests for the confessional show. Maybe you should ask yourself are you really cut out for this business."

"Oh for fuck's sake!" snapped Brooke as she stood up abruptly. "Why don't you try and get somebody your bloody self!" She turned and headed back to her desk.

She sat down in frustration. She was so sick of it all now, she could just walk out. Then she glanced down at the newspaper on her desk and saw a photo of Ricardo Martinez arriving at Dublin Airport with a load of screaming fans waiting for him. She picked up the paper and read that he was playing the O2 over the next three nights.

Ricardo Martinez was an international singing star who, with a clever mix of Latin and pop, had produced hit after hit over the past ten years. Still only in his thirties he was one of the biggest singing sensations around. She picked up the phone and rang a friend of hers in the PR department.

"Stella, it's Brooke."

"Hello there! How's it going with the guest-presentation?"

"Fine, working hard at it . . . I just wanted to ask you . . .

you didn't get any tickets to the Ricardo Martinez concert, did you?"

"I never had you down as a Ricardo Martinez fan!"

"Oh, I love him, he's so hot!" said Brooke, studying the photo of his chiselled Latino face in the paper. "I just love his new song . . ." she squinted as she read the title from the newspaper article, "'Baby, I Love Your Moves'."

"You want some tickets to the concert, I presume," said Stella.

Brooke knew the music promoters always sent concert tickets in to the PR department to keep them onside. She also knew they sent invitations to the after-parties of the concerts, which was what she wanted to get hold of.

"Well, actually I wanted to go to the after-party as well," pushed Brooke.

"But I've only got two tickets for that. I'm going and I promised I'd bring Sorcha in marketing."

"Please don't! Please bring me instead!" Brooke begged down the phone.

"Brooke! I never had you down as a groupie!"

"You'd make my year!"

Stella sighed. "I'll ask Sorcha does she mind and, if she doesn't, I'll take you instead."

52

The day of the concert Brooke slipped out from RTV in the early afternoon for a manicure and a visit to the hairdressser's. Then, back at RTV, she got one of the make-up artists to do her face. That evening she put on the cream dress Guy had bought her in Cannes, which complemented her French tan. She had to look as well as possible to try and get two minutes with Ricardo at the after-party. Looking anxiously in the mirror, she figured she might just manage to capture his attention for the required time.

Brooke collected Stella in a taxi and the two of them headed to the O2.

After they found their seats, Brooke sat through forty-five minutes of a support act she'd never heard of, before Ricardo Martinez came bounding on to the stage, all leather trousers, white T-shirt and super-fit moves. The crowd went wild and Brooke nearly had to cover her ears. She didn't like concerts as a rule – they made her feel claustrophobic and she always had an irrational fear the crowd would get so excited they would lose control and go stampeding over her en route to their idol. She would be left hoofed-over on the floor, a sacrifice to their adulation.

Stella seemed to be getting into the swing of things, dancing with the rest of the audience as Ricardo gyrated through his repertoire of hits over the next two hours.

"I thought you were his biggest fan ever!" said Stella as she looked at Brooke who hadn't got up from her seat once and looked as if she was barely tolerating the concert.

"I am. Loving every minute of it!" Brooke smiled brightly at her and gave her the thumbs-up.

Afterwards they managed to get a taxi and headed straight to Lillie's Bordello to the after-party.

"Seemingly, Lillie's is going to play his music on the system all night during the party as well," said Stella.

"Brilliant!" Brooke smiled falsely.

As the music blared, Brooke and Stella manoeuvred through the crowd in Lillie's, clutching their drinks as they vied for a glimpse of Ricardo.

"There he is!" squealed Stella as she spotted him and pointed. Ricardo was on a couch surrounded by security, management and pretty girls.

"Seemingly he always circulates and chats to people at the after-parties. I hope I don't faint!" sighed Stella.

"Hmm, me too," said Brooke as she scrutinised him. As he chatted amicably to the people beside him, he was scouring the crowd at the same time.

Brooke had done her research on him and chatted to some people in the know. Despite his Polish champion-skier girlfriend, Ricardo liked nothing better than a discreet night of fun with a girl when touring. Even though it was an open secret nothing had ever been confirmed in the press – a case of what goes on tour stays on tour. When Ricardo went on a scout around the club for his pick-up for the night, which apparently he always did, Brooke aimed to grab the opportunity and ask him if he would appear on the show. She would speak quickly and confidently and try to interest him in the show. If he didn't bite there and then, she would force her card on him and beg him to ring the next day to arrange the interview. It was worth a shot. It was the only chance she had to get near a star of his calibre.

The night whiled on and Brooke and Stella sat at the bar drinking wine and keeping one eye on the star.

"It would be impossible to get through that security and talk to him," said Brooke.

"You *really* are a big fan!" laughed Stella.

"You'd better believe it . . . watch out, he's standing up!"

They watched as Ricardo walked around the club chatting to people.

"He's coming this way!" squealed Stella.

"Come on then," urged Brooke as she jumped down off her stool and hurried over to the dance floor which was the direction Ricardo was heading.

Ricardo strolled on to the dance floor and started dancing slowly to one of his own songs. He was immediately surrounded by women trying to attract him with their best moves.

"Right, here's my opportunity," said Brooke as she walked on to the dance floor and headed in his direction.

"What are you *doing*?" cried Stella in shock after her as she watched Brooke elbowing away the opposition and managing to position herself right in front of Ricardo.

"*No shame!*" spat a gobsmacked Stella as she saw Brooke dancing as closely as she could to the star, short of wrapping herself around him.

"Mr Martinez, if I can introduce myself, my name is Brooke Radcliffe!" Brooke shouted over the music as she tried to imitate Ricardo's dance movements.

"It is nice to meet you!" Ricardo used his best seductive smile on her.

"I work at RTV and I'm a producer on a television programme."

"You are a good dancer!" complimented Ricardo as he moved even closer to her.

"Yes, anyway, I've been a huge fan of yours, well, for years!"

"You like me?" asked Ricardo as his seductive smile grew wider.

"Very much so. Huge fan. Bought all your CDs. My favourite song is 'Baby, I Love Your Moves'."

He studied her long chestnut hair and pretty face. "That is good," he said, "because, baby, *I* like *your* moves!"

"Yes, anyway, the thing is I'm trying to put together a show."

"I can't hear you. Let's go somewhere quieter to talk."

"Yes, I'd like that!" Brooke nodded her head enthusiastically, not believing her luck that she had got his attention long enough to maybe sell the show to him.

She followed him over to the couch he had been sitting on. Ricardo had a word with his tour manager and clicked his fingers. Before Brooke knew what was happening his whole entourage was marching towards the exit, her in the middle of them, following Ricardo.

She spotted a stunned Stella, still standing at the edge of the dance floor, who mouthed over the word *"Hussy!"* at her.

Not quite sure what was happening, Brooke followed the entourage down the stairs and out on to the street.

"Ricardo! Ricardo! If I could just continue that conversation with you!" she said as she stood in the street beside him, trying to get his attention and frightened he had forgotten her.

A limousine pulled up beside them and the back door was opened.

"Come on!" said Ricardo as he stepped into the back.

For a moment Brooke wondered if it was a good idea getting into a limousine with Ricardo Martinez. But, as she thought of the show and her determination to show Kim what she could do, she jumped in beside him.

The door was shut and she turned and looked around the back of the limo. It was luxurious to the point of being crass, complete with a bottle of champagne opened and two glasses. The car moved off.

Brooke was ecstatic. Having spent a week only getting through as far as the reception of the agencies of most major stars, she could hardly believe her luck to have Ricardo Martinez' undivided attention.

"Champagne?" he asked, filling two glasses.

"No, I'd better not. It's a school night!" she laughed nervously.

He just looked at her with a cynical look and handed her the glass.

"School night? So you are a teacher?" he asked, clinking her glass.

"What? No! As I was saying to you in the club, I am –"

"What is your name?"

"Brooke – Brooke Radcliffe, and I work at –"

"That is a very pretty name."

"Thank you."

"For a very pretty woman."

Brooke cringed.

"Has anyone ever told you look like Cheryl Cole?"

"Yes, recently," she said, wondering if she should ditch this hairstyle and go back to her normal image.

"So what do you teach?" he asked, smiling at her.

"No – I don't teach. But it is work I want to talk to you about."

Before she could continue, the car had pulled up outside the Merrion Hotel and a doorman opened her door.

"Madam," said the doorman.

She stepped out, wondering how she could make herself clear to Ricardo. There was definitely a lost-in-translation situation going on. She followed him through the hotel entrance and the hushed opulence of the hotel.

"Are we going to the bar?" she asked as his entourage disappeared and it was just the two of them in the lift.

"Yes – my bar," he said and the lift door opened.

She followed him down the corridor to a double door where there was a security man stationed. The man opened the door for them and Ricardo marched straight into the suite. She waited at the door, beginning to realise they were on totally different planets of understanding. She considered turning and getting out of there. But, as she thought of all those phones hung up on her, she marched in and the doorman closed the door behind her.

She looked around the sumptuous suite.

"Champagne?" Ricardo asked, smiling, as he poured two more glasses from another waiting bottle resting in another silver bucket.

"Oh – why not?" she sighed as she flopped unsexily down on a couch and quickly did a reality check.

He handed her a glass and chinked his glass against hers.

"You have most beautiful hair I have ever seen," he said as he began to stroke her hair.

"That's actually a hair extension you're stroking," she advised.

"'Scuse?"

"It doesn't matter."

"And your eyes. Eyes of brown, like pools of –"

"Ricardo! Mr Martinez . . ." She took his hand that was now caressing her face and gently pushed it away. "I'm afraid I've come here under false pretences. You see, I don't fancy you."

"I don't understand." Ricardo's face became a mask of confusion. "You don't like Ricardo?" He was incredulous.

"Well, no. Well, I mean, of course you're totally gorgeous. You're Ricardo Martinez, let's face it. But I have a boyfriend."

Ricardo visibly relaxed. "This is okay! I too have a girlfriend!" He went to kiss her.

She pulled back and gently pushed him away. "I'm sorry, Ricardo, I haven't come here for that. I'm actually not even a fan of yours, if the truth be known."

"What?" Ricardo jumped back in shock.

"I just wanted to have a chat with you about something."

Ricardo's face clouded with worry. "You a journalist?"

"No, honestly, it's nothing like that. If you'd just listen for a minute – I'm a producer and we have a new chat show airing next month and I want you to appear on the show." She looked at him hopefully.

"This is a crazy situation. I thought you came here for to fuck!"

"No, I came for a booking, on our show."

He stood up and backed away from her. "Why did you not contact my agent, like normal?"

"Because he would just hang up on me."

"So you come here and pretend you like me!"

"Well, I didn't actually say I liked you at all. I just said I wanted to talk to you and you misunderstood me," she quickly defended herself.

He viewed her suspiciously. "So what is this show you want Ricardo to appear on?"

"It's a guest presentation show for Joshua Green, who is one of the country's best-known chat-show kings. And exposure on this show would bring you an audience –" She stopped as she realised she had lost his interest already. She sat back and sighed. "The reality is we need you, because if we don't get a star of your calibre we're all fucked. Well, Joshua is. I think at this stage, as far as my own career is concerned, I'd be better off jumping ship at this stage. You see, being associated with Joshua and his show might tarnish me after what's been happening – he's being blamed for the fact that a guest on his former talk show committed suicide after. But she had suicidal tendencies anyway and it wasn't really his fault." She wondered how much of all this Ricardo was following, especially with his limited English. But in any case she had his attention and that was all that mattered. "And now I actually have the opportunity to move on myself if I push Guy to help me – he's my boyfriend who is our Director of Programmes. But I can't. Joshua probably deserves all the shit he's getting at the moment, but I can't walk out on him and the team in their hour of need. I've never been very clever with things like that. My heart rules my head, unfortunately."

Ricardo sat back down on the couch and looked at her. He should really call security and have this strange girl kicked out. But he wasn't used to somebody being as disinterested in him as she was. He couldn't remember the last time he was with somebody who wasn't staring at him, and treating him as if he came from another planet. He couldn't remember the last time somebody just treated him as normal.

"Your heart rules? So you are in love with this Joshua?" asked Ricardo.

"No . . . well, actually yes I was, if the truth be told. I guess I was kind of in love with him and I hadn't even admitted it to myself. Why else would I have showed up on his holiday with his wife and children?" she sighed.

"*Wife and children!*" exclaimed Ricardo.

"I know, don't judge me, Ricardo, I'm having a hard enough time judging myself." She reached into her bag and took out her cigarettes. "Do you mind if I smoke?"

"Eh – no, I guess," he shrugged.

"Do you want one?" she held out the packet.

"No, I'm not allowed them."

"Oh go on, I won't tell anybody," she pushed.

He slowly took a cigarette from her and she lit both cigarettes.

"Yep, he was married," she said, drawing from her cigarette and wondering why on earth she was rattling on like this about personal stuff. The truth was, she was afraid to stop now that she had his attention. "I shouldn't be telling you all this, Ricardo, but let's face it – you're not going to reveal this to anybody, are you?"

"So the affair is still on?" asked Ricardo.

"It's over. And I'm now with a lovely man who is everything I ever dreamed of. So there's no need for me to be jealous or angry about Joshua any more, is there?"

"Maybe not."

"I always think we only get bitter about past relationships if we're not happy where we are in life now, don't you think?"

He sighed and drew on his cigarette. "Perhaps."

"And I've never been happier, Ricardo. But still, I did love Joshua, and I feel really sorry for him at the moment – he looks a bit broken. And it doesn't suit him. And so I'm going to do everything I can to make his new show a success so he can get back to being the arrogant bastard we all love to hate." She swooped in for the kill. "And that's where you come in, Ricardo. You appearing on the show would pull in a huge audience. You know how popular you are. And then there's Soraya, his wife. I feel guilty and if I could get Joshua back on course it would be atoning for what I did. When we were on holiday, all they did was argue. I'd like to see them back the way they were."

"Most mistresses try to break up a marriage but you try and fix one, no? You have strange morals."

"I know . . . Will you help?"

"Look, I'd like to help but I will probably be touring at that time."

"I only ask that *if* you have nothing on you'll fly to Dublin for the show. We'll fly you, though not by private plane or anything. Your whole life is interviews and flights and publicity – I'm just begging you to squeeze us into your schedule."

He sighed long and hard. "I will ask my manager tomorrow, but I can't promise anything."

"Oh thank you, Ricardo!" She leaned forward and kissed his cheek.

He continued to look at her, perplexed. It was the first conversation he'd had for ages that wasn't about him.

53

Brooke picked up the ringing phone on her desk.

"They always say it's the quiet ones!" said Stella from PR down the phone at her.

"Stella, I can explain."

"Don't even bother. I heard a rumour that you were going out with Guy Burton?"

"I am."

"Well, you've a funny way of showing it! Running off with, wait for it, *Ricardo Martinez,* like that!"

"I just needed to talk to him, that's all."

"You really weren't bullshitting me when you said you were a fan of his, were you? I've never seen anything like it! Most people would be happy with an autograph, but not you! You practically threw your knickers at him!"

"It wasn't like that at all!"

"I wouldn't believe it only I saw it for myself. Do me a favour, next time somebody you're a fan of plays in Dublin, don't ring me to get tickets to go to the after-show party! I'm not comfortable in the role of pimp, you – you groupie!" Stella hung up the phone.

Brooke waited anxiously for the rest of the day for some word from Ricardo's agent as promised. When five thirty came and she had heard nothing she admitted to herself she was grasping at straws and they would not get back in contact.

Then she saw an email come in from Ricardo's management company.

Not bothering to knock, Brooke walked straight into Kim's office.

Kim, who was on the phone, looked up in anger.

"Will you get the fuck out of here? Can't you see I'm on the phone?"

Brooke reached over, took the receiver out of Kim's hand and replaced it.

Kim saw red. "Have you lost your mind? That was Henry King you just hung up on!"

Brooke triumphantly put the email from Ricardo's agent in front of her.

"Ricardo Martinez has agreed to appear on our *Tonight Show*. Is that a big enough star for you?"

She savoured Kim's reaction as she picked up the email and read it.

Then she turned and walked out, smiling smugly.

The next three weeks flew by as the team busily prepared for the guest presentation and pulled the show together. Everyone worked all hours trying to get detail correct. Everything had to be decided from the set design to the format to what Joshua would wear. Often it was just Kim, Brooke and Joshua working late into the night after everyone else had gone home.

It was like Joshua and Brooke were seeing each other with new eyes. Previously he had been the star and she the assistant. Then they had been lovers, which had moved on to them becoming enemies after the break-up. Now they were just work colleagues, both unsure and nervous of the future, which allowed them to just be themselves. For the first time Joshua took the time to get to know the real Brooke. He had to admit that in the past he knew she was in awe of him, and he had been happy to bask in that awe without taking the time to see what she thought about things. Now he realised how quick-witted, bright and innovative she was, and how lucky he was to have her working on his show. Brooke stopped seeing Joshua as the big star and treated him accordingly. She had seen him in his natural habitat with his family in France and realised his life was not some kind of *Privilege* magazine perfection but the same as everyone else's. And once he dropped the star act, and he seemed to have totally dropped it since France, he was warm, witty and even self-deprecating.

"So much rests on this show," warned Kim for the umpteenth time. "Not only our fortunes but the fortunes of RTV rest on your shoulders, Joshua."

"No pressure then!" said Joshua, winking over at Brooke. "We're all fucked in that case, if you're relying on me!"

Since Brooke had landed Ricardo Martinez, Kim had had a grudging respect for her that she was careful not to reveal. She wondered time and again how she had managed to land him. Brooke now answered Kim back regularly when she criticised her which also forced Kim to respect her position. She was refusing to be pushed around any more and gave Kim as good as she got.

After one blazing row between Kim and Brooke one night over the sequence of guests, Kim even had to admit eventually that Brooke was right.

"Impact, impact, impact!" Kim had raged. "Put the main guest Ricardo on first and knock the audience for six!"

"If you do that you're risking losing them once Ricardo has been interviewed," Brooke had insisted. "They might turn over once they've seen him. Put him on last and you're guaranteed the audience throughout the show."

Kim had eventually agreed with the format. Brooke was amazed Kim had conceded.

"I knew some of my brilliance would eventually rub off on you," stated Kim as she walked off.

One night back at Guy's, Brooke was stuffing herself with a Chinese takeaway as she spoke excitedly about the show.

"So it looks like you'll have to prepare a new contract for Joshua if his guest-hosting *The Tonight Show* comes off as well as I believe it will."

"We'll see."

He was as amazed as everyone else that she had managed to secure Ricardo Martinez.

"And Fiona Fallon has agreed to discuss the affair she had with that politician all those years ago," she went on. "That's an exclusive! You know how many times she has refused to discuss that affair in the past!"

Guy rolled his eyes. "I was wondering how long it would take until the traditional Joshua Green ethos would rear its ugly head on the new show."

"What do you mean?"

"It's what Joshua deals in. Scandal, affairs, sordid laundry being washed in public. It's just now he'll be dealing with stars' dirty laundry instead of poor unfortunates like Donna Doyle."

"Well, it is what audiences want, be it a good thing or bad! If Fiona Fallon came on and just discussed the weather, it wouldn't secure a big audience, would it?"

"You've definitely been hanging around Kim Davenport for too long!" He looked disapprovingly at her.

"I just want the show to be a success, that's all," she shrugged.

"But why?" he asked, perplexed.

"I don't understand?"

"Why do you want it to be a success? For Joshua Green and Kim Davenport to get all the credit and make their stars shine brighter?"

"I am a producer on the show as well," she pointed out.

"No thanks to them! Can I remind you how they treated you. She did everything in her power to get rid of you, and he treated you like an unpaid call girl!"

"He did not!" she snapped.

"Well, he didn't treat you well, let's face it. You are nothing to those people but an employee, a servant to run around and get them their lunch. You saved their bacon by getting Ricardo Martinez, but once they are up and running with that show you'll go back to being their skivvy. They are using you, and you can't even see it."

He stood up, gathered the empty plates and took them into the kitchen.

In the following days Brooke thought about what Guy had said. She felt he was wrong, that she wasn't being used, she was just doing her job. However, she knew there was some truth in what he was saying. All Joshua and Kim cared about was themselves and she was irrelevant. But she couldn't think along those lines too much or she would never further herself. She was riding their coat-tails, as much as she disliked them.

She was at her desk working away when she got a call. She saw the extension number was Martha in Accounts who she sometimes had a coffee with in the canteen.

"Hi there! And no I didn't sleep with Ricardo Martinez before you ask!"

Stella from PR was spreading the untruth around about her and Brooke was not impressed.

"It's not that," said Martha. "It's the Joshua website. Have you seen what they've put on it?"

Brooke got a feeling of dread in her stomach. She was hating this website and was just hoping there wouldn't be anything damaging before the guest presentation. She clicked on the website and saw there was a video link you could tap into. She pressed it and a second later a video of Joshua's studio came up on screen. She peered at it, trying to make out what was going on. She recognised herself, Lee and Joshua. Joshua was going mad – shouting and grabbing hold of Lee's arm. Brooke put her hand over her mouth as she realised it was footage from the day Lee had started work at RTV and Joshua had gone berserk.

Kim was over at Joshua and Soraya's looking at the video of Joshua on the website.

"Joshua!" Soraya was angry. "You look like a madman. You completely flipped your lid."

"You certainly won't win any Father of the Year awards with that little performance," said Kim, switching off the screen.

Joshua's face was buried in his hands.

"What was I doing? Lee isn't going to like this."

"How was it done?" asked Soraya.

"Somebody videoed with their mobile phone," said Kim.

"So it was somebody who was in the studio that day who is behind the website?" asked Soraya.

"Not necessarily. Again, the footage could have been sent to thousands of phones," said Kim.

"No, it was somebody there in the studio!" said Joshua. "I've always known it was somebody at RTV who is behind this campaign!"

"Who then?" said Kim as she thought and suddenly she looked up in surprise. "Donna Doyle and her brother were in the studio that day. I remember it because I was talking to them when I saw Lee."

Joshua stood up. "They also knew about there being no counselling. They are insiders on the show. And Aidan Doyle is very angry. He blames the show. He blames us for what happened to Donna."

"I bet if we check back the campaign started around the time they first were guests," said Kim. She began to nod her head in realisation. "I doubt Donna was behind this. She was too desperate to appear on the show. But Aidan was against us from the start. Even when we called over to the house he was using language that is used on the website. – not caring, exploiting guests for our ratings. I'm afraid it's Aidan Doyle behind all this."

Joshua sat in his car across from the Doyles' house. There had been people coming and going all evening but no sign of Aidan Doyle. Finally around ten in the evening the front door opened and Aidan Doyle came out and started walking down the street. Joshua got out of this car and followed him, finally catching up with him in a neighbouring street.

"Aidan!" Joshua called.

Aidan turned around and got a start to see Joshua. His face clouded over menacingly. "What the fuck do you want here?"

"I just want a word with you."

"You've done enough damage. Now fuck off back to your ivory tower and leave us alone."

Aidan turned to leave but Joshua reached out and grabbed his arm, turning him back around.

"Aidan, it's you behind the website, isn't it?"

Aidan looked at him, confused. "What the fuck are you talking about?"

"The website that was set up against me. I know you did it."

"You're on drugs – now fuck off!"

"Look, I feel terrible about what happened to Donna. If I could turn back time I'd never allow her on the show. None of us would. We didn't realise how sick she was."

"You're the sick ones, exploiting her!"

"You see that's it. That's what been said on the website. I know it's you. The campaign started just after the first time you appeared on my show. You knew there was no counsellor on the show and exposed that. You knew my son Lee was starting work on the show because you were there his first day. And then you used your phone to record me going mad at him. You blame us for what happened to your sister and you're out to get revenge. It has to be you."

Aidan studied him intently. "Well, I'm delighted it's got to you. You might just know a fraction now of how it feels to be exposed publicly."

Joshua sighed in relief. "So it was you all along."

"Yeah – why not?" Aidan said.

"It's not just me being affected by this campaign. My wife and my family are being hurt too."

"Good," said Aidan.

"I understand the pain you're going through about Donna so I'm not going to threaten legal action or anything. But I am pleading with you to stop."

"Do whatever the fuck you like," sneered Aidan and he walked off.

"So he admitted it," sighed Soraya.

"Yeah. It was just his way of getting back about what happened to his sister."

"I feel sorry for him. But let's hope he stops it now and that's the end of it," she said.

"I think he'll drop it now. I think now he's exposed it won't have the same kick for him any more."

54

It was the Saturday that Joshua's *Tonight Show* was due to air and the production team were in the studio with everyone rushing around getting things ready for the evening.

Brooke walked in, talking on her mobile, and then hung up.

"That was Ricardo Martinez' assistant – they just arrived in to Dublin Airport and are en route to the Merrion Hotel."

Kim was on the stage, standing beside two chairs, one which was empty and the other occupied by Joshua.

"Have you arranged a car to pick him up in time to bring him over?" asked Kim.

"Done," confirmed Brooke as she stepped up on the stage as well.

"I wish this show wasn't going out live," said Joshua, looking very worried.

Kim sighed. They had been through all this before. "They're considering you for a *live* show! *The Tonight Show* is a *live show*!" She grabbed his chin and looked him in the eye. "I want to hear no negativity today, do you hear me? You're going to do this show and you're going to do it excellently, do you hear me?"

Joshua smiled and nodded.

"Hello, everybody," said Soraya as she walked on to the set, accompanied by Ulrika and the children. "They wanted to wish their daddy good luck for tonight!"

Joshua gave her a hug and picked Danielle up.

At the top of the studio Guy was sitting unnoticed, watching it all.

The VIP room in RTV was upstairs behind the studio. It was here that the guests on a chat show and their entourage waited. It was a long lounge with a giant screen on a wall where the guests could watch the show as it was being filmed. A hostess was there behind the small bar, monitoring that everyone's glass was full.

Soraya had dropped the children and Ulrika at the house, changed into evening wear and headed back to RTV. She arrived into the VIP lounge to find Brooke there, dealing with the guests.

"How's it all looking?" she asked Brooke when she got a chance.

"We're all on tenterhooks, but so far so good," said Brooke.

"Between ourselves, Joshua is terrified," murmured Soraya. "Terrified he'll fuck the whole thing up live in front of the nation."

That's what we're all terrified of, thought Brooke.

Fiona Fallon, looking her normal glamorous self, came over to Soraya.

"I'm not sure I'm doing the right thing at all," said Fiona. "Agreeing to discuss that affair I had. It was years ago, and I've regretted it ever since."

It had been in the papers that day that Fiona was going to reveal all the details of the affair with the politician.

"My phone's been hopping all day with the media asking is it true."

"Well, you obviously think it's the right time to discuss it, Fiona, or you wouldn't have agreed to," Soraya pointed out.

"Right time, my ass! The ratings on my soap are dropping quicker than girls at a Ricardo Martinez concert. My agent said I had to go on a PR offensive to try and revive interest in me and the show. He thought a lurid account of my affair would do the business. It's a shocking life an actress has to endure, Soraya." Fiona shook her head in bewilderment. "Seemingly Mr Guy Burton wants to axe my soap and replace it with a costume drama that he hopes to sell on to the States. I mean, can you see me in period drama, Soraya?"

It would be hard to place her overly glamorous botoxed features in any period of history, thought Soraya.

"Well, then, it's not just our futures that rely on tonight being a success, it's your too," said Soraya.

The door of the VIP lounge opened and in walked Ricardo Martinez with his agent, stylist, secretary, PA, and publicist.

"And the circus has just hit town," said Fiona.

Joshua circulated around the VIP lounge, chatting to the guests. It was just an ice-breaker so the guests would feel relaxed with him. But it was also designed to make him feel more relaxed as well. He spent a while chatting to Ricardo and then headed over to Fiona who was still with Soraya.

"Now, you're to go easy on me tonight, Joshua Green," warned Fiona. "None of that shouting stuff you're known for."

"It will be a totally different approach, Fiona, I assure you."

"Thankfully. I'll be telling you things tonight I wouldn't even have told my diary before. I was always saw that affair as my pension plan – terrible I have to cash it in before its time just to garner a bit of publicity," she moaned.

Joshua leaned forward and spoke quietly. "To be honest, it's you everyone wants to hear tonight, not Ricardo Martinez."

"Really?"

"Of course. Everyone's been dying to find out what went on between you and that politician for years. What's a Latino super-star in comparison to real live gossip?"

Guy Burton walked into the room and looked around.

"That's all I need!" said Fiona. "Every time I see that man I know what Marie Antoinette must have felt like when she met the man who pulled the lever on the guillotine!"

Guy came smiling over to them. "How're we all doing?"

"So far so good," said Joshua.

Fiona viewed Guy coldly.

"Fiona," he nodded at her.

Kim came in and came straight over to them.

"Okay, Joshua, we need you downstairs now," she said in an

urgent and commanding way. "Fiona, you are the first guest on, so let's get you down and wired up."

Fiona got up and followed Kim out.

"This is it then," said Joshua to Soraya and Guy.

"Good luck, pal," Guy nodded to him.

Soraya and Joshua hugged each other for a long while, as Guy looked on.

"Joshua!" demanded Kim from the doorway.

Soraya kissed him and whispered, "Good luck."

Joshua then left the room.

"Do you mind if I watch the programme with you, Soraya?" asked Guy.

"I'd love that," smiled Soraya as they both sat down.

Half an hour later a hush fell instantly on the VIP room as the screen on the wall came to life and the music and credits to the show began to play.

On the screen Joshua came walking onto the stage as the audience began to applaud enthusiastically. As he began to talk and introduce the show, Soraya became nervous and grabbed Guy's hand. She squeezed it tightly before letting it go.

He looked at her curiously before concentrating on the show again.

He tried to look at the show objectively, which was difficult to do when Soraya kept grabbing him to calm her nerves. To his surprise, Joshua proved to be relaxed and in control. He conducted the Fiona Fallon interview with aplomb and professionalism, extracting enough details of her affair to titillate but handling the issue with sensitivity. The sportsman who followed her was similarly interviewed without fault. A well-known up-and-coming band were the music interval and Joshua chatted away to them after they had sung. Joshua then went around the audience having brief and amusing chats with them. And then Ricardo Martinez was introduced and Joshua finished off the show with an insightful and unusually deep interview with the normally over-polished star.

"What do you think?" asked Soraya nervously as the end credits began to roll.

"Eh – not bad," said Guy. "Not bad at all."

When Joshua and the rest of the production team came into the VIP lounge later, everyone began to clap and cheer loudly.

Brooke came over to Guy, smiling. "Well, that's a relief! All went without any major glitches!" She took a drink from the circulating hostess.

"Yes, it went smoothly enough," agreed Guy.

"What do you think then?" she asked impatiently. "Was it good enough to secure him the regular *Tonight Show*?"

"I don't know, Brooke. We'll have to see what the ratings were like and what the reviewers thought and audience feedback. These decisions aren't solely in my hands, unfortunately."

"I know," acknowledged Brooke, irritated he wasn't being more enthusiastic.

They looked over at Joshua and Soraya who had their arms around each other and were smiling broadly as people kept coming up and congratulating them.

"See, nobody's coming up to you and congratulating you, even though you did most of it," Guy pointed out.

"I don't care. I know I did a great job. And I'm genuinely happy for Joshua and Soraya. They seem back to normal."

"Until the next little tart comes along," said Guy.

Brooke looked at Guy, startled.

Lee came up to them. "Ricardo is leaving. He's asking for you, Brooke."

Brooke put her drink down, glancing at Guy unhappily before she followed Lee over to Ricardo.

As Guy continued to watch Joshua and Soraya, Kim walked up beside him.

"I was just on the phone to Henry King who was watching the show from home. He's delighted with how it went. He said he hadn't believed Joshua could pull it off, but he did. Said he sees Joshua in a whole new light!" She smiled triumphantly at him and then leaned close to him. "So whatever game you're playing with him, you might as well drop it now."

55

It was Sunday morning and Kim sat at the island in the kitchen of the Greens' home with the Sunday papers laid out in front of her. Joshua was cooking breakfast for them all while Soraya played with the children.

"Listen to this review," said Kim. "*Talk Show host Joshua Green displayed a whole new range of hidden talent when he guest-presented The Tonight Show. Viewers might be forgiven for expecting the usual rowdy and disrespectful approach from Green, so famous with his regular show. Instead we were treated to intelligent and probing interviews where the emphasis was on making the guests feel relaxed enough to confide in their host and, through him, the audience. There are rumours that Green will now go on to take over RTV's flagship Tonight Show. From last night's performance, it will be in safe hands with Green.*' What a review!"

"I'm thrilled," said Joshua as he served up the fry on plates.

"This paper here calls you a force to be reckoned with. While this one calls you multi-talented."

She went and sat at the kitchen table with Soraya as he handed out the plates.

"I'll just go and get Lee," said Joshua as he headed upstairs.

"It's all such a huge relief after everything that's been happening," said Soraya as she bounced one of the children on her knee. "I honestly thought it was over for him after Donna Doyle died. I didn't think he would come back from the controversy. And what's more, he didn't seem as if he wanted to. It was all looking so bleak. But hopefully this is a new beginning for us all."

"Well, let's hope so. We're meeting Henry King and Guy Burton this week to discuss Joshua taking over *The Tonight Show*."

That night Soraya and Joshua lay in bed.

"Soraya – I really want to thank you for everything. You keep us all together. You keep me together. I don't know what I'd do without you. I was a mess before I met you, and I'd go back to being a mess again."

"Well, you're not going to lose me," she said, hugging him tightly.

56

Joshua was in Kim's office prior to their meeting with Guy and Henry King.

"The ratings have come in. Your guest presentation show was the second highest rating last week!" Kim said delightedly.

"I can't believe it." He shook his head in astonishment.

"This guarantees you *The Tonight Show*. It guarantees *us* it!" She smiled happily. "This meeting with Henry and Burton is just a formality. They'll say they're interested in us for *The Tonight Show*. We'll say we're interested back. Your agent will then hammer out the deal. The whole team will be going to *The Tonight Show* with us, that's one stipulation." Kim looked out the window wall of her office at Brooke who was busy speaking on the phone. "Unless you don't want Brooke to come as well? This is a good opportunity to send her on her way. I'm sure Guy will find his new girlfriend a wonderful new job in production."

Joshua sighed. "Well, she hasn't said she wants to leave us, has she?"

"No."

"And she worked like a Trojan to make the guest presentation a success. I mean, if it wasn't for her we would never have got Ricardo Martinez."

Kim was tempted but thought better about disclosing to Joshua that there was a strong rumour circulating RTV that Brooke had slept with Martinez to secure him for the show. As far as Kim was concerned, she wouldn't put anything past Brooke Radcliffe any more. She would still prefer her away from her production team, but was willing to get on with it.

"It's up to you, Joshua. I actually can't fault the work she's been doing recently. So if you're comfortable with her working on the new show, it's your call."

"Yeah, we're both mature enough to put what happened between us in the past and forget about it. It was a massive mistake on my part, and I'm glad to pretend it never happened."

"At least you're seeing sense at last. Come on, the powers that be await us."

Brooke walked with a spring in her step down the corridor to get a coffee from the machine. As she put change into the machine a couple of men walked past her, looking at her furtively. She stared after them, wondering what their problem was.

The same thing happened later when she popped down to reception to collect a parcel. The girls on reception gave her funny looks and she heard them giggling as she walked off.

"If you take a seat, Guy will be with you shortly," said Jasmine from her desk to Kim and Joshua as they arrived into Guy's reception.

Jasmine and Kim were being very cautious with each other since she took up Guy's offer. They were being polite but distant with each other, their closeness temporarily suspended. It drove Kim crazy to think of her daughter being close to Guy. But she was backing off in case her disapproval pushed Jasmine further away.

"Busy?" asked Kim politely as Jasmine slowly typed on her computer.

"Very," said Jasmine with defiance. "I'm finding the work stimulating."

"Hmmm," Kim nodded.

The phone rang on Jasmine's desk and she picked it up. "Guy Burton's office," she answered aloofly before her face went red in embarrassment. "Oh sorry, Guy, I didn't see it was your line ringing me . . . Will do." She hung up the phone, turned to Kim and Joshua and spoke grandly. "You may go in. Guy can see you now."

Kim and Joshua stood up and went into Guy's office where they found a smiling Henry King and Guy.

"Well – here comes the star!" said Henry happily as he shook Joshua's hand.

"You can't complain about those ratings we got you," said Kim, taking a seat and smiling smugly.

"We're very pleased with how the show went with Joshua at the helm, aren't we, Guy?" said Henry.

"Ecstatic," Guy nodded.

"So let's cut to the chase," said Kim, crossing her legs and looking confident. "What are you offering us?"

Henry bellowed a laugh, "Kim Davenport, you never change! You're a hard bitch."

"Just professional, Henry, just professional. Give it to me, lay it on me."

"We are interested in Joshua taking over *The Tonight Show*," said Henry.

Kim leaned forward. "You're gagging for him to take it over."

Guy sat back, hiding his irritation.

"We do think that Joshua is the right man for the job," said Henry.

Kim sat back and smiled. "Good, because we think he is too. This is how it's going to be, boys." She focused her attention on Guy. "I want a full offer on my desk by Friday, outlining terms and conditions. Salaries, of course. There are a number of stipulations – I'll email them on to you. We'll be bringing our team with us naturally. Your offer of course will have to be looked over by our solicitor and Joshua's agent will have to approve the money. But other than all that – I can't see us having any problems."

Henry nudged Guy and smiled in appreciation. "I told you she'd be driving a hard bargain, didn't I?"

Guy nodded and managed to smile.

When Brooke went for her afternoon break in the canteen she was unnerved to see she was getting the same reaction as she had earlier. People giving her second looks, whispering to each other, giggling. As she sat down with her tea and Kit Kat she had a Eureka moment. That bitch Stella in PR was still spreading it around that she had slept with Ricardo Martinez! She began to seethe at all these people who were talking about something they knew nothing about. She spotted two girls she vaguely knew in the corner of the canteen, whispering and looking over at her. She stood up and marched over to them.

"Would you care to tell me what's on your mind?" she demanded angrily.

The two girls got a start and tried to look innocent.

"Don't bullshit me. I know you were talking about me. For the record, not that it's any of your business, I did not sleep with Ricardo Martinez!"

"*Ahem!*" one of the girls coughed.

"We weren't talking about that," explained the other girl. "That was yesterday's gossip. Today we're talking about –" She glanced at her friend nervously and the other girl nodded her approval. "Today we're talking about this."

The girl opened her laptop and turned it so that Brooke could see.

Brooke squinted at the screen, perplexed. It was opened on the 'We Hate Joshua Green' website. She sat down, pulled the laptop over to her and started to read.

'Joshua Green has to be the biggest hypocrite of all time. He portrays himself to be a devoted husband and father in magazine shoots and interviews. On his shows he preaches against infidelity and affairs. Yet he is guilty of doing the same himself. Joshua Green has been having an affair for months with a girl who works on his show. She worked as a researcher and then got promoted to being a producer because of who she was sleeping with. Green cares nothing for his family and his image is as false as himself.'

Soraya was playing with the children in the lounge when the phone rang in the kitchen. She got up and walked in to answer it.

"Soraya? It's your mother here," said Annabel, when she picked up the phone.

"Hi, Mum, I was going to call you later," Soraya said cheerily.

"Darling, I'm here with your father and we had to ring you . . . Maybe you should sit down."

"What's wrong?" Soraya became alarmed as she sank down on the chair. "Are you okay?"

"It's just that I've been following this website you told us about, the one that hates Joshua."

Soraya felt herself become angry. "Why are you reading that rubbish? Is that all you have to do out there? I don't want to know what's written on it if that's what you're ringing me for!"

"I think you have to know, darling. It's saying that Joshua has been having an affair – with the producer on his show."

Soraya burst out laughing. "With Kim! For God's sake, where do these people get this rubbish from? I've never heard anything so ridiculous."

"Well, I did wonder myself," said Annabel. "She didn't seem the type who'd be bothered with Joshua, to be honest."

"Well, you don't have to worry about it. I can categorically say Joshua has not been sleeping with Kim."

"Well, I just thought we'd better let you know."

"Thank you, Mum! I'll ring you later," said Soraya in a patronising tone of voice as she hung up the phone.

She smiled to herself. Joshua and Kim! Aidan Doyle or whoever was writing that website was really grasping at straws at this stage. Although this was actually making a false allegation as opposed to expressing an opinion. She wondered if they had crossed a line where Joshua could act legally and sue them or something.

She walked into the study, sat down at the computer, logged on and brought up the website. This stupid website, with everything going on it had sunk to the bottom of their priorities recently. She read the piece.

'. . . *having an affair* . . .' Soraya read from the website, '. . . *with a girl who works on his show . . . worked as a researcher but then got promoted to being a producer* . . .' Soraya looked up and spoke aloud. "But that's not Kim. She wasn't a researcher . . . they mean Brooke."

Kim and Joshua were just toasting the success of their new show, clinking two tumblers of Scotch whiskey together in her office, when Brooke came storming in.

"What the fuck is wrong with you?" asked Kim, seeing Brooke's stressed-out look, red face and tear-filled eyes.

"It's out. Me and Joshua, it's on the internet. On that stupid website."

"What are you talking about?" Kim said dismissively.

Brooke ran around the desk. Pushing Kim out of the way, she started to tap the computer keyboard and brought up the website. White-faced, Joshua got up and moved to the other side of the desk so he could read it.

"*For fuck's sake!*" Kim roared in disbelief.

"I don't understand – how did they find out?" Joshua shook his head in disbelief.

"It's the talk of the place!" said Brooke. "In the canteen everyone was whispering and staring at me."

"You're being paranoid," snapped Joshua.

"Am I? It was some girls in the canteen who *told* me!" Brooke shouted back.

"Will everyone calm down!" Kim demanded.

"This can't be happening!" Joshua was pacing up and down, one hand on his hip and the other on his head. "This cannot get out. This will ruin me."

"It'll ruin us all!" stated Kim.

"But how would Aidan Doyle know about our affair?" said Joshua.

"He probably saw the two of you acting indiscreetly and put two and two together," said Kim.

"No," said Brooke. "He wouldn't even have seen me and Joshua together except in the studio when there were loads of people around."

"Well, there's one way of finding out. Have you got his number?" Kim asked Brooke.

"I'd have it on file." Brooke got up and rushed to her desk outside.

Kim and Joshua eyed each other nervously as they waited.

Brooke came running back in, waving a piece of paper. Kim grabbed it and dialled the number.

"Aidan?"

"Yeah?"

"Kim Davenport here at RTV. You've just landed yourself in a whole load of shit printing the last episode on that libellous website you operate. What you've printed about Brooke and Joshua is untrue and I'm going to have a ton of lawyers descend on you quicker than you can say –"

"Ah fuck off, ya auld bag! I don't what you're talking about."

"Your website! The one you admitted to Joshua you set up."

"Oh that! I only said that to piss him off. I've never even looked at the crappy website, but good luck to them whoever they are!" He hung up his phone.

Kim put down her phone and declared, "It's not him."

"But he admitted to me –" began Joshua.

"He only said it to piss you off. I can tell by him – it's not him."

Joshua stared at her, horrified. "My God, you're right!" he whispered. "I'm thinking back to when I confronted him. He acted like he hadn't a clue what I was talking about in the beginning. I thought he was covering up. But, you know what, it was only when I insisted it was him and he saw how much the situation was affecting me that he said it was him."

"So we're no nearer knowing who's behind all this?" said Brooke.

"Never mind that now. How do we deal with it?" fretted Joshua.

"Okay, listen carefully, because this is what we're going to do," said Kim. "We deny it. This is an unfounded rumour from the internet. The internet has millions of unfounded rumours on it every day and nobody pays any attention."

"Actually, a lot of people do pay attention to them," Brooke disagreed.

"Shut up! Everyone does what I say – unless you two want to be ruined! Do you?"

Joshua and Brooke shook their heads.

"No matter what happens – deny, deny and then deny again!"

57

Joshua pulled into his driveway and paused for a while before going inside.

"Joshua?" came Soraya's anxious call as he opened the door.

He went into the kitchen.

"Where have you been?" she said. "I've been ringing you all afternoon!"

"Sorry, I had the phone on silent."

"Well, you shouldn't have had!"

He noticed her stressed face. "What's the problem?"

"The problem is I've had my mother on from France to tell me that website has said you've been having an affair!"

That fucking nosy cow Annabel, thought Joshua. "*What?*"

"Read it for yourself!"

She pointed to the laptop on the island and he dutifully went over and started to read it.

"It's shocking!" said Soraya heatedly. "It's just shocking that they can print these lies and get away with it. This is crossing a line, Joshua! I don't care what we have to do, we have to stop this Aidan Doyle from harassing us! We have to get our solicitor on to this tomorrow morning first thing. It's gone beyond a joke! And we'll contact the police and get them to investigate all this. This is libellous!"

"Calm down, Soraya!" ordered Joshua.

"How can I calm down? Mum thought they were accusing you of sleeping with Kim, of all people! But then when I read it I realised it was Brooke! The poor girl, if people read this!"

"Soraya, I need you to calm down!"

"How can you be so calm about it? I thought that website drove you mad. You should be hopping mad now – that's the worst things it's ever said about you."

"I just think we need to act sensibly. I won't be able to do anything until I talk to RTV tomorrow – their PR department, legal department." Joshua hoped to deflect her from doing anything herself.

"All RTV will do is sit on their hands and talk red tape. No, I'll contact Dad's solicitor myself in the morning and get his advice."

"I don't want your father's solicitor involved, Soraya," insisted Joshua, alarmed. He walked over to her quickly and enveloped her in a hug. "Just leave it all to me. I'll sort it, okay?"

Soraya turned over in bed that night, unable to sleep. Joshua lay sleeping beside her. She knew it was contradictory after trying to calm him down over things recently, but she wished he would have reacted more angrily about this latest gossip on that website. It certainly had got to her. She sat up in bed, put on a bedside light and viewed her husband sleeping soundlessly.

This was all her parents needed, to have an excuse to dislike him even more. Her mind went back to the holiday in France and what a disaster it had been. She thought about Joshua's mood swings. His anger when Guy showed up with Brooke. His unreasonable anger. His rudeness to Brooke. His unreasonable rudeness. The dagger looks she had caught him constantly giving Brooke. The sarky comments he continually made to her.

Still thinking, she got out of bed and went downstairs. She opened the back patio door and slipped out into the back garden. She stared up at the stars in the night sky and she kept reliving the holiday.

By the time the sun began to rise she was crying. She realised it was true. Joshua and Brooke had been having an affair.

Joshua came into the kitchen, tying his tie.

"Don't bother with breakfast for me. I'll grab something at

work," he said as he poured himself a cup of coffee and drank it quickly.

"Alright," said Soraya who was sitting at the table feeding Daniel.

He put down the cup, went over to her and kissed her. "See you this evening," he said.

"Yes, see you," she said back.

She waited until the front door slammed and she heard his car start up and drive away before standing up.

"Ulrika! Ulrika!" she shouted, picking up Daniel.

Ulrika came in, carrying Danielle. "What is the matter?"

"Come on, we have to get packed and get the children ready."

"Where we go to?"

"France. To my parents."

"To France!"

"Come on, I've booked us all on a two o'clock flight so we've no time to lose."

"But what about my English class tomorrow evening."

"Fuck your English class – now get a move on, or else I'll leave you behind!"

Lee was at his desk in RTV when his mobile rang.

"Lee, it's Soraya."

"Hi, what's up?"

"I'm just letting you know I'm leaving your father. I'm sorry to tell you like this."

"Where are you?"

"I'm about to board a plane for France. I'm with the children and Ulrika."

"I don't blame you for going – you've put up with him for long enough."

"We have to board now. I'll ring you later. I love you, Lee."

Lee put down his phone and his eyes welled up with tears.

58

Brooke spent the day on tenterhooks. She avoided the canteen or any place where there was a lot of people. She knocked off early and went home at four.

As she drove through the city her mobile rang. She didn't recognise the number and pulled over to answer.

"Brooke Radcliffe?"

"Yes."

"Brooke, hi, it's Jenny Hayden here from the *Daybreak* newspaper."

"Oh! How can I help you?"

"I just want to ask you to comment on the rumours circulating that you were involved in an affair with Joshua Green?"

Brooke's heart started beating wildly as she cut the call dead. She then turned off her phone and drove home in a trance.

"This cannot be happening!" she kept repeating to herself.

She drove into the car park of her apartment block and into her space. She grabbed her handbag and got out of the car, locking it behind her.

Suddenly as she walked across the car park she was surrounded by a group of photographers and journalists.

"Can you confirm you were sleeping with Joshua Green?"

"Is it true you were shagging the star?"

"Does his wife know, Brooke?"

Panic-stricken she walked towards the entrance of her block as fast as she could as the cameras kept clicking in her face. Once inside, she slammed the door shut on them. She ran to the lift and hit the button for her floor.

She only felt safe when she got inside and double-bolted the door. She went and looked out the window. The photographers were still gathered downstairs.

She grabbed her phone and dialled Guy.

"Guy, something terrible has happened. The press are after finding out about me and Joshua and they are outside my apartment and have taken lots of photos of me. I'm scared, Guy. What'll I do?"

"Fuck!" Guy said in a calm voice.

"Guy – you've got to help me!"

"Okay. Just don't leave the apartment because they'll take more photos of you. Just stay put and I'll think of what it's best to do."

The phone went dead. Brooke rushed to the kitchen and, shaking, poured herself a straight vodka.

Joshua drove down his street and saw a group of people gathered at his gateway. He drove in past them and to his astonishment photographers started taking his photo before he even got out of the car.

He stepped out and demanded, "What's going on? What are you doing here?"

"Joshua, can you give us a statement about your affair with your researcher?"

Joshua turned and walked quickly up the steps of the house and let himself in, slamming the door after him.

"Soraya!" he shouted, marching into the kitchen. "Ulrika!" He walked through the double doors into the sitting room where he saw Lee stretched out on the couch, playing a hand-held computer game.

"Where is everyone? And why didn't you warn me that lot were outside the house?" demanded Joshua.

"She's left you, Dad," said Lee, not looking up from his computer game. "Soraya has finally seen the light and done a runner."

"What are you talking about?"

"She left you a note in the kitchen."

Joshua turned and raced into the kitchen. He picked up the note on the island.

He read: *'Joshua, I know you were sleeping with Brooke. It's over, we're over. I've gone to my parents. Please don't try and contact me, Soraya.'*

Joshua held the note in both hands, disbelieving the evidence of his eyes.

Lee came sauntering in.

"Looks like it's back to just you and me, Daddy," he said, slapping Joshua on the back.

Joshua tried ringing Soraya a hundred times that night, but her phone was off. He tried ringing Ulrika, whose phone was also off. He tried ringing her parents' villa in France, again no answer.

The next morning he booked the first flight he could get on to Nice.

Joshua then rang Ben Pearson at RTV.

"There are these lunatics camped outside my house, Ben – you need to get rid of them."

"What am I supposed to do about them?" said Ben in a no-nonsense voice. "I don't know what to do here, Joshua. Is it true about you and this girl shagging each other?"

"Of course not! That's none of your business anyway, Ben. How dare you ask me that!"

"Whatever, Joshua. Let me give you some advice. Get your shit together and your story straight. Decide what you're going to say and stick to it. Otherwise you're fucked."

"I need to get to the airport. Can you send an RTV car over to collect me?"

"Are you kidding me? Henry King is going mad about all this.

He would go madder if you were sent a chauffeured car. You're on your own with this one."

Ben hung up.

Joshua picked up his suitcase, went to the front door and steadied himself. Then he opened the door and faced the cameras on his way to his car.

59

Guy hadn't phoned Brooke back the previous night. She tried ringing him later on but his phone just rang out. She felt under siege in her apartment and spent a sleepless night peeping out the windows to see if the media crowd were gone. They stayed until the early hours but, as she sneaked out of the apartment the next morning at seven she was grateful to see that they seemed to have gone away.

She got to RTV before most people had arrived to work and was scurrying across the reception when her eye caught the morning papers laid out on the coffee table. She did a double take and slowly walked over to them. She picked up the newspaper which had a photo of her taken the previous day in her car park under the headline 'Joshua Green's Mystery Woman'.

Brooke walked like a zombie to her desk, clutching a bunch of the newspapers under her arm. She got a start to see Kim was already there in her office, legs stretched out, feet on her desk, a half-finished bottle of whiskey beside her. Brooke walked to the open door and entered.

"And here she is! The woman of the moment!" said Kim, as she raised her glass and saluted Brooke.

Brooke saw that Kim already had all the morning newspapers on her desk.

"You're in early," said Brooke.

"Oh, I didn't go home last night. No, the press started ringing me for comments last night and they told me what was coming in the papers this morning. So I stayed here and drank the night away – on my own. Not even Jasmine for company."

"The reporters didn't leave my place until the early hours of the morning."

Kim started clapping slowly. "Well, congratulations! You finally got all the recognition you wanted!" She picked up the papers and dropped them in a heap on the floor in front of her.

"You're drunk," said Brooke.

"Ten out of ten for observation. To paraphrase an English politician – I may be drunk but I will be sober tomorrow – however, you will still be a slut tomorrow. A national one now, by the look of it."

"What should I do, Kim?"

"*You* are asking *me* for advice? That's a first! I'm afraid there isn't much you can do at this stage. You've blown it all sky high. Soraya has left Joshua. Took the kids and scarpered off to her parents. You are front page news, for the very worst reasons. Joshua's career is over. He won't be given *The Tonight Show* now, not after this. All that hypocritical shit he spewed out about being a loving husband and father. The public will stomach most things, Brooke, but they will not put up with hypocrisy. It's one of the few unforgiven sins these days. You can be anything as long as you admit it. And I guess my career is down the toilet as well, by association. You did a fine job, Brooke."

"It wasn't me. It was the freak who put it on the internet."

"You just keep telling yourself that, if it makes you feel any better."

Brooke turned and raced through RTV towards Guy's office.

"He's in a meeting," said Jasmine as Brooke strode past her desk to Guy's office door. Brooke ignored her and barged in. Guy was in a meeting with three men and a woman, all of whom looked startled by the intrusion.

"I have to speak to you now!" Brooke demanded.

Guy stood up and smiled at the others. "If you'll excuse me for a minute," he said before walking out and directing Brooke to a nearby empty corridor.

"What are you doing storming in like that? Do you know who those people are?"

"I don't care!" snapped Brooke. "Look at this!" She flung the morning's paper at him.

He took it and frowned as he saw the photo of Brooke on the front page.

"I don't know what to do," said Brooke. "I can't stay here with everyone talking about me. I can't go home in case there's a crowd of photographers there."

"Have you got the key to my place with you?"

"Yes," she nodded.

"Just go to my apartment and lie low for the day. We'll talk about it this evening."

"Thanks, Guy," she said and hugged him tightly.

60

It was six o'clock in the evening before Joshua's plane touched down at the Côte d'Azur Airport. Another hour passed before he had got off the plane, got through passport control and managed to get a taxi. The taxi then made the journey up through the hills to Soraya's parents' villa.

When they finally reached the property, Joshua was shocked to see the huge gates closed and padlocked. He got out of the taxi, went over to the intercom and started buzzing it.

"Yes?" came Laurence's voice eventually.

"Laurence, it's Joshua. Can you open the gates and let me in?"

"No, I'm afraid I can't do that, Joshua. Soraya doesn't want to see you."

"What do you mean she doesn't want to see me? Open the gates and let me in!"

"As I said, she doesn't want to see you. Go home, Joshua."

"I want to see my wife and children, you can't keep me away from them!"

There was no response.

"Laurence . . . Laurence!" Joshua shouted into the intercom but there was no response.

Laurence came away from the intercom and joined Annabel and Soraya who were on the couch.

"I told him to go away," he said.

Soraya's mobile started ringing incessantly. She turned her phone to silent.

"I don't know what he thinks he can say or do to make the situation better," said Annabel.

"He thinks he can talk himself out of anything, that man," said Laurence.

"Well, he's not talking his way out of this one – I'm never going back," said Soraya, looking determined.

"I hate to say it again – we told you so!" said Annabel.

"Then don't!" snapped Soraya.

In the distance somewhere down at the gateway they could hear Joshua screaming, "*Soraya! Soraya!*"

The taxi driver looked on half in amusement and half in concern as he saw Joshua scout around the property trying to find a way into the villa. However, thick foliage on the hill and secure fencing made the effort impossible.

"*Soraya! Soraya!*" Joshua continued to roar as he attempted to find an opening to allow him access. Finally he realised it was impossible and came back to the taxi in despair.

Taking out his mobile, he phoned Guy.

"She's left me, Guy. Soraya walked out on me," he said, almost in tears.

"Joshua! What the fuck is going on? It's all over the papers that you and Brooke were having an affair!"

"I know. That fucking website got hold of it and then the papers latched on to it."

"Where are you?"

"I'm outside their villa in France. That's where she ran off to, but the place is locked up like Fort Knox and I can't get in. She won't take my calls. She won't let me explain."

"Look, just book into a hotel tonight and we'll talk about it in the morning."

"I'm sorry. I'm just so sorry. And I'm sorry for not telling you about me and Brooke . . . I've no right to ask it, but will you talk to Soraya for me? Tell her I love her and I'm sorry."

"Alright, I'll try and phone her."

"You're a true friend," said Joshua.

As Guy hung up the phone he rolled his eyes. Selfish to the last. Not a word of how this might be affecting his and Brooke's relationship. Just all about him.

61

When Brooke heard the key turn in the lock of Guy's front door she jumped up. She had hardly left the couch all day but had stayed there, curled up, wishing this whole nightmare would go away and her normal life could start again. She had finally fallen asleep.

"What time is it?" she asked as Guy turned on the lights.

"It's nine."

"What took you so long to get home?"

"Packed day of meetings."

"You could have tried to get back a bit earlier – you know what state I'm in!"

Guy picked up one of the morning's papers with Brooke's photo on the front page.

"And to think," he said with a small chuckle, "that you didn't want to do internet dating because your old school friends would see your photo on it and you didn't want to have them laughing at you. Imagine what they're saying now!"

"Don't, Guy!" she pleaded in annoyance.

He read from the accompanying article: "*'Brunette beauty Brooke Radcliffe is also rumoured to include Latino superstar Ricardo Martinez on her list of conquests . . .'* It makes you sound like a real man-eater. At least they didn't throw my name into the pot."

"Ricardo Martinez! Nothing went on between me and him. All we did was talk."

"Unfortunately, no one is going to believe that now, are they?"

Brooke flopped down on the couch, while Guy went to the fridge, took out a can of Coke and opened it for himself.

"Joshua rang me this evening."

"What's he saying about it all?"

"Soraya has left him. Run off to her parents in France with the kids. Won't speak to him."

"Oh no!" Brooke buried her face in her hands.

"He's very upset. Although not half as much as Soraya is, I bet you. She's a classy lady, Soraya, though. No tears or scenes or accusations. She just leaves without a word. I admire that."

"Who'd have thought it would all come to this?" She shook her head in despair.

"Somebody a little less naïve probably," he said, sitting down on an armchair facing her.

She looked at him in anguish.

"Maybe you need a little time abroad yourself – just until this whole thing dies down?" he suggested.

"That's an idea," she nodded. "Could you get the time off?"

"Me?" He looked shocked. "Not a chance. I'm up to my eyes. Why don't you go on the net now and book yourself a flight for the morning?"

"No! I couldn't bear to be away from you. You're the only good thing in my life right now." She smiled at him as fresh tears sprang to her eyes.

"Well, em, you can obviously stay here tonight, but if you could leave your key behind you tomorrow on your way out?"

She was confused. "Leave my key? To your apartment?"

"Yes . . . I think it's a good idea if we didn't see each other for a while, don't you?"

"What? I don't understand."

"Come on, Brooke, you're a bright girl. It's impossible for me to continue seeing you under the circumstances. How would it reflect on me and my career? The situation is untenable."

"Untenable? You make us sound like a work contract that's run into difficulty as opposed to two people in love."

"I can't afford to be associated with you, Brooke. I've come too far for too long, and done too much shit to get here, to risk it over an association with – well, excuse me, I don't mean to be rude – but a mucky little scrubber."

She stared at him in total shock, unable to believe her ears. He looked back impassively.

Then she whispered, "You fucking bastard."

"Oh please – no scenes!"

"Don't worry, I wouldn't give you the satisfaction." She stood up and grabbed her handbag.

He crossed his legs. "What do you think about me and Jasmine? Is it worth a go? Do you think we might make a good couple. Is she a bit young?"

Tears of anger stung her eyes as she turned to go.

"Oh, and Brooke – don't forget my key."

She reached into her bag, grabbed the key and flung it at him.

"You can stick your key up your arse!" she shouted and stormed out.

Brooke was in a trance as she drove back to her apartment. She checked to make sure there were no photographers there before racing inside. There were loads of messages on her phone from her family, but she couldn't bear to ring them back. How could she explain things? There was no explanation that could show her in any other light but the worst. She was a stupid girl who had got ahead of herself. Who had got carried away. Thought she could be somebody important. That a bit of Joshua Green's glamour and Guy Burton's power would rub off on her. When she meant nothing to them and ruined herself into the bargain.

62

Joshua had booked into a hotel. Every day he travelled up to the villa and every day he found it was the same – locked, bolted and impenetrable. All calls to Soraya went unanswered.

Finally Kim rang him. "Get your ass back on a plane. We've a meeting with Guy Burton tomorrow morning."

"I can't leave, Kim. She won't see me."

Kim sighed loudly. "So you won't come to the meeting?"

"I can't leave until I see her."

"I guess I'll handle it on my own again, like I do everything."

Kim sat outside Guy's office, studying Jasmine as she tried to look busy at her desk.

Jasmine looked up as she pared a pencil and addressed her like she was a stranger. "He'll be with you any minute."

Kim nodded.

The phone rang on Jasmine's desk and she picked it up and listened before hanging up.

"He'll see you now," she informed Kim.

Kim stood up and entered Guy's office. She was surprised to see only Guy there and no Henry King. Her heart sank. Maybe Henry was running late.

"I thought Henry was coming," she said as she sat down.

"He sends his regrets but he's been held up."

Guy sat back and studied her.

"Well, this is an unfortunate situation we've all been thrown into."

Kim nodded. "I did warn you at the beginning that if this affair got out the aftermath would be very destructive. That's why I begged you to get rid of Brooke at the time."

Guy sighed loudly. "Alas! You were right and I was wrong. If only I had listened to your advice. But what is done is done and we can't rewrite what's happened . . . So, to use your own expression I'm going to cut the bullshit and get to the facts."

"I'd be grateful if you would."

"RTV will not be offering Joshua *The Tonight Show*. Neither will we be recommissioning *The Joshua Green Show* this season."

It was like the breath had been knocked out of her to hear the words.

"We can't, Kim. You've been in the game long enough to know he can't come back from this, not for a long while. He's exposed as a hypocrite. He sold the public an image that is now exposed as a sham. Particularly considering the nature of the show he was involved in. It was all about being sanctimonious, judgemental. Putting people down for their human errors. And then for him to be seen as the biggest sinner of all! As I said, the public have turned. This in the wake of that Donna Doyle tragedy. The phones have been hopping with complaints. The press baying for blood. People like Joshua in the public eye are paid a lot of money and have a wonderful lifestyle, and all that is expected back from them is . . . to behave."

Kim nodded. "And this is final?"

"Yes, no need to go running over to Henry King. A quick flirt won't save your show this time. He has rubber-stamped the decision. He didn't want to be here. He wanted to save himself and you the embarrassment, you being such old friends and all."

"So what now?"

"The production staff will wind up the show's department. Their jobs are safe, they'll just be relocated to other programmes.

They are all on permanent contracts with RTV. The only ones not on permanent contracts are Joshua and of course . . . you."

"So I'm finished from today?"

Guy nodded.

She stood up and looked at him. "I can see you're not too upset."

Guy shrugged. "*Comme ci, comme ça!*"

"You had it in for us from the beginning. Why? You wanted us gone from the beginning. What were your reasons?"

Guy looked at her blankly. "My job here is to raise the standards of television. That could never be done with you and that show spewing its filth. I don't like your show. It's exploitative. And I don't like what you represent. You don't care about anything but ratings and success. I think today is a very good day for RTV."

She stared at him challengingly. "You might think very differently in a year when your ratings and your revenue have dropped considerably and they hold you responsible. And they will, Guy. Then we'll see how smug you are. How long you last. Television is a reflection of life, Guy, and that's about survival."

"Well, if it is, then it's just caught up with you. I guess every dog has its day."

Kim walked to the door, opened it and walked out. On the other side she closed it tightly and leaned against it, closing her eyes.

"Mum?" asked Jasmine.

Kim quickly opened her eyes and saw Jasmine and the other PAs looking at her in concern.

"Is everything alright?" asked Jasmine.

"Y-yes –" Kim's voice cracked and she willed away the tears that were threatening. She quickly marched from the reception and rushed down the corridor outside.

"Mum!" Jasmine called after her, but Kim kept on going.

She raced through the building and out to the car park. It was only when she reached her car that she realised Jasmine had been following her all the way.

"Mum! What's wrong?"

Kim turned and faced her and Jasmine got a shock because she had never seen her mother cry before. She had never even seen her look vulnerable, but now the tears were streaming down her face.

"They've got rid of me, Jasmine. I'm finished."

"Oh, Mum!" Jasmine cried out as Kim collapsed in her arms. "Come on, let's get you home." She led her to the passenger side of the car and gently sat her in.

"Give me the car keys," she ordered.

Kim managed to reach into her pocket and handed them over.

Jasmine sat into the driver's seat and, taking out a handkerchief, she gently wiped away her mother's tears.

"Let's get you home before any of these bastards see you like this."

63

It was the fifth day that Joshua had shown up at the locked gates of the villas. Soraya listened to the incessant buzzing of the intercom.

"Oh, I can't take this any more," she suddenly said, standing up. "I came over here so I wouldn't have to listen to him or deal with him."

"Where are you going?" demanded Annabel as Soraya marched to the front door.

"I'm going to get rid of him," said Soraya as she left the house.

"Don't, Soraya!" pleaded Laurence.

Joshua saw Soraya appear, marching down the long winding driveway, and grasped the iron gateway.

"You don't know how pathetic you look there," she said.

He was shocked that her voice sounded so harsh and cold. He'd never heard her like that before.

"Soraya, I need to speak to you."

"Well, I don't need to speak to you! That's why I came to France – to get away from you."

"But you left without even speaking to me."

"And you screwed that slapper without any thought for me!"

"Soraya –"

"Don't try and deny it. I'm not having my intelligence insulted any more."

"I'm not going to try to deny it. But it meant nothing to me. I love you, I must have been mad. I –"

"Why don't you try telling somebody who gives a shit. Because I don't. Our marriage is over. I won't be talking to you again. My solicitor will be in contact shortly to arrange access and custody for the children. I won't deny them their father, despite what I think of you. You can have the house and everything else. I don't want a thing off you, so it should be a very straightforward and quick divorce. The grounds being adultery. Alimony not required, and custody shared. We should have this wrapped up in matter of weeks. Now goodbye, Joshua."

She turned and walked back up to the house, ignoring his pleas shouted after her.

64

Guy walked confidently into the Westin Hotel and surveyed the half-empty bar looking for Joshua. He spotted him in a discreet corner and went to join him.

"Hi," said Guy, sitting opposite him.

"Thanks for meeting me. I really appreciate it," said Joshua.

He looked dreadful, Guy thought.

"When did you get back from France?"

"Late last night." Joshua filled a glass from the bottle of wine and handed it to Guy.

"Did you get to speak to Soraya?"

"No, only a few words through the gate, when she told me to piss off. She seemed so removed from my normal Soraya, I hardly recognised her."

"I guess she doesn't recognise you any more after learning what happened between you and Brooke."

Joshua nodded sadly. "I know . . . How are you and Brooke?"

"We broke up. You should have told me about your affair, Joshua."

"I know. I was in an impossible situation. I didn't want anyone to find out about us. I was trying to warn you about her in a roundabout way in France."

"Very roundabout. I guess you were 'the married guy' then?"

Joshua nodded. "I'm sorry. I'm sorry about the whole bloody mess."

"Did Kim tell you about RTV? About you not getting *The Tonight Show* and your regular show being cancelled?"

"Yeah, she's devastated."

"Are you not?" He looked at him curiously.

"Of course, but I haven't even thought about it to be honest. The only thing I can think about is Soraya and the children. She wants a divorce!"

"I see." Guy looked surprised.

"I need you to talk to her for me, mate. Just have a word with her. Try and tell her how much I care. Just get her to sit down with me to talk."

"What makes you think she'll listen to me?"

"She really respects you, Guy. She has a lot of time for you. You're the only person we both know who's on my side."

"I don't know –"

"Please, Guy!" Joshua leaned forward and grabbed his arm.

Guy sighed loudly. "Alright. What do you suggest? A phone call? Go out there and try and talk to her?"

"I'll owe you for ever, but if you could meet her face to face you might get through to her. Her phone is off all the time anyway."

"Alright – I'll go this weekend."

"I don't know how to thank you."

Guy came whistling into the reception of his office and saw Jasmine packing all her belongings into a box.

"What are you doing, Jasmine?"

"I'm quitting my job with you."

"Are you crazy? You won't get another opportunity like this again."

"Probably not, but family comes first. I can't stay working for you after what's happened with my mother."

He shook his head in disappointment. "That's really stupid. I thought you were a clever girl."

She picked up her box of belongings and said knowingly, "No, you've never thought that. Have you?" She walked off.

65

Soraya was shocked to answer the phone and find it was Guy Burton telling her he was in the South of France and would like to meet her.

She agreed to meet him in the local town, naming a small restaurant that looked out on the port.

He sat at an outside table wearing a cream linen suit and sunglasses, anxiously surveying the passing tourists. He spotted her in the distance, walking gracefully and standing out from the crowd. He got up as she reached his table and they kissed each other's cheeks.

She sat down. He took off his sunglasses but she kept hers on. He wondered if she'd been crying.

"This is a surprise," she said.

"Well, let's face it, there have been a lot of surprises lately."

"You can say that again."

"How are the children?"

"A bit too young to realise what's going on. They just think they're on holiday at their grandparents' . . . He obviously sent you over and I'm sorry but you've had a wasted journey, Guy. I'm not going back to him."

"He's devastated."

"Well, imagine how I feel then. At least he can blame himself."

"He just wants to talk to you."

"The only talking will be through our solicitors."

He observed her. "I never thought you would come to such a quick and decisive resolution. I thought your home life meant everything to you."

"It did mean everything to me – that's why I can be so clear-thinking. It's ruined now and I can't go back to it."

"His shows have all been cancelled."

"I know, Lee told me."

"What will you do now then?"

"Well, my parents are already driving me mad here, so I guess I'll return to Dublin soon. I'll move into their house in Ballsbridge. And I'll file for divorce in time."

He looked at her in amazement. "And Joshua and the children?"

"Ulrika can take them back and forth between us."

"I'm sitting here in awe of you. You're being so strong."

"I have to get on with it. My heart is broken, Guy, but I have children to consider. I don't want them caught up in the blame game and rows and screaming matches."

Guy looked down at the red-and-white checked tablecloth. "I wish I could be as strong as you."

"Oh Guy, I'm so sorry. I'm so wrapped up in myself I didn't even think about you being tangled up in all this with . . . *her*."

Guy nodded sadly. "As soon as I found out about the affair I broke it off with Brooke. I just couldn't believe that she had done it."

"It knocked me for six as well. She fooled us all."

"But to come over here on holiday and stay in your house. It really takes some doing."

"I certainly will never be as trusting with people again. I've learned my lesson well."

"Neither will I, Soraya. I really thought she was the *one*, do you know what I mean?"

"Oh Guy, I'm so sorry!" She took off her glasses and he saw her eyes were red and swollen.

"We had discussed marriage, babies, settling down, the lot."

"I know what you're going through."

"I just think, Soraya, is this my lot? Am I just unlucky in love?"

"You've just been unlucky in your choices, that's all. I mean, she took us all in – you can't beat yourself up about that."

"I believe she was seeing Joshua at the same time as me."

"Oh Guy!" Soraya shook her head sadly.

"And I've been told she slept with Ricardo Martinez as well when she was supposed to be going out with me!"

"What kind of a bitch is she?"

"I think she was just using me to get ahead in RTV. But it hurts, Soraya, you know it hurts."

She leaned across the table and clasped his hand tightly.

"When are you going back to Dublin?" she asked.

"Tomorrow."

"You know, you've had a terrible time with all this. Why don't you stay out here a few days and give yourself some time to recover. You need some time out over something like this."

"Yes, I think you might be right. Thanks, Soraya."

Guy spent the rest of the week in the South of France. He booked into a local hotel but met up with Soraya every day. They mostly went down to the beach with the children. Soraya found him relaxing company. And she was delighted with company other than her triumphant parents and whinging au pair. She found him to be an excellent listener who didn't judge her as she opened up about her marriage with Joshua. She felt it was like therapy for her.

Soraya and Guy climbed up on the rocks and looked down at Ulrika and the children playing on the beach.

"Has Joshua been on to you?" she asked.

"Of course – every day."

"If you want to be a proper friend to him and me, make it clear to him there is no future for us."

He nodded.

"I'm so angry with him. I'm more angry than hurt. You're hurt over Brooke. But I'm angry with Joshua. That he ruined our marriage and our family over a dirty little affair. That he thought so little of us, of himself even."

"I admire you so much, Soraya. I would have thought you'd have behaved more like a victim in this – felt more sorry for yourself. I don't know why I thought that because you never played that role before. I just thought you were soft and might have fallen apart. But no – far from it."

"I was brought up to be self-reliant. That's what's getting me through this. And I was never a bitch, but I'd love to do the same back to him. Make him realise what this feels like, to have this done to you." She looked at him with a mixture of fury and upset in her eyes.

He put an arm round her and nodded in understanding.

Later Guy was sitting with Laurence and Annabel on the patio at the villa.

"Well, I for one am delighted it's finally finished between her and Joshua," said Annabel. "She'll be much better off without him. I never liked him."

"Do you think she'll be able to cope with the children on her own and everything?" asked Guy.

"Of course she will!" insisted Laurence. "She's the one who keeps everything going. He'd have fallen apart years ago if it wasn't for her. She'll be much better off when she only has to take care of herself and the children."

"She does seem to be coping amazingly well with the break-up. I'm surprised," said Guy.

"She's very stoic," said Annabel. "People underestimate her all the time and always have. Because she's charming and kind, they sometimes think she's a pushover. But she has a core of steel. Something people only find out when it's too late, like Joshua has now."

"She was always like that, remember?" said Laurence. "Growing up she would be the most loyal and good friend. But if somebody treated her badly, she would just walk away and never look back at that friendship."

"No second chances," agreed Annabel. "How much longer are you planning on being out here, Guy?"

"I hadn't really thought. A couple of days probably."

"Well, it's ridiculous you staying in a hotel in the town when you can stay here with us."

"I couldn't," Guy shook his head. "It would be imposing and Soraya might not like it."

"Soraya would insist. Besides, you're a very welcome distraction from all that's going on."

66

Brooke never thought she would think it, but as she sat at her desk and looked into Kim's empty office, she actually missed the woman. Kim hadn't returned to RTV since everything blew up, and neither had Joshua. A memo had gone around to the production staff on the show saying it had been cancelled and wouldn't be recommissioned, and they were to wait for further instructions.

HR had then been in contact with each and every member of the production staff and deployed them to other programmes, everyone except her. Even Lee had been carted off to be a researcher on some new dynamic current-affairs programme. She waited and she waited, but no call came from HR for her. Finally she had rung HR and asked where she was being redeployed. She had been frostily told they didn't know where to send her and to stay put for now. So she sat at her desk in the empty department tidying up, surfing the net and thinking about how fucked-up her life had become. She remembered the inquisition from her parents and family.

"Is it true you went out with Enrique Iglesias?" asked her mother, always one for mixing up the finer details.

"No! It wasn't Enrique Iglesias, it was Ricardo Martinez."

"You slept with Ricardo Martinez!"

"No! I didn't sleep with him or any other Spanish superstar."

"But you did have an affair with Joshua Green?"

And what could she say to that? Guilty as charged your honour? The sentence – a lifetime of shame and humiliation. With nobody left in the office she put on music and let it blare. She kept replaying Adele's "Rollin' in the Deep". She felt herself to be in a strange maelstrom of juxtapositions. On the one hand she felt like the world's biggest bitch, being responsible for the break-up of a marriage. On the other hand she felt a complete victim and miserably sorry for herself because of the way Guy had treated her and discarded her.

But what comes around goes around. Karma is a bitch, she thought, a real bitch.

67

Guy waited at the Arrivals Hall at Dublin Airport. He checked the monitor again and saw the flight from Côte d'Azur had landed forty-five minutes ago. He wondered what the delay was. At that moment Soraya emerged with Ulrika and the two children and waved over at him.

"There was really no need," she chastised as they embraced. "We could have grabbed a taxi."

"Nonsense, I wouldn't hear of it."

She walked alongside him to the nearby car park, with Ulrika and the children behind them.

"It is comforting to have a friend there waiting for us, given the circumstances we are coming back to," she said. "I could have called one of my other friends, but I would have had to go through sixty million questions with them and I'm not ready for that yet. Whereas you, well, you know everything. You've been involved since the beginning."

He nodded at her and smiled and they headed out to his car.

Guy had thought Joshua and Soraya's house in Sandymount was impressive, but it hadn't prepared him for Annabel and Laurence's house in Ballsbridge. It was a Victorian manor house on Shrewsbury

Road. He tried not to look too impressed as he followed her up the steps and she opened the door.

"So, eh, this is where you'll be living now?" he asked as he stepped in and looked up at the high ornate ceilings.

"Yes, it makes the most sense. Mum and Dad spend so much time in France they hardly ever use their home here now. It's a bit too big for us, but we'll cope."

Guy had smiled wryly at Soraya's idea of 'coping'.

He had spent the rest of the day with her, going to the shops, helping her get all the things she needed for the house.

"Where to next?" he asked as they loaded up his car outside Tesco.

"Emm, I suppose we'll drop these off home. And then maybe go to a toyshop and get some new stuff for the children. There's so much practical stuff I have to rebuy."

"Is there anything you want me to get from your old home? I'm sure Joshua would let me get it for you?"

"No, Guy. I want nothing from there. Any interaction with him will result in giving him encouragement, and I don't want that. Look, you've been too good already. I can go to the toyshop by myself."

"I wouldn't hear of it," he said, smiling, and holding the door open for her.

She smiled as she sat in. She took out her mobile. "Another five missed calls from Joshua. Does he never give up?"

"Look, I'll go and tell him face to face how you feel. That you've made up your mind."

"Thanks, Guy. If he'll listen to anybody, he'll listen to you."

"Guy!" said Joshua when he opened his front door. "I've been leaving messages for you. Come in!"

Guy stepped inside and took in Joshua's appearance. He had lost more weight, was unshaven and pale. He didn't look like the glossy well-manicured star any more.

Joshua followed him in to the kitchen where a half-drunk bottle of vodka sat on the island.

"Drink?" asked Joshua, pouring himself a neat vodka.

"No, I'm fine."

"So what's she's saying? Will she meet me?"

Guy shook his head sadly. "She says it's over. She says she never wants to see you again."

"I don't believe her. She's only saying that, making me suffer for what I did."

"She's not, she means it. I'm telling you now, Joshua, as a friend, for your own sanity, you have to move on. Stop trying to contact her. Start living your life without Soraya."

"I can't! I can't move on! I love her too much. Living my life! I've no career any more. I've no wife. No family. No future."

"You still have the children. And Lee."

"Lee! He won't even talk to me any more. Blames me for messing up with Soraya and driving her away. And he's right."

"You've no choice but to get on with it, Joshua. She won't be coming back."

"I'll never give up on her."

The children had gone to bed and Ulrika was out on a date. Soraya was serving up spaghetti bolognese in the kitchen for herself and Guy.

She sat down opposite him and raised her glass of wine. "Cheers!" she said, clinking it against his glass of Coke.

"Cheers!" he responded.

They began to eat.

"This is wonderful," said Guy.

She smiled and they continued to eat in companionable silence.

Eventually she paused and gazed at him. "How did Joshua look?" she asked.

"The very same," said Guy. "Healthy-looking, suntanned even."

"Well, he mustn't be as heartbroken as he's pretending to be, in that case," said Soraya. "He'd be too vain to let himself go anyway."

"He would not accept it was over, though, no matter how much I told him so."

"Well, he's just going to have to get it into that thick head of his that it is."

"He seemed very committed to you."

"Pity he wasn't as committed when he was poking the payroll!" she said and she managed a little giggle. "That was almost funny."

He turned and looked at her. "It's good to hear you laugh again."

She shrugged. "If I didn't laugh I'd cry. The only reason I'm not jumping into that bottle of wine and feeling sorry for myself is because you're here. Making me feel better."

He placed his hand on hers and smiled. She smiled back and then took her hand away to pick up her fork again.

"Maybe you should serve divorce papers on him," suggested Guy. "That would make him realise it's totally over."

She flinched slightly. "I don't know if I'm ready for that just now. I want to do it and I will do it. But I need a bit more time. It's so final."

68

If RTV had the equivalent of purgatory it was the data-compiling department. And when Brooke finally got the call from HR for redeployment that's where she found herself headed to. Her new job there didn't compromise her contract as she was still a researcher, all reference to her elevation to assistant producer now forgotten. But instead of being a researcher on a television show she was now researching and compiling statistics on things as exciting as internet usage within RTV. It was a dead-end job in an office on her own all day, without much benefit to anybody except maybe deciding on future budget allocations. Brooke did her penance quietly and without complaint, remembering how very briefly she had been on the ladder to everything she had ever wanted.

Joshua sat at the kitchen table reading the 'We Hate Joshua Green' website. The Police's "I Can't Stand Losing You", was blaring from the sound system.

Since the website had revealed his affair with Brooke, the site was more popular than ever, having been mentioned in the press a lot as the source of the revelation of the affair.

'Rumours abound that Joshua Green will not be getting The Tonight Show, despite the fact his guest presentation got surprisingly large ratings. The exposure of his tawdry affair put an *end to that. And also The Joshua Green Show is not being renewed in RTV's future schedules. At last – sanity! No more exploitation of other people's misery, now that Joshua Green has been exposed as the biggest hypocrite of all time – lecturing people on marriage when he was cheating on his poor unfortunate wife all the time!'*

Joshua took a swig from his vodka glass and said out loud to the screen, "Who are you? *Who are you?*"

The front door opened and closed and Lee came into the kitchen and looked at his father.

"Have you even left the house today?" said Lee, shaking his head in disgust.

"Were you speaking to Soraya?" asked Joshua.

"If I was, it's none of your business. I'm getting ready to go out." He shook his head again. You look pathetic!" He pointed at a bottle of pills on the table. "I hope you're not taking those anti-anxiety tablets you have stashed all over the house with that alcohol. It's a dangerous mix, you know. The last thing the family needs now is *'Was It Suicide? Ex Talk Show King Bows Out'* headlines."

"Of course I'm not!" snapped Joshua. "They're just my headache tablets."

"Well, maybe you should save them for your hangover tomorrow!" He turned to leave the room. "I'm going over to stay with Aunt Helen. I don't even want to be in the same house as you, with you like this."

69

Soraya put on her earrings and looked at herself in the mirror. Guy was picking her up any minute. He had persuaded her to go to the cinema. She hadn't been out anywhere since breaking up with Joshua and Guy had convinced her she needed a night out. The cinema seemed a good idea, as she could get lost in someone's else's life for a couple of hours.

She thought about how good Guy had been to her. She wouldn't have been able to get through the last few weeks without him. He was easy company and cared about her. He was the only person she could really relax with.

The car beeped outside and she got up to go.

As Guy drove them back to her house after the cinema he discussed the film intently, dissecting the plot and characters.

"You really were paying attention!" she said, astonished by his level of observation.

He laughed lightly. "I can't help it. I studied film."

"What did you want to do with that qualification?"

"Oh, I knew exactly what I wanted to be. I wanted to be a director. I wanted to be an Alfred Hitchcock, Martin Scorsese, Neil Jordan, a Claude Chabrol. An Oliver Stone."

She saw there was great regret in his face. "Why didn't you pursue it?"

"I couldn't get the right breaks. I needed to pay the bills. So I went into programming instead." He smirked over at her. "At least I get to decide what everyone else gets to watch, even if I'm not making it myself."

She smiled back and nodded. "You've done very well for yourself."

He pulled in to her drive.

"Nightcap?" she asked.

"Yeah, thanks," he nodded.

Soraya marched through the large hall, taking off her shawl. "Fix me a Martini, would you?" she asked as she headed up the stairs to check on the children.

He walked through the double doors into drawing room and over to the drinks cabinet. He fixed her drink and poured a Coke into his own glass.

She came down a few minutes later. She was wearing a black wool dress, her hair loose down her back.

"Fast asleep," she smiled, taking her drink from him. "What are you drinking?"

"A Tia Maria."

She took a drink from her glass and sat down on the sofa.

"So tell me more about your film career," she said as he sat down beside her.

"There's nothing to tell unfortunately. I was a runner on a couple of sets after I finished college. That's about the size of it."

"Then television beckoned?"

"Something like that."

"It's funny the destinies people have, isn't it? Another turn here, a twist there, and everybody could be leading completely different lives. If other doors opened for you, or you made different decisions, then you might be a Hollywood director." She smiled at him.

"I'm glad I'm not," he said.

"Why?"

"Because then I would never have met you."

He stared at her and she looked at him curiously and then was staring back. He leaned slowly forward and put his lips on hers and began to kiss. She responded.

"I'm sorry!" She suddenly pulled back and stood up.

"No – *I* am!" He stood up quickly too.

"I wasn't expecting that!"

"Neither was I!"

They looked at each other nervously before she burst out laughing. His face showed a mixture of disbelief and concern. "Soraya?"

"I'm sorry – I didn't mean to laugh! I just – I didn't think you felt that way about me. It came as a bit of a shock."

He sat down. "I shouldn't have done it. I'm sorry."

She sat down beside him and put an arm around him "No, you were right to do it, if you felt like doing it . . . Look, if I'm honest, I can't imagine a nicer person to get involved with other than you. It's just – it's too soon."

He looked at her. "But I thought you were adamant about getting on with your life . . ."

"I am. And actually, fuck Joshua, there's no reason why I shouldn't get involved with somebody else. It's just I know he's suffering at the moment. Even though it's his own fault. It wouldn't be nice of me to go with you, his friend. Even though I might even feel like doing it. If I did I might be doing it out of revenge and that wouldn't be fair on any of us, especially you. You've been hurt enough by Brooke. I don't want to add insult to injury." She leaned forward and hugged him closely.

"I'd better go," he said eventually, standing up.

"Will you still come round for dinner tomorrow as planned? But I'll understand if you don't want to."

"I'll be over at seven," he said and winked at her before leaving.

She heard the front door slam and she sat on the sofa with her legs crossed for a long time, deep in thought.

70

Tom Davenport came into the lounge and saw Kim stretched out, reading a magazine.

"What are you up to today?" he asked.

"Well, I imagine I'm going to be reading, eating, drinking and watching TV. Since I've nothing better to do all day long."

"Where's Jasmine?"

"Gone to enrol for another media studies course for the next year."

"And what about you? What are you going to do next?"

She looked up from her magazine and viewed him cynically. "What's this, Tom? Interest from you at last?" She then continued to read.

"I just thought you might be trying to put together a new programme or applying for new producer's jobs."

"There's no point, Tom, nobody will touch me. I've done what the wonderful world of television will never forgive."

"And what's that?"

"Failed. And been outsmarted."

"Nobody could ever outsmart you, Kim."

"Is that a compliment from you, Tom? After all these years? Things must be bad . . . Go to the bank, you'll be late for work."

Ulrika opened the door to Guy the next evening.

"Hello. She is inside the kitchen cooking dinner again," she said in a bored voice.

"Good evening, Ulrika, how was your date the other night?" he asked as he stepped in.

"It was okay. I think I don't like Irish men so much. I think they are fucked up." She looked in the direction of the kitchen. "I think all Irish are fucked up."

Guy grinned and followed her into the kitchen.

"Hi there," said Soraya, smiling at him warmly.

"Hi – I brought you these." He handed over flowers and chocolates.

"Thank you!" she smiled at him. "It should be me giving you presents. You've been so helpful to us."

They all sat down and Soraya began to serve beef stroganoff which Daniel and Danielle immediately began throwing around with their spoons, to Ulrika's loud-voiced annoyance.

"Sorry for the crowd this evening," Soraya said, nodding in the direction of the others.

"Don't apologise. I love being in their company."

She smiled at him and gave him an extra serving.

Soraya came into the drawing room and closed the doors behind her.

"I told Ulrika not to disturb me for the rest of the night. She's a good girl really, but if only she could *smile* once in a while. It's me going through the marriage break-up, not her!" She sat down beside him with her glass of wine.

Guy laughed and they sat awkwardly for a minute until he turned to her "Soraya, I hope I didn't offend you last night –"

"No, of course you didn't. I was very flattered. It was an ego-boost I needed after discovering my husband no longer found me attractive."

"As if you could ever not be attractive!"

"And if the circumstances were different, you wouldn't be safe in my company!" she said with a smile. "We've been a huge crutch to each other and sometimes the lines get blurred. But I think it's too soon for me."

Soraya's mobile started to ring.

"Who is this?" she sighed, reaching out for her mobile and

looking at the screen. "My mother!" She rolled her eyes and answered the phone. "Yes, Mum?"

"Darling, I don't know if I'm doing the right thing or not –"

"When did that ever stop you?" asked Soraya.

"But I figured if I didn't tell you, somebody else would. And I would prefer for you to hear it from me."

"What is it, mother?"

"Well, it's that website about Joshua . . ."

"Are you still reading that?" Soraya was annoyed.

"I know I shouldn't, but I can't help myself. Anyway there's a new posting – is that the right word? – on the website . . ." She paused.

"Go on," ordered Soraya in a bored tone.

"It's about Joshua's past and his first wife. It's quite disturbing and I think you should know about it."

Soraya's face creased in worry. "Alright, I'll take a look, thanks for telling me." She turned off the mobile.

"What is it?" asked Guy.

"That dammed website again. Seemingly there's something new on it."

She stood up, walked out of the room and went down to the study, followed by Guy.

She sat down in the leather swivel-chair behind the large mahogany writing desk and started to Google the website.

"Here it is," she said and started to read aloud: "'*Why does Joshua Green never talk about his first wife? Is it because he has something to hide? Was it because he treated his first wife as badly as his second? Driving her to drink with his affairs? Treating her so badly she ended up trying to kill herself with an overdose? Driving her to an early death. Joshua Green was revelling in misery long before he made a living out of it. The misery he caused his first wife.*'"

"I can't believe this!" said Soraya, standing up and beginning to pace up and down.

"Is this true?" asked Guy, rereading the blog.

"Who is writing this stuff? Where are they getting it from?" demanded Soraya. "How do they know so much?"

"So it is true?" asked Guy, his face confused.

"I don't know! I don't know any more what's true or false!"

He came over to her and grabbed her shoulders. "Calm down, relax, you're fine – you're with me. Nothing can harm you."

"Guy!" She fell into his arms and held him tightly. "I don't want my children mixed up in all this shit! I'm so sick of Joshua and all the pain he's causing us."

"Then don't let him cause you any more. End this now. End your marriage with him."

She stared into his eyes and, leaning forward, began to kiss him.

Joshua stood in the study, staring at the website, reading what it was saying about him and Lee's mother. He took up his vodka bottle and hurled it at the computer screen, breaking the bottle and cracking the screen.

"*No!*" he screamed at the broken screen.

71

The doorbell of the house rang and Joshua went to answer it. Opening the door he found a young nattily dressed man of about twenty-five there, smiling from ear to ear.

"I thought it might be you when I saw the name on the envelope," said the man cheerily.

"Can I help you?" asked Joshua, confused.

"Yes, I'm just delivering this," said the man as he handed over an envelope with Joshua's name on it. "You know I used to love your show. I used to try and never miss an episode."

As the man twittered on, Joshua tore the envelope open and read the contents. It was divorce proceedings from Soraya.

"Now, I just need you to sign for that. And also, if I could be so bold, ask for another signature? An autograph for me? Do you know you can sell autographs on eBay? I mean, I'm not sure what yours would be worth any more. But it would be nice to have."

Joshua slammed the door shut and walked back to the kitchen as the man started shouting through the letterbox. "Mr Green!"

Joshua spent the day on his laptop, reading the website dedicated to destroying him, the divorce papers beside him with the letter from RTV formally telling him his position with RTV was over.

At six o'clock that evening Lee put his key in the door and let himself in. He put his slim briefcase down on the floor and looked around. Music was blaring from the lounge and he made his way in.

Joshua was seated there with A-ha's "The Sun Always Shines on TV" playing loudly.

"Have you finally lost it?" said Lee, taking up the remote and lowering the sound.

"Good day at the office, son?" asked Joshua, staring at him.

"Not bad. Better than your day by the looks of it. You know, you really need to give yourself one of those boring motivational speeches you used to give me."

"Yes, they really were very effective on you – in the long run. Did you have any free time today?"

"Not much – that new programme I've been assigned to keeps me very busy."

"Not much time then to mess around on the internet?"

"No, as I said I've been busy."

"Not much time to write another piece on your website then?"

"What are you talking about?"

"You know exactly what I'm talking about." Joshua stood up quickly. "I should have guessed it was you. It all makes sense. You started off like a diary pouring out your scorn for me. But like anyone with a twisted mind that wasn't enough, was it? You had to go further and further."

"Will I call a doctor for you?" Lee looked at him disdainfully.

"Soraya used to warn me not to underestimate you. Of course she meant it as a compliment, not realising what you're capable of. So when you got the job at RTV and got access to all this information, you just couldn't help yourself, could you? You started off with the programme – we didn't employ a counsellor. Then revealing my losing my temper with you in the studio – you got the footage from one of the studio cameras, right? It wasn't somebody's mobile phone. I knew then it was not some random geek with nothing better on their mind than to mock me. I knew it was somebody connected with RTV. And then you went further, didn't you? You found out about me and Brooke. Did you just put two and two together, or did you hear some gossip around the canteen in work? So you reveal it to the world on your website. You must have been delighted with the outcome of that. You managed to break me. But why stop there? You had to come back for some more. And you revealed about your mother and me. But that was your mistake. That narrowed it down to just you, me and your mother. Well, your mother is dead. And I certainly didn't do it."

Lee held his gaze defiantly.

"Well? Talk to me. I know it's you. Why are you doing it?"

Lee laughed but there was nothing mirthful in his laughter.

"Well, it's all the truth, isn't it?" he said. "I didn't say anything that wasn't true."

"Do you know what you've done to me? You've destroyed me!"

"You destroyed yourself. I just told the world what you were like."

"But why? Everything I did I did for you."

"Everything you did you did for yourself! I know what you did to Mum and you are now finally paying the price. It might have taken me a long time to get there, but I've paid you back."

"For what?" Joshua threw his hands in the air in despair. "For trying to keep a roof over our heads? For trying to deal with your mother who was a paranoid depressive with a drink problem?"

"Don't speak of her like that! You didn't deserve her."

"Nobody deserved her and what we went through with her!"

"She was a martyr to you!"

"She was a martyr to herself! Lee – you were a small kid – you only saw what she wanted you to see. You only heard the version she wanted to give you. You weren't old enough to know right from wrong. Please think about this rationally as an adult. Think of what she was like."

"You never loved her, you didn't want to marry her!"

"I loved her. We got married because she was pregnant with you. Of course that's true, I never denied that. Me and your mother were hardly going out a wet weekend when she got pregnant. It threw me. We didn't come from money and I wanted to make something of myself. I'd just started selling advertising for a radio station when I found out you were on the way. It changed everything. But I never regretted it, not one moment. Soon after you were born your mother started acting strangely. Mood swings, violent mood swings. Depression. She'd been like that before but I hadn't known. And the drinking started. It was a nightmare. So I threw myself into my work. I just wanted some kind of success so we could get a nice life for ourselves."

"And so you could start screwing around," Lee accused.

"That's the bit that isn't true. I was never unfaithful to your mother. Not that she believed me. And she fed you those lies that you believed and put on your website all these years later."

"Your affairs destroyed my mother in the same way you tried to destroy Soraya, but Soraya was stronger than my mother and she got away from you before you could ruin her the same way."

"I never had an affair while I was with your mother. The marriage was eight years of hell that nearly sent me to the loony bin, but I never cheated on her. Even though our marriage became a sham."

"Bullshit."

"Finally I had to leave. Think back to what she was like, Lee, think about it rationally. Remember when you were eight. Remember what she did."

"Stop it!"

"Remember she had dressed you up like a little waiter. Complete with white towel over your arm and holding a silver tray in the other –"

"*Stop it!*"

"And she was in bed and she got you to bring her in all her pills on a silver tray to give them to her, one by one. She was getting you to serve the pills for her to kill herself!"

Lee went to race from the room but Joshua grabbed him and held him tightly.

"*Let me go!*" screamed Lee as he broke down.

"I know we never talk about it, because it's too painful. But that was the state of her mind. Lee, think about it. She survived that time. And she didn't need to kill herself in the end – she had done so much damage to herself with her drink and prescription pills that her heart gave out soon after."

"I hate you! I hate you for what you did to her! I hate you for what you did to me! You killed her and I never want to see you again!" Lee pulled away and ran from the house.

72

Brooke's new position at RTV was driving her to early dementia. Sitting compiling statistics all day was not what she was cut out for. As she sat in her office, looking at the paperwork that lay in front of her, she decided that maybe what she needed was a clean break. To get away from it all. There was no point applying for anything else at RTV, she wouldn't be given a chance. She went on the internet and began perusing other television channels' job sites to see if there was anything of interest. Jobs looking for somebody with her experience were scarce. But she managed to find an assistant producer's job for a new lifestyle programme on the BBC. She read through the job description and it sounded exciting and intriguing. She doubted she had enough experience but it was worth a try and she filled out the application form online.

Joshua waited patiently for his guest to arrive. He had phoned Lee's Aunt Helen, his first wife Catherine's sister, to come over. He'd always liked Helen and got on with her. She was the polar opposite to her sister, a no-nonsense practical woman who had done very well in banking and liked to live the good life. She had never married or had children, and had been very good with Lee when his mother died. She has graciously taken a back seat once Soraya arrived on the scene but still played a part in her nephew's life.

The doorbell rang and he hurried to answer it.

"Well, I've seen you look better," said Helen as she stepped inside and gave her former brother-in-law a kiss on both cheeks.

"I've felt better, believe you me." He closed the door and showed her into the lounge.

Helen was an elegantly dressed woman with a bob, her appearance matching her personality.

"Drink?" he asked.

"Fix me a gin and tonic, would you, darling?" she said, sitting down on the couch, placing her handbag on the floor beside her and crossing her legs.

"So to what do I owe the pleasure of this invite?" she asked as she took the drink from him.

"Lee. What else?"

"What else indeed? What's he been up to?"

"Oh, everything's gone disastrous, Helen." He shook his head disconsolately.

"Doesn't it always?" she quipped. "Why do you think I have neither chick nor child? I couldn't face the demands of it all. I read about your exploits in the newspapers with your researcher. All true, I presume?"

"Yes," he nodded. "Soraya and the kids have left, she's filing for divorce."

Helen smiled sadly. "Why do we feel the need to destroy everything we have, eh?"

Her sympathetic look threw him. "Don't be nice to me, Helen, I'm not used to it at the moment and I don't deserve it."

"I'm sure you don't." She took out a small mirror and began to fix her make-up. "Well, I'm sure you didn't call me over here for a shoulder to cry on. What can I do for you and, more importantly, Lee?"

"He blames me for what happened to Catherine. He holds me fully responsible."

"That's daft, Joshua. My sister, much as I loved her, was as mad as a bag of frogs. She put us all through the mill in her time."

"Well, Lee doesn't see it like that. I'm to blame, and he hates me. He's been attacking me on the internet on some website he set up."

"Website?" she asked as she tossed off her drink.

"I think I'd better pour you another drink," sighed Joshua and he began to unfold the story.

Ten minutes later, he ground to a halt, having filled her in on all the details of the website and his encounter with Lee.

"Obviously he's more affected by everything than we thought," said Helen, sighing. "How can I help?"

"I was hoping you'd speak to him. Make him see how things really were with his mother."

"I can try, Joshua, but who can say how Lee will react?"

"Thanks, Helen." He took her hand and squeezed it.

The doorbell rang.

"Who's that now?" said Joshua irritably as he got up and went into the hall.

As Helen looked around the room she reflected on how the house seemed with everyone gone. She heard banter in the hall and then Joshua came back in with a tall good-looking man.

"Helen, this is a friend of mine, Guy Burton."

Guy looked startled to see her there.

"Nice to meet you," said Helen, standing up and shaking his hand.

"Helen's my sister-in-law," explained Joshua.

"Sister-in-law?" asked Guy, looking confused.

"She's my first wife's sister."

"Don't I know you from somewhere?" asked Helen.

"No, I don't think so," said Guy.

She studied his face. "Anyway, I'd better be going. I've a date at nine and I'm late. Nice meeting you."

She nodded at Guy and Joshua showed her to the door.

Kim heard the front doorbell ring and went to answer it. She was surprised to see Joshua standing there.

She looked at him wearily. "Come on in," she sighed.

He followed her sheepishly into the living room.

"You look like shit," she informed him.

"Cheers!"

"Drink?" she asked, raising her whiskey glass.

"Why not?"

She poured him a drink and handed it to him, then raised her glass and said, "How the mighty have fallen!"

"You'll get back to where you were again."

"You know, it took me twenty years to get where I was. If it takes me another twenty years to get there again I'll be getting my bus pass."

"I'm sorry, Kim. That it came to this."

"Not half as sorry as I am."

"I found out who was behind the website."

"Really?" she said curiously.

"It was Lee."

"*What?* The stupid little shit! What did he do that for?"

"He's got problems, and he blames me for it all."

"But he destroyed you!"

"I destroyed myself really, didn't I? He just told the world what I was doing."

She sighed loudly. "Well, I wish the two of you had gone for group therapy or something instead of flinging muck on the internet! I might still have a career if you had."

"I wish I'd done a lot of things differently." He stared into his drink.

She studied him. "Is it still off between you and Soraya?"

"She's filed for divorce."

"That girl doesn't hang around, does she?"

"Nope. Guy says she won't even meet me to talk."

"*Guy!*" She spluttered on her drink. "What's he got to do with it?"

"He's been acting as a go-between."

"What's it got to do with Guy Burton?" She was incredulous.

"He's a good friend to both of us."

She stared at him in horror. "He's no friend of yours, Joshua."

"He has been. He's been ringing me through all this constantly . . . Which is more than you have, by the way. I thought we were a little more than just work colleagues, you and me – you could at least have kept contact. You used to practically live in our kitchen on Sundays."

"Oh, shut up about me! Joshua, can I warn you not to trust Guy Burton? He's not on your side."

"You're wrong. I mean he's got me through this. I wouldn't mind but he was going through his own shit breaking up with Brooke. He broke up with her when he found out about our affair."

"Bullshit! He knew about your affair with Brooke from practically the first day he started at RTV!"

"No, he didn't!"

"Yes, he most certainly did."

"How do you know that?"

"Because *I* told him!"

Joshua gaped at her. "I don't understand."

"I predicted that this would happen if your cheap affair got out. So I went to Guy Burton and told him about the situation and tried to get him to fire Brooke."

"You did *what*? I can't believe you'd go behind my back like that!" He shook his head in disbelief.

"And I can't believe you've ruined both our careers! But, hey, guess what – shit happens!"

"So Guy – he *knew* about me and Brooke?"

"Yep. So I was shocked when, after I divulged the information to him, he promoted the idiot instead of getting rid of her. I was even more shocked to learn he started going out with her. And just flabbergasted when he arrived over to France to you with her."

"Why would he do that?" Joshua was bewildered.

"Probably for the same bizarre reasons – whatever they are – he tried to get your show axed continuously since he took over RTV!"

"I don't believe you. You're making this up to get back at Guy!"

"Oh, shut up, Joshua, you know me too well to believe that. And besides, I've nothing to gain or lose at this stage by telling you. . . He tried to get the show rescheduled to afternoon. He desperately tried to get the show axed after the whole Donna Doyle fiasco and tried to stop you getting a shot with *The Tonight Show*."

"He told me he saved the show that time!"

"My arse! It was *I* convinced Henry to continue – you can ask him. And he was certainly behind the final axe. He's done everything in his power to finish you off, Joshua, so I wouldn't be taking marital advise from him, if I were you."

The intercom buzzed and Brooke got a start. The journalists hadn't been around for a long while, and she hoped it wouldn't be one of them back trying to rekindle the story.

"Hello?" said Brooke into the intercom.

"Brooke, it's Joshua, can you let me in, please?"

Startled, she said nothing.

"Brooke?" he pushed her.

She pressed the buzzer to let him in and opened the front door. A few seconds later he came out of the lift onto the landing and she let him into the apartment and closed the door.

They viewed each other cautiously.

"To what do I owe the pleasure?" she asked.

"Can I ask you a question and you give me a straight answer?"

"Depends on the question."

"Did Guy Burton know we were having an affair before you started seeing him."

She opened up her packet of cigarettes and lit one. "Joshua, I don't want to talk about this any more. It's ruined my life. My name is mud not only in RTV but in the press as well! They've stuck me in the most boring job of all time collecting data on internet use! I can't take any more."

"My heart bleeds for you, Brooke. At least you have a job, mine is over. As is my marriage."

She got a shock. "When did that happen?"

"Straight after the story about us got out. She packed herself, the kids and the au pair and fucked off."

She dragged on her cigarette and sat down. "I didn't think she'd walk out on you. I thought Soraya would be the type to put on a brave face and suffer in silence."

"She's gone," he confirmed with a nod.

She sat down and waved him to a seat.

"Yeah, he knew," she said eventually. "He called me to his office one day and asked me outright. I didn't deny it. He took me off guard. He knew all along."

"And he still brought you to France?"

"It was he insisted I go with him. And I, the fool, went."

"He's been working against me all along."

"I'm still dealing with how he treated me. He was vicious, Joshua. He was deliberately cruel. I've never met anybody like him."

Joshua looked at his laptop screen a long time before finally logging on.

He typed in 'We Hate Joshua Green' and waited for the site to come up.

An announcement came up on the screen saying the website had been closed down permanently.

73

Brooke couldn't sleep that night as she thought about Joshua and Soraya's broken marriage. She was racked with guilt. She had destroyed the marriage she had been so jealous and envious of. But she was only so envious because they were so much in love and right together. She couldn't believe Soraya would walk out on it without trying to give it a second chance. The next day at work she couldn't concentrate and decided she couldn't just walk away from the situation without at least trying to rectify it. If Soraya knew how obsessed Joshua was with her, she might meet him and talk to him.

After work, she set off to find Soraya. She knew where the house was because she remembered Joshua pointing it out to her. She had looked at the house with inevitable envy.

As she walked down the street she saw Soraya's Range Rover parked in the drive, confirming it was the right house.

She braced herself, walked up to the front door and pressed the bell. She heard the bell echo inside and she hoped the dipsy au pair wouldn't answer. The door swung open and there stood a smiling Soraya. The smile lasted all of one second before it was dropped.

"You've got some nerve," said Soraya, eyes widened in disbelief.

"Soraya, I know I'm the last person you want to see."

"The understatement of the century."

"Could I come in for a minute? I need to talk to you."

"No! I've no need to talk to *you*!"

"You see, Soraya, I haven't come for forgiveness or atonement," Brooke said quickly, "or anything for myself."

"What do you want?"

"It's just that I hear you and Joshua are breaking up and, Soraya, you don't know how much in love with you he is."

"Did he send you over here?"

"No, of course not. Listen, all he did whenever I was with him was talk about you! He's mad about you. I meant nothing to him, I knew I meant nothing to him."

"It didn't stop you though, did it?"

"This isn't about me. It's Joshua and you I'm concerned about. If you could just talk to him, you'd understand how much he loves you."

"I think you've interfered in our marriage enough, don't you? I don't want you talking about me or anything concerning me any more, do you understand me? I don't want you near my house, my children, me."

"But –"

"Why did you do it? All I ever did was show you kindness and open my home to you when you came over. Made you coffee, food, chatted as friends."

"I know!"

"I even got Joshua to invite you to parties! All I did was be nice to you, and you were laughing at me all along."

"I wasn't laughing at you – I envied you!"

"You came to my parents' house and laughed and joked and ate with us!"

"I know, Soraya. I'm so sorry," Brooke said as she saw tears spring to Soraya's eyes.

"Are you alright, darling?" said a male voice in the hall behind Soraya, giving Brooke a fright.

Suddenly Guy appeared behind Soraya and put his arm around her.

Brooke looked on in bewilderment.

Soraya looked at Guy and nodded. "I'm fine. This – lady – is just leaving."

"Go away, Brooke, we don't want you here," said Guy.

Soraya looked at him and they kissed each other, before Soraya firmly closed the door in her face.

Guy led Soraya into the drawing room and held her tightly.

"Are you alright?" he whispered.

"I am, but only because you're here. How dare she come here? Has she not caused enough trouble?"

"She's a tramp, she knows no different."

"I wanted to hurt her. I wanted her to see that you and me were together and let her see how it feels. She was standing there with sympathy on her face, trying to tell me that my husband was in love with me! I hate people feeling sorry for me. People thinking I'm a victim."

"Nobody thinks that, love."

"I want everyone to see I'm getting on with my life. That I'm not broken. I want Joshua to see he's not broken me."

"Well, let's show them then. We've done no wrong. We've nothing to hide. Let's go out to dinner tonight. I'll book Town and Grill."

She nodded and smiled. "Okay."

Brooke took out her mobile and, her hands still shaking, managed to ring Joshua.

"What is it?" he asked, surprised to hear from her.

"I think you need to sit down. Your wife has a new boyfriend. Guy Burton."

74

Brooke sat in Joshua's sitting room, watching him angrily pace up and down.

"I'm going to go over there and sort him out!" he threatened.

"There's no point, Joshua. What good would that do?"

"It would give me some satisfaction."

"And he'd use it against you to get even closer to Soraya. Do you want that?"

"No." He sat down. "What the fuck did you go over there for anyway?"

"I thought I could get her to see how much you loved her. That I didn't mean anything to you. That you never had any feelings for me, and I was just a bit of fun."

He stared at her guiltily. "You say that without sounding too bitter."

"I've given up being bitter. It takes too much effort. And I always end up coming out worse anyway."

"Thanks for trying anyway," he said.

She looked around. "The house seems very quiet without them all bustling around."

"It's unbearably so." He shook his head.

"Where's Lee?"

"You tell me. We've had a terrible falling-out. I guess you have a right to know. It was Lee behind the whole website. He was the one who set it up, and revealed all those things about me, and you for that matter."

She stared at him. "I knew you two had problems but I didn't think he hated you that much."

"He obviously does."

"But did he not realise the consequences of what he was doing?"

"I think he did. I think he wanted those consequences."

"How did you figure it out?"

"The last stuff he put up. He revealed stuff about his mother, my first wife Catherine, which nobody else would know. I confronted him and he admitted it all."

"I'd like to kill him! For all the damage he's caused."

"It's not his fault, it's mine."

"Oh come on, Joshua, you might never win Father of the Year awards, but how could he do that to you? Why couldn't he just confront you like anyone normal?"

"You've answered your own question, I don't think he is normal. I think his childhood has fucked him up too much. I should have got him better help along the way. I was so busy trying to forget the past that I didn't stop to think how Lee was dealing with it."

"So what is the story with Lee's mother. Who is she? Where is she?"

"Her name was Catherine. She worked for a radio station. I met her there. You see, I left school burning with ambition – wanting to be somebody. I always had the gift of the gab, so I ended up doing advertising sales for the radio station. She worked there in the promotions department. She was a beautiful girl, full of fun and life and really ambitious too. We'd talk about our dreams for hours. I wanted to get into television presentation. She wanted to get high up in broadcasting. We didn't have a qualification to our name, no money, but we had our dreams. It was a bit of a shock to us when she got pregnant with Lee. We hadn't factored that into anything. And even though we were mad about each other, marriage had never been talked about or anything. But we got married quick enough and Lee was born. We rented a small flat, did what everyone did I suppose."

"Then what?"

"Life cruised along for a while. She gave up work to look after Lee. After a while she started to have panic attacks. Nothing much at first. Just, she wanted to avoid crowded places, that kind of a thing. I didn't think much about it, to be honest. I had kept badgering the boss of the radio station I worked for for a chance to do presenting, and he finally let me do a few stints, so I was focused on that."

"Where *The Joshua Green Show* cut its teeth?"

"Yes. Catherine then started getting paranoid about things. She thought the neighbour hated her and so we moved. But then the next neighbour hated her as well, so we had to move again. Then, when I was given a regular slot presenting on the radio and my career started to get busy, she started saying I was going to leave her. And she wouldn't listen to sense. It got worse and worse and she started ranting a lot and raving. She wouldn't see a doctor. She then accused me of having affairs. Which I wasn't, incidentally. I finally got her to see a doctor who said she was suffering from depression and he prescribed pills. They helped for a while, but she kept slipping back into terrible black moods. And when she was down there was no talking to her. I spent every day trying to coax her out of the moods, but it was impossible. By the time Lee was seven we didn't have a marriage any more – and I had a woman who had lost herself and was completely paranoid about me. She wanted me out and so I left. I was glad to leave then. But I left Lee with her."

"Well, that would have been the norm then," said Brooke.

"I know, but she wasn't in the right state of mind to look after a child, and he shouldn't have been left with her. She tried to poison him against me. Telling him I was with other women all the time, and treated her badly and abused her. I'd have him for weekends, but even then I could see he was putting up a wall against me, created by her. Then when he was eight, she tried to kill herself."

"Oh, Joshua!"

"But the worst of it was, she involved Lee. She dressed him up as a waiter and got him to bring her the prescription drugs on a silver tray and feed her them one by one. He rang me at work and said he couldn't wake her."

"What happened?"

"She survived, and blamed me for it. But then she was dead in a few months anyway, from alcohol abuse. Lee came to live with me. He was nine by then but very angry with the world and especially me. My career was flying at that stage. I was with the national radio and had a top-rating talk show on it. And I know people think I exploit all those people on my shows. But in actual fact, I understand them. Because I've been there. I know what it's like to deal with a desperate situation. That's why I can communicate with them the way I do."

"I see," she nodded.

"So, it was just me and Lee for the next four years. I obviously went out on dates which made him think that I did cheat on his mother all along. Then I met Soraya. He was thirteen by then. And she managed to work magic with him. She managed to communicate with him and when we got married we managed to provide a real home for him, and a family when Daniel and Danielle were born."

"And then I came along and blew it all apart," said Brooke, sighing.

"No, I blew it all apart. But what surprises me is that he would hurt Soraya that way by exposing our affair. I thought he genuinely adored her and wouldn't do that to her."

"Well, I guess he thought he was protecting her by exposing the affair. He didn't want her going the same way as Catherine, his mother."

"It makes sense, I suppose," mused Joshua. "I just didn't think he would have the heart to hurt her publicly like that."

"Lee obviously is capable of anything," said Brooke. "As you said, he's damaged from all that happened. What are you going to do about him?"

"I don't know. I've asked Catherine's sister, Helen, to talk to him. They always got on well. He might listen to her . . . But none of that helps with the situation Soraya is getting herself into with that creep. I don't know how to warn her."

"You know what we need?" said Brooke suddenly. "Kim

385

Davenport. She's the most devious person I know. If anyone can outsmart Guy Burton, she can."

Lee waited in the canteen for his Aunt Helen to arrive. She had badgered him into meeting her for lunch, so he'd finally agreed to meet her at the RTV canteen. He saw her come in and make her way over to him.

"I feel blessed to be granted an audience," she said sarcastically as she reached him, kissed him on both cheeks and sat down opposite him.

"I've been busy," he said.

"Yes, so I've heard. Now you're a big television executive."

"Don't take the piss."

"Perish the thought."

"Do you want something to eat?"

She looked down disdainfully at his sausages and chips. "I'll pass, thanks all the same. I'm meeting friends at Patrick Guilbaud's . . . Now what's all this I hear about you launching an internet campaign or some such nonsense against your father?"

Lee's face went red. "I don't regret it."

"No, we never do at your age. However, I do not like you spreading lies on the internet about my deceased sister, young man."

"I didn't spread any lies about Mum," said Lee.

"Writing that Joshua drove her to her death is a lie, Lee."

"It's not! I know what happened. I was there."

"And so was I, and had the benefit of being an adult. Your mother was a very ill woman, Lee, I should know. I went to the doctor's with her on many occasions. And what you're doing now to your father and the memory of your mother and to us, her family, is cruel and unnecessary."

"So he just gets off scot-free?"

"Whatever Joshua has done or failed to do in life is one thing, but being responsible for Catherine's death he is not. And by the looks of him I certainly don't think he's got off scot-free from anything. He looks broken, thanks to you and your poisonous website."

"Oh, easily known he put you up to this!" Lee stood up quickly.

"Oh, sit down and finish your sausage and chips, Lee, and don't be such a prima donna!" snapped Helen.

He shoved the tray over to her. "No, you finish them, you look as if you need a good dinner." He walked off.

Helen sighed, before reaching for a chip, dunking it in ketchup and eating it. She got up and walked out of the canteen.

She spotted Lee at a distance, deep in conversation with a man she recognised as the same one who had been at Joshua's the other night. Guy.

She suddenly started having flashbacks.

A young woman was walking by and Helen stopped her. "Excuse me, that man over there – Guy. What's his surname again?"

The woman looked over to where Helen was indicating and her face took on a reverential look. "That's Guy Burton," she said as if everyone should know that.

"I see. Thank you," said Helen and the woman walked off.

She stepped into a shadow and observed them. Guy looked as if he was trying to calm Lee down. Then he put his arm around Lee's shoulders and they walked into a spare office and closed the door.

"Guy Burton. Now that's a name I thought I wouldn't hear again."

Helen hung around RTV for an hour, keeping an eye on the office that Lee and Guy had gone into. Finally they emerged and Lee headed off in one direction while Guy set off in the other. She quickly followed Guy as he made his way to reception.

"Oh, hello there again!" she said as both of them arrived into reception at the same time.

He looked startled to see her. "Yes – hello."

"Joshua's sister-in-law, I met you at his house." She stretched out her hand and smiled.

"Yes, how are you?"

"Very well."

"Joshua doesn't work here any more if you're looking for him," said Guy.

A. O'CONNOR

"Yes, I know – it was my nephew Lee I was meeting."

"Oh, I see."

"Do you know him?"

"Vaguely," said Guy, beginning to walk away.

Helen walked alongside him.

"You know, I'm sure we've met before?" she said.

"I get that a lot, I've one of those faces."

"Not at all . . . How long have you known Joshua?"

"Not long. I haven't worked at RTV that long." He stopped and gave her a brief smile. "I need to get going to a meeting. Nice to meet you again."

Guy strode off. Helen looked after him, thinking hard.

388

75

Kim was not amused to receive a call from Joshua, anxiously asking her to call to his house. There was an "urgent matter" he wanted to talk to her about. She tried putting him off, but he threatened to call to her house again. She didn't need Joshua annoying her right now. She was getting over her life falling apart. And Joshua's irresponsible behaviour was a huge contributing factor to why her life had fallen apart. But regardless of her career being over, she did have Jasmine back which was the main thing. And she did see how Soraya's leaving had affected Joshua.

And she was curious.

"What's all this about?" she asked as he led her into the sitting room.

She got a start to see Brooke sitting there.

"Isn't it a bit too soon to be having a reunion?" asked Kim as she looked from one to the other.

"Kim, sit down. Let me get you a drink. Whiskey?"

"Whatever," she said, seating herself and staring at Brooke.

Joshua handed her a generous glass of whiskey and sat opposite her.

"Kim," he said, "we've discovered that Soraya is now seeing Guy Burton."

Kim raised her eyes to heaven. "There really is no accounting for

389

taste. From the fire to the frying-pan. And you've called me here to tell me that?"

"Well, doesn't that concern you?" asked Joshua.

"Frankly no! It's none of my concern. And to be honest it shouldn't be your concern either."

"But we've only just figured out everything Guy has been doing. How dangerous he is," said Brooke.

"I think you'll find I was always aware how dangerous he was. It was you two who were falling over yourselves to be his friend and lover."

"We've been completely naïve, we accept that now," said Brooke.

"Good. Let's hope you learn from the experience and won't be stupid next time – and won't leave complete destruction in your wake."

"But we can't just leave Soraya to him, to ruin her life as well!" said Joshua.

"I think you'll find you two have done a very good job at ruining poor old Soraya's life on your own!"

"Kim, we need your help," said Brooke.

"Joshua, you just want to get Soraya back – and, Brooke, you just want to cleanse your conscience. However, I've done nothing wrong, my conscience is clear. Soraya is an adult, with an unfortunate taste in men, but responsible for her own decisions. I'm not getting involved." Finishing off her whiskey, Kim got up to go.

"Remember how you felt when Jasmine was working for him?" said Joshua. "Did that not frighten you?"

"Yes, but she is my daughter."

"And Soraya meant nothing to you? All those times we socialised together? You practically lived in this house, you spent so much time here. We were like family. That was all a show on your part, was it? Soraya and I were just a meal ticket when your career was dependent on us?"

"You forget, Joshua, I don't do guilt. You're wasting your time with that one."

Joshua gave her a pleading look.

Kim sighed. "I'm actually extremely fond of Soraya. But I just find the idea of the two of you trying to rescue her a farce! You're the two people she wants to be rescued from!"

"Exactly. She won't talk or listen to us. That's why we need you."

Kim sat down again. "Why me?"

"Because you're the person who can outsmart everyone. You're the person who finds everyone's weak spot and exploits it," explained Brooke.

"Well, Guy Burton found all our weak spots and finished us off. I bow to his superiority," said Kim.

Joshua's mobile rang and he went out to the kitchen to take the call. Kim looked at Brooke wearily.

"Also, don't you want revenge on Guy Burton?" asked Brooke. "For finishing off your show?"

"Is this what it is for you, revenge for him using you and dumping you to get to what he obviously really wanted – Joshua out of the way and him with Soraya?"

"You were more right in what you said the other night. I *am* looking for some kind of atonement for what I did. Something bad will happen to Soraya if she stays with him. Whatever games he plans to play on her, it's only a matter of time before he starts. And she's gone through enough already. She's vulnerable after what happened and I don't want to see her go through any more."

Kim looked at her and lowered her voice. "You know, if you gave it a shot, you might get something going with Joshua now. Soraya's out of the way, he's at a low ebb. You might get your relationship back on a permanent basis."

"I don't want that. I now realise I never loved him, I just had an infatuation. And he certainly doesn't love me."

"Soraya won't thank you for all this. Meddling further in her life," warned Kim.

Joshua came back in and turned off his phone.

"I'm sorry," said Kim. "I think you're so used to me dealing with all the shit at work and sorting it out that you think I have the answer to everything. I don't have the answer to this. I'll see you around."

Kim got up and left.

Brooke let herself into her apartment and, taking off her coat, she began to open her post. As she tore open the envelopes she spotted the BBC headed paper and read the letter from them, expecting it to be a rejection letter for the job she had applied for. Instead it was an invitation to an interview. She read the letter again and again before grinning happily.

76

After Brooke had left, Joshua was sitting brooding when he heard Lee come in the front door and make straight for the stairs.

"Lee?" said Joshua, following him up the stairs.

"Don't worry, I'm not staying. I've only come to pack a bag and go."

"Where are you going?" asked Joshua, following him into his bedroom.

"I'm staying with a friend for a couple of nights. Then I'm going to rent my own place."

"You're too young to be renting your own place," said Joshua.

"As you constantly remind me, you were working and supporting yourself at my age. So I can do it as well."

"Lee, I want to talk to you about the other day."

"There's nothing to talk about. You now know it was me who wrote all those things on the internet about you. And you know the reasons."

"Did you meet with your Aunt Helen?"

"Oh, I met her alright. You really brainwashed her too, didn't you? But then you always had a way of getting women to do what you wanted."

"Lee, I want you to know that I don't blame you for writing those things on the internet. I just wish we had a relationship where you could have come and said them to my face and given me a chance to explain."

"Well, we don't."

"But it's not to late for us to start now."

"Of course it is."

"We never talk about your mother but I want to now. I want to explain properly how things were, instead of sweeping things under the carpet. You know, I made my living in getting people to open up about themselves and try to sort out their problems by talking to each other. And I wasn't capable of doing it myself."

"That's because there was no money involved."

"No, because it was too painful. She was a very complicated woman. And I shouldn't have left you on your own so much with her. Yes, I wanted to get somewhere in life. But I never cheated on her. In the end I couldn't cope so I moved out for a while, and that's when that night happened."

"I don't want to talk about it," snapped Lee.

"When she got you to serve her the pills."

Lee sat down on the bed and put his face in his hands as he had a flashback.

His mother told him she had a very special job for him to do. She got him to dress up in a suit she had bought him and then place all the jars of pills and tablets on the silver tray. She called them her sweets. He remembered the towel over one arm and carrying the silver tray in the other and bringing it into her room as she had told him. She sat up in her bed, smiling, and told him to put down the tray on the bedside table. Then she got him to hand her tablet after tablet as she swallowed them with the help of a glass of water. Until she had drifted off to sleep.

Lee stood up abruptly. "Why aren't you angry with me? Why don't you want to kill me after I exposed everything you are?"

"What's the point? Most of it was true." Joshua looked at his son. "You look as if you want me to be angry with you."

"Yes, I do!"

"Because you'd feel satisfaction then that you've got to me?"

"Yes!"

"Then if that makes you feel better, you have."

"Good," said Lee as he grabbed his bag and left.

Helen had spent ages at home going through old family albums and photos. She usually kept them locked up in her study as it often caused her pain to relive memories, especially about her sister. She smiled as she sifted through the photos of her dead sister, remembering her when she was a young vivacious woman full of life, before her mind started to disintegrate. She smiled to herself as she saw photos of Helen and Joshua when they just started going out together.

"Little did you know what was ahead of you," she sighed.

And then she continued sifting through the photos until she found the one she had been searching for.

She stared at the photo and said, "I knew it!"

When the doorbell rang Joshua hoped it would be Lee coming home, having forgotten his key as per usual, but was surprised to see Helen on his doorstep.

"Oh it's you!" said Joshua, looking disappointed.

"I've had warmer welcomes!" said Helen.

"I'm sorry, come in. I've had a row with Lee and he says he's moving out of home. I thought it might be him coming back."

He closed the door after her and they walked into the sitting room.

"Have you heard from him today?"

"No."

"Ring me if he turns up at yours, will you? I'm that worried."

"Of course I will."

He saw her worried expression. "Everything alright, Helen?"

"I don't think so. I think I should show you something."

She held out a photograph.

Joshua took the photo and sat on the sofa.

"I don't understand," he said, shaking his head as he stared at it.

Helen was fixing herself a gin and tonic. "I knew I recognised him as soon as I saw him. But it's been that many years, and I've met a lot of men since then, believe you me," she smiled wryly, "that I couldn't place him. He's changed a lot. His appearance is very different, all suave and sophisticated now. And where did he get that Americanised accent?"

"He worked in New York for years," said Joshua.

"Any bitters?" she asked, perusing the drink's cabinet. "Oh, it'll have to do," she said, taking a gulp of the drink and making a face.

She came and sat beside Joshua and looked down at the photo of a very young Guy, smiling, with his arm around Joshua's first wife Catherine.

"Don't you remember him at all?" asked Helen.

"No, but why should I?"

"Because Guy worked at the same radio station as you and Catherine back then. He went out with Catherine before you. She dumped him for you."

"I don't remember her even talking about seeing anybody else."

"No surprises there. She was kind of seeing both of you at the same time."

"What?"

"Catherine and Guy had been going out about a year. I never really liked him, he was very intense. Very jealous if she spoke to another man, and you know what Catherine was like – she never stopped flirting with other men. And then you arrived to work at the station, and quite literally turned her head. She never stopped talking about you. This dashing new guy. Then you became a presenter. That was the icing on the cake! And when you showed interest back, well, she wasn't going to let Guy get in the way of her being with you. I don't like speaking ill of her, but you know what she was like, Joshua. She kept Guy there until she was sure it was going to work out with you. Then she dropped him. He took it very badly. He wouldn't take no for an answer. Anyway, finally he left the station."

"Why did she never tell me about him?"

"She was frightened it might scare you off. I think she was secretly enjoying Guy's infatuation. Besides, Catherine liked playing games with people, until her games caught up with her . . . in her head."

They both stared down at the photo.

"That's how I like to remember her. Beautiful, vivacious, the life and soul of the party," said Joshua.

"Yeah, me too," sighed Helen as she looked at the photo and rested her head on his shoulder.

Guy was in his apartment listening to classical music when the intercom sounded. He frowned at the interruption and, choosing to ignore the caller, raised the volume of the music. The buzzer rang again and again.

"For fuck's sake!" he snapped, getting up and turning off the music. He went over to the intercom.

"What?" he snapped in to the intercom.

"It's Joshua Green. I want to talk to you."

Guy sighed irritably. "Well, I don't want to talk to you. Now fuck off!"

"I'm going to keep pressing this bell and all your neighbours' bells until you let me in."

Guy thought for a moment and then pressed the button. He unlocked the front door and moved back into the lounge. A couple of minutes later Joshua came into the apartment, followed by Helen.

Guy looked very uneasy when he saw her. "Oh, you again," he said casually.

"Yes, me," said Helen, closing the door behind her. "Are you beginning to recognise me yet?"

"I don't know what the two of you are doing here, but I'd like you to leave now," said Guy.

"Well, we don't always get what we want in this world – you should know that by now, Guy," said Joshua.

"I always get what I want. But then I'm not a loser like you."

"Wasn't always the case though, was it?" said Helen and reaching into her handbag she took out the photo and handed it to Guy.

He took the photo and paled, then flushed.

"You made a lovely couple," said Helen. "Pity she didn't agree."

Guy crumpled the photo in his hand. "How do you know what she thought?"

"I was her sister. She told me everything," said Helen.

"We were very happy until *you* came working at the station!" Guy pointed viciously at Joshua. "Thinking you were something, marching around as if you owned the place. You were going to be the big star and, boy, didn't you let everyone know! And you pursued Catherine until you got her. And she fell for all your bullshit."

"She fell for me, mate," snapped Joshua angrily.

"We were going to get married," stated Guy.

"No, you weren't," Helen objected. "She never even hinted at that. Catherine had more boyfriends than you had hot dinners before she met Joshua, and you were just one in a long line of them. She loved them and left them. She was notorious for it. You weren't the first to fall for her guiles. But you were the last, before she settled down with Joshua."

"And what did you do when you married her? Treated her like shit! Drove her to madness with your carry-on. She didn't deserve that. You didn't deserve her!"

"But you did?" asked Joshua incredulously.

"I made her happy," stated Guy.

"Oh, nobody could make Catherine happy, Guy," insisted Helen. "She was restless beyond compare. Joshua couldn't deal with her, and you certainly wouldn't have when she started getting very bad in her head."

"So this is what it's all about?" said Joshua. "Trying to destroy me – taking my career, my wife, my son even, because I took your love all those years ago. I can't even remember you. She never even mentioned you. You meant nothing to her, you fool!"

"Didn't I?"

"No."

"You know, Brooke isn't the only woman we were seeing at the same time. Catherine didn't just finish with me and start seeing you. I found out when she finished with me that she two-timed me with you for a long while."

"Yes, she liked to keep her options open," said Helen with a sigh.

"So what?" said Joshua.

"So, I left the radio station when we broke up and I headed to New York. But I've done the arithmetic. She was already pregnant with Lee when I left for the States."

"*What?*" said Joshua.

"With me gone, when she found out she was pregnant perhaps she didn't think too carefully who Lee's father could be. Especially if she had set her cap at you – well, a pregnancy was a great way to cement your relationship."

"You think Lee is yours, is that what you're saying?" asked Helen incredulously.

"I think it makes perfect sense. He's absolutely nothing like you," said Guy.

"No, that's because he's so like his flaming mother!" said Joshua.

"Maybe you always suspected he wasn't yours. Maybe that's why you're angry with him so much?"

"I'm angry with him so much because he's so like his mother I'm terrified he'll end up just like her! I'm just trying to keep him on the right path!"

"I don't buy it," said Guy.

"I don't care what you buy," Joshua's voice rose in anger. "Lee is my son."

"Are you sure?" Guy asked mockingly.

"Yes, I'm sure. It never even crossed my mind he wouldn't be."

"Well, I've done the maths and I reckon he's mine."

"Shut your mouth!" Joshua shouted, moving towards him.

Helen gave a light laugh and sighed. "He's not your son, Guy."

"How would you know? Because she told you? She wouldn't even know herself."

"No. But I know he can't be your son."

"Why?"

"Because Lee has brown eyes and Catherine had beautiful blue eyes and you have blue eyes, steely cold blue eyes. Two blue-eyed parents can't have anything but a blue-eyed child. Lee with his brown eyes can't be yours, Guy."

Guy stared into Joshua's brown eyes and his face became red with anger.

"Get the fuck out of my apartment!" he said through gritted teeth.

"And you get the fuck out of my family's life!" shouted Joshua.

"No, me and Soraya are for keeps, you might as well get used to it. Now you'll know what it's like to have something you loved taken away from you."

"If you do anything to her, you'll pay for it! She's not a pawn in your stupid games for you to use or discard as you see fit!"

"I'll treat her anyway I want. It's not up to you."

"If you hurt her . . ." warned Joshua and he grabbed Guy's shirt.

"Then I'll be hurting you too," said Guy, smiling.

Helen moved between them and pushed Joshua back. "Come on, Joshua, let's get out of here."

Glaring at Guy, Joshua let himself be led away by Helen.

Guy was in his apartment, staring out at the Dublin skyline as the sun set. He uncrumpled the photo they had left him of himself and Catherine from all those years ago. It seemed like another lifetime. It was another lifetime. At least another life. When he had been fired from Lagarde's film that time, he was lost when he realised he wasn't going to get another break in the film world. So eventually he decided to try and carve out a career in the next best thing: broadcasting. He was just a runner at the radio station where Catherine worked.

He was amazed when she showed interest in him. He was at a low ebb and feeling bad about himself and life, drinking too much. And then Catherine had come along and changed everything. He didn't recognise the Catherine they described, the disturbed paranoid Catherine. He remembered a beautiful fun-loving girl who gave him a reason to be happy again. Until Joshua came swaggering in and swept her off her feet. He pleaded with her not to leave him. Told her he would do anything for her. Even turned a blind eye when she cheated on him with Joshua. When she finally dumped him he was desolate and emigrated to New York to try and slowly build his life again.

When he was offered the job at RTV it seemed too good to be

true. The station where Joshua Green was a star. Guy would make his triumphant return. He was no longer the backroom boy, he was a force to be reckoned with. He anticipated meeting Joshua again, shocking him by how powerful he now was and showing how he could crush him at a whim. Then he decided it would be more satisfying to manipulate Joshua and undermine him secretly.

Catherine was no more, of course, replaced by the beautiful Soraya. Nobody ever even referred to her. This motivated Guy even more strongly to take everything from Joshua the way he had taken everything from him – starting with his mistress, then his career, then his wife and even his son.

He hadn't even known Catherine was pregnant when he headed to America. Then he'd done the arithmetic and figured Lee could be his son. This idea was reinforced by the fact that Lee bore no resemblance to Joshua. He started to believe that Lee was his. But now, thanks to Helen's knowledge of eye-colour genetics, he realised he had been kidding himself. Lee was not his son.

The intercom buzzed. He turned and looked at the video screen on the intercom and was surprised to see Lee there. He buzzed him in and unlocked the front door. A minute later Lee arrived into the apartment carrying a large bag, which he placed in the hall.

"I've had enough of him this time. I really have," Lee said, coming in and sitting down.

"What has he done now?"

"Nothing. Everything. Another argument and another confrontation. All he does is sit around feeling sorry for himself, drinking."

"It must be tough for you to live with," Guy sympathised.

"Yeah, well, I've had enough," said Lee. "I've moved out of home."

"Have you?" asked Guy, looking concerned.

"Yep. Packed my bag and told him I was out of there."

"I'd say he was annoyed?"

"He didn't want me to go. But I feel free, Guy. For the first time in my life I feel free. Free from him."

Guy glanced over at the oversized bag in the hall. "Where are you planning on moving to – exactly?"

"Well, I was thinking, well, I was hoping that I could crash here for a while."

Guy studied Lee's brown eyes and said, "Here?"

"Yeah."

"Ah, that could be a little awkward."

"Oh?" Lee was startled.

"Yes, you see, I'm seeing someone new. And she's spending a lot of time over here. And she's quite private. And well, you know, three's a crowd and all."

"Oh, eh, sure." Lee went bright red.

"I mean if it wasn't for that, you could stay here no problem. I'd love to have you stay."

Lee nodded, embarrassed. "Em, I'd better be off then."

"You're okay for a place to stay tonight though, aren't you?" asked Guy, looking concerned.

"Of course, I've loads of friends I can stay with. Loads."

Guy relaxed and smiled. "Good. I thought you would."

Lee felt awkward and got up quickly. "Right. I'd better be off then."

77

Brooke had booked a very early morning flight to London to allow herself enough time to avoid any usual Brooke Radcliffe fuck-ups en route to the interview at the BBC. So she arrived in plenty of time at the television centre and took in the atmosphere and ambiance of the place. She tried to stop herself from getting too excited at the prospect of working there because she wouldn't be able to cope if she got her hopes too high and they were then dashed. She had to be realistic. The competition for the job would be intense and it was amazing she had even been called for an interview.

She had done plenty of research on the producer of the new show, Molly Grinder, who had won plenty of awards and was well respected.

She steadied her nerves as she was shown into Molly's office promptly at two in the afternoon.

"Hello there, delighted you made the trip to meet me," said Molly in a broad north of England accent, smiling warmly.

Brooke liked her immediately. She had a friendly face and spiked hair and was dressed in bohemian clothes – quite unlike the sharply dressed and sharp-tongued producers Brooke was used to.

"Please take a seat," urged Molly after shaking Brooke's hand and Brooke did what she was bid. "Did you have nice flight?"

"Yes, very, thank you," nodded a smiling Brooke.

"That's good. I was so looking forward to meeting you. I was so impressed by your accolades and attitude," said Molly.

"Really?" said Brooke, delighted and getting quite excited by this encouraging talk.

"Yes, definitely. I'll just briefly tell you the process that brought you here. All the applications are sifted through in HR who then forward suitable candidates down to the programme here. Then my assistant Tilly goes through the CVs and she condenses them into brief notes. Then I go through the notes and decide who I want to meet. And I have to say yours was top of my pile."

Brooke's heart started beating quickly in excitement.

"My assistant Tilly is a great girl – I couldn't do without her," confided Molly. "She can be a bit scatty at times, particularly after a heavy night the night before. But she has a heart of gold. A tart with a heart."

I should fit in just fine then, thought Brooke wryly.

Molly glanced down at Tilly's notes. "Now the first thing I was impressed by, and what I'm really looking forward to talking to you about in detail, is the fact that you never eat anything that you haven't grown yourself. That's amazing. Very *The Good Life*, init? How do you manage to be so disciplined?"

Brooke's face dropped. "Em – I'm afraid that's not true."

"You what?" Molly's face dropped in turn.

"Em – I don't produce any of my own food. I live in an apartment with only a tiny balcony so, even if I wanted to, it would be an impossibility."

Molly looked crestfallen. "Oh – I see. Tilly must have got mixed up somehow with somebody else's CV." Molly began to smile again. "Anyway, at least you're a vegan. I like to employ vegans as we're all on the same wavelength, aren't we? I tell you, when I was growing up in Wigan, I was the only vegan in a ten-mile radius. When the other girls were having competitions to see who could down the most lagers in an hour, there I was with my beans and lentils. I was such a disappointment to my parents, they didn't know what to make of me . . ."

"I'm not a vegan!" Brooke suddenly blurted out.

"I'm sorry?"

"I'm not a vegan."

"Oh!" Molly looked stunned. "Vegetarian though?"

"I'm afraid not," said Brooke.

"I see . . . I don't know what Tilly was thinking of when she compiled your notes. It must have been a very heavy night on the booze the night before . . . Anyway, maybe we should move on to your actual work history."

"Yes, it might be safer," smiled Brooke.

"So," Molly glanced through the notes quickly, "you've been the producer on a current affairs programme for the past five years."

Brooke blinked a few times and bit her bottom lip.

Molly spotted Brooke's worried expression and asked, "Weren't you?"

"No. I've been an assistant producer."

"On a current affairs programme?"

"On *The Joshua Green Show*."

"Joshua Green!"

"The talk show," confirmed Brooke.

"*Confessional* talk show," said a disturbed-looking Molly. "Silly Tilly! It's slap-on-the-wrist time for you later!" She pushed the notes to one side and looked at Brooke. "Well, at least you're an Aries. I love working with Aries. I always say you know where you are with an Aries. You mightn't *like* where you are with them but at least you know where you are . . ." Molly trailed off as she saw Brooke slowly shaking her head.

"You're not an Aries?" asked Molly.

"I'm a Libran," said Brooke.

"A Libran! But my brother-in-law is a Libran!"

"Not a good thing?" checked Brooke, sighing.

"No, definitely not. I'm practically allergic to Librans."

Brooke nodded, resolved to her fate, as she reached into her handbag and took out a cigarette and lit it.

"A smoker to boot!" exclaimed Molly, horrified.

"Yep! You might as well get to know the real me while we're at it."

As Brooke sat on the plane that evening heading back to Dublin, going over the details of what must be one of the worst job interviews in the BBC's history, she didn't know whether to laugh or cry. She decided to laugh.

Guy and Soraya had dinner with the children and, after the little ones had gone to bed, they sat in the drawing room.

"I was speaking to my parents today. They said hello," said Soraya.

"Were they, eh, surprised to hear about me and you?"

"Yes, they were, of course."

"But not upset?" he checked.

"No. They were very worried when Joshua and I broke up, wondering how I would cope. So they're just glad I'm getting on with things."

Soraya looked pale and had been quiet, he thought.

"And any more word from Joshua?" he probed.

"No. I think the message has finally sunk in. The divorce papers did it – you were right."

He sat nearer to her and put his arm around her. "Listen, next week we're unveiling the winter schedule at a do at RTV. I'm giving a speech. Why don't you come?"

"I don't know, Guy. I don't know if I want to go in there after all that's happened."

He smiled at her crookedly. "It was you who said you wanted to be seen getting on with things. Not be pitied. What better way than to show up with me?"

Soraya thought and nodded. "Yeah, why not?"

The doorbell chimed through the house and Soraya made her way through the hall and opened the door. She got a surprise to see Lee there carrying a large bag.

"Lee!" She enveloped him in a hug and kissed him. "How are you?"

She led him inside to the drawing room. Guy had gone out of the room.

"I'm okay. Missing you," Lee said.

"And I've missed you so much!"

They sat on the couch and she held his hand.

"You told me on the phone you got a new job in RTV."

"Yeah. It's still a researcher job, but the programme is interesting. Politics."

"Excellent . . ." Her face clouded over. "And home?"

"Not so good. All he does is sit around feeling sorry for himself. We've been rowing a lot."

"Oh Lee!"

"I need some time away from him or I'll kill him, so I moved out a couple of days ago."

"Where have you been staying?" she asked, concerned.

"Over at Ross's family. But he has a ten-year-old brother who's driving me mad."

"You can't stay there indefinitely."

"I know . . . I was hoping . . ." He looked embarrassed.

"Lee, you can stay here," she said decisively, guessing his question.

"Are you sure?"

"Of course I'm sure. You're my family. I don't want you staying anywhere else unless you're with your father."

"Thanks, Soraya," he said and hugged her tightly.

She drew back. "Lee, there's just one thing – and you might be a bit surprised."

"What is it?" He didn't look too concerned.

At that moment Guy walked in, holding a glass of Coke.

"Hi, Lee, how are you?" asked Guy with a smile.

Lee's face dropped and he looked quickly from Soraya to Guy.

"Lee, myself and Guy have started seeing each other," explained Soraya.

Lee continued looking from one to the other in amazement. "When did all this happen?"

"Not too long ago," said Soraya. "I've no reason to feel guilty, Lee. I haven't done anything wrong. I'm a free agent now, I've filed for divorce and everything."

"I know. No, I'm just a bit shocked. But you're right, I guess. There is nothing stopping you."

"So you're pleased for me?" asked Soraya.

"If you're happy then I'm pleased," he said, still looking shocked.

"That's good," said Guy. He came over and sat on the other side of Lee, putting an arm around his shoulder.

Suddenly there was crash upstairs and the sound of one of the children crying. "Soraya! Soraya!" Ulrika shouted.

Soraya rolled her eyes, saying, "There's always something, isn't there?" and went out of the room and upstairs.

Guy smiled at a still shocked Lee and then he got up and closed the door.

"This is a turn-up for the books," said Lee. "You sleeping with my stepmum."

"Ex-stepmother," Guy corrected, going over and standing by the fireplace. "I overheard you asking about staying here."

"Yeah."

"I don't know if that's such a good idea," said Guy slowly.

"Huh?"

"Soraya is quite a woman, isn't she?"

"Yes, she is."

"I don't think I've ever met anybody like her. Beautiful, classy, kind, rich but not spoilt. I really think we could make a go of it."

"Maybe."

"It's just, you know, that the beginning of a relationship often is the most important part as it sets the tone for the rest of it. I don't know if having Soraya's ex-husband's son around is the most conducive scenario for romance to blossom."

"I don't get you."

Guy approached him. "If life is a stage, then everyone must know their part, and more importantly their exit. And your exit has just arrived."

"You don't want me staying here?"

"I always said you were a bright kid. When Soraya comes back, just make your excuses. Say you've thought about it and you can't leave your dad in his time of need. She'll appreciate your loyalty to him, I'm sure."

Half an hour later Lee was walking down the street away from Soraya's home in a trance. He took out his mobile and started going through all the names in it. He paused as he came to Brooke's number. He hesitated before dialling her number.

"Brooke? It's Lee. I don't know who else I could call."

78

Guy had got a wonderful video show-reel compiled of all the new shows he had commissioned. To a background of funky music in the auditorium, the video would showcase the winter schedule to all the staff at RTV. He was going to introduce the video. Henry King and all the directors would be present as well as the staff and he was delighted with the new schedule he was unveiling. Delighted too that Soraya had agreed to accompany him.

The day of the screening, he waited patiently in the hall for Soraya to finish getting ready. RTV was sending a car to collect them.

"Car's here!" he shouted up the stairs, hearing it arrive outside.

"I thought my days of going to these events were over when I left Joshua," she said as she walked down the stairs, looking lovely in a white dress.

"Never say never!" he said.

He kissed her and took her hand. They went out to the waiting car.

Henry King had heard rumours that Guy was seeing Joshua Green's ex-wife and when he saw them arrive in together he realised it was true. The whole year had been such a roller-coaster of events that he was hoping for a quiet period from now on. All his personal favourite shows were gone, axed by a non-compromising Guy

Burton. Joshua Green was finished in disgrace. Their top-rated soap starring Henry's favourite actress Fiona Fallon had been axed, with Guy citing poor production and bad acting as the reason. Of course Fiona Fallon was a bad actress – it was part of her charm that endeared her to the public. Guy Burton had certainly stirred things up.

Henry smiled at Soraya as she sat down beside him in the front row and all the other staff from RTV began to pile in and take their seats.

"Nice weather we're having for the time of year," Henry said, not knowing what else to say under the circumstances.

She smiled back and nodded.

Guy went up to the podium and adjusted the microphone as everyone quietened down.

"Good afternoon, everybody. Good to see you all here," said Guy, smiling. "As we go into the winter schedule we are looking at a very different television service, I'm glad to say. Changes can be unsettling for people, but I think they are necessary in order to move forward."

As he spoke he saw Brooke enter by one of the doors at the top of the auditorium and stand there with her arms folded.

"So you will see by the promotional piece we are about to view that a lot of old faces will be missing, and a lot of new ones introduced . . ."

As he spoke, another door at the top of the auditorium opened and Kim came in and also stood at the back staring at him.

"We say goodbye to some old soaps which are to be replaced by excellent quality dramas. We say goodbye to some controversial talk shows as we replace them by intelligent conversation programmes."

Finally Joshua came in through the third exit and stood there, also looking fixedly at him.

Guy paused and looked from one to the other of them before continuing. "All this with a host of well-produced documentaries that will bring RTV to the very top of the television world. I hope you enjoy the following piece."

Guy stepped down from the podium and went and sat beside Soraya and Henry.

The large screen behind the podium flickered and came to life. But instead of the promotional piece, footage of Lee sitting on a chair came on.

Soraya looked at Guy in confusion. "What's going on?" she asked.

"I don't know," said Guy, astounded.

"Hi, my name is Lee Green," said Lee on the screen. "You might have seen me around as I work at RTV as a researcher. My father is Joshua Green. The reason you're watching a video of me instead of the winter line-up is because I've a confession to make. I know you've all been following the 'We Hate Joshua Green' website and all its thoughts and revelations. Well, it was me that created the website. I started the website, designed it and got it up and running. I said all those negative things about my father. But only up to a point. I wasn't responsible for all the revelations that appeared there. You see, when I started work at RTV, I became friends with Guy Burton."

"I think we've seen enough of this crap," said Guy going to stand up.

"No, I want to hear it," said Soraya, gripping his arm and forcing him to resist.

"Let's hear what he has to say," said Henry King, looking at Guy.

"I became good friends with Guy Burton," said Lee on the screen. "And I confided in him about the website I had created. He thought it was a great idea. In fact, he thought it was such a good idea that he took it over from me. I had nothing more to do with it after that. It was Guy Burton who wrote about there being no counsellor on the show. It was Guy who revealed the affair between my father and Brooke Radcliffe. I didn't even know about that until I read it like the rest of you. But he had discovered it and he revealed it on the website. And I had confided in him about my mother and the relationship she had with my father. He revealed all that on the website as well. I never wanted the website to be used for all that. I was angry with my father and it was just a way for me to vent my anger and write annoying things about him. I didn't want it to be used to destroy him the way it has. Why didn't I ask Guy to stop? I did, but he talked me round. I thought I owed him a lot. I thought I could trust him. I'm sorry for the damage I caused."

The video ended and the screen went blank as the auditorium erupted in loud conversation.

Soraya turned and stared at Guy.

"It's rubbish, absolute rubbish! A stupid boy making up lies!" said Guy, half laughing.

Soraya shook her head, then stood up and walked through the auditorium. As she reached the exit she saw Joshua standing there.

"Soraya," he said as he moved towards her.

She glared at him for a moment and left.

Henry leaned over towards Guy. "I think we need to talk."

Kim walked over to Joshua and said happily, "Well, what do you think?"

"You arranged all that?" He was incredulous.

"Me and Brooke. Lee rang me a few days ago and confessed everything and asked me to advise him how best to deal with it."

Joshua pointed to the screen. "And you thought that was the best way of dealing with it?"

"A wonderful piece of theatre if I say so myself," she beamed happily.

"How dare you organise that behind my back!" he spat and walked out of the auditorium.

Kim looked after him, bewildered, and then went storming after him.

"Hold on a second. What's your problem? A thank-you would be nice!" She caught up with him and grabbed his arm.

They faced each other.

"A thank-you! For what?"

"For exposing Guy Burton for what he is. For showing Soraya exactly what she was dealing with. For basically doing everything you approached me for and asked me to do."

"By making a cheap bit of confessional video tape?"

"That's what it took, yes."

"Not with my life! Not with my son! I don't want my son used like that. I would never have allowed him to confess to that website or any involvement with it or Guy Burton in that way. You've made him a laughing stock."

"You see, this is why I just went ahead and did it. Because I knew you would stop us if I warned you. It was the same when I was producing your show. If I'd listened to every negative reaction or hesitation or doubt we'd have never produced even one show!"

"This isn't a television show, Kim, it's my life. My son!"

"So it's alright for you to expose every one else's family problems, but not yours? Joshua, what I've done in there might, just might, give you another shot at a broadcasting career. People will now sympathise with you –"

"I don't want another shot at a broadcasting career."

"They'll see Guy Burton was working against you. Henry King might even be worried you'll bring a case of bullying against RTV with this campaign waged against you by the Director of Programmes. This could give you another chance. A strong bargaining position."

"Is that all you care about?"

"Yes!"

"I don't want a broadcasting career any more. Not like the one I had. Not if it comes at the expense of exposing Lee like that."

"You just don't know what's good for you, that's always been your problem."

"No, my problem has always been that you tried to manipulate me and pull the strings. If you treated me like a person instead of some commodity none of this would have happened. If you had come to talk to me about my affair with Brooke instead of going to Guy Burton, this whole thing wouldn't have started."

Kim looked at him in amazement. "Don't try and make this my fault. Tell you what, Joshua, next time you need help with something do *not* call me. Next time you need some shit in your life sorted out, do it yourself!"

"You know what? I will!" Joshua turned and walked off.

"I should have left you in radio!" she shouted.

"Yes, you should have!"

"It's true what they say. No good turn goes unpunished!" Kim shouted after him.

"Find yourself a new performing poodle!" he yelled back.

"I will! Fellas like you are two a penny! It takes someone like me to turn them into stars!"

"Then you shouldn't have much trouble creating someone new. Good luck, Kim!"

Joshua looked for Lee in all his usual haunts but there was no sign of him. Finally he had an idea and drove to the cemetery where Lee's mother was buried. In the distance he could see Lee at the grave, and he waited patiently in the car. As Lee came out of the cemetery, Joshua pulled up beside him and opened the passenger side door.

"Come on, Lee, sit in," he urged.

Lee hesitated and then sat in.

Joshua drove away.

"I've been ringing you all afternoon," Joshua said.

"I had my phone on silent."

"I saw your video. Along with the whole of RTV. Why did you film all that on video and let everyone see it?"

Lee shrugged. "I was shocked when I saw Guy with Soraya. And then I realised he had been using me all along. And he didn't want to know me any more because I was of no use to him any more. I was so angry. I didn't have anywhere to go or anyone talk to about it."

"Why didn't you come and talk to me?"

"How could I? I've never been able to come and talk to you about problems. So I rang Brooke and went over to hers. She was really good and calmed me down. She said Kim would know how to handle it and then Kim arrived. And she said to finish Guy off, he had to be exposed, in front of everybody, and so we filmed the video. I don't regret doing it. It showed Guy for what he is."

Joshua sighed. "It certainly did that. But it exposed you as well, Lee. It showed you in a very negative light for starting the website in the first place."

Lee turned quickly to him. "But I didn't write those other things, Dad. I didn't write about your affair, or expose the show or talk about Mum."

"I know, I believe you."

"I just wanted to get at you a bit. Not destroy you. But Guy has a way of drawing you in, telling you things, and getting you to tell him. And I trusted him. I wanted him to like me."

"You don't have to tell me anything about Guy Burton that I haven't already discovered. But, when I guessed you were involved in this website, why didn't you tell me Guy had taken it over from you and written the very damaging stuff?"

"I didn't want to betray Guy. I thought he was my friend. He did so much for me. He was always there for me, giving me advice, giving me jobs at RTV. Giving me a role in life."

"If I hadn't neglected my role with you, he wouldn't have been able to step in and take advantage. Where have you been staying?"

"Just with friends."

"Come home, Lee. I need you there."

Lee sighed. "I want to go home, but Soraya and Daniel and Danielle aren't there any more. I really miss them."

"So do I. And that's my fault. But that's why I need you more than ever."

"Okay."

"We've a lot of things to work out. I was talking to some people who said you might benefit from talking to a doctor. I think you're very angry with me and your mother. I think it would help you to talk to somebody. Rather than expressing your anger on the internet or confiding in people you can't trust like Guy Burton."

"I'll think about it," sighed Lee.

79

Guy sat in the grandeur of Henry King's house.

"Well?" asked a stern Henry King, seated opposite him on a gold embroidered sofa.

"Well what?" Guy shrugged with a smile. "The boy is obviously demented. The whole family are as far as I'm concerned."

"So you're saying you didn't write all that stuff about Joshua Green?"

"Of course I didn't."

"It will be a case of your word against his then."

"The word of a highly experienced, respected and qualified Director of Programmes against a delusional twit of a kid? No contest, Henry."

"We will have to conduct an internal enquiry. We have to take it seriously. It would be unacceptable for the Director of Programmes to seriously slander and undermine one of our premier stars."

"*Allegedly* is the word you're missing from that sentence. Besides, I don't think there was any slander involved. It was all true, wasn't it – what was written?"

"We're in a very complicated situation."

"You might see it that way. I don't. Business as usual as far as I'm concerned. Now, if you'll excuse me, Henry, I've a winter schedule to get going."

Guy stood up and walked to the door.

416

"Oh, Guy!" called Henry.

"Yes, Henry?" Guy turned around and smiled.

"It might be an idea for you to hire yourself a solicitor. You should get independent legal advice."

Guy stared at him and walked off.

Guy drove back to RTV deep in thought. Henry King and his internal enquiry! He needed to retire and stop meddling. Of course when King found out Kim Davenport was involved in Lee's video, he probably would turn to jelly. The two of them flirting with each other in that silly schoolyard way they did. Oh Henry, you are awful! No, Kim, *you* are so awful! The two of them were awful in Guy's opinion. But the fact remained RTV was going to try and get rid of him. Henry King had just stated it when he said if he planned on trying to stay he would need a solicitor. They would like him to just leave. To go now so they wouldn't have to have any messy enquiry and all that would entail.

The thought of the enquiry filled Guy with fear. But he wasn't giving up. They hadn't reckoned on how smart he could be. He would find a way to discredit Lee and his accusations. He already was working on an idea.

Guy marched into his office and slammed the door behind him. He got a start to see Joshua sitting at his desk.

"What are you doing here? You shouldn't be here. You don't work at RTV any more."

"And why don't I work here? Because of you and the tricks you pulled."

"Get out, or I'll call security."

"Using my son to find out everything you could to use against me on that damned website!"

"Your son is half mad, as far as I'm concerned, and I doubt anybody believes him."

Joshua stood up and walked up close to Guy, glaring in his face. "Watch what you say about Lee. You're not hiding behind the internet now."

"Come on, Joshua, you know what Lee's like. You've told me all about him yourself. Drugs, unreliable, attention-seeking. How is anybody going to believe him?"

Joshua grabbed Guy's tie. "I'll make sure they do."

Guy grabbed Joshua's hand and forcibly removed it.

They stared at each other warily.

"I'm going," Joshua said. "There's nothing left for me here. You thought you were so clever, working us all up against each other. But you were found out in the end. You made the mistake of underestimating my son. Lee adores Soraya. There was no way he was going to let you anywhere near her once you made the mistake of exposing your real self. Now Soraya is safe away from you. She'll never have anything to do with you again."

"Or you!" Guy spat back.

"That may be. But at least Soraya has been moved away from you. That's all I care about."

"Pity you didn't give your first wife as much consideration."

"You meant nothing to Catherine . . . Get over it."

80

Kim was sitting with Jasmine in her living room.

"The ungrateful fool! Joshua Green! Who had heard of him before I discovered him, and who will ever hear of him again now he is no longer with me?"

"No one," confirmed Jasmine.

"You know, I'm coming to the fast conclusion he isn't very bright. He could never have dealt with Guy Burton on his own. I had to be ten times smarter than Guy – otherwise he would have wriggled his way out of this the way he does everything else. He can't wheedle his way out of this one. Everyone heard what Lee said about him. He's as good as finished. I'm surprised I haven't heard from Henry King yet, offering me something new."

"You seem very confident he will?"

"Yes, Henry loves me. I might have gone down with the *Titanic* that is Joshua Green, but now that Guy is disgraced as well, Henry will be panting to have a familiar and trustworthy face back on his team."

The phone started ringing and Jasmine looked at the number on the screen.

"It's Henry King on the phone for you," she squealed excitedly.

Kim quickly took the phone from her and purred down the phone.

"Henry, what a pleasant surprise."

"I heard you were in RTV at the winter-schedule screening but I missed you."

"Oh Henry, you know you have to move quickly if you want to catch me!"

Henry gave a little laugh. "But if I ever caught up, what a catch!"

The two of them laughed a flirty cackle down the phone.

"I don't know what's going on with Joshua Green and websites and accusations of all sorts," he said. "But I think you might have been right about Guy Burton."

Kim winked at Jasmine. "But don't you know yet, Henry? I'm always right."

"There's a rumour floating around that you were behind the Green kid's video."

"May I take the Fifth Amendment on that?"

"It had all the hallmarks of your confessional TV, in my opinion."

"You can't teach an old dog new tricks."

"I'd like you back at RTV, Kim."

"Of course you would. But what would Guy Burton have to say about that?"

"I don't think Guy Burton is going to have much of a say about anything, is he?"

Kim licked her lips in excitement. "So what are we talking about, Henry. Joshua's show back?"

"No, we can't have Joshua Green back through the doors. He's tainted and tarnished. Not good for our image. But you're not tarnished, and with Guy no longer making decisions I think we can get you producing another show on the winter schedule."

Kim stood up and started pacing excitedly. "Give it to me, Henry, what have you got for me?"

"I think we need to keep you away from anything controversial for a while. I was thinking a move, say, to lifestyle programmes?"

"Interesting – go on."

"There's a gardening programme that I think you would be just right to produce."

"*Gardening?* Have you lost your marbles?" she shouted.

"It's the only programme left on the schedule without any producer. It's the only show in town."

"But I don't know anything about gardening. I'm cut and thrust, not cut and weed!"

"Kim, these gardening programmes get huge audiences. It will be a new feather in your boa."

"Gardening! I don't believe it!" Kim was disgusted.

"It's the only thing on offer. Take it or leave it?"

"I'll bloody well take it then, as I have no choice. But you've a bloody cheek, Henry King!"

"Ta ta, sweetheart!" Henry hung up the phone.

Kim threw the phone down on the sofa. "He wants me to produce a *gardening* programme. *Gardening!*"

"Oh!" Jasmine pulled a face.

"I know what's he's trying to do, the old bastard – keep me on side but keep me out of trouble. If there's legal trouble ahead with Guy Burton he wants me on his side as a witness." She looked in a mirror and patted her hair. "He also loves me being around – he's always had a soft spot for me. But gardening!"

"Well, you know these gardening programmes aren't what they used to be, Mum. It's not all the right time of year to plant your geraniums any more. It's people having makeovers of their gardens, being outlandish and adventurous."

"I suppose." Kim was thoughtful. "We could approach it from a psychological point of view. Get into families' relationships as they do up their gardens. Run a competition between neighbours who hate each other to see who can do the better garden."

"Yes!" said Jasmine, getting excited.

"Turn it into a – reality show!"

"You could revolutionise the world of television gardening."

"I'm loving it. But what do I know about actual gardening? I'd need to learn about it."

Kim and Jasmine looked at each other knowingly and both said together: "Dad!"

81

Joshua dropped Lee off to his psychiatrist.

"I'll collect you at six," he said as Lee got out of the car.

"Okay," nodded Lee.

Joshua waited as he watched Lee go up the steps into the building. Only when he saw he was safe inside did he turn the car and drive home. Most of his time had been taken up with trying to sort Lee out. First of all he had got him referred to the psychiatrist. The doctor had recommended that Lee continue his job at RTV and so Joshua had met with Henry King. Henry had seemed quite nervous at the meeting in the light of the revelation about Guy Burton. Joshua had explained he wouldn't take any action against RTV, but in return he wanted their help with Lee. He insisted that the internal enquiry had to be handled as sensitively as possible with Lee. Henry had confided off the record that he wished Guy Burton would just leave, but that Guy was giving no indication that would happen and was prepared to defend his position with the enquiry.

Joshua sighed as he pulled into his driveway. He got a shock to see Soraya's Range Rover parked there. His heart began to beat quickly as he made his way up the steps and let himself into the house.

"Soraya!" he called.

"Yes," she answered from the kitchen.

He hurried to the kitchen and found her sitting at the table there.

"Hi!" he said.

"I rang the doorbell and, when there was no answer, I used my key to let myself in."

"Of, course, it's still your house. Your home."

"It doesn't it feel like it any more. I'm here because of Lee. I'm very concerned about him after I saw what he said in the video and I want to check how he is."

"He's over at a psychiatrist's now."

"Oh good, he's seeing somebody."

"Yeah, I got an appointment straight away."

She looked at him warily. "I thought you might be angry with him about the website. I was frightened your relationship might have deteriorated more."

"I wasn't angry, just worried that he felt he had to do that. And that somebody like Guy Burton could take advantage like he did."

"Well, I guess we all fell for Guy Burton's act. Including me."

"Yes, we did. I didn't think I would see you again."

"As I said, I've been really concerned about Lee."

"You're a really strong person, Soraya – the way you just moved out without a word and got on with your life."

"I'm not that strong, I just had options. A lot of people get trapped in bad marriages and have to stay because they've nowhere to go. I had. I had support. I had money. I had an au pair to help with the children. I could afford a solicitor."

"Why do you always put yourself down? Why don't you give yourself credit for who you are?"

"I guess there was no room for my ego to grow when yours was taking up so much room, Joshua."

"I'm sorry for everything."

"So am I . . . We need to put something permanent in place for you to have access to the children. They miss you terribly."

"I miss them terribly. I miss you terribly. I'd do anything to get you back."

"And I'd do anything to get us back to the way we were before all this. To get my life back. But you can't go back. Some things can't be fixed."

423

"There's an answer to everything, you just have to look hard enough."

"What about your career? What are you going to do about that?"

"My agent has had a few offers from radio stations, trying to cash in on the controversy. I'll have to start again, I suppose."

"You'll get back to the top again. Your type always does."

"I'm not going to do anything for a while though. I just want to concentrate on Lee for now, and the children."

"Okay, I'd better be off. Ulrika is in one of her moods today. Relationship trouble, don't you know." She went to the door and turned to him and said, "Why did you do it, Joshua? Why did you throw it all away?"

"I got carried away. I thought I deserved all the attention I was getting. And when I came back home it was coming back to the real world. And I couldn't adapt. After being in the studio all day, being the centre of attention, I'd then come back here and be just a normal guy to everyone."

"But that's life, Joshua. That's real life, and no matter who you are you still have to do normal things at the end of the day."

"I guess Brooke just extended the attention I was getting when we all left the studio."

"Well, I hope it was worth it."

"Of course it wasn't."

She reached the front door and turned to face him. "This whole thing with Guy Burton has unsettled me. I don't trust my own judgement now. You deceived me and then I pick the worst possible choice on the rebound."

"Is that all he was, a rebound to you?"

"I suppose. Anyway, I'm taking the kids back to France for a couple of weeks. When I get back we'll sort out the custody situation."

He nodded sadly. "Whatever you want."

She walked out.

"Soraya!" he called out after her. "I love you!"

"Yeah, it's a pity you didn't remember that before you slept with Brooke Radcliffe."

82

It was afternoon and Brooke was in her office, compiling her next report on internet usage at the station, when she heard her door open and close. Looking up, she got a start to see Guy standing there.

"Hello there," he said pleasantly enough and came and half sat on her desk.

She felt frightened and told herself to cop on as there was no reason she should be.

"How are you enjoying the new job?" he asked, taking up a pile of papers on her desk and leafing through them.

"It's fine," she said.

"Stimulating!" he said sarcastically as he read her reports and cast them back on her desk. "A little birdie tells me that you were behind Lee Green making that video and screening it to RTV."

"Lee came to me for help when he realised you had double-crossed him and then we both went to Kim who came up with the idea," she said evenly.

"What a perfect production team you made. Lee researched the story, you the assistant producer compiled it and brought it to the producer, Kim, who put it all together. Pity you didn't all work as smoothly together on Joshua's show."

"We all had a common aim and enemy this time. You!"

"Do you hate me that much? To set me up like that in front of everyone? To try and destroy me?"

"I was only doing back to you what you did to me and everyone else – to try and stop you from doing it to anyone else."

"Soraya?"

Brooke nodded.

"There's to be an internal enquiry on the whole matter. They'll try and discover if I was really behind the campaign against Joshua."

"Good."

"Of course they've no direct evidence. The website was all written from internet cafés. I'll deny I had anything to do with it."

"The truth always comes out."

"Does it though? You'll probably be called as a witness. You'll have to repeat what Lee told you about me."

"I've no problem with that."

Guy reached forward and gently touched her hair. "You could always say that Lee told you he was making it up about me, to get himself out of trouble with his father."

Brooke pulled back from him and pushed his hand away. "I'm not lying for you, Guy."

"If you did that for me, you wouldn't be in this crummy job for long. I would guarantee you any job in RTV you want."

"Are you for real?" She shook her head in disbelief.

"Come on, Brooke, I want you to think seriously about this. You are destined to spend the rest of your life compiling these dull reports. You'll never be given another chance after you were shown up in the press. Opportunities like I'm offering you are once-in-a-lifetime chances. You could be a great producer, and I'll give you the opportunity to be one. I'll give you whatever show you want."

"You're mad!"

"No, I'm not."

"Yes, you are. Kim is mad but at least she knows she's mad. You're mad but you think you're normal."

"Think what you like. But think about what's best for you."

She looked at him, her face creased in thought.

"Come on, Brooke, you know the people who get on in life are

426

the ones who grab opportunities like this. Aren't you sick of always being the last in the queue? The one things always go wrong for? You have to bend the rules a bit and think a bit deviously to get to the top."

"Like you?" She eyed him dubiously.

He shrugged. "You could learn a lot from me."

"I thought I was learning a lot from you until you dumped me without a second thought. 'Mucky little scrubber', wasn't that how you described me?"

"I'm sorry about that, I really am. I actually really like you. We worked well together. We were a great team."

"You were using me to get to Joshua, and Soraya."

He reached forward and started stroking her hair again. "We could always give it another shot. Try it again."

She started laughing. "If I tell this lie for you to the enquiry? I don't know if that says more about you or me. That you would prostitute yourself to get me to lie. Or I need to rely on bribery to get a partner!"

"It's not like that at all. We're two of a kind, you and me. We could be great together."

She got up and went to her window and stared out. He came and stood behind her, so closely she could feel his breath on her neck. She started to shiver. He leaned forward against her and started to kiss her neck.

"What are you doing tonight?" he whispered.

"Nothing planned," she said.

"Why don't I come around to yours and we can discuss it in more detail? More intimately?"

She stared straight ahead.

"I'll be over to yours around seven," he whispered and, turning, walked out of the office.

She waited until she heard the door close before she went to her desk and sat down quickly. She stared at the door for a long while before dropping her head and putting her face in her hands.

83

Kim followed Tom around the Botanic Gardens, listening attentively.

"Now you see this one," he said, pointing to a flower. "This is a Dutch amaryllis."

"An amaryllis," she repeated as she jotted it down in her notebook.

She had spent nearly every spare minute over the past couple of weeks with her husband, touring garden centres, great-house gardens and every other public garden they could get access to as she tried to gain an education for her new gardening show. Tom was delighted to talk about his favourite subject incessantly and thrilled to have a pupil in Kim who was desperate to learn.

If Kim was going to be producing a gardening programme, then she was determined to produce the best gardening programme around. And that would entail gaining as much knowledge on the subject as possible. And who better to impart that knowledge to her than her husband?

As she watched him quickly walk off to the next resplendent display of flowers, she paused and thought. Who would ever have thought, after all these years of marriage, that they would finally have something to bond over? That two people who had nothing in common would finally come together over a combination of their two favourites subjects – gardening and television.

As Tom began to lecture on the next array of plants, he turned

428

around and saw her some way back, standing and looking at him.

"Come on, Kim!" he called over to her with a smile. "Try and keep up! We've a lot to get through today!"

"Just coming!" she smiled and hurried after him.

As he pointed out an exotic plant, she reached out for his other hand and held it and gazed at him. He looked at her, surprised, then squeezed her hand back.

84

In her apartment that evening, Brooke looked at her watch. It was just after seven and she was expecting Guy any moment. She crossed over to a mirror and quickly gave herself a once-over. She had changed into a cocktail dress and looked very well with her hair falling over one shoulder in Guy's favourite style. She stared into her eyes in the mirror and forced the worried look to leave her face.

The intercom buzzed.

"Come on up," she said, pressing the buzzer, and unlocked the front door.

She went to the coffee table, picked up her packet of cigarettes and lit one. Guy came through the front door a few seconds later and closed it behind him.

"You look great," he complimented, seeing she had gone to an effort for him.

"Thanks. Drink?" she asked, refilling her wineglass.

"No, I'm okay for now," he said, studying her intently.

She sat down, drew on her cigarette and crossed her legs.

"I didn't think you'd ever be back here," she commented.

He looked around the apartment. "I had some of my happiest times since I came to Dublin here," he said.

"Sure you did! That's why you went rushing off to Soraya's mansion on Shrewsbury Road."

He looked at her and smiled. "Ah –that!"

She viewed him coolly. "Yes – that!"

"I guess I owe you an apology. I haven't treated you very well, have I?"

"You've been a complete bastard to me. I thought you were different, special."

"I know. I'm sorry . . . Soraya never meant anything to me. I was impressed by her wealth and her background and her manners, looks. She was a conquest, that's all."

"How very gallant of you!"

"I'm just telling the truth. The truth is we've nothing in common. She would have bored me very quickly. She's not like you. Like me and you together. We're dynamite."

"If we were so good together, why did you set out to destroy me by putting my affair with Joshua on that damned website?"

"Look, that's all in the past." He sat down beside her quickly and took her hand. "I want to talk about the future. Our future, you and me together."

"Our future which all depends on me covering for you?"

"Just say Lee admitted to making the whole thing up about my involvement in his website. That will stop this stupid tribunal they are putting me in front of and I can get back to doing my job. If you said that, the case against me would be dropped immediately. Lee would be shown up for the crazy dysfunctional kid both you and I know him really to be."

"And what's in it for me?"

"I told you. You can have the job of your choice in RTV. I'll promote you to produce whatever programme you want. It's a simple choice. Stuck in this dead-end job or becoming a great producer . . . being alone or being with me. You actually don't have a choice with this. Everyone, at last, would be jealous of you."

He reached out and kissed her neck and she nuzzled her neck into his mouth. "I don't think I can do it, Guy. It would be too bad a thing to lie like that."

"Come on, Brooke! Don't pretend to be something you're not. You went out with Joshua for months without giving it a second thought. You only felt bad because you were caught. You're just like me. Has Joshua or Soraya rung you to thank you for exposing me to them?"

"No," she acknowledged.

"Of course they haven't, because you're nothing to them. They only care about themselves. Has Lee rung you to thank you for your help?"

"No, he hasn't."

"Exactly. Why should you ruin the rest of your life for people that you don't matter to?"

"You put forward a good argument." She pulled back. "But how could I trust you?"

"Because you'll always have this over me . . . this will be your protection against me. Do you need some time to think about it?"

"No, I don't think I do."

"So you'll help me?"

She inhaled her cigarette and blew the smoke into his face. "I don't want some assistant producer job. I want to produce my own talk show. I choose my team, my guests, even my budgets."

"Whatever you want."

She was trembling and quickly took another drag of her cigarette.

"All I have to do is lie for you?"

"Yes."

She ground out her cigarette.

"Do we have a deal?" he urged.

"I'm afraid . . . no. We don't have a deal." She stood up.

"Brooke –"

"*You can come out now!*" she called to the bedroom door.

The bedroom door opened and Joshua and Soraya walked out. Guy's mouth dropped open.

"You lying bitch!" Guy leapt to his feet.

"You can talk!" Brooke spat back.

"Soraya – I –" began Guy.

"I don't want to hear any excuses. You've taken me for a fool long enough, Guy," said Soraya.

"You know that expression," said Joshua. "You can fool some

of the people all of the time, and all of the people some of the time, but you can't fool all of the people all of the time. You've just been totally exposed."

"You think you're all so clever," said Guy.

"No, it's *you* who thinks *you're* so clever. Well, not any more, see you at the tribunal," snapped Brooke.

"And we'll be telling how you tried to bribe Brooke to lie for you."

Guy walked to the door. He turned and smirked at them before saying, "What a charming team you make – the cheating husband, the cheated wife and the cheat mistress!"

He left, slamming the door behind him.

Lee looked at his mobile again and realised his father was now nearly an hour late for collecting him from the psychiatrist as arranged. He'd tried to ring him a few times but no joy. He was fed up waiting in the clinic's reception and, though he was trying to make an effort to co-operate with his father, he decided enough was enough and headed off into town.

This was the area where Brooke lived and he momentarily toyed with the idea of dropping in on her, but decided not.

Guy went storming down the street, with a throbbing headache. He relived the scene at Brooke's. How she set him up. Exposed him. Destroyed him. She had completely outsmarted him. Who'd have ever thought? He passed a pub and a strong smell of alcohol hit him from inside. He paused and inhaled deeply and savoured the familiar old smell of the stale booze. Suddenly he was walking through the doors of the pub and marching up to the bar.

"A whiskey," he ordered. "A double!"

Lee had got a start when he noticed Guy striding rapidly down the other side of the road ahead of him. He'd dropped back a bit and cautiously followed. Then Guy had halted abruptly outside a pub, before walking quickly inside.

Lee was intrigued. This wasn't Guy's normal behaviour. He waited a while and then darted across the road and slipped into the pub which was crowded with punters downing a few before heading home from work. From where he stood a the back of the crowd he saw Guy down a large whiskey and then order another.

Joshua, Soraya and Brooke had been having a brief post mortem on the episode with Guy.

"Does anyone want a drink – after all that?" said Brooke.

"No, I'm going back to the children." Soraya walked to the door, then turned to them. "I only came here to protect Lee and what Guy Burton was trying to do to him. It doesn't make me change what I feel about the two of you." She walked out.

Brooke took up her cigarette packet and lit herself another one.

"Do you want one?" she said, offering the packet to Joshua.

"No, I'd better be going too. I have to pick up Lee from his psychiatrist and I'm running really late."

Brooke nodded.

"Thanks for letting me know what Guy was planning and for exposing him," said Joshua.

Brooke nodded. "I did what I had to do."

"See you, Brooke," he said and he walked out of the apartment.

"See you," said Brooke after the door had closed.

She sighed loudly as she sat down and picked up her glass of wine. She didn't know what was upsetting her most – the dramatic events of the past few months, or the very undramatic and uneventful future that now lay ahead of her.

Lee was wondering how he could get a pint for himself without Guy spotting him. Suddenly his mobile started to ring and he answered it.

"Sorry, son, I got held up and couldn't get away. I'm on my way to the clinic now to get you."

"No, don't – I left. I'm on my way into town."

"Tell me where you are and I'll pick you up."

Lee took a final glance at Guy ordering another drink and left the pub.

Guy looked at his watch and saw it was nearly half past ten. He had been nearly two hours in the pub and had just ordered his fourth double whiskey. He held the glass under his nose and smelled the whiskey before taking a drink. He had forgotten how good it tasted. And how good it made everything seem. He wouldn't let them destroy him. He would think of something. His mobile rang and he was surprised to see Lee's number come up.

"Lee?" he said cautiously.

"Hi. I wondered if you were around. I think we need to talk."

"Sure, where do you want to meet?"

"Eh – your apartment?"

"I'll be there in thirty minutes – see you then." Curious, Guy downed his drink and went out to the street to get a taxi.

85

It was eleven o'clock at night and Soraya was in the drawing room gazing unseeingly at the television, a glass of wine in front of her, thinking about her conversation with Joshua. Thinking of the cruel words she had heard Guy say about her. She heard the front door open and close and few seconds later a smiling Ulrika walked into the drawing room.

"Hello!"

"Hi, Ulrika. How was your date?" Soraya turned off the television.

"It was okay. In fact, it was better than okay," she said, smiling.

"Really?" Soraya was surprised. All of Ulrika's dates inevitably ended up being miserable events.

Ulrika sat down. "Yeah, it was really good."

"Ulrika, is this not the fellow who stood you up last week?"

"Yes, same man. But he is very regretful now."

"Well, it's easy for him to say that, but he left you in Eddie Rocket's for an hour and a half staring into your strawberry milkshake, and you arrived back here in tears."

"I know that. But I like him!"

"Well, that may be true. But you don't want to be somebody's doormat either, Ulrika."

"I don't plan to be a doormat. But if you like somebody, you need to work to make it good."

436

"I'd prefer to keep my pride, thanks all the same."

Ulrika looked at her curiously. "Is Guy coming over tonight?"

"No, we're finished. It was stupid going out with him anyway. I was at a low ebb, and wanted to get back at Joshua."

"Did it work?"

"No."

"You must still love Joshua if you wanted to hurt him in this way."

"Of course I still love him."

"And does he still love you?"

"So he says. But he's ruined it."

"He made a big mistake. But do you want to throw everything away? If you still love him and he loves you, it is best to try one more time, no?"

"My pride won't let me."

"Pride can lead you to a lonely place." Ulrika stood up. "Goodnight. I am going to bed."

"Goodnight, Ulrika."

Ulrika left the room.

Soraya took a drink of wine and thought for a while.

Guy waited anxiously in the penthouse for Lee to arrive. He hadn't sounded angry or agitated on the phone and Guy was intrigued as to why he wanted to meet. Thinking about it, he realised it would have made more sense to have worked on Lee to change his story rather than Brooke. Brooke, who had been around the block too many times and was world-weary at this stage, had been too much of a risk and it had backfired terribly. A woman scorned looking for her revenge. But Lee was a totally different matter. A kid, a damaged one at that, who hung on Guy's every word. He was the obvious choice to work on. Better again, they would have to drop this tribunal if their chief witness refused to testify.

The intercom buzzed.

"Lee?"

"Yeah."

"Come on up," said Guy.

He opened his apartment front door and waited until the lift doors opened a few seconds later and Lee came out.

Guy greeted him with a big smile. "Lee! Great to see you!"

Lee looked at him cautiously as he entered the apartment.

"Is it?" he asked as he entered the lounge and sat down on one of the sofas.

Guy sat opposite him. "Of course it is," he said. "It's always good to see you."

"I thought you'd be angry after what I did."

"I'm not angry with you, Lee. I'm angry with myself for letting you get the impression I wasn't there for you when you needed me."

"I was just upset when I fell out with Dad and I turned to you and you didn't want to know."

Guy sat forward. "But you misread me! Of course I wanted to help you, I just didn't think it was a good idea for you to move in with Soraya at that time. I'm sorry if you got the impression I didn't want you around. Nothing could be further from the truth! I was going to ring you and give you a deposit to rent your own apartment so you could be independent!"

"Were you?" Lee's eyes widened.

"Yes. But then you did that DVD and showed it to everyone in RTV." Guy sat back, looking disappointed.

"I'm sorry, Guy. I'm sorry I did it. I felt I had no one to turn to. So I contacted Brooke who contacted Kim and suddenly they were telling me what to do. And they said to make the video to expose you."

"I know what bitches those two can be, believe you me." Guy sat forward again, picked up a glass of whiskey in front of him and took a gulp. "The trouble is, Lee, that video and the accusations you made on it have landed me in a lot of hot water. Do you understand me?"

Lee bit his lower lip and nodded. "I didn't realise they were going to put you in front of a tribunal. I didn't want that."

Guy sighed. "That's why you have to be so careful what you start in this life, Lee, because you can set in motion a chain of events that you can no longer control, and that's what you've done now." Guy took another drink from his whiskey. "Remember me telling you about the time I was working with the great film director, Lagarde?"

Lee nodded. "I do."

"He taught me so much. But I was young and naïve like you and I fucked up my big chance by just not keeping my mouth shut and landing Lagarde in trouble with his wife. It meant everything to me to be a film director, and then my dreams were shattered and it was never going to happen. So I started to see real life as a film and people as characters that I could manipulate. Life is art, that's what Lagarde taught me. Every so often you come across somebody like Kim Davenport who is impossible to manipulate. But generally people do what you want them to do."

"And was that what I was to you? Just somebody else whose life you could play with?"

"No, of course not. I saw in you somebody very much like me. Somebody who had the strength of personality to get what he wanted and didn't care how he got it."

"I don't know what to do about this tribunal."

"I'll tell you what to do. Refuse to give evidence. Say Kim Davenport and Brooke Radcliffe manipulated you into saying those things about me and you want nothing more to do with it."

"But – that'll affect my career in RTV."

"No, it won't - not with me still at the helm. If I stay on as director, I'll make sure you go to the top, Lee."

"I want to trust you."

"Then do!" Guy sat forward. "Listen – remember when I told you to go for the job on Joshua's show?"

"Uh huh."

"And I filled out the application form for you?"

"Yeah?"

"Well, I also made sure you got the job. *I* was the one who contacted HR and said to fix it to give you the job."

"You fixed it?" Lee's eyes widened.

"Yes. Come on, Lee you were up against some serious competition to get that job. If I hadn't interfered, you wouldn't have stood a chance."

"So I didn't get it on my own merit?"

"No. But I saw the potential in you and I still do. And all I need now is for you to withdraw the accusations you made."

Lee nodded slowly while thinking deeply.

Guy looked down at his empty glass and handed it over to Lee. "Go fix me another whiskey, will you? The bottle is on the counter in the kitchen."

Lee took the glass and went into the kitchen. He put the glass on the kitchen top while he unscrewed the whiskey bottle and filled the glass three quarters full.

"Dad told me this evening that you were trying to get Brooke to say I was lying," said Lee from the kitchen.

"*What?* That's not true, Lee. Don't listen to that crap."

"He said you said some pretty nasty things about me." Lee slowly reached into his jacket pocket and took out the bottle of pills he had taken from the bathroom at home – his father's anxiety medication. "He said you said I was mad and nobody would believe me."

"That's just bullshit, Lee. You know, if the truth be told, your father is just jealous of the friendship we have. Because we're much closer than you and him could ever be. And hardly surprising, the way he treated you over the years. I've seen the way he speaks to you. It's a disgrace."

Lee unscrewed the bottle of pills as Guy talked on. He took the pills out one by one and crumbled them into the glass of whiskey, watching them quickly dissolve.

Once he had put in the required amount he took a spoon and stirred the drink, before replacing the bottle of pills in his pocket.

"Ice with that?" he called.

"Yeah," answered Guy.

Lee scooped some ice from the ice bucket and filled the glass. He then looked around and, seeing a tray, he placed the glass on it, and folded a towel over his other arm.

"The trouble with your father, and Kim, and Brooke and even Soraya is that they don't respect you, Lee. They think you'll do what they want. And they are using you to get to me."

Guy watched in surprise as Lee approached, with the glass of whiskey on the tray.

"What's this – silver service?" he asked with a smirk.

Lee took the glass and placed it on the coffee table in front of Guy.

Guy took up the drink and swallowed a large gulp of it. I'll have some confession to make in my AA meeting next week, he thought.

"You're right, Guy," said Lee, sitting down opposite him. "I think people do underestimate me. They think they can manipulate me, and I hate that. I hate when people do that."

"Well, this is your chance to stop that," said Guy, taking another long drink. "So will you refuse to testify at the tribunal?"

"Yes," nodded Lee. "If that's what you want, then that's what I'll do. There will be no tribunal, believe me."

Guy sighed loudly and sat back in the couch, looking visibly relieved. "You don't know what that means to me. It's a weight off my shoulders. Now they can all go and fuck off with their accusations and their tribunals. Without you as a witness, they haven't a leg to stand on. I've won."

Guy put his head back against the cushions of the couch and closed his eyes.

Lee continued to watch as Guy stopped talking and began to drift off. Finally Lee got up and took a last look down at Guy before he left the apartment.

86

Joshua was surprised when the doorbell rang so late at night. He was even more surprised to see Soraya there when he answered the door.

"Hello," he said as she stepped inside.

"I'm not staying long," she said, following him into the sitting room.

"Is everything alright?" asked Joshua.

"Yes, everything's fine. Where's Lee?"

"Out."

They sat at either end of the sofa.

She looked at him awkwardly and hesitated before speaking. "It's going to take me a long time to recover from your betrayal, Joshua."

"I know that."

"I don't think I'll ever be able to trust you again," she said, smiling wryly. "And after Guy Burton, I'm not sure if I can trust anybody again."

"I know."

She sighed. "I still love you, Joshua. But it's a damaged, weary love at this stage."

He nodded and looked down at the floor.

"If you want I'll put a hold on the divorce proceedings . . . for now."

He looked at her, his face lighting up. "Of course it's what I want. But why?"

"I just think we had too much together for me to be able to just walk away without at least trying to see what went wrong."

"Are you saying you're giving me another chance?" he said as if he thought he was dreaming.

"I'm saying we'll see how it goes. But I need to take it very slowly and very cautiously. I don't want to be hurt again."

He leaned towards her, his eyes glowing. "I'll do everything in my power to make it work this time. You'll see, just give me time."

"We'll see. Time heals – they say."

He reached out tentatively and took her hand and she didn't pull it away.

Brooke came into her apartment and locked it behind her. She had endured a particularly boring day at work and she was glad to be home. There was no bringing work home with her in this new job like she used to with Joshua's show.

The difference being she had loved doing work at home before because she enjoyed it so much. Back then she'd thought her life was sad, with her work folder, bottle of wine, and television on, but she now realised in actual fact she had been happy.

She sat down and opened her post quickly. As she tore open an envelope she spotted the BBC headed paper and realised it was the rejection letter for the BBC job she had gone for. But as she read the letter, she realised it wasn't a rejection after all but an offer of the job. She read and reread the letter, hardly believing it. How could they offer the job? The interview had been a disaster. Maybe the producer's scatty assistant, Tilly, had sent out the letter of offer to the wrong applicant. Let's face it, the girl had form for doing such things. The letter said to contact Molly Grinder, the show's producer, to accept the offer. Brooke couldn't wait to find out if there had been a mistake or not and decided to ring the programme's office even though it was after normal work hours.

She waited patiently for somebody to answer.

"Hello, Molly Grinder at the BBC speaking," said the friendly familiar voice.

"Oh Molly, it's Brooke Radcliffe here. I didn't think I'd get you at this time. I just received your job offer and I wanted to check if there hasn't been a mistake?"

"No mistake, love. I want you as my assistant producer."

Brooke's eyes started welling up with tears as she smiled at the same time.

"I'm just very surprised. I thought my interview didn't go that well, due to – well, due to the fact you thought I was somebody else."

"True, but I liked your honesty and your chutzpah. You could have just lied and pretended to be a vegan and everything, but you didn't. I really liked that."

"I've learned secrets and lies are not a good idea."

"So – do you want the job or not?"

"Of course I want the job! More than you'll ever know."

"Excellent. But I think I'd better warn you – expect the unexpected. We're a mad lot here."

"That sounds wonderful. Believe me – I'm used to working with mad people."

If you enjoyed
Talk Show by A. O'Connor
why not try
Full Circle also published by Poolbeg?
Here's a sneak preview of Chapter One

FULL CIRCLE

A. O'CONNOR

POOLBEG

CHAPTER 1

2010

Blanche Launcelot looked down at Dublin stretched below her as the plane continued to circle around the city. She glanced away from the view and down at her Cartier and was alarmed to see the flight was now forty minutes delayed for landing. Reaching forward, she took her glass of champagne from the small table and sipped at it while she looked around for a flight attendant.

She saw one making her way down the Business Class section and beckoned her over.

Smiling broadly, the attendant approached Blanche.

"Yes, Mrs Launcelot, can I get you something?"

"What time are we actually going to land this plane?" Blanche asked in exasperation.

The attendant's face became worried even though her smile was rigorously maintained.

She was saved from answering by the pilot suddenly announcing: "Ladies and gentlemen, I apologise for the delay. There's been a problem on the ground which has now been resolved, and I'm pleased to say we are now beginning our descent to Dublin Airport."

"At last!" said Blanche.

"Shall I just take this glass?" suggested the attendant, reaching forward and taking away the champagne glass, fixing up the table at the same time.

Blanche sat back in her seat and fastened her seatbelt, looking around the half-empty business section. As the plane continued to make its descent, she spotted the Launcelot plane hangar on the outskirts of Dublin Airport and sighed, reminding herself that her days of flying by private plane might be well and truly over.

Blanche made her way through Dublin Airport, several shopping bags in each hand. Her luggage was being pushed in a trolley beside her by an airport attendant.

Blanche was fifty and cut a glamorous figure. Dressed in an elegant silver-grey business suit, her figure was that of a woman twenty years younger. Her jet-black hair swept past her shoulders. Her beautiful features were often the topic of gossip as people speculated if she'd had any work done. She hadn't. As she came out of the airport she glanced around and spotted the black Mercedes waiting for her.

"Just over here," she instructed the attendant with the trolley.

On seeing her, the driver of the Mercedes got out smartly and opened the boot of the car, took the luggage and put it in. Blanche tipped the attendant, put some of her shopping into the boot and then got into the back of the car with the rest of it. There, waiting for her, was her lawyer William.

He smiled warmly at her.

"Sorry I'm so late," she said, closing the car door. "The pilot felt he needed to give us a tour of the Dublin skies."

"Good flight otherwise?" asked William.

She shrugged. "Fine."

As the car whooshed away from the airport, she reached forward to the shopping bags on the floor and handed William one.

"A little present from Fifth Avenue," she said.

He was surprised. "You shouldn't have." He reached into the bag and took out a brown-leather attaché case. "You really shouldn't have bothered!" He was embarrassed.

"Nonsense. You've been putting in a lot of hours recently."

"You get billed for them," he said.

She shrugged.

"Any luck in New York?" he asked, getting down to business.

She smiled sadly and shook her head. "No . . . when you're down, you're down. Have you had any luck here?"

"I found a few things in company law that might unfreeze funds, but it would take far too long to start court proceedings. I'm afraid the company would go bust before we'd even have our day in court."

She shook her head. "This is unbelievable. There must be something we can do. I have an awful lot of people to pay at the end of the month. If we can't release funds by then there will be a riot."

"I know." He wasn't used to seeing Blanche look desperate. It was a look that didn't suit her and he wanted to reach out and hug her and tell her it would be alright. But he would be lying.

He looked down at the rest of her shopping and spotted some bags from FAO Swartz, brimming with toys.

"Blanche?"

"What?"

"How is your grandson?"

"Fine. I can't wait to see him."

He spotted the first glimpse of happiness on her face.

"Blanche . . . I want to speak to you . . . not as your lawyer, but as a friend." Maybe the only friend you have left, he added silently.

"Go on," she shrugged.

"Blanche, I know how much you love the child, but hasn't this gone on long enough? Don't you think the rightful place for any child is with its parent?"

"It depends on what kind of parent it has!"

"I know, but –"

"But nothing, William. You know what situation I rescued him from."

"Look, Blanche." He reached over and forcibly grabbed her hand.

"What they are doing to you is a scandal. Trying to take away everything you've worked for, everything you own, is cruel. But the child is something else. I don't want you to get confused about what's right and wrong with everything else that's happening."

Blanche quickly pulled her hand back. "It's not up for discussion, William. He is my grandchild and his safety and happiness are my first priority . . . I'm all he's got!"

And is he all you've got? William asked silently.

If you enjoyed this chapter from
Full Circle by A. O'Connor
why not order the full book online
@ www.poolbeg.com

POOLBEG WISHES TO
THANK YOU

for buying a Poolbeg book.

If you enjoyed this why not
visit our website:

www.poolbeg.com

and get another book delivered straight
to your home or to a friend's home!

All books despatched within 24 hours.

POOLBEG

WHY NOT JOIN OUR MAILING LIST
@ www.poolbeg.com and get some
fantastic offers on Poolbeg books